THE
PEDESTAL

DANIEL WIMBERLEY

Design Vault Press, LLC
www.designvaultpress.net

First Edition: February 2014

The characters and events in this book are fictitious. Any similarity to real persons, living or dead, is coincidental and not intended by the author.

Library of Congress Cataloging-in-Publication Data
Wimberley, Daniel.
The Pedestal / by Daniel Wimberley. – 1st ed.
p. cm.
1. Life on other planets – Fiction. 2. Bioengineering – Fiction.
3. Apocalyptic fantasies – Fiction.

Book design by Giovanni Auriemma.

ISBN: 061593708X
ISBN-13: 978-0615937083

For my son, Luke.

Prologue

It starts with an upset stomach. Bearable at first, soon uncomfortable enough to send the man dashing home from a poker game on a perfectly gorgeous Friday night, forfeiting twenty credits to a twitchy, red-eyed apothecarist along the way. Shuffling through his front door, the man chews a fat antacid tablet, bemoaning the unconscionable price of such bitter, antiquated medicine to his empty condominium. Later, still suffering, he downs two more to no avail. The discomfort worsens with each passing minute until it can no longer be written off as just another of middle-age's petty tolls.

Something is undeniably wrong.

A man of proud stock, he's powerfully resentful of his implant—technology better suited for the hopeless youth, in his opinion, who brandish their lazy constitutions like the engorged bellies of ticks—but when the heat in his gut becomes unbearable, his lifelong posturing over such things loses focus; he calls upon his NanoPrint like a prodigal son, and he's far too despondent to feel any shame.

The implant tingles in a short burst, flooding him with merciful relief in milliseconds and drawing from him a scoff of grudging amazement. He'll wrestle with guilt in the morning, no doubt, but for now he feels like a new man.

Minutes later, sitting in his favorite chair, he draws a glass of chilled Chablis to his lips, smiling even as he drinks. Maybe he's misjudged the value of his implant after all.

Beneath the skin of his wrist, the tiny body of his implant begins to oscillate in steady spurts. At once, the burn of reflux resumes, this time with maddening intensity. The Chablis smolders like hot coals in his stomach. Simultaneously, the room seems to yaw, spinning around him like a broken carnival ride; he worries that he should sit down before he falls, but—of course—he's already sitting. Sweat seeps from his pores, yet his body shivers.

What's happening to me?

In answer, the contents of his stomach spew from his mouth like rodents fleeing a flooding burrow, toppling him off his chair and sending his drink sailing. Prostrate on the floor now, the man groans. The floor tilts in and out of kilter, gathering speed. His chest seems to compress as if a fat man is climbing aboard. It's becoming maddeningly difficult to breathe with his lungs heaving in sporadic gulps—and for a few terrifying seconds at a time, not at all. His NanoPrint is still now, but he suspects the damage is done.

I'm dying.

There's no one to help, no friendly neighbor to run to his aid, no automaid resting on its charger, waiting patiently for a command. Hardly the time to entertain loneliness, yet it creeps in nevertheless. For many years, he's lived in the shadow of death— alone, separated from the woman he loves; now, as the end is upon him, the wastefulness of fear is made plain. He wants to cry out, to scream for justice, if not for help. Even if he could summon the energy to bother, his voice would scarcely penetrate the soundproofed walls of his condo.

In desperation, he submits an emergency ticket on his NanoPrint. But he's a pragmatic man; help will arrive too late, and he knows it.

As if to vindicate this bit of black cynicism, the emergency submission hiccups and then fails; it slips quietly into a background queue where he hopes it will idle only briefly before reprocessing. Gliding across his retinas, though, a connection error dispels even that feeble hope.

... Fatal error encountered.

... Connection failed.

... The nexus is not accessible with your current NanoPrint configuration. Please seek the immediate assistance of a nexus administrator.

Tears cloud his vision. He's been cut off from the nexus, and thereby from everything on the planet, living or otherwise; however lonely he felt only a moment ago, he's truly never been as alone as he is now. And still, the room spins and spins.

Oh God, why won't it stop?

In a last-ditch effort, the man attempts to launch his MentalNotes—to document these final seconds, for whatever they're worth—but nothing happens. A sob forms in his throat, yet he can't catch a decent breath to send it on its way. His implant whirs to life again, and for a scant millisecond his hopes rise.

Perhaps there's still a chance—

Crawling to his knees, the man suddenly buckles as an immense pain seizes him, goring through his chest like a giant, dull knife. Beneath the chaos, despite the pain, his thoughts race with detached clarity. His NanoPrint isn't arbitrarily failing him, he realizes—it's attacking him. The unthinkable—the stuff of conspiracy tales—has come to pass. He's known for some time that his end is near; he's spent many sleepless nights worrying over the how and when, but he never imagined that his own NanoPrint would be weaponized against him. He's terribly afraid now. Of dying, naturally, but equally for those he's leaving behind, the few who have made life worth living.

It's now or never, he realizes. Everything he's worked for—all that he's endured to protect his loved ones—it all boils down to this moment. The realization gives him an ounce of bitter courage, and he digs into his NanoPrint process queue. Sequences cycle there at dizzying speeds, resolving too quickly to interpret in the best of circumstances, but that doesn't matter. As the dying man issues his final command, a victorious smile rises above the agony of death.

_execute file pedestal.exe;

His implant responds instantly.

... Fatal error encountered.

... Connection failed.

The smile flickers off like a popped filament. Just like that, it's over. He has failed. Nothing remains but to die.

Abruptly, as if cast away by a great wind, the bondage of his implant leaves him; the persistent signage, the gentle chemical prompts he's endured every moment of his life—they're quiet for the first time, and in their absence, the silence is sweet bliss.

Blackness engulfs him, and though he longs for the plush nothingness of that soft abyss, a lone thought gives him pause on the very precipice of death.

There's only one hope now—but who will protect the boy?

Part One:
Ignorance Is Bliss

One

August 21, 2105

There's an expression: once you've bedded down with death, she'll never leave your side. Some guy said that over a hundred years ago. It must be very profound, because people continue to parrot this bit of nonsense as if it truly explains everything. I don't really get it—the image that comes to my mind is a pretty morbid one. I'm hardly an intellectual, though—a little on the lowQ side, in fact, if my genomap is to be believed—so what do I know?

Not much, as you will undoubtedly come to understand.

Until early this morning—so early, in fact, that it still felt like yesterday—I really thought I was at peace with my mortality; death and I had an understanding, you see—and no bedding down was required.

She doesn't come looking for me; I don't tempt her by wandering into oncoming traffic.

It's frightening how quickly things can change—like a worn-out toggle switch, completing a circuit at the slightest touch when one would rather wade through transition gradually, as if into cold water.

Just like that, death has plumed around me like a thick, clinging mist; I feel it condense on me like morning dew, and I wonder if I'll ever be clean of it again. Certainly, I'll never take death slightly again.

>>*Silly, Wilson ... you're awfully sexy, but did you mean to say 'never take death* lightly'*?*

Oh, uh, please excuse my nexus interface—Marilyn has a tendency to interrupt. To her credit, she's considerably more pleasant than the other available interfaces. And I don't suppose it hurts that she's modeled after a wonderfully voluptuous pin-up model. Actually, I sometimes look forward to Marilyn's corrections. Who am I kidding? I goad them when I get a little bored.

It should come as no shock to you that I am single.

Anyway, I stand corrected: take death *lightly*. The point is, I should've slept right through the waking hours. If I'd been granted even a tiny inkling of what was to come, surely I'd have covered my head with a pillow and smothered today from my future.

Speaking of sleep: though I crave it deep in my bones, rest is completely out of the question. I stayed up much later than was responsible last night, playing the odds that I'd manage to squeeze in a little break-room catnap during lunch today—it seemed like a good bet last night when I was riding an unnaturally hot streak at the poker table. A hectic morning at the ER wasn't even on my radar.

And so here I am, headed to my office aboard a crowded tram with scarcely a few grudging ounces of gray matter left awake to man the helm. I know it's hardly the appropriate time to notice, but the sun is kissing the clouds through the window in stunning pastels, and the air is crisp with autumn beginnings. Everything's so beautiful, so disproportionately alive. It's a slap in the face to cliché, whose script calls for a Gaussian haze of cold drizzle. Still, it's an exceptional morning; I wish I could pause it in midstride to revive it on a day when I'm in better form to appreciate it.

What can you do?

I smile mechanically at a lady seated opposite me on the tram—not because I hope to engage her in conversation, but because she's pretty, and society deems this worthy of a respectful, if not admiring, smile. She nods politely—not because I'm reciprocally handsome, but because it's considered socially responsible to humor the plain among us—and looks promptly away with a subtle cringe. She doesn't dare look again. The man next to me sniggers under his breath.

Yup, that's me: chick magnet.

It's okay, I'm used to it. Actually, while it often depresses me, I'm completely unfazed this morning. I'm far more dismayed—and likewise distracted—by the incessant nagging in my stomach. It isn't some trivial, back-of-my-mind *did I leave the milk out again?* sort of nagging, either. You can ignore those, with enough practice—trust me on that; I'm an expert in the art. This one lingers at the forefront of my awareness, casting my thoughts in balmy shadow.

I've been hanging on a single strand of hope, and it can only stretch so far. As much as I long for some invisible force to save the day, I know logic doesn't mesh with such mysticism—and disregarding logic certainly won't do me any good.

I've been up for more than twenty-four hours, and I'm in dire need of sleep or caffeine—or both. Since leaving the hospital this morning, my thoughts have continually returned to just how surreal the world has become; I feel strangely betrayed that life and commerce continue to bustle with such energy, irrespective of my plight. It makes me want to make others as miserable as me.

I didn't see any of this coming. If there were signs along the way, I somehow missed them. Yesterday, Arthur—my longtime friend and mentor—treated me to Gizi's Trattoria for my thirtieth birthday. Today, he's in a hospital bed with a heart that's only twitching at all by the magic of some determined machine. I can't fight off the primal need to scramble, to generate some kind of last-minute salvation by the sheer tenacity of my willingness to try.

But what can anyone really do for anyone when his number's up?

If you knew Arthur at all, you'd assume someone of his intellectual means—a man knee-deep in the tides of progress, nose buried deeper in the nexus than just about anyone—was surely first in line to opt in for medical monitoring on his NanoPrint. And you'd be wrong. Mrs. Grace, my elderly next-door neighbor, is convinced her implant will catch fire and cook her from the inside—like that's happened at all in the last fifteen years—yet even *she* had the common sense to opt in; there's just no downside.

But not old Art.

He's a paradox: he spends his days developing technology that few among us can fathom, and he's almost vehemently opposed to enjoying it. To be fair, it isn't the technology itself he takes issue with; it's our eager, worldwide reliance on it—the nexus, specifically. It's our global crutch. "One day," he's fond of ranting, usually over—or perhaps under the influence of—a tall glass of Cabernet, "the pedestal of this arrogant civilization is going to collapse. It's a historical inevitability. We've lost our animal instinct."

He's a good friend—the best, actually—but at the moment, I want to give him a good kick in the nay-saying rear. If his aversion to all things normal wasn't so freaking acute, his health problems would've been detected long before they could fester.

But then, I guess he wouldn't be Arthur.

Passing swiftly into the lobby of my office building, I grab my usual extra-large coffee from an automated kiosk. Please don't judge me for my addiction to manual caffeine infusion—there are far worse things to be addicted to, after all. I make a careful run to the elevator, where Keith Billings, my recently transgendered boss, is already onboard. We slingshot to the seventh floor. I expect her—er, *him*—to offer some tacky, preemptive condolence as if Arthur has already passed—because Keith's just the sort of socially retarded person who would do something like that—but he doesn't say a word.

At least, not right away.

He waits until we've already walked into the office to open his mouth, and when he does, his androgynous voice pitches to a level of condescension one might normally reserve for a six-year-old—I mean, if there's a mother out there with so little regard for her maternal responsibilities that she'd even allow a weirdo like Keith near her kid.

"Hey, Wilson. Didn't see you there," he says. "How's it going?" Sheesh, he might as well drop to one knee and put a hand on my shoulder—*What do you wanna be when you grow up, little guy?*

For a split second, I imagine my coffee soaking his face, washing away that stupid smile and a pound of blush.

Seriously? Like we didn't just ride the elevator up here together?

Like I didn't just hold the door for you two seconds ago?

Like you don't already know that I've been sitting in a hospital room for the last four hours?

This is exactly the sort of thing that drives me crazy about Keith. I used to be more tolerant of his disregard for social mores, perhaps because I thought I saw a light at the end of the tunnel. Unfortunately for us all, his little, uh—*procedure* didn't resolve his extreme eccentricities. Worse than ever, his weirdness routinely breaks free from the good old parentheses of gender confusion and bleeds into everyday interaction, where it manages to make even the most innocuous of social situations utterly unbearable. So pardon me if I'm a little intolerant. I think I've earned it. This particular incident is pretty mild, I suppose, but recognizing that doesn't make me want to backhand him upside his fat head any less. So I dig deep, clench my fists and—

A wave of chemical calm ebbs through me, and for a split second, I nearly forget why I'm upset at all.

"Doing fine, Keith," I say in a voice that seems far away.

That'll show him. Okay, weirdness aside, he's still my boss.

"Too bad about Arthur, huh?" he says. With my irritation re-enflaming, I don't respond in word; rather, I look at him like he's a crank wearing mascara because—well, in part because he actually is, but more so because he doesn't get to chum up with me by the watercooler of my dying best friend—and frankly, I can get away with a nasty look when nasty words might just get me the boot.

He waits about two seconds longer than is socially acceptable and then decides to move on. "Well, anyway, I guess you know we're all gonna be pretty swamped for a while; hope you're up to the challenge."

That last statement wasn't exactly phrased as a question, but I can definitely sense one in there, buried in Keith's careless inflection—as if I suddenly get a vote in my workload and can just say, *No, I'm a little tired this morning; just ignore me for a while so I can go watch cartoons, would you?* For a moment I think he's hinting that we have a new contract coming down the pipe. I cringe at the very thought, reflecting back over the countless weekends and late nights I've sacrificed to the god of career advancement as new contracts are broken in by Innovative Design Systems—my renowned employer and, in times like this, my Alcatraz. We're already sacrificing our Saturdays just to keep up with the workload—for once, I think we can afford to say no to a client or two. But then, as Keith busily miscalculates my reaction in another swell of awkward silence, I realize what he's actually getting at.

Arthur's not likely to return—time to face facts—and that means someone here needs to take on his immense workload until more permanent arrangements can be made. Unless I've misinterpreted Keith's shoddy imitations, that someone is going to be me.

>>*Silly Wilson ... you're so kissable, but did you mean to say 'Keith's shoddy* intimations*'?*

Whatever, Marilyn—*intimations*. If you weren't so smokin' hot—

Anyway, the point is: *yikes!*

I work nine or ten hours a day, and I'm a zombie by day's end; Arthur's been putting in a minimum of twelve a day since before I was born, juggling a million hats to keep our projects on target. He's sort of a jack-of-all-trades around IDS. He's as much a fixture here as any of the equipment we rely on every day—more so, when you think about it: he's been around a heck of a lot longer.

More to the point, he's a department of one. If he dies—when he dies—the rest of us will only be able to speculate about what he did all day long.

Sure enough, when I walk into my office, I find one of Arthur's project drives on my desk. I sip my coffee with a scowl. Don't get me wrong: I'm a team player. I've always been willing to go the extra mile in my professional life, and I don't intend for this situation to be an exception. But I'm irritated. It's not necessarily the extra work—which is pretty significant, by the way—it's that I'm neither equipped nor trained to handle the tasks that have been tossed so casually into my lap. It's a recipe for failure, and I don't relish the likelihood of coming up short. Ironically, the one person with the necessary skill set around here to train me was never given time or priority to impart his wisdom when it counted.

So now, when it's too late, I'm supposed to perform a miracle with my hands tied.

This isn't the first time Keith has pulled something like this, either. He often tries to play like I should know what the heck Arthur does all day long, since we happen to be buddies. It doesn't appear to matter how many times I explain to Keith that I am not

Arthur by proxy. Actually—and my boss is fully aware of this, even if he likes to feign ignorance—my work at IDS has almost no overlap with Arthur's. It hardly seems appropriate for me—or anyone else in my tiny department—to absorb that level of accountability. Arthur and I work in two completely insulated worlds. My department writes procedures for the nexus; Arthur secures them.

Sip, scowl.

Case in point: for several months now, I've been working on a proprietary add-on named IntelliQ, whose title is a pretty lame convergence of *intelligent* and *queuing*. Don't blame me—my opinion on the matter died a horrible death the moment the marketing department got their CamelCase-addicted hands on it. Anyway, unlike our usual projects—which are generally proposed and commissioned by our clients—this one is of my own design and volition. If it makes it into the marketplace, restaurants will be able to use the nexus to seamlessly manage their table turnover, waiting lists, and even their supply inventory. And I'll finally make my mark on this company.

I'm very excited about it, yet in the entire time I've been working on it, I don't think I've ever done more than toss around its market potential with Arthur.

Why?

Because the guts of IDS programs simply aren't germane to our friendship. They are, however, germane to my tale. So please forgive the following explanation.

IntelliQ is a patron analysis suite. Unlike native nexus analytics, which are leveraged exclusively for logistics management, IntelliQ endeavors to quantify the eating habits of restaurant patrons—what they typically order, how often they leave room for dessert, how long they like to linger for leisurely conversation, how much they tend to tip, et cetera—and calculates the likely resource investment and, ultimately, the profit margin associated with each dining party before they ever walk through the door. Patron statistics are carefully guarded throughout this process in accordance with nexus privacy protocols, but the statistics aren't the point. The real payoff begins at the moment when a patron makes a formal entry to the daygrid on his—or her—implant, favoring a particular restaurant; as these data points

12

become available to the nexus, IntelliQ fluidly adjusts projections for consumer turnout at the restaurant and modifies its efficiency plan for seating, menu preparation, staffing, et cetera. It will shave a minimum of twenty percent off the average restaurant's operating costs.

A fringe benefit for patrons is that if a venue is over capacity or running a waiting list, IntelliQ can be used in conjunction with the nexus to issue notices to customers' daygrids with real-time alternative recommendations based on their preferences, proximity, traffic and so forth. Of course, that's a selling point that we'll only tout from one side of our mouths, since no restaurant will appreciate their customers being redirected elsewhere when they could instead be made to wait. Nevertheless, once the nexus is in possession of the ball, tram and shuttle schedules will remap accordingly to compensate—all in an instant.

If the program tests well—and I have no reason to believe it won't—it'll be a shoo-in for the government's next add-on roundup. If that happens? Oh, man ... I tremble with bliss at the thought. It'll mean billions for IDS over the next few years—of which a percentage will be justly mine. And not only will the enhancement benefit restaurants—which will pay well for it in the form of taxes—commerce in general will become that much less volatile, paving the way for even higher-profile government contracts with IDS.

I know. I'm awesome. By the way, this is just the sort of dinner conversation that has kept me single for most of my adult life.

Anyway, Arthur comes into play the moment my programs land on our test partitions. Even then, he's not terribly interested in my programmatic procedures; his concerns revolve around which gateways I'm using, which scripting libraries I've imported from the codebank. What he does—I think—is plug our programs into the nexus via our corporate portal, which in turn releases them into the market stream behind the appropriate firewalls across the global network. Without Arthur, my program's dead in the water.

Hey, let's just call a spade a spade: without Arthur, IDS is doomed.

If Keith seriously thinks I stand a chance at filling Arthur's enormous shoes, he's as asinine as he is socially retarded. Whether he's prepared to acknowledge it or not, our top contracts are in serious danger right now—the government isn't known for giving second chances. We've done a good job for them over the years, but there's no loyalty in business or bureaucracy. A single mistake, and they'll drop us like a rotten egg.

I swipe the drive over my terminal reader and chew my lower lip as its contents splay across my screen. I sort the file list by modified date, as if that's going to help. I don't know what the heck I'm looking at. I open a few files and scan their contents in my code editor: it's all nonsense. I recognize a virtual host configuration script here, an .htaccess file there, though I have only a vague idea of what they do. I know they hearken back to the days of the dotcomosaur, before its abrupt evolution into the nexus, but that's it. I only recognize them at all because I took an immersive course on the history of programming in my college days. It was a mind-numbingly boring download that examined bits of old-world computer technology to prove that, while technology continues to advance, programming concepts remain fairly consistent. Apparently some of the programming itself managed to stick around as well.

I close down the files in rapid succession. I'm about to dismiss the drive altogether when a file catches my interest. Well, really, it isn't the file itself that has my interest—it's the extension. At IDS, we work with proprietary file types, unique not only to our industry, but to our company. In other words, we make up our own extensions and assign them internally to different compilers as needed; and we do this to an absolute fault—no exceptions. So finding an .rtf file extension on the list raises an eyebrow.

If you're not a fellow nerd, let me explain: I'm looking at a run-of-the-mill rich-text file—one that by design is readable on just about any technological platform known to man, with or without the nexus. To preserve the integrity of our security, IDS prohibits the use of these, so finding one on Arthur's drive throws me off—at least until I open it.

At once the confusion is gone, and in its place is grave concern. My stomach cinches into a quivering fist as I survey a list of names—names I recognize from all walks of prominence.

Scott Heber, Envirosec CFO: 100,000;

Amanda Van Burr, NSA Operations: 60,000;

Ronald Weistmeisser, FAA Operations: 70,000;

Leah Carlisle, Miritech (more notably, the vice president of Unified freaking America, for crying out loud!): 110,000;

Mannford Waters, Global Freight and Logistics: 60,000;

Et cetera; the list goes on and on and on.

In and of itself, this file is circumstantial, if not meaningless—at least, a court of law would say so. But around here, many of these names carry significant weight; not only are they general points of authority my company routinely encounters as we spec out new projects, these are the very names that grease the wheels of progress in this country.

Envirosec is the single largest security firm in the world, tasked with maintaining the global integrity of NanoPrint technology and its legal implementation in commerce.

The NSA is very much a governing force in the overall scheme of budding computer science, as it has been for hundreds of years—nothing happens without their permission.

The FAA is responsible for vetting every single NanoPrint add-on to determine its compliance with wireless transmission guidelines.

And so forth.

If any one of these guys gets a bad taste in his mouth for your product, you can bet it'll never see the light of day.

I don't want to read too much into this file, but I can't think of a single benign explanation for its existence. My gut tells me this is bad news, not only for IDS, but for me. Unless I'm just being paranoid, somehow Arthur—and by extension, IDS—has landed smack dab in the middle of something sinister. Something I'm not supposed to know about.

Before anyone can get an unauthorized eyeful over my shoulder, I swipe out of my workstation, gather a few things from my desk, and head for the door. Keith looks up from his desk as I pass by his office, a manicured eyebrow hiking toward his hairline—I know, it's messed up; he tossed his biological heritage out the window, yet he's holding fast to many of the behaviors that came with it. Fifty cred says he still pees sitting down.

Oh, gross. Why'd I go there? Now I'm thinking about Keith's body—Keith who used to be Keisha with boobs, until she paid someone handsomely to have them chemically lopped off in the name of equality.

I really just stopped in to get some files together. Given what's happened, I wasn't planning on staying long; already this feels long enough. Keith gives me a *hey, what's the deal?* sort of look, but I don't bother with a detailed explanation. I just nod toward the elevators and say, "Be back in a little while." No point in wasting breath, anyway; experience tells me that Keith will likely consult my proximity stats on the nexus, heedless of what I say. A more respectable person might call up my daygrid to determine if I'm headed out for a late breakfast or a dental appointment, or whatever. But Keith has no respect for anyone's privacy, least of all mine.

Two

Fifteen minutes later, I walk into the hospital. The odor of the elderly and otherwise terminally infirm wafts over me, and I now fervently wish I'd stayed at the office. I guess the grass is always greener.

Arthur looks terrible; that much is obvious even from the hall. I intend to go in there and see how he's feeling—and to demand answers, if I can bring myself to be so callous—but framed by the doorway, my friend looks so pitiful, so unnaturally frail, that I'm suddenly unsure that I can face him. It's all but impossible to juxtapose him against any ledger of wrongdoing; he isn't only my best friend, he's always been a monument of integrity. Yet, though it pains me to admit it, I'm already seeing him differently after opening that file. I feel like the worst kind of friend for withholding any benefit of doubt from him, a man who I know deserves better.

I lean against the wall outside Art's doorway, where I hope to be unseen, should he happen to open his eyes in my direction. I remember the last time I was here for any length of time, four years ago, when my aunt Gertrude passed away. Somehow, though she still holds a dear place in my heart, this seems worse. Maybe it was the abruptness of her death that made it more bearable; before

I even learned that she'd been involved in a freak accident, she was already dead. There was no room for hope, no slow easing into acceptance.

One moment she was here, the next she wasn't.

This is different; the onset of Art's condition has similarly come from nowhere, but unlike Gertrude's, Arthur's fate is an island on the horizon toward which he slowly rocks to and fro. I have no doubt he'll eventually reach its sandy shore, but it's impossible to pin that moment on a timeline.

The hospital is virtually empty; healthcare is a dying industry—if you'll pardon the pun. Don't get me wrong: I'm sure emergency rooms will remain forever abuzz with the broken limbs and bloody lacerations that prove we're all still human and fallible. But whoever got the bright idea to chemically override the natural life cycle of cellular development turned the healthcare model on its rear forever. The—

>>*Oh, Wilson ... you make me all warm and gooey inside, but did you mean to say 'turn the healthcare model on its* ear'?

What? No—ear? Now, how does that even make any sense, Marilyn? What I mean is, the life expectancy of a healthy human being, left unchecked, anyway, more than tripled on that day, so I can see why it must've seemed like a great idea at the time. I'm sure the guy never considered what should happen to people when they outlive their societal value.

The indignity of the nexus—or at least, the political powers that oversee the nexus—deciding how and when I'm going to kick the bucket enrages me if I allow myself to dwell on it. Politicians were never meant to don the reaper's cape, of that I'm quite sure. Nevertheless, even if my cells are still dividing and synapsing like little champs, their days are literally numbered.

I guess I'd be less offended if I didn't also feel systematically sapped of my free will while I'm still alive; everything I do, for example, is logged, classified, and then plugged into projections, which are then used to either influence or predict the commercial value of my next move. I can't go number two without the wipe dispenser advancing six squares because at some point the nexus sensed a trend in my number two behavior and applied its conclusions to my global preferences. I don't care that six squares is the perfect amount and that, if given a choice, that's the number I'd invariably pick anyway. The fact that I don't get to be spontaneous about it makes me want to squeeze my cheeks together and hold out for a day when I can rip off eleven squares— or use a crank bidet without consulting the nexus—just for the sake of mixing things up.

A nurse passes me and gives me a vague, sympathetic smile, which reminds me that I have more pressing concerns than hygienic wipes and bidets. I nod politely, then take a breath and step inside Arthur's room. As soon as I reach his bedside, I know something's wrong. The machinery to which he's umbilicaled is still. In fact, all the gizmos and electro-widgets that were sustaining him earlier appear to have been powered off. When I left here early this morning, Arthur's room was a tone-deaf choir of beeping and mechanical swishing, pulsing to the twinkle of countless LEDs and tiny backlit panels. Now, the musicians have retired, and the lights have gone home to sleep off the nightmare. By all appearances, my friend has been abandoned, left here to die.

But that can't be true, I know. They must've done all they could here—and he died anyway. All the medical gadgets in the world are useless at some point. Still, they could've covered him with a sheet or something—or has that tradition fallen by the wayside just like everything else of value in this age? And the part that's really bugging me: why didn't someone tell me?

No one should have to die alone, least of all Arthur.

I reach out to touch his hand and find that my own is trembling. I'm breathing heavily now, through my mouth because I'm afraid that the smell of death will overpower me. I've never seen a dead body before, and I'm not ashamed to admit that the experience is creeping me out a little.

Before I can overthink it, I take his hand in mine and give it a tentative squeeze. It feels smooth and uncalloused—spared from the wear-and-tear of manual labor—like my own. Yet it's cool against my skin, and there's a stiffness that shouldn't be there.

I have to remind myself that this isn't some slab of meat—this is *Arthur*.

Arthur, the family friend who took me to my first carnival when I was six years old.

Arthur, who became a father to me when life deprived me of a more legitimate one.

My buddy Art, who used to have me over for dinner every Thursday night, until his wife Mitzy became concerned that I'd never learn to be independent.

Art, the worst poker player in the world.

Arthur, my colleague who went out on a limb to get me hired on at IDS when my résumé wasn't quite up to snuff.

Arthur, the stranger who apparently decided his monthly credits weren't enough and got himself mixed up in something ugly.

Arthur—my best friend, to whom my last words—something stupid and wasteful, like *Be back soon, Art. Don't bother flashing the nurses, they've seen it all before*—were hopelessly inadequate.

I begin to cry, as much in anger as grief. It doesn't take much effort to dream up a target deserving of my rage. Mitzy left Arthur a couple of years ago. Last I heard, she was living off her alimony with some bum, slurping Mai Tais on the beach and snorkeling over the Great California Reef. I hear it's something to behold, and it makes me sick that Mitzy is experiencing it when her ex-husband—whose credits she is shamelessly burning through—will never get a chance.

Other than me, Arthur has no one; he may be a longtime darling of the rockstar technological community, but like many brilliant men, he's armed with the social prowess of a cinder block. Few have been diligent enough to wade past the awkwardness, and though I sometimes feel elite to the point of snootiness for being among them, that charm has now completely lost its luster.

I suppose that's only part of why I'm angry right now. Perhaps more than anything else, it hurts that Arthur has kept me in the dark. Because I—like him—have few people in my life. And of that few, I trusted Arthur exclusively and wholeheartedly. My best friend may have kept secrets from me, but I have never dreamed of keeping one from him.

I hear a faint shuffling behind me and turn to find a short, plump doctor there. I'm momentarily stunned by his oblong physique—not that there's anything wrong with plumpness, it's just not something you see every day. The night-burner in our implants zaps surplus calories by default, after all. I don't think it does much for me, but only because skinniness is already in my genes.

"Sorry about that," the doctor says. I cock my head slightly at this; I'm not sure if he's apologizing for startling me, his obesity or for the state of neglect his hospital has left Arthur in. If he's referring to the latter, I sincerely hope he's prepared to do better than that. "We weren't sure who to notify," he explains, as if that should clear up the whole matter.

I clear my throat, giving him a moment to recant this ridiculous statement. Just underneath the awkwardness, I feel our implants shake hands, buffering my periphery with a few megabytes of useless trivia—am I honestly the only one who truly doesn't care to know everything about every person I encounter? I purge my buffer without a second thought. The rotund doctor merely smiles grimly and shrugs. He must know how stupid he sounds—I mean, how is it possible to *not* know—especially given Arthur's prominence? It crosses my mind that perhaps Arthur's celebrity loses steam outside of techie circles, but in any case— ignorance is no excuse. There are laboratory animals capable of learning what this hospital is apparently too lazy to bother with.

I guess my expression is sufficiently dubious—and perhaps

something a little more alarming—because the doctor takes a half-step back. I feel something dark stir within me at the sight of this; I suppose it strikes me as an admission of guilt, and that only validates my sense of indirect victimhood.

"Exactly how long has he been left here?" I ask. "Like this, I mean." My words are sharp and overannunciated; I hardly recognize the exaggerated timbre of my voice. I feel my NanoPrint send out the shut-up juice and for a moment, I'm disturbed by my rudeness. I look again at Arthur, though, and I feel instantly vindicated.

"An hour, give or take," says the doctor. "I understand he was already deceased when he was admitted this morning."

He's covering his butt, and I guess I can't really blame him for leaping to the defensive. I nod, not at all to let him off the hook, but because I sense that my emotions are getting the better of me, and I don't trust myself to speak just now. What he's said is true, after all. When I arrived this morning—only minutes after Arthur—the ER staff had just resuscitated my friend. They were coldly unoptimistic about his chances, explaining it had been more than twenty minutes since his heart stopped, according to his implant. Knowing little about modern medicine, I found some false encouragement in their successful resuscitation. Later, I learned that Arthur's implant was electronically stimulating a heartbeat and that no measurable brain activity was responsible. Eventually, his implant would give up and power down.

And that would be that.

Nevertheless, and despite everything I've been told, I unconsciously clung to some vaporous hope for a miracle. It was stupid of me. But honestly, what else could I do?

"Listen, Mister—?"

"Abby," I say with annunciation that can only be described as something resembling a feline spit. "Wilson Abby." *Check your stupid proximity sensor, jerk.*

"Right. Mr. Abby, my name is Dr. Philip Seymore."

I nod, but make no move to shake his hand.

"I wonder, Mr. Abby, if you have any idea how we can reach his next of kin? We really need to make arrangements before the state takes possession of his body."

I give him a blank stare. "You mean other than the freaking nexus directory?" I'm doing the best I can to keep a lid on my snippiness—because for all my grief and indignation, I understand that my flesh is crying out for an excuse to lash out—but this guy's really going out of his way to make himself a target.

Seriously: next of kin? C'mon, you couldn't hide that information if you tried. You gotta be limping along with a broken helix to miss it.

Again—laboratory animals, people.

"Yes, well, that's proven to be surprisingly problematic," the doctor says. His voice is slightly aflutter with what might be nerves, or—more preferably—shame for making such an idiotic statement and keeping a straight face. Whatever the case, I feel a little guilty—and a tinge proud, if I'm being completely honest—to be the source of it. It's never been in my nature to be hateful, so I'm appropriately appalled at my behavior. Yet somehow, I feel liberated by it.

Huh. Being a jerk isn't supposed to feel this good, is it?

Well, while I'm at it, would it be petty of me to mention that this poor excuse for a physician has one of those stupid little moustaches? I suppose in the right context, the right sort of guy might just pull one off—a millionaire playboy, perhaps; Dr. Seymore is most certainly not the right sort of guy. Not only is he freakishly plump, he's uncomfortably asymmetrical, out of square in a way that flesh was never intended to be. It's like he's been cobbled together from bits of genetic leftovers. Based on these inadequacies, it seems logical that his brain has suffered similarly, in which case I should probably have some sympathy.

Despite my mental tantrum, I wisely hold my tongue. I realize that regaining even that small bit of decorum is a victory. I choose to take credit for this over the fresh rush of chemical influence coursing through my veins.

Dr. Seymore has a uniquely vulnerable quality; I get the sense he's both accustomed to insult and completely unprepared for it. Which seems to beg the question: what's with the look? I mean, when you think about it, it would take a fair amount of effort to circumvent your night-burner; it's a native NanoPrint function, which excludes it from the scope of user preferences, so you couldn't disable it casually. And the moustache?

As I ponder this, I begin to wonder if the doctor and his deceased patient might have been chummy under better circumstances; perhaps they shared an equally yoked distaste for society's predications for unnaturally prolonging life.

>>*Silly Wilson ... you're the best kisser in the whole world, but did you mean to say 'society's unnatural* predilections'?

Oh, um, she's just kidding. About the kissing, I mean. Pardon me for a moment.

open NanoPrint admin

config nexus attributes

modify globals

... Modifying nexus globals is highly discouraged. Erroneous configuration may result in unpleasantness such as poor connectivity or physical death. Are you sure you want to proceed?

confirm;

open global preferences;

disable NanoPrint digital assistant;

Marilyn slides into retinal view and gives me an angry pout at full, scornful opacity.

>>*Well, somebody's being a crank fuddy-duddy.*

Sorry, Marilyn.

apply settings;

... Configuration saved.

exit;

Marilyn gives me a rueful sigh and a great, invisible wind

billows her white skirt around little hands that only just protect her modesty. With an indignant *Hmph!* she blows off my retinas like a deflating balloon.

Where was I? I've lost my train of thought, but fortunately, Dr. Seymore is right here to keep me on track with another brilliant witticism. "You see, Mr. Billings left us no medical records or living will, and there's a small problem with his NanoPrint."

I breathe a deep, therapeutic sigh through my nose and project a flat smile. A security guard appears at the door and begins to hover patiently. A moment later, when he's joined by another, my eyes begin to narrow suspiciously. "Okay, I'll bite. What sort of problem?"

Dr. Seymore looks me sharply in the eyes, sustaining the glance as if it might say something all on its own—although exactly what is beyond me—and shifts his attention to the officers at the door. For a split second he seems frightfully uncomfortable. I guess I can understand, even if I can't personally relate; getting the dress-down in front of a corpse probably hasn't been the highlight of his day. Then again, I'm not exactly having the best of days either.

Then, just when I've begun to think he has forgotten about me altogether, the doctor opens his funny moustached mouth to speak, and the words that come out plunge into my chest like little auditory fingers, squeezing the breath from my lungs with flesh-like dexterity.

"Well, I guess there's no easy way to say this, Mr. Abby, so I'll just say it. It's gone. His implant has been, uh ... well, somebody removed it."

At once, I understand with horror why Art was left uncovered, why hospital security is waiting to pounce on this room as soon as I depart it. Looking once more upon Arthur's inanimate body, my inner lens starts to come into sharper focus.

Good Lord, this isn't merely Arthur's deathbed—it's a crime scene.

Three

I push past Keisha—dang it, *Keith*—and into the racks. The whine of servers and auxiliary fans is so intense here that most don't dare venture inside without hearing protection. Actually, on most days, I'm quite careful to heed this precaution—it's been somewhat of a belabored point at IDS since one of our interns sued us a few years ago, back before it occurred to us to mandate the use of earplugs.

Under the circumstances, a little hearing loss is the least of my concerns.

I make a beeline to the back wall, where Ryan and Tim—our resident server and database gurus—are locked in heated debate over nonsense.

"There's no way Telia is hotter than Gillian—she's got a crank third arm!"

"I'm not talking about on the show, idiot. I'm talking about in real life. Besides, you're not considering the potential of a third arm, Ryan."

"Ugh! You're a lonely man, Tim. A sad, lonely man who needs a pet. And a therapist. A three-armed therapist with a license to lobotomize."

"*I'm* lonely? The last time you went on a date ... wait, I'm sorry—have you ever been on a date?"

Tim's wearing a t-shirt that says, "Don't hate me because I'm beautiful; hate me because I'm smarter than you," and I almost crack a smile. On any other day, you know?

I wait patiently for a polite break-in, but their volley is as fluid as it is juvenile. I realize a few minutes in that my presence is somehow prolonging their exchange rather than drawing it to a close—I've given no sign of amusement, but apparently they consider a bored audience to be better than none at all. At four minutes and twenty seconds, I can wait no longer.

"Listen up, guys," I bark. The whining of fans is already rousing a headache. "We have a big problem." The banter falters; they both look at me with deadpan eyes and—as if sharing one brain—ask in unison, "Where're your earplugs?"

Ignoring the jab, I hastily explain the mystery surrounding Arthur as they listen with mouths round and agape—they're like kids hearing their first ghost story. And believe me: in our industry, that's exactly what this is.

When I've finished, they whip into immediate action. For a solid half hour, they bounce from console to console, consulting our numerous nexus access portals in a blur. Finally, exchanging a glance of grudging defeat, they face me in tandem.

"He's gone, Wil," Ryan confirms. "Completely gone. No GPS coordinates, no electro-magnetic proximity signature. No transaction history. No daygrid. No update log. Nothing."

"It's like he never existed," Tim adds with a scowl.

I'm bewildered, and don't mind showing it in front of these cranks—they're used to dealing with dimwits; actually, I think that's what they prefer. "How is that even possible?"

Tim passes Ryan a sidelong glance, as if requesting permission. Ryan responds with a weak shrug. Tim looks back at me and clears his throat.

"In theory? It's not. You couldn't destroy a NanoPrint if you tried—corpses from seventy years ago are still online."

"What about dodgers?" I ask. "They don't even have implants, do they?"

Ryan shakes his head. "That's not how it works, Wil. Having your implant removed doesn't take it offline. It may power down, but it's always threaded in the system."

"Besides," Tim adds, "dodgers usually have their implants hacked to maintain functionality. It takes a special kind of person to *really* go off the grid, you know? Dodgers usually just want a little more privacy."

"Oh," I say, deflated.

We stand there in silence for a few seconds—well, we didn't speak; there is, of course, no such thing as silence in the racks. Ryan makes a sudden whistling sound between his teeth, which peters out into a clicking of his tongue. "You know ..." he intones, as if dangling a bit of candy to a child. Tim and I both peer at him plaintively, hopefully.

Ryan smiles—one of those thin, crooked smirks that he must know annoys the pee out of everyone—and pauses for effect. My eardrums are beginning to smart, so I'd just as soon dispense with all the drama.

"Spit it out, man!" growls Tim.

Yeah, what he said! I add with an exasperated tossing of my hands.

"I'm just saying," Ryan explains reasonably, "I mean—it isn't technically possible for a NanoPrint signal to disappear. As long as ..."

Until 2086, the capital of Florida was ... anyone? Anyone?

Tim's eyebrows slowly rise, scrunching his forehead into an epiphany of skin rolls. He gets it now, even if I don't. I clear my throat—my own dramatic contribution—which is only just audible above the noise. Turning to me, Tim blessedly completes the fragment of thought that I've proven incapable of completing on my own.

"As long as it's still on the planet."

I've been knocking on Uncle Stewart's door for a while now with no response. He isn't in the best of health these days. Now, I'll grant that he's pretty spry for a man in his seventies, but he's been coughing lately. A lot, in fact. It's hard enough to keep from dwelling on the looming of his eightieth birthday, when his NanoPrint will automatically shut him down. Lately, I'm not sure he'll make it that long.

I happen to know that Stew never enabled medical monitoring on his implant. It's a shame he and Arthur never got along; they certainly had that in common. I've tried more times than I can count to steer the old man toward reason. He isn't just stubborn; he's utterly incorrigible.

My knocking crescendos into pounding, fueled by a lifetime of abandonment issues. Behind the panic, I'm acutely aware that I've begun to draw some unwanted attention from the neighbors. But some things justify extraordinary behavior—like the idea that my uncle Stewart is lying in the throes of death, helpless to let me in. I'm on the verge of kicking the door in when a shuttle lowers in front of the building. Uncle Stewart steps out of it and, spying me on his doorstep, shakes his head with mild irritation.

"Don't you ever read your updates?" he grumbles. "I ran out of Earl Grey."

Oh, Stewart. Blessed Stewart.

I don't, incidentally. If I had my druthers, I'd delete my NanoPrint updates out of hand—and Uncle Stewart knows that perhaps better than anyone. They remind me that my every moment is theoretically mapped out before me—whether I like it or not—and I hate that.

"Sorry, Stew," I wheeze, rushing him on the sidewalk with an uncharacteristic bear hug. I'm so relieved my eyes are stinging.

If there's a god out there, thank you.

We sip our weekly cup of tea—decaf for Stewart, since he's

an old fogey and has probably been ready to hit the sack since noon. He's already heard about Arthur, who he's known vicariously through me for many years, but never really clicked with in person. I want to tell him about the list and Arthur's missing NanoPrint, but I suppress this urge. The last thing I want is to worry Stewart unnecessarily with such things. He's the type of person who cares too much to be an idle listener.

Once, when I told him that Keith had me working mandatory overtime while another programmer was on an unplanned vacation, Stewart actually stopped by IDS to tell Keith what a miserable boss he was; I barely intercepted him at the elevators in time—ten seconds later and I'd be painting office buildings and hanging my hat in the ghetto stacks. Another thing: he's always trying to get me to eat when I've already eaten—*You're too skinny; a boy your age shouldn't be so skinny*—as if he doesn't share a skinny gene with me. Come to think of it, I don't think he's ever let me out of his apartment without a piece of fruit for the road. I don't have the heart to tell him that I usually toss them without taking a single bite.

He annoys the daylights out of me. And I love him all the more for it; he's one of a dying handful who cares enough about me to bother.

Heading home, I'm so immersed in my thoughts—worrying about Stewart, wondering what I'll ever do without him around, now that I've learned to fear death—that I almost don't notice the stranger loitering at the front of Stewart's building. I only notice at all because he's trying so hard to be unnoticed—at my approach, he seems determined to avoid eye contact, yet I could swear he's watching me from the corners of his eyes as I wait for a tram.

Huh.

After three long days of vigilant analysis, I've come to one solid conclusion regarding Arthur's files: if I'm truly our last hope to get things back in order at IDS, we'd all better start revamping our résumés. I'm brain-fried and frustrated beyond measure, and I have absolutely nothing to show for my considerable time and energy.

There's no point in delaying the inevitable. I'm simply not the man for the job; no amount of staring at Arthur's files is going to change that. So I corner Keith in her—dang it, *his*—office, prepared to officially throw in the towel.

"I can't do this, Keith."

"What do you mean?" he asks, eyes widening innocently, like he honestly doesn't know the difference between one of his junior program analysts and his former A-game security administrator.

"Arthur's files; I can't make heads or tails of them. You're gonna have to find someone else to work with them. Maybe hire a consultant or something."

"Huh," he grunts. "That's surprising. They're that cryptic, huh?"

"And then some."

Keith leans back in his chair, which screeches as if it might buckle under his considerable form—and trains a reptilian gaze on me. "No change logs or read-mes? Nothing like that?"

I feel my blood slow, my eyes narrow.

"I kind of thought Arthur was highQ enough to leave a breadcrumb, or something we could use. Something in a language the rest of us could understand."

Okay, this is getting weird—the way he said that last part? It's like he's trying to steer me—like he already knows. "What, you mean like a text file?" I ask, my voice filling with gravel and steel.

Keith smiles slightly and shrugs, tapping his desk with a fat, hot pink-nailed hand. "Sure, why not?"

Angrily, I turn to leave, but he calls after me. "Wait a second, Wil. Just hold your horses." With a great creak, he heaves out of his chair and steps toward the door. Squeezing past me, he peeks through the open door and then shuts it.

Suddenly, I can feel my heart racing. It's been doing that a lot lately, with everything that's been going on; I wonder if in some high-rise, Nike analysts have taken notice of the trend as well, deducing that I've finally gotten into exercise and am now a worthy cause for marketing.

"What is this, Keith?" I demand. He smiles—it's all in his mouth, though; nothing at all friendly in the eyes—and returns to his desk with slow, deliberate steps and hands clasped, as if he's on a stroll through the park.

"Why don't we just settle down for a minute, Wil? I can tell you're upset, losing your buddy and all."

"It's Wil*son*."

"Fine. Wilson. I know you like to think you have a monopoly on caring about this company, but I can assure you that IDS is just as important to the rest of us. And a few of us have a heavier burden here than you can imagine." He pauses to make sure I don't have anything wise to crack. I do, naturally, but now isn't the time. "The problem we face as a company," he continues, now with a professorial air, "is making money when everybody out there has a hand out, looking for his piece of the action. If it were easy to make a profit in that kind of climate, everyone would be doing it."

I feel him taking me down a path and, though I can't quite see where it leads, it smells a little fishy to me. "Last I heard we were turning a nice profit, Keith. So I'm still waiting for the part where you justify accepting illegal kickbacks. We don't need to make money on those terms."

Keith blinks. "Kickbacks?" He scoffs, covering his mouth to absorb the force of a magnificent guffaw. "Jeez, Wil," he laughs. "You got your head on upside down and backwards, kid."

Wait for it ... here comes my trademark dumb expression. "Uh, what do you mean, *upside down*?" Backwards I hear on occasion, so maybe there's something to it. Upside down is a new one.

Keith plops back into his chair and sighs. "Nobody's on the

take here, okay? It's the other way around. Listen, Wil—"

"It's Wil*son*!"

Keith sighs and taps his desk with a pen. "Wilson. It wasn't always like this. There used to be a time when we could all just come to work, bust our butts and keep the world running. Everybody was happy—we all got a nice paycheck, our shareholders made some fat coin. But then something happened." Keith sighs and begins chewing thoughtfully at the inside of a cheek, forming a makeup-spackled, pocked, dimple on the outer surface. "You ever hear of Palmer Gunn?"

The air around me seems to smack me in the forehead. *Whoa.* Didn't see that coming. At the invocation of that name, I feel the blood drain from my face. "Who hasn't?"

"Exactly. Only, when he first started sniffing around this place, none of us had. Didn't take long to figure out what the score was, though. That's for sure. Told old Pinrose he had to pay the toll—you remember Pinrose? Way before your time."

He was before my time, but among programmers around here, the guy's still a legend—he and Arthur practically built this company from the ground up.

"Anyway, if you know anything about Pinrose, you know he didn't take any circuit scrap from anyone. So when Gunn came in here, throwing his weight around like he owned the place, you can imagine it didn't sit well with Mr. Pinrose. Way I hear it, he had Gunn tossed out like a piece of trash."

My eyes must be bugging.

"Crazy, huh? These days, Gunn'd probably wipe a guy's entire family off the map over an undercooked steak. But those were different times—I guess he was still cutting teeth. Anyway, green or not, Gunn didn't give up there. Sure, Pinrose had some spine, but there were plenty of others who didn't. So he got in their pockets instead."

"So, what are you telling me? Those people are just passing the expense on to us?"

"In a manner of speaking, yeah. Cost of doing business these days."

"But it's illegal, Keith. Surely that crossed your mind!"

"Listen, Wilson, let's make one thing real clear. This wasn't my doing; you got a problem with the way things are done around here, look no further than your pal Arthur. He set the standard long before I came up the ranks. When a guy like Arthur tells you to look the other way like your career's on the line, you look the other way."

"Is that what you're asking me to do, Keith? Look the other way?" I feel my NanoPrint at work, trying to calm me down with some hormonal concoction, but my indignation is too concentrated to be reasoned with. "Why didn't you just clear the file off the drive to begin with? I can't believe you dragged me into this."

Keith plaintively shows me his palms. "I didn't know what else to do, all right? If someone doesn't step up to the plate, we're all gonna go down in flames. And I thought I knew you well enough to know you wouldn't let that happen. Guess that was my mistake, huh?"

"Let me tell you something, Keisha—"

"It's *Keith*." *Ding! Score one to Wilson Abby.*

"Whatever! You don't know anything about me. You think I'm just gonna pretend nothing's happening? Jeez, how'd you think this was gonna play out? If Arthur went along with this, it's because you or some other scumbag had something on him. Good luck finding anything on me."

Oh my God, that felt good.

Yeah, I know I'm seriously burning my bridges with Keith; any chance I had of walking out of here with a better understanding of what's going on poofed out of existence the moment I opened my stupid mouth. Keith's face twitches, his cheeks darkening a few notches right through his makeup, and it occurs to me that I've probably just torched my job. Watching that painted troll rise slowly from his chair, I realize that losing my job may be the very least of my concerns—because man or woman, this crank can take me, hands down.

I don't give him the chance; in one fluid motion, I swivel in place and yank the door open, bolting for freedom with a surge of adrenaline. Keith stomps after me. "You're making a mistake, Will!" he bellows. "You're gonna wish you could take this all back, but it'll be too late."

Fat chance, Keisha.

I find a hole-in-the-wall pub and seat myself near the back, where the lights are low and the air is stale with the humidity of electronic cigarettes. I run my finger along the table menu and swipe my finger twice next to some kind of Scotch, ordering a double on ice. Six credits. I'm not exactly an expert on the subject—this may be my fifth bar excursion ever, actually—but six credits seems close to giving it away. A soft drink costs twice that, in fact. I can't imagine how these guys manage to stay in business.

Minutes later, a filthy bot delivers my drink tableside. I take a careless sip and it all makes sense. Never before have I wondered what a mixture of spoiled butterscotch and pig urine might taste like. Now I know. I'm beginning to question the sanity of whatever urge brought me here when something extraordinary happens.

The most stunning woman I've ever seen sits at a nearby table and, looking directly at me, smiles.

I honestly can't explain just how things progress from there. One minute I'm grimacing at the tang of bad Scotch, the next I'm dropping bad lines—the sort that might normally buy a man a kick to the diodes—on this spectacular lady, and somehow they're working. It's like I can't say anything wrong. I buy her drinks, she laughs at my stupid jokes. She spouts wit like old faithful, and I laugh with genuine abandon. Deep down, I know she's just looking for a few free drinks, though a woman of her caliber really ought to set her sights on a classier place than this.

The thing is, though—the way she looks at me? I've seen that look before, just never trained at me. As bizarre as it sounds, there's little doubt that she has an interest in me. There's a connection happening here, and despite all logic, it isn't completely one-sided.

Her name's Adrian Stone. Pretty, huh? She's exceptionally beautiful—way too hot to be wasting her time on a loser like me, but I'm too enamored by her presence—and more than a little inebriated—to question my luck. As we walk outside and a tram pivots against the curb to envelop us—where we're headed isn't even a concern, just that we're headed somewhere together—the sports store next door begins to spam my NanoPrint, causing it to spew a barrage of Nike signage. I laugh. Long and hard, like I'm trying to dislodge something within, and I don't stop until Adrian kisses me.

I'm really not sure what to expect from work today—my belongings waiting unceremoniously in a box at the lobby desk, perhaps? A lengthy, unpaid suspension? As it turns out, it's neither. Rather, it's like nothing ever happened. Keith stops by my office and, to my shock and relief, trades Arthur's project drive for a set of unrelated project specs. It's as if yesterday was a figment of my imagination, except that as Keith walks off, he gives me this weird conspiratorial wink—like we're sharing an inside joke now.

Fantastic.

Around noon, I eat some kind of health wrap in the cafeteria and watch the news on the Viseon wall. I'm feeling warm and fuzzy, ruminating over last night and wondering if Adrian is really just a dream—I guess I'll know if she ever calls like she promised. At some point, the news begins to compete for my attention. Vice President Leah Carlisle is onscreen. With a quick adjustment to my

NanoPrint, Carlisle's voice is streaming directly to my auditory nerves. She's proudly tooting her own horn in a way that only pandering presidential candidates can do without blushing.

"My company, Miritech, spends billions every year toward the development of new medical advances. As well, we're active participants in the War On Drugs. We fund the operation of multiple rehabilitation centers and law enforcement task forces to put a stop to illegal drug use. Why do we do this? We do it because we care about the people of this great nation. With my help, we can—" she blathers on and on. It makes me a little sick to hear her voice, especially knowing what I've learned. I mute her with a scowl. I can't help but notice she's wearing huge olivine earrings. Somehow—however irrational—I feel certain they're the real thing, carved from the core of some fantastic chondrite meteor. And there's little doubt in my mind that these superfluities were paid for with credits scraped from IDS pockets. And, of course, she's bolstering her stupid campaign at the expense of my company.

Yeah, I'm probably being a little unreasonable. She was bleeding blue long before IDS came along to fatten her credit accounts, after all. Acknowledging this doesn't help, though; in a way, it actually makes things worse. She doesn't even need our money—she just saw a wounded victim and thought she'd get her pound of flesh along with everybody else.

In disgust, I toss the rest of my lunch into the nearest bin, ignoring its shrill beep of protest that my plastic fork hasn't been separated from the biodegradables. As I storm out, my NanoPrint tingles, alerting me that I've just been fined for this indiscretion.

Dang it.

It's very late and pleasantly dark with just a sliver of moonlight seeping between my drapes. Despite two glasses of Merlot and a rather slow mystery on my retinal display, I can't sleep. I could remedy this easily, if I really wanted to. I have several sleep-aid add-ons at my disposal, any of which could have me sawing logs almost instantly. The truth is, I think I'm enjoying the struggle, dwelling on Adrian like a teenage boy who's just seen his first bra.

Did I mention she called this evening? I guess she isn't just a dream after all.

Four

Arthur was a master storyteller, when the mood struck him—a cool glass of wine on a warm night generally got him going, in the right company. The man could conjure fiction from thin air like some sort of magician. Most of his tales stemmed from life before he was even born, the era he affectionately called *the good old days*— when a man carried his fortune in a billfold and anyone of sound mind could manually operate a motorized vehicle. These nostalgic accounts, while wildly entertaining, were too terrific to believe. Even more fascinating than the stories themselves was the excitement with which Arthur talked about life before the nexus— his mannerisms, the way his eyes would lose focus as he lapsed into a state of pure longing—it's as if he had fallen in love with a time he never knew. Though he never spoke the words, I sometimes got the impression he believed the nexus has ultimately caused more harm than good, which is ridiculous, of course— downright blasphemous.

Nevertheless, Arthur's stories have foddered my daydreams since I was a kid. I don't fantasize about a futuristic society where my every whim is catered to, where a NanoPrint add-on can flavor the blandest gruel, or perhaps make me irresistible to women— well, that last one comes and goes. I dream of a land where vegetation still grows according to nature's design, where people still know how to cook and engineer contraptions in their workshops. Where being a neighbor means more than physically residing next door to a stranger. I dream of a world in which people are prized in part for their roots. Surely there's really nothing wrong with having cultural differences; dismissing our ethnicity doesn't make it any less a part of us, even if our entire global society is ostensibly devoted to quashing the concept of heritage—in the name of peace, of course.

Anyway, dreams are just dreams. Thanks to the nexus, though, I have access to an endless supply of old movies in which these fantasies are repeatedly lived out vicariously across the backs of my retinas—or on my Viseon walls, when I have company.

Incidentally, I know I've finally found my soul mate when Adrian one day confesses that her guiltiest pleasure also happens to be old movies. I mean, seriously—what are the odds? I can count on one hand the number of people I've met in my life that have seen a single movie released before 2050. I feel like I've just won the lottery or something!

Together, Adrian and I admire the antiques of cinema, enjoying the palpability of real people on film, projecting from a single wall—long before 4D processing dragged us into a movie when the movie was too weak to pull itself off on its own, even before film stardom made the shift from live personalities to digital avatars—until I fall asleep in her arms.

Generally speaking, I don't normally wake up with the urge to seek out my dead best friend's ex-wife. There was a time when I really liked Mitzy, when I cared for her a great deal, in fact. But when she left Arthur high and dry, I quickly grew to despise her, dismissing each fond memory of her when I could, characterizing the rest as moments of normative fiction. It wasn't just that she and

Arthur could no longer see eye to eye—that sort of thing happens to the best of us—it's that she made such a gratuitous show of exercising her newfound freedom.

I know how much Arthur must've hurt, yet he kept it all to himself. He was like a citadel standing tall amidst the rubble of a sacked city. So stoic, so forgiving. After all she'd done to wound him, he still wouldn't permit a single ill-spoken word against Mitzy in his presence.

Like it or not, I have to find her. Otherwise, Arthur will be unceremoniously recycled, the flesh of his former essence ground into the landscape alongside a multitude of this super-city's unclaimed vagrants.

I have no intention of allowing that to happen.

I take a sick day—yeah, I know my NanoPrint will forsake my fake cough, and I'm way beyond caring—and spend the entire morning tapping the nexus for leads. I've never been very good at this stuff, mostly because I'm too antisocial to keep up with the enormously progressive tools available for social networking. It was child's play for Arthur—not because he was any more socially apt than me, but because he understood the basis of the technology—but he's not exactly available for customer service.

An hour before lunch, I finally stumble across something I can use.

Mitzy has dinner reservations tonight at a restaurant in the Bellagio in Vegas. I'm not sure why, but I feel my distaste for her sharpen as I learn this; perhaps it's the impression that she's gambling away Arthur's hard work. Or maybe it's that life is serving up dinner as usual for her while the man she once vowed to stand by is dead on a table.

I submit a contact request through the nexus and sit back to wait. If I'm lucky, she'll respond in the next few minutes and I'll get this over with.

An hour later, my NanoPrint remains utterly still. Mitzy's avoiding me. Perhaps I should leave it at that, but now my ego is raising its hackles. I should probably eat, but my stomach is filled with the rocks of apprehension. I submit another contact request—this time to Adrian, letting her know that I'll be out of town until tomorrow. With a scowl bitterly affixed to my face, I take a shuttle to the airport. By seven p.m., I'm in Las Vegas headed toward the renowned strip with my scowl quickly losing steam; I guess it's hard to stay grumpy when you're surrounded by the bling of Sin City. I've been using my pocket terminal to check the nexus as I travel; as of now, Mitzy is still presumed to be on time for dinner.

If all goes as planned, I'll be waiting for her.

It hasn't even occurred to me that I should make my own reservations until I arrive to find the restaurant packed with an hour wait. I know what you're thinking, and you're right: it *is* too bad—IntelliQ could've prevented this. Fortunately for me, I'm not here to eat, anyway; I just need to be ready when Mitzy walks through that door.

But as time snails ahead and the tables slowly turn over, my nerves begin to rebel. It's a little past eight o'clock now, and I've detected no sign of her. By now, my stomach is cussing and gurgling a rude reminder that I haven't eaten since breakfast. I check the nexus again to see if Mitzy has rescheduled, and my guts perform an unpleasant flip-flop.

According to her proximity sensor, she's already here.

Shrugging off the protests of an ultra-chic host, I push my way into the restaurant and begin scanning the tables. It's a large restaurant, gaudily adorned with oversized chandeliers and colorful frescos. But despite its size and likewise sizeable clientele, I'm certain I'll find Mitzy if she's in here.

Only, I don't.

I'm about to leave when—thanks to the now irate host—security decides to graciously help me along. I land on my rear on the steps outdoors, bruising both cheeks. I've never taken the phrase *thrown out* literally until now—I guess they don't mess around in Vegas.

For a few minutes, I'm overwhelmed by bewilderment; the best I can manage is to sit on the steps where I landed, rocking from one wounded buttock to the other as I try to pinpoint where my plan went wrong. My next move is unclear. Logic dictates that I wait right here, because eventually she's got to come out—and when she does, she'll have no choice but to walk right past me—but my gut is chiming in, and not merely out of hunger.

Something is wrong, it whispers.

How could I have missed her coming in? I'll cede that I'm hardly trained at this detective stuff, but I watched the entrance very carefully, and I simply can't imagine how she managed to slip past me. That ship has sailed, unfortunately.

I'm not about to allow the next to follow suit.

Using my pocket terminal, I edit its notification settings to alert me of any activity on Mitzy's daygrid. Then, I do something I've never before considered an option: I put a formal proximity trace on Mitzy's NanoPrint. Proximity traces aren't really prohibited, but they're greatly frowned upon. I'm sure a few million stalkers and jealous ex-husbands think they're great, but the rest of us find them a little unsettling. Nevertheless, my desperation outweighs my shame for the moment, so I sit back to wait.

As it turns out, I don't have to wait long—at least, not when compared with the waiting list inside.

A half hour after my gymnastic exit from the Palagio, my pocket terminal begins to vibrate like mad. I get my feet underneath me as a small crowd exits the restaurant and spills onto the stairs. Not a crowd, really, just five people who are loud enough to give a crowd-like impression. Among them, there are two smartly dressed men arm-saddled to gorgeous ladies, and a fifth, unaccompanied woman, who is pretty, though considerably less so than her peers. I scan their faces, though it's obvious that Mitzy is not among them. At their approach, I'm forced to step aside to allow them passage down the stairs. All the while, I keep a frantic eye peeled for my quarry, who ought to be here, yet somehow is not.

I check my terminal and discover with mounting frustration that Mitzy has somehow gotten past me again. Her daygrid has updated, reporting that she's headed to a nearby nightclub, just a few blocks down the strip. I step toward the shuttle queue but think better of it—I'm in a hurry, and to be honest, I could use a little break from sitting—and begin walking in a brisk stride down the strip, passing by lurid posters and beckoning marquees. When I finally approach the club ten minutes later, my trace reports that she's already inside.

Following her trail, I forfeit an ungodly number of credits just for the privilege of walking through the door. It's dark, lit primarily by strobes in opposing corners. The music—if I can call it that—is loud enough that my ears might well begin shooting blood at any second. The flickering lights are messing with my vision a little, but it looks like—yes, I see something. In the corner, seated at the bar without her beautiful friends, is the pretty lady from the Pelagio, nursing a watery drink through a long straw. Actually, though I perceive her to be alone, she's all but surrounded—yet completely ignored. At first I can't make sense of what I'm seeing: a pretty lady in what appears to be a thriving singles bar, without a bite on her lure? She seems sad, resigned. She's swaddled in the sort of melancholy that makes her all but invisible to those around her, and though nothing about this situation makes sense, I feel my heart ache for a beat. I check my pocket terminal to confirm my suspicion, and sure enough, it's her.

Except that it isn't.

At once, my empathy turns cold. Instinct tempts me to swarm in and expose this little con of hers—and if I choose to do so, I'll be completely within my rights; nexus fraud and identity theft are tantamount to murder these days—but something tells me that's not the right move. So instead, I squeeze alongside her at the bar and introduce myself.

I'm terrible at this in real life—I don't doubt that women have been pushed over the very edge of sexuality by my romantic ineptitudes—but the situation in which I've just found myself doesn't quite seem real. It seems so surreal, in fact, that I very nearly spit out a fake name and crash and burn right out of the shoot. I try to buy her a drink, but that goes nowhere fast; the music is just too loud and the lighting is so sporadic that lip-reading is a complete impossibility.

Suddenly—and mercifully—she throws me an unexpected bone.

Slugging back the clouded dregs of her drink, she takes my hand and leads me outside. With the blare of music at our backs, she laughs nervously. "Take two, if you don't mind," she says. She speaks in a clipped tone that is at once guarded and approachable. In the harsh neon of the strip, her eyes shine like smoldering chrome. "I'm Mitzy."

I let that percolate for a second before opening my mouth to respond. Maybe I didn't expect her to be so bold with her alias, or maybe I'm just finding it hard to marry such a familiar name with the face of a stranger. Either way, I'm taken aback—and therefore immediately at a disadvantage. "Uh, Wilson," I reply. "My friends call me Wil." We shake hands like businessmen, and she giggles as our implants do likewise. Her xchange stats upload to my NanoPrint almost instantly; for once, I don't purge it.

"Well all right then, Wil. Are you going to ask me to dance, or is it too old-fashioned to expect something like that from you?"

I chuckle with a cringe. "Oh, I'm plenty old-fashioned. But I'm a miserable dancer." Believe me, this confession is understating reality to the point of absolute irresponsibility—imagine a chicken burning alive in slow motion, and you'll be on the right track.

"Thank goodness," she exclaims with a nervous titter. "My roommate says my dancing is more than likely the reason I'm still single."

"Suddenly I feel like I'm missing out on something."

"Believe me, we're all better off." She apparently realizes the contradiction in her behavior thus far—leading me down a path to dancing, when in fact she has no interest in following through—because she immediately follows up with a disclaimer. "Sorry, I guess I'm not very good at cutting the ice." Her eyes lose focus for a split second and she blushes. "I mean, *breaking* the ice." A breeze brushes past us and the pheromones of her faint perfume perk me up.

It suddenly dawns on me that I've been flirting with a pretty sexy lady, and for some reason she hasn't run away in tears yet. Maybe there's some truth in what they say about men becoming more attractive simply by entering a relationship. Perhaps this woman can sense my unavailability and is subsequently helpless under its strange power. "How about a cup of coffee?" I offer. She smiles her assent and offers an elbow.

"What about your friends?" I ask, though I don't hesitate to link arms with her. "Won't they miss you?"

"Oh, sure. They'll be heartbroken to lose their fifth wheel."

We find a little diner that serves breakfast and pie all night long and I order a cappuccino and a slice of blueberry pie. I could do some pretty substantial damage to the entire menu, but some adolescent psychology has me feeling weird about eating real food in front of her. I keep having to remind myself that this isn't a real romantic encounter—that this girl is an imposter—and that whatever attraction I may be feeling for her is just another product of her deception. Then, to my surprise, she orders a cheeseburger and fries, and rounds it out with a chocolate milkshake. Noting my boggled face, she laughs with a cute roll of the eyes. "Don't worry, we'll go Dutch."

"Oh, uh—"

>>*Go Dutch?*

...*In a courtship situation where both parties are assumed to have a similar financial standing, the traditional custom of the*

*man bearing the financial burden may be forgone in the ritual of
"going Dutch"; the origin of this ritual is often attributed to the
Netherlands where—*

Jeez, forget I asked.

"Um, tell me about your name," I say when our waitress
leaves us. "It's a little unusual."

"It was my grandmother's."

"Really. Where was she from?"

"You wouldn't know it from the name, but she grew up in
France. A little south of Paris. I went there once when I was a kid.
They still speak French there today, if you can believe it."

I scoff. Leave it to the French to defy world order while the
rest of us speaks Unified English.

"She and my grandfather died when I was fourteen.
Automobile accident—some crazy guy rammed their tram with
one of those old gas cars. They both died instantly."

Her explanation sobers the mood a little; if she's lying, she's
very accomplished at it. I ask about her job, her hobbies, her
favorite things about the city—all subjects intended to reveal
inconsistencies in her identity, which are easy enough to cross-
reference against the xchange stats hovering in my social buffer.
Interrogation or flirtatious curiosity, she's either too highQ for me,
or she's the real thing. Not one of her responses seems to be
anything other than the honest truth.

And the way she keeps looking at me? Wow. I haven't the
slightest idea what has attracted her to me, but let's just say I could
very easily forget that I'm not on the market.

"You're cute," she announces abruptly. My heart flip-flops.

"Um, I think your definition of cute may be a little off." She
laughs and I feel my cheeks flush.

"Maybe," she admits. "I think it goes deeper than appearance,
though. You're different than other guys I've met."

Relaxing a little, I sip at what's left of my cappuccino. "How
so?"

"Oh, I don't know," she mutters shyly. I shrug and level a patient stare; there's no unringing that bell. Mitzy realizes this and eventually relents with a grudging smile. Her pretty eyes narrow as she takes me in, slowly and methodically. A moment later, she sighs. "Well, for one, you don't exactly dress the part, do you?"

"What do you mean? What part?"

She giggles. "You know, a ladies' man."

I scoff at the absurdity. "Me? Oh, that's funny. What else?"

She bites her lip, gaze pushing through my eyes to some plane far beyond them. I sense that the conversation is about to go a little deeper than I've been in a while, but I don't stop her. I'm not sure I could if I wanted to. "I kind of get the feeling you don't quite... um, belong."

I feel my heart deflate, but I try to smile anyway. "Wow. How flattering." I lean back in my seat, crossing my arms.

Mitzy covers her mouth with a cringe. "I'm sorry, I shouldn't have said that."

I wave off her apology. "It's fine, really. Besides, you're right. This place," I nod toward the window, into Vegas's pretentious cityscape, "isn't really my thing."

The brightness in her eyes fades a notch and her mouth forms a bittersweet curve. "That's not quite what I mean," she says softly.

Meeting her gaze, I nod slowly. The truth is, I know exactly what she means.

I feel her hand seek out mine and the world seems to flicker. "The thing is, Wilson," she says quietly, "Neither do I."

An hour or more later, I walk her outside to the street. As we stand by the tram tracks, radioactive in the glow of blinking neon, I realize she really is exceptionally pretty. Just not necessarily in the conventional way—her charm is a vital component, and with it added to the equation of her allure, she's truly a delightful creature.

A tram clatters through the moment and cinches against the curb at our feet. I'm hesitant to let her go; after talking with her, I feel more confused than ever. I'm afraid of what might happen if I dare to stick with her—because there is some undeniable chemistry happening between us—but I'm equally afraid of letting her out of my sight until I've unraveled this tangle of pretense.

Mitzy seems to detect—if not understand—my apprehension, and before I'm aware of what's coming, she steps boldly—yet somehow timidly—into my arms and touches my lips with hers.

The moment we connect, I feel like I'm drowning in electrified honey. It's a sweet, unpracticed gesture that feels more real than any human contact I've ever known. Images of corn fields and homemade apple pies enfold me. I try not to think, to just bask in the moment—but from the periphery of my mind, a voice berates me. I should probably listen to it, because even now, with lips tingling and cheeks aglow, I recognize that what I'm doing is not only wrong—it's dangerous. Yet I can't seem to grab hold of common sense; it tosses about like a kite in the wind—and before I know it?

Well, I suppose what's done is done.

Like it or not, my heart has just divided. When I return home to Adrian, a piece of me will undoubtedly remain here, with this lady. Long after her tram departs, I stand there in a daze.

Oh, crank. What've I stepped in this time?

Five

I hole up in a cheap hotel—a good mile from the strip, where an average Joe like myself can still afford to sleep indoors—and spend the next several hours fact-finding on the nexus. I'm getting better at it. Plus, I'm better able to focus my efforts with Mitzy's xchange profile at my disposal.

Stuffing my face from a second-rate room service menu, I find the first bit of interesting news: in February of 2091, a woman named Mitzy Renard was in fact killed—along with others, including her husband—in a freak automobile accident in Paris. The driver of the other vehicle, an eccentric local historian named Etienne Aucoin, was purportedly obsessed with the antiquities of transportation. Only a year before, he was arrested for operating an illegally restored motorbike after losing control of the machine and colliding with a road sign. He survived—miraculously, by the tone of the article—only to repeat his insanity later, this time with irreparable consequences.

This situation is starting to show all the hallmarks of data corruption, or perhaps misaligned data feeds. Fifty years ago, this sort of thing supposedly happened all the time. Records of like individuals sometimes became entangled through a variety of early-nexus hiccups and subsequently spawned broad confusion that lasted months or even years. These days, our records are uniquely keyed to our DNA profiles via our implants, rather than to the implants themselves. As a child, I remember hearing about these twins who had some weirdness with their implants because they shared the same nuclear DNA. But even that nonsense is ancient history. It simply isn't possible for one person to be electronically confused with another.

Or so I thought.

I'm not sleeping well at all. My sleep add-ons have individually been mildly helpful, but while each seems effective at putting me out, I repeatedly wake with a start, uncomfortable and confused about where I am, and none of them seems capable of keeping me out. Part of the problem, I know, is that I'm simply overwhelmed by the sheer variety of disconcerting situations in which I've found myself over the last several days. My mind simply won't shut off, and no amount of pleading makes a difference. Perhaps more than that, I'm a creature of habit, and I've betrayed my nature. This little adventure of mine feels less like a casual broadening of my horizons than an unpleasant stretching of my coping skills, which I've coerced well past their reasonable limits.

I can't wait to get home and curl up in my own bed, on the pillow I've spent years deforming to the curvature of my head. I can't wait to look out my own window at a view that is—while virtually featureless—blessedly familiar and perfectly void of the gaudy lighting and tacky architecture for which Las Vegas is both loved and hated the world over.

More than anything else, though, I can't wait to see Adrian. That kiss with Mitzy has awakened a lustful beast in me that I can't wait to unleash.

Dawn eventually crawls from a drunken coma and, peeking grudgingly over the window sill, finds me already showered and repacking my overnight bag. I feel my NanoPrint shiver an alert of my early checkout to the nexus. When I step outside, a tram is already waiting for me, prepared to cater to my every unpredictable whim. For all my complaining about the nexus, moments like this help me appreciate just how convenient it can be. I'm too tired to be chasing down a ride.

I'm home by noon. I rummage through the fridge and throw together a sandwich, watch a little of the news. I have contact requests from Keith, Stewart and Adrian that I've ignored out of habit, but I give them my attention now. I delete Keith's in midsentence—it's clear from his tone that he knows exactly where I've been, and that I'm not at all under the weather—but who cares? Stewart's left me a hearty grumbling about the evils of Sin City—admonishing that the house always wins—and Adrian says she misses me and can't wait to see me.

I know Adrian's probably at work, and I'm guessing Stewart's taking his midday nap because—well, that's what old people do, right? Nevertheless, I can't stop yawning, so I hit the sack for a nice, long nap of my own.

I awake to a knocking on my door. I'm hoping for Adrian but settle for Uncle Stewart as he trudges in out of an ugly drizzle.

"Wilson, you scared me half to death," he snips. I shut the door and, though he puts up a vigilant fight, manage to steer Stewart into the kitchen. I load two mugs with Folgers tablets, fill them with water, and set them aside to steep on the counter.

"Don't you read your updates?" I parrot with a sarcastic frown.

"Very funny. As a matter of fact, I did. And I took a junky tram over here to talk some sense into you"—unlike me, Stewart prefers the air-cushioned comfort of a shuttle over the Spartan utility of the common tram. I guess they're a little hard to come by after five o'clock—"but you were already gone." His mouth stretches thin and his milky eyes glisten. "When your planner said you were in Vegas last night, I nearly had a stroke."

Scrap. "Sorry, Stew. I should've called."

He nods, but his face remains taut, a mask of concern that prods my guilty heart. "What're you doing, Wil? This isn't like you—skipping out on work to gamble, not telling anyone where you're going or when you'll be back." He pauses to shake his head, which is possibly his greatest weapon in any argument, and then adds, "I'm worried about you."

I want to point out that I wasn't in Vegas to gamble, but I have a hunch that he already knows this; his body may have seen better days, but his mind and his well-earned intuition are still razor sharp. I'm thinking that where I've been isn't as much of an issue as my going there without first giving him the opportunity to talk me out of it. He really does seem worried, though. Yet as terrible as I feel about that, I'm just as annoyed by the kid treatment.

"Stew, don't blow this out of proportion. I just needed a day to get my head on straight. Everyone needs to blow off some steam once in a while."

"That's all this is?"

I hate lying to anyone, especially to Stewart. But, as I've intimated before, I prefer not to fuel his overt need to protect me from the elements of daily life. So I make a rare exception—well, I guess it's becoming less rare—and hope that I can pull it off.

"Of course. What else would it be?" I chuckle, throwing in a *don't be silly* wave for good measure. I sip my coffee, which is steaming hot and perfectly doctored with cream, no-calorie sweetener, and just a hint of cinnamon. Dang, it's good. Remember all that stuff I said earlier about wishing we still cooked from scratch? Yeah, disregard that nonsense. You just can't beat a good cup of no-prep coffee.

Stew is staring at me hard, mulling over my performance—which is one of my best, in my opinion—like a critic who's teetering on the fence. I lean back against my kitchen counter and wait for the verdict. A moment later, he sighs, shoulders visibly drooping as if a great weight has just been lifted away. He takes a loud slurp from his coffee—a rarity, by the way; I more than half-expected him to ignore his mug, or perhaps even pour it out, in his usual display of tea-loyalty—and finally rewards me with a smile.

"I was afraid that—" he begins to confess, but cuts himself off with a dismissive wave and a sheepish grin. "Well, I guess it doesn't matter. As long as you're okay."

"I'm good, Stew. Really." He nods his grudging acceptance and, as we exchange a truce smile, I'm suddenly aware of how glad I am to see him—and of my rumbling stomach, which hasn't quite forgiven my poor stewardship over the past twenty-four hours. "How about I whip up some dinner?" I tempt, happy to change the subject. "You hungry?"

Stew gives me a toothy smile and rubs his diminutive potbelly, and I know we're back on familiar ground. "Does a bear poop in the parking lot?"

I nearly cross my eyes over that one. "I don't even know what that's supposed to mean, Stew. But I think I'm gonna have to ask you to leave my kitchen."

"Oh, get over it. It wasn't that bad—just a little before your time."

"Seriously, Stew. That was just nasty. You're spoiling history."

I have breakfast with Adrian the next morning. Her silken hair is pulled back in a loose ponytail, demonstrating the effortless beauty that has every girl in the bistro scowling contemptuously, and every guy gawking at me with envy. Well, they're mostly staring at Adrian, but occasionally they glance at me, too, wondering—just as I often wonder—how such an incongruous matchup is even possible.

I tell her about my trip yesterday, minus a few details, naturally. I know what you're thinking, and you're right: lying is becoming just a little too easy for me. In my defense, what possible good can the truth do in a situation like this? Besides, it's more of a lie by omission, which isn't technically in the same category, is it? I tell her about the unexpected authenticity of Mitzy's backstory, and Adrian is appropriately surprised. She sips coffee and nibbles at a piece of toast with jam, stroking the back of my hand with a primly manicured fingernail.

Sheer bliss.

"You in any trouble with your boss?" she asks, pushing Mitzy to the back of my mind.

I shake my head no, but I really don't know yet where things stand. I guess I'll find out soon enough. If it'll help offset my recent binge of dishonesty, I suppose I can admit that I'm not looking forward to a confrontation with Keith. I'm not really worried per se, just dreading it like I dread waiting in line for a haircut.

"So, was she pretty?" Adrian's right eyebrow is peaked in warning. My gaze is drawn to a tiny scar at its outer edge, where she had three stitches when she was a kid. It's sexy, just like everything else about her.

"Good Lord, no. Pretty is not a word that should ever be used to describe anything about Keisha—er, Keith." I feel the contents of my stomach churn as my mind conjures images of Keith plucking his disgusting eyebrows, applying makeup before a heart-shaped mirror. "Jeez, that ruined me. I may never eat again."

Adrian giggles. "I meant the girl, dork. Mitzy."

Oh. "Next to you, my dear, pretty shrivels into dust."

"Oh, it better."

Dr. Seymore calls just as I'm headed out the door for lunch. I take his call and my Viseon wall alights with his gawky likeness.

"Any luck on locating Arthur's next of kin?" he inquires. There's a stain on his lapel that looks suspiciously like mustard.

"None. I'm not finished trying, though." He nods, but the expression on his face isn't encouraging. "Everything okay, Doc?"

He smiles. Now that I've had some time to grieve a little, I've lost my animosity toward him. I'm starting to view him less as an incompetent practitioner, and more of an eccentric one. "Thing is, Mr. Abby, we're pretty well out of time on this thing."

My jaw clenches, and though I know exactly what he's getting at, I feel compelled to ask anyway. "What the heck does that mean?"

Dr. Seymore gulps and some of the blood appears to drain from his face. "I'm sorry," he says plaintively. "You have to know that, Mr. Abby." I suppose I do, but it's not what I want to hear. Since I haven't replied, he forges ahead. "But since no living will has been located, and no family members have stepped forward, the hospital is required to honor state protocols." He pauses and swallows visibly again. "Arthur will be turned over to the city later this morning. More than likely, he'll be recycled by the end of the day."

Although I've been expecting this all along, it hits me like a wrecking ball. I'm too stupefied—to horrified, really—to speak. This city that I thought I knew and loved is preparing to shrug off the remains of my best friend—an icon in this town—like an old ratty coat. I imagine his ashes smoldering in a back-alley garbage can.

"Really, Mr. Abby, I can't tell you how sorry I am. I know how much he meant to you, and if I had any say in this at all, I'd—"

"It's fine," I cut in. Of course, it isn't—not by a long shot. How can this be happening?

I disconnect and turn to leave, but I'm not hungry anymore.

With a grave sigh, I return to my desk and begin making calls. After ten minutes of bouncing from office to office, I finally reach a cordial woman who explains that the city has already scheduled a pauper's wake for Arthur this afternoon—and as Dr. Seymore has already warned me, this process can only be overridden by the formal instructions of a family member.

I've got to do something.

I head toward the server room and snatch a set of earplugs off a hook by the door. Ryan's at lunch, but Tim's poking around as usual on an array of terminal keyboards.

"Hey, Wil. What's scrappenin?"

"Tell me you have something on Arthur's implant."

"Nah, man. My guess is we may never figure that mess out."

I tell him about Arthur, and he's appropriately disgruntled. Then I bring him up to speed on Mitzy and my cross-data contamination theory; he's intrigued and immediately begins to call up her profile in the nexus. He's smiling like a giddy schoolgirl, sifting through her purchase history—lo mein noodles from a street vendor, a scented candle from a perfume shop, underwear from Victoria's Secret, et cetera—with the gusto of a tried-and-true stalker. Suddenly, his demeanor shifts, smile fading, eyes narrowing.

"What is it?" I want to know, trying to wipe the fantasy of Victoria's Secret from my mind—how I can even think about that girl with Adrian in my life is a mystery.

"There's an anomaly here, see?" Tim directs my attention to the screen with a bony finger. All I see is a meaningless data grid, and I tell him so. "Right here, Wil. Look at this—see the profile ID for her NanoPrint? Now look at the profile ID tied to her credits and her proximity sensors!" With the aid of his finger, I do. They don't match.

"I don't get it," I confess with a tired shrug. "That's not supposed to happen, right?"

"Exactly. The only way it could happen is for someone to

manually alter the database."

"Okay, well that's a start, isn't it?"

Tim gives me a poignant frown. "The thing is, other than Ryan, the only person who's ever had direct access to the database—at least in our patch of the circuit—is Arthur."

Whoa. The room feels as though it's a giant tilt-o-whirl. "Hold on, are you saying Arthur did this? Why would he do that? It doesn't make any sense." Only, even as the words pass my lips, I realize that it does—well, sort of. Suddenly Arthur's split from Mitzy seems to take on a new light. Arthur was never the emotional sort—I sometimes wonder if he believed outward displays of emotion to be signs of weakness—therefore he never so much as cracked a frown when Mitzy left him. I feel as though a small piece in a giant puzzle has quietly merged with another, yet the overall picture remains obscured.

Tim shrugs, as if to say, *Stranger than fiction, right?*

"Listen, Tim. I need to ask you something—and it's important that you tell me the absolute truth." I need to know just how deeply Arthur was immersed in this little extortion racket, and I'm rapidly running out of leads. "Was Arthur involved in anything, you know—unethical—or anything?"

"Jeez, Wil. You're asking me? He was your best friend."

"I know, I know. It probably sounds weird, me even bringing it up. But have there been any—I don't know—rumors or anything? You know, things that maybe people talk about but would never mention with me around for fear of it making it back to Arthur?"

Tim pales, and I know I've hit paydirt. "C'mon," I prod. "I really need to know."

"Well, there's sort of been a rumor going around that he's been getting a little, uh, action on the side."

I blink. Just like that, there it is—right out in the open, where it's much harder to deny. "How long?" I manage to squeak out.

"I don't really know when it started. Right before he got

divorced, I guess. We all kind of figured it was a contributing factor and all—I mean, nobody cheats on a woman like Mitzy, you know?"

Uh—say what? "Wait a second, are you saying Arthur was having an affair?"

Based on Tim's expression, I surmise that I've just reached a level of dimwittedness previously reserved for the truly extraordinary. Mom would be so proud. "Hi, I'm Earth. Have we met?" he says. "What the heck have we been talking about, man?" He shakes his head and then pauses to appraise me, suddenly worried. "You sure you're okay?"

"Yeah, sorry. Just misunderstood you, that's all. So has anyone actually ever seen the other woman?"

"I'm thinking Rupert—you know him, right? Works on the first floor?—seems like he's the one that got all the bugs scuttling. Think he saw them kissing once when he was running some lines behind the building or something."

"Did he say what she looked like?"

"I don't know, man." I give him an incredulous glare, to which he replies: "C'mon, we're talking two years ago. At least."

"Yeah, okay." My vision pulses slightly, warning that my lunch break is now half-over. "Thanks, Tim. I appreciate your help." I'm about to leave when I realize the burden of populating Arthur's impromptu ceremony has fallen on my shoulders. "I guess Arthur's wake is this afternoon," I explain. "Any chance you can make it?"

Tim gives me the deer-in-headlights look. "Oh. Uh, I should probably stay here. Gotta leave a man on deck, right?"

I smile flatly at this pragmatic and perfectly reasonable excuse. But inside, my heart aches because I know most of the guys around this place will find equally reasonable excuses to bow out.

"Yeah, I guess," I agree with as little disappointment as I can manage. "I'll see you later, Tim."

Six

Though I've been given no reason to believe it will do any good, I have nevertheless decided to ensnare Dr. Seymore for a final plea before the cogs of progress irreversibly spring into motion. As it turns out, I'm wasting my time: Arthur's body has already been transferred to a nearby recycling facility. Not a funeral home, where he might actually get an ounce of the respect he deserves, but a wretched compost plant—a meat grinder for human souls. Apparently, this was in motion before I even left the racks. I learn this halfway to the hospital, my fingers wringing each other into nervous taffy. If I was alone in this tram, I'd scream at the top of my lungs.

I just can't seem to catch a break.

Upon redirecting my tram, my NanoPrint bursts a notification to the nexus. I wish I could rip it right out of my body. A few stops down the road, and suddenly I have the tram completely to myself. The availability beacon changes from green to red, yet I hardly notice. By now, the compulsion to scream has passed, but it's still nice to be alone with my grief. Oddly, traffic seems to part before me, clearing a distinct path through Chicago's bustling arteries like death itself. It might be my imagination, I suppose. Much of today has felt a little like this, though I haven't realized it until this very moment—like I'm passing between the clockworks of time, the minutes rasping away faster than I can experience them. Like I'm allowed to watch and to disapprove, to throw fits and wail like an angry toddler if I choose to. But I'm prohibited to participate, to interfere. To influence the course of fate.

Then, as I glance out my window at the pedestrians outside, noting their curious, sympathetic expressions, I realize what's happened. I don't know what triggered it—the implication of my destination? A rogue thought? Some hidden functionality in my daygrid? I can't even imagine. One way or the other, though, thanks to the nexus, my tram has become a funeral procession of one.

I'm not even sure how to feel about this. Normally, I'd be angry. Indignant, at the very least. Rather, I'm embarrassed—and maybe a little grateful, too.

I've never been to a human disposal plant before, though I have an image in my mind of what one should be like: cold and dismal, tightly clad in concrete, streaked gray by the perpetual duress of rain and sadness. Inside: pale linoleum, drably painted cinderblock, tarnished fixtures, industrial steel everywhere. When I step inside the real thing, I discover that my preconceptions couldn't have been more inaccurate. This place is plush and tastefully nouveau, from the serene garden in the foyer right down to the warm, inviting carpet.

A matronly woman greets me at the front desk and explains that this facility—for all intents and purposes—really is a funeral home, meaning that the business end of human disposal lies elsewhere. When my questions stall, the woman politely offers to help me navigate the facility. It's a large building, octagonal with a large fountain situated at its center. My escort leads me through an endless corridor which skirts its perimeter—the figurative circle of life, I guess. We pass a series of thematic viewing rooms along the way, most of which are not currently in use. I've lost count of them when the woman deposits me at an open door and, with a tidy bow, leaves me to my devices. From the hall, I hear soft music within.

I poke my head in bashfully, peering around the strange space, afraid to commit my body to its unexplored belly just yet. My nostrils are pleasantly teased with a faint waft of peppermint and jasmine. The music is ethereal, calming.

It's nice. So I ease inside.

The room is unoccupied, save for Arthur's casket and a few rows of padded chairs. The casket is constructed from some sort of translucent, glowing resin. I step forward and notice tiny fossils suspended in the resin, trapped like insects in ancient amber. I suppose this is supposed to be symbolic of something—and it truly makes for a beautiful effect—but I'm too emotionally impaired to give it my full appreciation.

But I have no doubt the nexus has taken note.

Arthur looks good for a dead guy. His face is lifelike and peaceful, like he's merely dreaming. I'm grateful that someone went through the trouble of restoring his pallor and shaving the scruff from his face; given that Arthur's is a pauper's wake—generally reserved for the homeless or otherwise unclaimed—I assumed every expense would be spared. I've never been happier to have been wrong.

I touch his hand—it's stiff, kind of waxy—and let my fingers glance off his wrist, not really repulsed by the stitches there as much as I am disturbed by the notion that he might have been alive to feel the pain as someone carved out his implant.

I glance around the room, soaking in the distressing emptiness of the space. The efforts of architects and interior designers can only take things so far; at some point, people have to show up. I feel immensely sad to be alone here with Arthur, to discover with certainty what I've grown to suspect—that I was his only friend. "Arthur, my friend," I whisper, "I'll never forget you." I lose my grip for a second and a thick sob slips through my net.

Then another. And another.

I hear a faint rustling behind me, like fabric against fabric, and swivel my gaze just in time to see a figure—a woman, I think—disappear through the door.

"Wait!" I cry out, but she's gone. I rush to the door and erupt into the hall; I catch a brief glimpse of her before she rounds the corner and disappears—tall and willowy, long auburn hair splayed down a black mourning dress—but I resist the urge to chase her.

Just then, like a lumbering hoard of socially inept degenerates, a small army of my fellow nerds appears around the bend, looking lost and confused, trying hard to look cool. My heart does a flying leap into my throat, and it's all I can do to keep from sobbing again. Leading the charge is Ryan, who I know never really got along with Arthur, but always respected him.

Thank God for him.

At his approach, I reach out to shake his hand, but observing my own quaking like a leaf, I shove it in my pocket instead. Ryan, who normally lives for moments of weakness in his competitive rivals—technically, I'm not his rival, but he's treated me like one since the day we met—draws no attention to this and gives me a comforting shoulder squeeze.

I return to the viewing room, this time reinforced by the presence of my coworkers. My thoughts are unapologetically frazzled, yet I have the presence of mind to appreciate that the nexus has managed to notify everyone about the wake. At the same time, I'm bitterly ashamed to have made so little effort beyond my paltry conversation with Tim. Thank goodness my coworkers, unlike me, are willing to heed their updates. But despite the volatile range of polar emotions I'm enduring for the moment—gratitude versus shame—one thought is persistently pressing things like them out, fighting tooth and nail for my undivided attention.

Ryan sits next to me and smiles. It's weird how tragedy does this—brings together people who are otherwise happy to be apart—and, before I've had a chance to think it through, my mouth has opened to speak my mind. "Did you see that lady in the hall?"

The smile falters, but doesn't disappear altogether. "What

lady?"

"You didn't see a lady in the hall, right before you guys found me?"

A nervous frown. "No, I don't think so. Pretty sure the hall was empty." Ryan's eyes dart around the room as his voice abruptly drops to a conspiratorial whisper. "Why, who was she?"

I sink deep into my seat. "Good question." My gaze is drawn to Arthur, where the others are busy paying their respects in a somber queue. I blink as I recognize Rupert among them, taking notice of the fossil-infused casket just as I had done earlier. I should probably sideline him now while I have a chance—we work on different floors, so I rarely see him around the office. Today is perhaps my second or third Rupert sighting in the last month—but I don't. It's not that I'm angry or tired. Maybe I've subconsciously concluded that I don't really need his testimony to affirm what I've already begun to believe.

And I don't even have to look at Ryan to know he's thinking exactly what I'm thinking: that I've just narrowly avoided meeting Arthur's mistress.

Good thing it was me here rather than Mitzy. Divorced or not, something tells me Arthur's ex would've torn that poor woman to shreds.

Adrian's in a protective mood tonight, repeatedly asking me how I'm doing, if I need anything. Saying things like *poor baby* and *I can't stand to see you hurting*. We have dinner in and watch a movie. Adrian's taking a sabbatical from old movies. I don't understand why, but I'm trying to be accommodating. Dumb flicks like the one we're watching now make that seemingly trivial task particularly difficult. It's yet another bland facsimile of a century-old chick flick that wasn't any good the first five times it was remade, but Adrian laughs and cries like it's the best thing she's ever seen. Worse, she revels in drawing the film space around us like a cloak, so she can feel a part of the story. Why she would waste 4D features on a movie with absolutely no action is a mystery to me, but who am I to judge? About halfway through, I stop watching the movie, silence my NanoPrint—there's nothing more aggravating than trying to watch a movie as your implant interrupts every other minute with useless film star trivia and snack advertisements—and begin watching her.

The view is far more entertaining.

The last thing I remember before closing my eyes is thinking, *How did I get a hottie like this?*

At two in the morning, I tread through darkness into the bathroom to pee; I'm committed to sleep, so my eyes are barely open in slits—it may be wasted effort, but I'm hoping that keeping them just so will allow me to return to the exact dream-state I awoke from. To my irritation, at the precise moment when I flush the toilet, my NanoPrint whizzes to life and a queue of unacknowledged contact requests unfolds down my retinas.

Goodbye, sleep. How I loved you so.

The first request is from Tim: "Never mind, Wil," he says. "I'll get with you in the morning. But be warned: you're gonna owe me big time when you see what I found."

The next one is from Mitzy. Wondering how I'm doing, if I might like to meet her for lunch sometime. If there were any remnants of sleep still lingering in my system, hearing her voice squeezed them out in an instant.

I think of Mitzy; I think of Victoria's Secret. I think of Mitzy wearing Victoria's Secret. I think of Mitzy no longer wearing Victoria's Secret.

Dang it.

I return to bed and lie there in the darkness, trying to work out what it is about Mitzy that has me so infatuated. In theory, she shouldn't even compare to Adrian, who is gorgeous in all the conventional ways, sexy to an absolute fault. Yet here I am, heartstrings singing at the mere thought of Mitzy—a girl I hardly even know. A young woman I'd thought to be a con artist only a short time ago.

I shouldn't be dwelling on these thoughts, I know, and I feel terrible for failing to ward them off. Despite my erratic behavior of late, I'm truly not a disingenuous or duplicitous person. I have no interest in deceiving the people around me, nor do I find the prospect of infidelity to be anything other than disgusting.

But.

What can I say? There's just something about Mitzy. Maybe in another life, another world where there is no Adrian or nexus fraud, we might've been something.

Seven

It's too early. I get into the coffee right out of bed, sucking down two cups before I even consider showering. Alas, it fails to medicate my caffeine deficiency fast enough, and for once, I turn to my implant for help. I recognize that it's an ill-conceived plan, but my brain is too sleep-deprived to come up with any less of a gamble. Wouldn't you know it? As common sense surely predicted, the coffee finally decides to kick in just moments after it's no longer needed, and now I'm more wired than I've been in a long time—possibly ever—and what's really weird? The sensation isn't entirely uncomfortable. I feel as though all the sharp corners—the unseemly burred edges of consciousness—have magically softened. It's like my mind is jaunting a half-step ahead of my body.

Waiting for a tram, my hands patting out an arrhythmic tribal cadence against my thighs—completely of their own accord, incidentally—I notice a couple of pigeons nearby. My interest is piqued when one of them begins some weird jiggling dance for the other, puffed up and bobbing about, effervescing like some gelatinous oil slick. The second bird cringes and turns tail as if offended—

Wait, wait, wait: can pigeons cringe? I may have imagined

that part.

—and abruptly flees in a rude applause of feathers. I erupt in boisterous chortling at this small-scale reenactment of my own romantic life, and a few of my fellow pedestrians shuffle away from me, as if standing within earshot might contaminate them with whatever I've been infected.

I pick up my usual large coffee in the lobby out of respect for my morning ritual, but now that I have it in hand, I'm afraid to drink it. All the way to the elevator, it sloshes about, dribbling onto my skin like brown lava. I'd leave it on the elevator if not for a surly-faced woman who would certainly object.

"Coffee?" I offer with a maniacal grin. She glares at me and turns to give me her back. It takes every ounce of my humanity to keep from dousing her. I'm not sure what department she works for, but I suspect no one would complain much if deprived of her glittering company for the morning.

Upstairs, Tim is waiting for me by my office door.

"Tim! Timmy-Tim, my man," I rattle loudly. "What's happening?"

One of his feet is tapping impatiently, but its metronome rapidly flags, and then stops altogether at my approach. His face is slightly flushed, probably from the temperature of the outer office, which is a good fifteen degrees warmer than the racks. On second thought, maybe it's just that he's excited; his eyes are sparkling.

"Got something you need to see," he says. His voice is a steel cable under tension—stretched taut, barely restrained. He escorts me to the racks, where I happily toss my coffee and we both slap on ear protection before plowing inside. Ryan's hard at work and doesn't even look up as we crowd his workspace. Tim zips to the NanoRack and I follow dutifully.

"Check this out, Wil," he says with a thin smile, then turns to the rack.

"What is it?" I peek over his shoulder, but there's nothing to see yet—he's frantically navigating menus, burrowing into the nexus with the precision of a concert pianist.

"I did some plunking around yesterday after you left. And I found some interesting stuff."

"Like what?" I probe. He moves with lightning speed that I can't begin to follow, and until he arrives at wherever he's headed, I'm just begging for motion sickness.

"Like, remember how Mitzy's profile ID was cross-contaminated on the nexus?"

"Yeah, so?"

"Well, I followed the other profile ID to see who it belonged to, and I think I'm on to something."

At our backs, Ryan interrupts our conversation. "C'mon, Tim. We don't have time for this nonsense."

I turn to look at him like he's on drugs.

"We have a new contract to spec out this week," he explains. "I need you both completely focused if we're gonna hit deadline."

A new contract? Oh, man. Good thing I'm in high gear right now. But wait: "Is it a rush job?" I demand, because if not, it can wait five minutes, as far as I'm concerned.

"Aren't they all?" Tim snipes from the side of his mouth.

"Cool it, Tim. You guys can play detective on your own time."

I give Tim an exasperated grimace, as if to say, *What the heck crawled up his rear?* Tim shrugs and grumbles, "To be continued. The nexus-master has spoken."

Ryan rolls his eyes and says, "Stop calling me that, man." But the corners of his lips are tugging into a smile he can't quite keep at bay.

To be continued turns out to be the next afternoon, and then only when the swell of my impatience compels me to skip lunch and corner Tim in the racks. Unfortunately, by then Tim has inexplicably switched teams.

"You know what, Wil?" he says with forced—and completely unconvincing—flippancy, "I don't know what I got all excited about. I'm pretty sure it was just a truncation error or something."

I reward this flip-flop with as much venom as a glance can inject. When that alone doesn't prod further explanation from him, I launch a full-fledged examination. "But you said that kind of error can't happen on the nexus without help from a human. You said that someone had to have intentionally overwritten the data."

Tim's ears are beginning to flush red. *Good.*

"Yeah, I know what I said, and I'm sorry for getting you all bent out of shape." He smiles sheepishly and buries his hands deep into his pockets. "Turns out it was nothing."

I stare at him with my mouth working silently, like a fish in the throes of death. My thoughts wander to old crime television— *Matlock, Murder She Wrote, Perry Mason*—trying to remember what you're supposed to do when someone turns your witness. Unless I'm misreading the cues, this is the part where I'm supposed to badger him until he jumps from his seat and exclaims, *Yeah, I did it; and he had it coming, too!*

"I don't believe this, Tim!" I bark. "What the heck's gotten into you?"

Tim, who's never seen me lose my temper before—even in this artificial context—is understandably taken aback. "Nothing, man. Jeez, don't make a huge thing out of this. It was just a misunderstanding, that's all." His eyes wander toward the back of the room, and I have a sneaking suspicion that Ryan's standing by unseen, overseeing this little scene like the director of a really scrappy play.

It seems a change of tactics is in order. Lowering my voice, I place a gentle hand on Tim's shoulder. "What's going on here, buddy?" I'm trying to project an air of protectiveness, like I'm the only person on the planet he can talk to openly—I know, I'm impressive: from bad cop to good cop within thirty seconds. Tim's eyes are a little bloodshot, and they widen at my touch. I notice his mouth is twitching just a tinge.

I can't speak for Matlock or Ms. Fletcher, but I feel certain that Perry Mason would be proud: I've about got this perp cracked.

Unfortunately, he's cracking in a way I wasn't shooting for. "Back off, Wil," he snaps, shrugging off my hand like it's dripping fire. His nostrils are flaring, fingers curling into puny fists at his side. "You gotta let it go, all right?"

I'm speechless. He may be a good guy—my friend, in fact—but he has his limits just like anyone else. And just like anyone who has just stepped past his, I can tell that Tim feels guardedly remorseful for losing his cool.

But that doesn't mean he's changing his story.

"Listen, I've got a lot of work to do," Tim pleads. "And so do you, you know?"

I shake my head in disbelief and direct my feet toward the door.

"Wilson," Tim yelps. I turn my head and stop in midstride. His face is pained, torn. "Sorry, man. Don't mean to be rude or anything." He looks appropriately deflated, considering that he's just let down a buddy in need. I really don't have any idea what's at play here, but I'm not exactly brimming with sympathy.

"Whatever, Tim."

I rip off my earplugs and blast out the door without another word.

I spend the next half hour locked in my office trying to ferret out something useful from the nexus. Unlike Tim, I have neither the clearance nor the intellectual capacity to manually cross-reference NanoPrint data. The best I can manage on my own is to check up on Mitzy—my Mitzy, not Arthur's. Looks like a late lunch at a sushi bar in about fifteen minutes; no dinner scheduled yet. No surprise there—I still haven't gotten around to making dinner plans either. I don't know why I'm stalking this girl, and I'm feeling more than a little slimy for making excuses. I leave Adrian a meaningless, guilt-driven contact request before heading down to the cafeteria.

I'm still angry with Tim; if I run into him on the elevator, there's a good chance I might lock him in a sleeper hold until he passes out. And if I'm gonna bother going that far, I might as well leave him with a Spanish moustache for good measure—with permanent ink.

The elevator's all mine, though. Just me and my problems. Me and my lackluster, nexus-hacking, witness-interrogating self.

Me and my sorry, divided heart.

Ryan and Tim aren't the only guys I know with liberal access to nexus profiles; they just happen to be the only ones with any obligation to give me the time of day. Following lunch, I make some calls. College professors, former employers and coworkers, fellow alumni—even some dork I met at a conference last year, who I'm pretty sure drank from my water glass during a luncheon—and I get nowhere. Not a single call manages to squeak past a receptionist, one of whom is even bold enough to claim her boss—who dated my college roommate's little sister, and who still technically owes me ten credits on a lost bet—is out of the country, when his proximity sensors show he's in the office.

I'm about out of ideas here. Maybe Tim's right—maybe I should just drop it after all. I mean, what exactly am I hoping to accomplish, anyway? The list that more or less started all of this is out of my hands now, so it's no longer my problem. Right? Sure, my company is knee-deep in a financial scrapstorm, but that's hardly unusual in an industry as prolific as ours.

By the end of the day, I'm exhausted and immeasurably

frustrated. What I need more than anything is to relax, to give my mind a much-needed—if not well-deserved—rest. Instead, all I can do is think. And the more I do, the more agitated I become. At this point, I'm not sure which is more disconcerting: that Keith so thoughtlessly dragged me into a mess that I'm too much of a simpleton to sort out, or that I was so close to making sense of it, to no avail. Part of me is still wounded that Arthur kept me in the dark, because that same part of me needs to be validated by a third party—to prove that I'm not a complete waste of flesh and energy. I hate that Arthur didn't feel he could trust me, that I couldn't handle the truth. Most of all, I hate that he might've been right to doubt me.

Adrian agrees that I should try to forget about all this. "Why don't you just think about me?" she wisely suggests, and she kisses me.

Sold.

Eight

It's Friday. I'm resolute, and after a good night's sleep, I'm firing on all cylinders, ready to take my life back. I take a flying leap into our new project specs. I spend two solid hours mapping out programmatic components and checking them against our codebank—no reason to duplicate existing functionality if we can avoid it. I'm feeling pretty good about my progress so far—it's actually a pretty good set of specs: well-constructed, plenty of contingency plans—and about my decision to move on with life.

Until I see it.

Buried in the specs is a flow map of databases—one of which contains NanoPrint profile IDs. My eyes bug for a second as I realize that—in one fatal swoop of fate—I've just gained access to the same database tables I failed to identify after many fruitless hours yesterday. I know I should ignore this and get on with the project. Indeed, the sensible side of me demands it. Yet, though I'm completely convinced that no good will come of indulging my morbid curiosity, I simply can't rein it in.

With a nervous sigh, I begin writing a program—nothing fancy, just some quick and dirty code to export NanoPrint data into a temp database, index the tables for scanning, and run a query for women in Unified America with the first name Mitzy. I expect millions, considering the enormity of our population here. I end up with less than one thousand.

I rerun the query several times, adding filters as I go—
>>*Domestic Geography = 'Las Vegas, Nevada'*
>>*Minimum Age = '25'*
>>*Maximum Age = '35'*
Et cetera.

—until I've narrowed my results down to three. I save their profile IDs to my MentalNotes, feeling confident that one belongs to the woman I've begun to think of as *my* Mitzy.

I should get back to my actual job now. I want to, in fact—I was really on a roll. But as they have so many times, my genetic proclivities prevent me from leaving well enough alone. I don't know what Tim uncovered, but he pretty well told me all I need to know to unearth the truth on my own.

Well, almost.

Through creative querying, I can access schedules and even proximity sensors via the public nexus directory. With a little time, I can even access transaction grids. But the only way to access a person's records by profile ID is by manually querying the databases. And the only way to do that is by accessing the nexus server matrix directly in the racks. This is turning into some sort of a secret-agent mission, only I lack any of the slick gadgets that give agents their legendary edge. I feel as if I'm gonna be taken out any minute—or, more likely, I'm gonna suffer through some stress-induced diarrhea.

I spend a few minutes fleshing out an overly elaborate con, and once I'm good and primed to pull it off, I jump to my feet and rush with bold determination toward the racks—where I promptly chicken out and run back to my office. Back at my desk, staring at the project specifications spilled across its surface, I realize there is one other way to do this.

The lights automatically engage as I slip inside IDS. My heart is throbbing like I've been running sprints. I'm in no danger of meeting anyone at this hour, yet I feel as though either Ryan or Tim is hiding behind every corner. My NanoPrint is in privacy mode, which is something I rarely allow. As much as I dislike my lack of privacy, hiding one's day-to-day affairs from the nexus is an invitation for scrutiny; ostensibly, only thieves and adulterers have something to hide.

This situation is a case in point.

The door to the racks is locked. I'm neither shocked nor dismayed by this, because I expected nothing less. I pass my NanoPrint against the door scanner and the magnetic lock releases. I predicted this too, because our security system is integrated with our project requirements—the moment Keith assigned a project to me involving our databases, he also opened my access to their home in the racks.

God, I hope I don't have to explain my presence here to anyone in the days to come—I'm a terrible liar, in case you're wondering.

Since I'm already throwing caution to the wind, I don't even bother with earplugs. If this all falls apart, the least of my concerns is becoming a little hard of hearing. Besides, I don't want to risk anyone sneaking up on me.

As I walk through the racks, the lights flicker on to light my path and back off again as I pass—it's an economy mode that I'm supposed to be using at home. One of my dirty secrets? Me and Stew disabled mine after I first bought my condo. I hate the feeling of walking around in a moving spotlight at night; it creeps me out. Thankfully, Stew sympathized with my plight enough to lend me his electronic genius.

When I reach the NanoRack, I realize for the first time just how naïve I've been to think I can pull this off on my own. The rack is filled from floor to ceiling with humming server blades; these aren't even the tip of the iceberg, I know. The real nexus doesn't call any one server-farm home—it's everywhere. Our NanoRack is really an array of database clusters; from here, we can access NanoPrint data as if it were our own, thanks to our security clearance as a certified nexus development firm. I swipe my wrist across the scanner on the rack door and wait for the magic beep.

Nothing but the whine of fans.

A couple more tries yield similar results. *Now what?* I try the door and find it unlocked. I'm simultaneously relieved and outraged by the carelessness of this.

I pull out the rack keyboard and monitor, which are folded neatly into the space like a pizza box. When the monitor lights up, I encounter my first real problem.

Username and password, please.

Ah, scrap. Leave it to Ryan to pull something like this. Billions of credits running through this place in the name of technological advancement, and we're using flimsy twentieth-century login technology? What a joke.

Naturally, it's enough to stop me.

My assumption is that a generic set of credentials is floating out there, and that if Keith wanted me to have it, I'd have received it along with my project specs. I take a few stabs with no luck.

Then I get to thinking.

Any IDS employee with a need for something sensitive from the nexus will ultimately find himself on Ryan's doorstep. Until now, I assumed this convention existed because he was the only one with the requisite expertise. Now, I'm developing a new hunch. Something tells me Ryan's not only fiercely competitive in the workplace, he's also a control freak. If I'm right about that, there is no generic login. Rather, he'll have given his own login global permissions in order to keep the flow of data under his scrutiny. The rest of us must beg for mercy.

I give it a shot, hoping against hope that Ryan was lazy

enough to use something other than a random password. I type *RWHITE* into the username field, tab to the password field and watch the cursor blink.

Hmm.

I try a few of the old-school favorites—

>>data

>>darwin

>>stars

>>god

>>000000

>>123456

—without success. Then, out of sheer frustration, I try something too sarcastic—too blatantly mocking—to possibly work.

>>nexusmaster

I nearly soil myself when the login goes through. I'm laughing with glee, but I'm also immensely disturbed. It takes a special kind of arrogance—or carelessness, at the very least—to leave a NanoRack unlocked. It takes an absolute moron to use his own nickname—assigned in disrespectful jest, mind you—as a login credential. If I manage to get through tonight, remind me to report that scrapbag, will you?

I take a deep, cathartic breath. From here, the rest should be easy; our database administrative consoles launch automatically, so running my queries should be as simple as identifying a database and drilling down to the relevant tables. But since that would be too easy, the naming convention of NanoPrint tables turns out to be completely foreign. Instead of meaningful field names, like *NanoProfsByID* or *NanoProxByID*, they're random sixty-four-character alphanumeric strings. Forget looking for a needle in a haystack—this is looking for a needle in a haystack factory.

I'm starting to sweat. Despite outsmarting Ryan, this excursion isn't going particularly well—I gave myself twenty minutes tops for the whole operation, and I've been here for over thirty. I'm considering throwing in the towel and getting out of here while I still can with a little dignity when I have an idea.

I plunk around on the admin console, navigating through menus until I locate the activity logs. The onscreen frame lists the day's processes, which scroll in real time—faster than I can keep up with the interlacing. I sort the processes by time stamp and filter out the automated processes to reveal what's left, and that's when I find it.

It's some fifteen hundred rows down, so I'm very lucky to have noticed it. What caught my eye was the word *delete* in the description field, which is certainly not something I expected to see. The record is time-stamped just after two o'clock this afternoon. I select the row to expand the full transcript and begin reading. At first, I can't believe what I'm reading—it has to be a mistake—but it gradually becomes very clear that it's nothing of the sort.

DELETE FROM TO_BASE64 ("master_nano_user_profile") WHERE TO_BASE64 ("nano_profile_id") = '747719554136';

Command processed successfully in 0.000000000101 seconds.

It's basic SQL, and it's the first time I've seen it since college. I've never had the occasion to use SQL, but I know exactly what I'm looking at, even if I don't understand what motivated it.

We use stored procedures for absolutely every programmatic interaction with the nexus—proximity searches, transaction queries, activity logs, testing stats—everything. Running an update or delete query on any of the nexus databases is essentially circumventing every security measure we hold dear at IDS—and it's a surefire method for getting yourself blackballed in this industry.

Furthermore, at IDS, we have no procedure stored for deleting a user. Deleting a master user record is pretty much the Holy Grail of thou-shalt-nots—not only at this company, but at any facility with direct access to the nexus. When the nexus stumbles across an orphaned set of data—meaning child records that are tied to a nonexistent master, or parent, record—it automatically begins an internal cleanup process. Any data referencing the phantom master record is purged in a split second, never to be seen again.

As you can imagine, deleting a master record by accident would mean literally and irreparably cutting a person off from the rest of civilization. Only official nexus administrators—which we are not—are permitted to modify user records. So I'm more than a little shocked that the offending command wasn't rejected—I doubt the president herself could gain clearance to run a deletion query—but I know that if anyone can manipulate the system to make something like this possible, it's Ryan.

All of this begs the larger question: why in the world would Ryan delete a master record from the nexus?

Wait a second.

I call up my MentalNotes and locate the profile IDs I saved earlier today. Comparing them to the master ID in the query on my screen, I catch my breath.

Sure enough, one of them is a match. It seems that with a little help from Ryan, Mitzy has been absorbed by the identity of a complete stranger.

As for the meaning in all of this, I can only extract one bit of incontrovertible logic: Mitzy—the real one—has been completely deleted from the nexus. Now, I'm actually a firm believer in the beauty of coincidence, but I'm finding it hard to wrap my mind around one in which a man's NanoPrint physically disappears from the planet—which has never happened—and the master NanoPrint record of that same man's ex-wife disappears from the nexus— which seems like a much more plausible scenario, yet has also never been documented.

As usual, whatever is amiss is too deeply buried for me to plumb on my own. I need the benefit of wisdom that exceeds my years.

For once, I know just what to do.

I call Adrian on my way to Stewart's. I tell her I'm not feeling well and encourage her to carry on without me tonight. The crazy thing is that I'm too freaked out to feel guilty or to consider how poorly I've sold my story—even if it's not entirely untrue. I've just blown off a Friday night—the highlight of my week—with the best thing that's ever happened to me. And I've done so for no tangible reason. My genetic helix must finally be cracking! Seriously, what's wrong with me? All I can think about is profile IDs and databases, and how you never really know people.

Stewart is visibly annoyed at my dropping by this late, despite a ten-minute warning—he's a stereotypical old fart: dinner by four thirty, in bed by seven; up again every half hour to pee—but he lets me in anyway. His pajamas are reminiscent of prison garb in old movies—drab, striped, and ill-fitted. He emits a strained little cough as I follow him inside, and if I wasn't already frowning, I'd frown now at the ominous sound.

With every step, I know he's gearing up to light into me, so I wait for it. Perhaps to passively admonish me, he doesn't say a word; he just surreptitiously glances at my face as he walks, which must reveal my disquiet, and shakes his head sadly—not in judgment, mind you, but as if in observation of a dog he's just witnessed a tram blow down.

It's just a dang shame, Wil, his eyes seem to whisper.

Out loud, he finally remarks, "Ah, Wil. What'd you get yourself into now?"

I'm feeling a little shaky, so I let Stew lead me to the couch. It's an old, saggy piece of furniture with a dated damask pattern woven into worn upholstery. Stewart can easily afford to replace it, but I know he'll never get rid of it. I run my fingers across a shallow dent in one of the cushions, where my Aunt Gertrude used to sit with her feet curled beneath her, nibbling on pretzel sticks and warming our hearts. It's never been discussed aloud, but neither of us ever sits on that sacred cushion. Gertrude may be gone, but she'll always have a place here with us.

Stewart disappears into the kitchen for a moment and then almost immediately reappears with a mug of hot chamomile. I'm not yet sure which of us it's meant for. He sits in his chair with the coffee table between us, where he can look me in the eye. His hands are shaking a little, and when he realizes I've noticed, he quickly grasps his tea cup to busy them. This is a new symptom. Added to the coughing and his recurring lethargy, his ailments have my worry meter rising. But what can I do?

Besides, as far as shaking hands are concerned, I have little room to talk—mine are trembling worse than his. Stewart takes a cautious sip of his chamomile and settles back into his chair.

"Tell me," he says, and stifles a brittle cough.

So I do.

Nine

I keep thinking of something Stew said as I was walking out his door. *"Be careful, Wil,"* he whispered. *"You know what they say about putting the cat back in the bag."* His words are foreboding enough alone, but they aren't solely responsible for my wariness. There was also something unspoken, a sense of defeat buried in his limp posture. Watching him stand at the door in his prison pajamas, it was if he was seeing into the future, glimpsing something terrible. Something too saddening to put into words. Then, just as I hit the sidewalk, he called out to me in a voice marbled and tremulous with worry: *"Love ya, kid. You know?"*

At two thirty, I give up on sleeping and make some coffee. My stomach is in knots, but I gulp the stuff down anyway, both for the caffeine and the distraction for my restless hands. I'm looking through my pantry for something to snack on when my NanoPrint vibrates. I shouldn't be startled—this is something that happens with such regularity, after all; I'm still getting notifications every time Nikes go on sale down the street, for crying out loud—but I guess I suddenly have a bad feeling. I close my eyes and filter through my updates. A couple of hundred have accrued since I last checked them; I scan to the most recent, past all the junk—

No, I don't need more stamina in the bedroom.

No, I'm not ready to take my love for the cosmos to the next level.

No, I don't want to see a directory of lonely women in my quadrant.

—and settle on the last notice. I read the words, and my blood freezes in my veins.

The police station is abuzz with the usual suspects: prostitutes, drunken vagabonds, wife-beaters, teenaged vandals. I'd like to think I'm too upset to notice these details, but the truth is that my curiosity is the only thing grounding me to reality. Without it, I might just collapse. In fact, that's exactly what happens when I remember why I'm here. I try to keep calm, but it's an exercise in futility. I have no control over the sobs that overtake me and batter me with seismic tremors.

A detective named Rackley takes me back to his office and asks me questions: when was the last time I saw Stewart; who were his friends; who might've had a beef with him; on and on. It's pretty easy to infer from this line of questioning that Stew didn't die of natural causes, and that makes his passing infinitely more difficult to accept.

At some point, my composure begins a wounded progression from shock to grief, and finally to indignation. Why do they need to ask all these stupid questions? All they have to do is check the nexus—law enforcement agencies have their own portal to the nexus, which is reputedly far more powerful and user-friendly than anything I've ever worked with—and they'll have all the information they need. Yet as the detective continues to exhaust this line of questioning, I realize he's shaking this bush for a reason.

And as the implications of this burgeon in my tired little brain, I become more than a little uncomfortable.

Rackley doesn't arrest me—thank God—but the look in his eyes as he escorts me from the building tells me he's got his man all picked out. I take some comfort in knowing that he bears the burden of proof—and that none exists to incriminate me. Still, I know my every move will be scrutinized from here on out, and that isn't good news.

I suppose this doesn't bother me as much as it probably should. Frankly, I can recall feeling similarly since time imprinted against my very first memories—the feeling that every decision I make will someday come back to haunt me. That fear has never ceased to crowd my decisions, even if I've become used to its relentless presence—even now, it remains the dark, foreboding figure at the back of the tram: we all eventually grow accustomed to him, but most of us will never let ourselves forget that he's there.

What bothers me more is that as long as Rackley remains fixated on me, the real killer is free to kill again at his leisure.

It's eight thirty by the time I get home. I'm so exhausted I can barely see straight. I stumble into my room and literally fall into bed. Forget work, forget food. Forget everything—I just want to sleep or die, and I honestly don't favor one over the other right now. I feel my NanoPrint nagging at me, but it's only just discernible as I tumble into blissful unconsciousness, where nothingness graciously obscures the repeating theme of death and grief in my life.

Someone is pounding on my door. I groan and pantomime a shriek of frustration into my pillow, yet I drag myself from the comfort of my bed and across the footprint of my condo to the front door. On the adjacent wall, my door monitor illuminates the digital representation of Adrian, who looks so haggard with worry that her prettiness only just prevails.

Cripes.

I let her in, an apology spilling out of me before the door is half open. She grapples me into a desperate hug, squeezing me like she more than half-expected me to be dead. Then she releases me and commences to slap me silly.

I raise my hands in defense. "Hey, what're you d—"

"Don't—you—ever—do—that—to—me—again!" Each word is emphasized by a stinging slap against my bare skin. *Do what?* I wonder. Did I black out and force her to delete her scrappy movie collection?

"Okay, let's just settle down and—"

Slap. "Don't tell me to settle down!" she seethes. "How dare you disappear without any explanation and not even bother to let me know you're okay!"

Jeez, I think. If she'd just looked at my daygrid, she'd have seen that I was here—and that I spent half the morning at the police station. Suddenly, as if on cue, my NanoPrint shivers and throws a notice. For once, I take a second to read it.

When I do? I want to cry.

Are you sure you want to remain in Privacy Mode? This is your sixth notice; to disable this recurring notification, simply change your privacy preferences to—

Oh, no.

That explains a lot, I realize. How I must've looked to Rackley, inaccessible to the nexus even as I labored to answer his questions with nothing to hide. How I must look now, to Adrian. I feel like I might throw up.

"I'm sorry, honey. Really, I just forgot I was in privacy mode yesterday and—"

"Who is she?" she interjects in a voice thickened by distrust. "What's her name? Is it that Mitzy tramp?"

"Wait a second, now. You're jumping to the wrong conclusion, okay?"

She pauses for a second, then another. I can't believe she's giving me a chance to explain myself. Actually, now that she is, I'm not sure what to say. Her nostrils are flaring, cheeks flushed red. For a second, despite the inappropriateness of my timing, all I can think of is how sexy she is when she's angry.

"Well, I'm waiting."

Have I mentioned that I'm a terrible liar? My deficiency in this area prevents me from trying often. Normally, this is a practice that has served me well. But given the extraordinary events that I've been through in the last few days, I doubt the truth will be any more believable than anything I can make up. I'm too tired to embellish, though.

I tell her about poor Stewart and my interrogation, my narrative picking up momentum until it drifts outside of my control. I lose steam after a while and fall into tearful silence.

"Why is this happening?" I want to know. "First Arthur and now Stewart?"

"Poor baby," Adrian croons. "Everything's gonna be fine now."

I want to believe her—desperately, perhaps more than anything—but I can't. My life is falling apart around me, and as much as it hurts, I know deep in my gut that the heartache is only just beginning.

Ten

Keith greets me with a frown, and though I'm disrespectful of his authority as a general rule—treading the line of insubordination for the sheer joy of it, in fact—I have to admit that I've been remarkably flaky lately. Not only have I cashed in several untimely absences in the past week, I've also made no effort to warn my coworkers—much less my boss—that I would be out. Unlike some of the guys around here, and in spite of my tenure, I'm quite expendable. They could easily teach a monkey to do my job. Of course, if they dared, charges of animal cruelty would surely follow, considering how deliriously boring my job can be. Honestly, if it wasn't for IntelliQ, I'd fall into a protective coma immediately upon arriving at work—and I'd have absolutely no leverage at this company.

I follow Keith back into the womb of his office, wishing I had taken the time to prepare a defense, or that I had the energy to cough one up now, on the fly.

Sigh.

I'm just so tired of this, all the limelight and cloak-and-dagger scrap. I want to come clean, to have my old, boring life back.

But Keith has other plans. Instead of seating himself behind his desk, he stands directly in front of me, leaning forward with his rear hinged against the edge of his desk. The expression on his face isn't one of disappointment—it's pity. He's hunched forward with his head cocked slightly to one side—I think he's going for an air of sympathy and approachability, but he looks more like a sexless bear with a bad crick in the neck. And what's worse? Courtesy of a popped shirt button, Keith is inadvertently providing a free, eye-melting peepshow of his man-boobs, which seem to come and go throughout the months—and are more there than not, at the moment. Tim has a theory, incidentally, that Keith's amorphous body hasn't given in to all the formulaic hormone treatments, and is attempting to menstruate as it was originally designed to do.

In case you're wondering, my genes don't keep me thin all on their own: mental rabbit holes of this repulsive variety are pretty effective appetite suppressants. Right now, for example, I'm so grossed out that I have to breathe through my mouth and look at the floor just to keep my breakfast down. I can feel it churning in my belly like a quivering ball of baby snakes.

Keith takes this as some sort of grieving cry for help—remind me to give Tim a good smack upside the head the next time I see him—and puts a fat hand on my shoulder. With a groan, I swallow back a little bile that has slithered up my throat despite my best efforts.

"I know it's hard," he says. "We're all going to miss him."

I feel my cheeks flush, and though I'm trying to be on my best behavior, I involuntarily slap away his hand. I guess I'm a little more chafed than grossed out now. "Please don't act as if you knew him," I warn. I don't mean to be hateful, but my indignation at this unnecessary false familiarity sets my nerves aflame.

His face opens up with bewilderment and he squeezes farther against his desk, putting a little more distance between us. "Don't be like that, Wilson. I've known him as long as you have. We're all shocked, and we're all hurting just as much as you."

What the heck is he talking about? As far as I know, Keith and Stewart have never knowingly shared breathing space on the same block. My incredulity must be blatant, because Keith slithers away and reverts to his comfort zone behind his desk, his eyes darkening by the moment.

"Listen, Wil, he left something for you." He immerses a hand into his desk drawer and it emerges with an envelope. What in the universe would prompt Stewart to leave something for me through *Keith* of all people? Before I lose my temper—which is possibly closer than it's ever been to completely escaping my grasp—I snatch the envelope and stomp into my office. I sit at my desk and seethe for a moment. When I've had a moment to cool off, I get back up and shut my door.

My eyes are brimming with tears. Poor Stewart. I can't believe he's dead, that someone killed him. I remember when he taught me to tie my shoes as a child, back when my parents were still around but were too busy to bother. He taught me so many things, things I can't describe because their combined depth escapes words.

And though I still can't claim to understand the mess I've gotten myself into, I'm beginning to believe that my uncle died because of me. Because I dragged him into something I should've been man enough to bear the brunt of alone.

I return to my desk and wipe at my face with the back of my hand. Before I can overthink things, I rip into the envelope, hoping for some explanation of how my beloved uncle came to be associated with my coworkers. Instead, I find something far more frightening. Inside the envelope, a single sheet of paper is sloppily folded into thirds. Stretched flat, its surface is void but for one word—a word that at once fills me with trepidation and steals my breath away.

Run.

You don't have to tell me twice.

I rise to leave, but suddenly Keith is in my doorway. I'm not pleased with his lack of knocking etiquette—but I'm not about to waste a moment harping about it, either.

"Please tell me he left you the password," he says, a sheepish frown splitting his wide face.

I look at him dumbly.

"Figures," he growls. Leaving me confused, he walks out of my office and into the common corridor, yelling, "Does anyone know the password to the NanoRack?"

A mental tumbler clinks in my head.

Oh, no.

I blow past him into the rack room and find it empty. "Ryan? Tim?" No answer. I dart about the rack corridors like a mouse in a maze. I hear a sort of gagging sound—weird, but undoubtedly human—and follow my ears past the humming servers into the back, near the emergency exit.

Slumped against the wall with his butt on the floor is Tim, eyes gushing, nose dripping like a faucet. He's trying for all he's worth to contain a sob, and when it finally erupts, it does so with enough intensity to seize his entire body.

"Tim, you okay there, buddy?"

He looks at me and shakes his head.

"It's my fault, man."

"No, Tim. It isn't. It isn't anyone's fault," I tell him, though I know in my heart that, in fact, I am to blame.

Tim looks at me desperately, like he wants so much to believe me and is right on the precipice of doing so, if I can just push him over the edge.

"We should've left it alone, Wil," he cries. I think I'm supposed to say *We were just doing our jobs, Tim,* or something—anything to grant him permission to put away the guilt. But I'm too self-absorbed, too confused and hungry for understanding to worry about mollifying him right now. "Left what alone?" I demand.

"The nexus, man."

"What are you talking about, Tim?"

"Ryan did something he shouldn't have—and now he's dead."

"You mean deleting that master record?"

Tim's eyes bulge. Maybe I shouldn't have tipped my hand—

again: I suck at lying.

"C'mon, man," I assure him. "I know it's a big no-no, but people don't die for causing data confusion, do they?" I try to smile as I say this, to give an impression of assurance—yet I'm shaking in my shoes, too.

"You don't see it, do you?" he whispers, barely audible amidst the cacophony of fans. No, in fact I don't see it. Whatever is going on here has escaped me since day one.

"Tell me what's going on," I beg him.

"He was just trying to help."

"Help who?"

"Us, man! God, you're so lowQ sometimes."

"Noted. Pretend I'm a crank intern and spell it out, Tim."

"Ryan didn't want me getting my hands dirty with that whole Mitzy thing. He knew if I kept poking around, my queries were bound to get someone's attention. So he figured he'd just get rid of the evidence altogether."

"But what good does that do anyone? There's a girl running around right now living under the assumed identity of Arthur's ex-wife!"

"Exactly, Wil. That's the way Arthur wanted it."

"What?"

"I think we really screwed this up, crank. I don't think Mitzy ran off with another man the way we all thought. I think she's in hiding somewhere."

"Hiding from what?"

"The same people who threw Ryan off his terrace last night, that's who. The same crazy freaks who killed Arthur."

I'd like to chew on this for a while, but Tim's not finished yet.

"If you have any doubts, let me tell you something no one else seems to know yet."

"What's that?"

"Ryan's NanoPrint? It's gone. Just like Arthur's."

My head is about to explode. "I don't understand this. If

Arthur was so scared, why didn't he go into hiding with Mitzy? Why stick around at all?"

"I have a theory."

"Which is?"

Tim wipes his nose with his sleeve and gives me a sidelong glance. "You."

On my way out, I pop my head into Keith's office and say: "Nexusmaster." His manicured eyebrows scrunch, and I'm gone. I don't bother with a resignation or a request for time off. I just walk out the door. Mind ablaze, I plummet to the ground floor on an empty elevator, step through the swishing door—

—and literally into Inspector Rackley.

"Mr. Abby, just the man I'm here to see."

"I'm a little busy right now, Inspector. Can this wait?"

He smiles at me like I've just proven a point he's already made to himself and says, "Time waits for no man."

A tram pulls to the curb and jettisons a few passengers; I step past the inspector and toward the waiting tram. "Why don't you make an appointment with my receptionist, Inspector?" I suggest with unveiled agitation.

To my back, he replies, "You don't have a receptionist, Mr. Abby."

I pause with one foot in the tram and offer an ironic smile over my shoulder. "Huh. Well, I guess that explains a few things." I step inside and the door dismisses Rackley with a hydraulic *swoosh.*

Eleven

It's after one in the morning. I'm sitting up in bed with my heart trying to blast a hole through my chest. I don't know what disturbed my sleep, but whatever it was didn't exactly lull me awake like a kiss on the cheek. Probably my morbidly obese upstairs neighbor, who I have recently learned is a sumo wrestler in training.

I try to still myself to listen, yet the beating of my heart fills my ears like muddy lake water, and I suppose I know on some level that sumo footsteps aren't to blame. I don't want to disturb Adrian; I just lie there, trying to tell myself that everything's fine. But I feel as though a wild animal is cornered in my flesh, moments from bursting free to escape something too sinister for my brain to grasp.

Then I hear it. It's a knocking, so faint it might've been my neighbor coming or going. Only I can't imagine Mrs. Grace doing anything at this hour. No, it's definitely a knocking.

Leaving Adrian to sleep, I shut the bedroom door and creep through my condo, ill at ease in the captivity of my own home; every shadow is an assassin, poised to attack if I dare to look away. I reach the door no worse for the wear, save for my poor heart, which has taken quite a beating lately. My antiquated door monitor isn't much help in the darkness; I see a figure on the screen, and that's as much detail as I can discern. I shouldn't answer the door, I know. If I were a smart man, I'd call the police right now.

Please, send someone right away! Someone just knocked on my door!

Okay, so maybe that's not such a good idea. Still, considering all the craziness going on lately, I really shouldn't open—

Knock-knock.

I flinch involuntarily. Man, I'm terribly spooked. "Who is it?" I whisper.

Staring at the monitor, I listen intently for a response, but I hear nothing. And then, just audible above the hum of inner city silence, I hear her speak.

"It's me," the voice says. "It's Mitzy."

I haven't seen her in a couple of years, but I'm no less shocked at what I see when I open the door. This woman has no trace of the regal beauty that was Mitzy's hallmark. Her eyes are hazel, where Mitzy's were a soft blue. Her nose seems rounder, maybe a little shorter. Even her hair seems wrong, though I'm enough of a man that I can't pinpoint how it's different. Everything I see here tells me this woman isn't Mitzy, yet when I look deep into her eyes, there's no doubt.

"Hello, Wil," she says. Despite her appearance, her voice is the same—and against all logic, it warms me. "It's been a long time."

I want to say something witty for some reason, something that artfully betrays my dissonance with what I've always believed to be her shameful parting with Art—something that lets her know that I know what the score is. I'm not sure why this feels so important to me, considering I don't know the score at all. I'm a fly nabbed in a sticky web of deception. I search the directory of my mind for something to say, but I come up empty.

So I just step to the side and let her in.

It isn't until she's in my apartment, looking around with a

wistful sadness—like everything's familiar, yet completely changed—that our implants shake hands. Almost greedily, I sift through her xchange profile. What I find there doesn't make sense to me, so I check again to be certain. There's no mistake.

"Misty Edwards?" I ask, my wariness regaining a foothold.

The woman who is and isn't Mitzy laughs. "I know, creepy, huh? I'm walking around with a dead woman's implant. I keep waiting for somebody to call me out, but I doubt that'll ever happen. Art did an excellent job."

He had. I lead her to my couch—from behind, something about her is eerily familiar, though only slightly—and we both sit.

"So tell me about yourself, Miss Edwards."

"Missus, actually. Well, let's see. Fifty-nine, born and raised in Pittsburg, married for thirty years—no children—widowed at fifty-four."

"Misty, huh?"

She sighs. "Just Arthur being funny; people were always calling me Misty,"—I can empathize; I still get an occasional post-introduction *William*—"plus, I'm not very good at subterfuge. I needed something close enough to my real name that I'd at least react when someone addressed me. You can't imagine how strange it is, Wilson."

She's right; I can't, and I admit as much. I scrutinize her face—no rudeness intended, of course. She looks remarkably different; I'm not sure I'd have picked her from a lineup before now.

"Strange, huh? It's been two years and I still flinch every time I pass a mirror."

At once, I find myself thinking about how bizarre—how horrible—this all must've been for her—to give up her home, her husband, her career. To become a stranger, to pretend that her memories never happened, and to collect someone else's as her own.

"So who's the girl walking around with your hard-earned

name?"

"Oh, she's a bona fide Mitzy—she earned it fair and square. Sweet girl, too." Her eyes flicker to mine and an absurd little smirk tugs at her pursed lips. "But I guess you already know that, huh?" She laughs deep in her throat, and I blush appropriately. "Anyway, as you've discovered, a cursory search for me on the nexus points to her. Of course, anyone who lays eyes on her can see that she's half my age."

"Is she in any danger?"

"Not at all. Arthur was very careful about that. The fact that she's still alive proves that much."

I give her an appraising glance. Despite the new getup, she looks good. I'm reminded of balmy Saturday nights, playing cards with her and Arthur out on their veranda. Man, those were such good times.

"So, how have you been?" I ask, in part because I'm interested, but mostly to fight off the onset of awkward silence.

"Alive. I guess that'll have to do for now."

I hesitate, then say: "I guess you know about Arthur."

She blushes, and I suddenly realize I *have* seen her before, if only a glimpse as she fled Art's wake. In that same moment, it dawns on me who actually footed the bill for the ceremony. I should've guessed; the city of Chicago isn't exactly renowned for its benevolence.

"You know," she says, "when we were younger—when *you* were younger—Arthur used to think of you like a son. But then, as you became a man, his perception of you changed. You weren't just an honorary adoptee, Wilson. You were his best friend. He'd have done anything for you."

This is too much, too raw and unexpected. It's bitter and sweet, swaddled like an infant in a blanket of time I'll never get back.

"They killed him, Mitzy."

A pained expression unfolds on her face. "I know."

"What's going on? Too much is happening; I can't make sense of it all."

"I'll tell you what I know, Wil. And then I'm going to leave—and we'll never see each other again."

I sigh deeply, and then nod.

"You might think this has something to do with IDS."

"Doesn't it?"

"Yes. And no," she says drily. "It started with me."

"What?"

"Just listen, Wil. It'll all make sense."

I nod again.

"Okay. About the time you hired on to IDS, I was drafted into the ranks of an executive marketing team at Premiere Global Research Services." I look at her with wide eyes. *Mitzy? A corporate executive?*

"Don't look so surprised. I put in twenty years at Premiere before they even considered me; once I was promoted, I was working alongside men who'd put in less than ten in the industry—some less than five in the company. Anyway, I was excited at first. It was what I'd been working toward my entire adult life. But then, I got an introduction to our first project. Premiere was working on preliminary testing for a new drug back then, one of the first formulaic NanoPrint add-on patents to ever hit the market."

I'm baffled that Mitzy—who I've known as long as I knew Arthur, on a much shallower level—was such a pioneer in medicine. And that I never had any inkling. Formulaic patents are a dime a dozen these days, but there was a time when drugs had to be physically introduced into a person's body. In case you're not already aware, formulaic drugs are produced on the fly by our implants; technically speaking, they aren't drugs at all, but procedures that trigger the natural production of hormones and proteins in our bodies as needed to address specific conditions. Virtually everything from headaches to rheumatoid arthritis can be treated and/or cured using these procedures. Not only that, these same procedures now work hand in hand with medical monitoring technology to actively prevent heart conditions, discourage cancerous activity, et cetera. And every formula equals huge profits for drug research corporations, because no one formula does it all.

"Then what?"

"At first, it was just the company cutting corners. We glossed over a little anomalous data here, skipped a test filing there. Nothing to lose any sleep over, except it really bothered me that we would do that with so much at stake. Why invest billions in R&D, only to invalidate our data with sloppy documentation and testing? Turns out what I took for careless behavior was actually quite deliberate. We knew the drug was solid; but NanoPrint technology was still a bit shaky back then. Occasionally, an implant would misfire in administering the drug—nothing fatal, mind you. Once, a woman treated for an infection on her foot developed a tumor at the infection site. Another time, a man developed a chronic bladder infection following treatment for colon cancer. Any time something like that happened, the NanoPrints turned out to be the culprit. Our CEO was convinced these problems would work themselves out as NanoPrint technology advanced—and in the long run, she was right."

"But in the meantime, Premiere covered up the undesirable test results," I offer helpfully.

"Exactly. But that was just the beginning. A few years later, just when I was reestablishing some respect for the company, a new era of research began. Formulaic drugs remained our bread and butter, but we began subsidizing research for new drugs—and I don't mean the healing kind."

"Why? That doesn't make any sense."

"Didn't seem to. But eventually, it did. The market for hallucinogens has never waned, but medical monitoring via our NanoPrints made it impossible to mask drug use. For a few years, there were countless manufacturers of formulaic hallucinogens—

and they sold like hotcakes. Drowners must've thought heaven fell to Earth. But eventually, the keepers of the nexus caught on. You couldn't get high like that if you tried, now. Even if you managed to get an add-on installed, the nexus would shut it down and report you to the authorities before a single chemical process could take place.

"So Premiere went old school. We began experimenting with bioengineered plants—cannabis, coca and whatnot—trying to enhance and domesticate their naturally occurring properties. Those of us in the fray had no idea what we were working toward, believe it or not. Formally, Premiere was revisiting nature for inspiration. We may have been fooled for awhile, but eventually a few of us caught on. Suddenly, all of our tried-and-true clinical tests went out the window. Our research leaders became closed-mouthed, and many of us lost faith.

"I should never have complained about all this to Arthur. But you just can't help that sort of thing when you're married. He'd ask over dinner, 'How was your day?' and I'd get a glass of wine in me and tell him all about it. If I had even an inkling of where it would all lead, I'd have kept my mouth shut.

"Anyway, a month or two went by, and suddenly Arthur became distant. We argued a lot. He wanted me to quit my job, and he wouldn't give me any explanation why. I refused, of course, resented that he'd even ask that of me. I'd worked too hard to get where I was, and I guess I thought I could wait out the storm. Goodness, it sounds so selfish when I say it out loud. Especially now."

I want to console her, to tell her it doesn't sound selfish to me. But I'd be lying, and she'd see right through me. "So then what happened?"

"Well, nothing for a lot of years. But then, one day Arthur came home and he was terrified. 'You're being used,' he said. 'By who?' I wanted to know, but he wouldn't say. All he would tell me was that I was in serious danger and that we had to flee. I wouldn't dream of it, naturally. I told him no. He insisted, but I wouldn't give in.

"Then, one night after work, someone attacked me in the lobby of our building. He was big and hairy." Mitzy pauses, her eyes losing focus for a moment. "I remember he smelled like onions and cheap aftershave. He stabbed me. If not for Arthur, I'd have died that night. He came running down the stairs, screaming and brandishing a gun. My attacker was about to stab me again, but when he saw Arthur coming down those stairs like an angry bull, he ran for the hills and left me bleeding on the floor."

I feel my mouth parting in a gape; I never knew.

"The blade missed my heart by a half inch, so I lived. But that was it. Neither Arthur nor I had any doubt that we couldn't just continue on with business as usual. So I left him. I wanted him to come with me—demanded it, actually. But he convinced me that we were both better off like this, and that it was only temporary."

"Why?"

Mitzy looks me squarely in the eyes and smiles shyly.

"Because of you, of course."

My pulse races and sends my head into a slow spin. If I wasn't already seated, I'd have to sit down. "What are you talking about?"

"The thinking was that if I left, I'd be hunted. Arthur was confident we could beat that. If we both left, whoever wanted me dead would use you to draw us out. We couldn't risk your life."

It's clear to me that Arthur hasn't been truthful with Mitzy; she doesn't know about Palmer Gunn and his extortion racket. As a result, she's been carrying on with an unfair burden of guilt. I'm compelled to lighten the load.

"Mitzy, I think there's something I should tell you. I don't think Premiere had anything to do with the people chasing you."

"What are you talking about?"

"Arthur was caught up in something at work. Something he never shared with me or anyone else, to my knowledge."

Mitzy falls silent and leans forward. "Are you referring to

Palmer Gunn?"

I'm stunned.

"Still don't get it, do you?"

"Apparently not."

"Premiere was using us both; they promoted me and made sure I was in the loop with all their covert research. Then, they approached Arthur to drag him aboard."

"What could they possibly need Arthur for?"

"Because the drugs we were working on? They would never make it past the nexus without help."

"So they thought they could use their hold on you to manipulate Arthur?"

"More or less, yes. It started out as *Get on board, or your wife'll be out of the job*. When that didn't work, it escalated to *Get on board, or your wife is dead; she knows too much*."

I must look stupefied, because Mitzy laughs—not with any humor, but as if it has suddenly dawned on her that she's become so desensitized to her situation.

"I know, it's crazy."

"And then some. I guess I just never imagined gangsters would get their hands into something like this. It doesn't really seem like their territory. The tactics sort of fit the stereotype, though."

"It's a brave new world, Wilson. For once, Palmer Gunn isn't the one calling the shots."

"What?" Oh, my brain hurts.

"Let me ask you something, Wil. Have you ever dealt with Premiere Global Research Services before?"

"Sure. Couple of times; nothing really memorable, though."

"So what do you know about the company?"

"Other than what you've told me? Virtually nothing."

"Then it might surprise you to know that Premiere is a thriving subsidiary of Miritech."

Miritech. I rack my memory, trying to remember where I've

heard the name. It's in there, I can tell. But I can't place it—and then I remember.

"Wait a second, as in Vice President Carlisle's company?"

"Bingo."

"Are you saying that the Vice President of Unified America is indirectly funding and overseeing the research of illegal narcotics?"

Mitzy smiles bitterly. "Exactly."

"Oh, my God."

"I'm sure you can imagine the political fallout if that information was to leak."

"Holy scrap. So that's why you ran."

"More or less, yeah. Arthur was supposed to stick around long enough for things to blow over. But I never really thought they would. I just knew it somehow, you know? I told myself it would be okay, that if we just stuck it out, we'd be together again. But deep down, I knew they would never let him go."

"I don't understand why Arthur thought they'd spare him."

"Because he agreed to give them what they wanted. He pushed the drug through."

I feel my cheeks warm at this terrible revelation. "What? Why in the world would he do that?"

"Don't judge him, Wil. Arthur was a good man. He did what he had to do to protect me. And you."

I feel sick with the knowledge that my best friend sacrificed his integrity—and ultimately, his life—for my sake.

"I guess they decided to take him out of the equation after all," I say.

"Yeah, it looks that way. Which is why you have to make a tough decision, Wil."

"What's that?"

"There's a good chance they'll be coming after you now."

I swallow a mouthful of cotton. "Why would they do that?"

"Because you're a loose end. Just as I am. I could be wrong—

maybe they won't bother with you at all. But one thing is certain: they haven't stopped looking for me. Knowing that, I have to believe they'll eventually latch onto you as a resource. And when they've finished with you, Wilson, they'll kill you."

I want to dispute this, to water it down so I can more easily digest the end of life as I know it. But what's the point? Save for Adrian, my life has lost all meaning and order. I'm considering a new bout of questions when I hear Adrian stirring in the bedroom. She calls my name and Mitzy looks startled.

"It's okay, it's just Adrian."

"I'm sorry, I didn't realize you weren't alone."

"Yeah, that's kind of a recent development."

"I've got to go, Wil."

"Wait, please. Give me just a second, will you?"

She's reluctant, but she doesn't refuse.

I pad softly to the bedroom and peek inside.

Adrian squints at me in the darkness. "What're you doing?" she grumbles. "It's after two in the morning."

"Sorry, babe. Having trouble sleeping, that's all."

"Who're you talking to out there?"

"Just an old friend. I didn't mean to wake you."

It's a little too dark to tell, but it sort of feels like her eyes are trying to pierce me. "Define *old friend*," she says in gruff monotone. Warning bells begin to ring in my head. Before I can respond, she's suddenly up and out of bed and screaming in my face—just to be clear, there's nothing sexy about her being angry this time. "Do you have an ex-girlfriend here?"

An ex-what? I guess I've neglected to tell Adrian that not only is she my first live-in girlfriend, she's technically my first *girlfriend*. "What? No, Adrian. It's nothing like that."

But she's not listening. Before I can react, she whips past me and storms the living room like a vengeful demon, eyes ablaze with hellfire. I follow in a mad rush to intervene, but there's really no need.

The front door is slightly ajar, and Mitzy is gone.

Twelve

Adrian is an enigma. A lifetime of cinematic stereotyping has led me to believe that women are internally wired to drool over romantic getaways. An all-inclusive, luxury cruise to Australia, for example. Pre-booked with a nonrefundable deposit, just to demonstrate my commitment to her happiness. With no other frame of reference, it's hard to decide if Hollywood has intentionally duped me, or if my girlfriend is simply an exception to the rule. Either way, I'm baffled. I might as well have pitched a nice hike through a recycling plant.

"It'll be relaxing," I plead. "A chance for us to spend some real quality time together. Isn't that what you want?"

"I can't just blow off my job, Wilson," she says. "Besides, I get seasick." I try not to let my irritation show, but it's hard. She's been at her job less than a month, and so far, she's done nothing but complain about it. And the inner-ear stabilizers built into her NanoPrint are calibrated to counteract motion sickness simply by enabling an add-on. It takes no effort at all.

She knows I'm upset, but she's not budging. Instead, she offers a weak mollification. "Some people get seasick for a reason, Wil. We aren't all meant to sail. Besides, I hate relying on my implant for things like that. It just seems petty."

Wow. Suddenly, she's a budding purist. I'm normally incapable of perceiving hints—particularly from the opposite sex—but I'm getting this one loud and clear. We aren't going anywhere.

I'm pretty sure that if I share the truth with Adrian, she'll cave. We'll be on the next plane out of here, and everything will be okay. But I'm not positive—what if, knowing what I know, she still refuses to flee?—and even the smallest doubt leaves room for cowardice to work. So far, the few people I've opened up to have died; I'm a curse to everyone I've ever loved. And with Stewart gone?

My God, this woman is literally all I have left in this world to cling to.

Through my indignation, Adrian must sense my anxiety—and that it goes deeper than a romantic gesture gone awry—because her demeanor abruptly softens. "Why don't we just play hooky here for a few days? I just don't like boats, that's all."

My automaid picks this precise moment to roll by with its bristles whirring against my baseboards. In that brief moment of distraction, my confused little brain forms a thought and sends it on to my mouth.

"Adrian, as much as I'd like to spend some quality time with you at home, the point of this trip was to get away from here. You know, to get some perspective." *Oh my God, did I really just say* perspective? As if my innate inability to talk to women isn't enough of a crux, my stupid automaid has clearly been programmed to kick me while I'm down.

Not that we haven't already been struggling a little, me and Adrian. Things have been a little tense. I'm not exactly sure when things changed between us; one moment she's lugging around an overnight bag, the next her stuff is all over my condo and her apartment is on the market. Now I'm talking about needing *perspective* like I regret her living with me? Good Lord, is there no bottom to the pit of my ineptitudes?

"Some *perspective*?" She hisses the word as if it was made of something utterly repulsive.

Oh, scrap. Here it comes.

Just as I feared, her eyes are narrowing dangerously, her lips stretching into a thin, menacing line. It might be my imagination, but her nails appear to grow before my eyes, curving into feline claws. This is not a woman to be trifled with.

I need to get this tram back on the track. "Not perspective, really—sorry, wrong word," I blurt with a nervous laugh. *Chugga-chugga, chugga-chugga. We can do this, Wil.* "I mean, um, I just don't think I can really relax here with everything that's going on right now. Do you understand?"

I expect her to drag up last night, to demand again—as she did for nearly an hour—to know everything there is to know about my unexpected guest. To my relief—and confusion, that anyone can shift emotional gears with such ease, I mean—Adrian smiles suddenly and reaches out to take my hand in her own. The claws have retracted. *Choo-choo!* "Of course I do," she says in a throaty purr. "Tell you what: why don't we just take it easy here tonight, and tomorrow we'll figure something out. Maybe we can fly to Australia—that would give us more time there anyway."

Until this moment, my instincts have been pushing me away from here—as quickly and as far away as possible—but as the moments pass, my sense of danger begins to feel more and more irrational. Before long, it begins to feel almost dreamlike, as if from the onset, it was nothing more than my overactive imagination. Also not helping: Adrian's so incredibly beautiful, and everything about her body language promises that I'll be handsomely rewarded for playing this her way.

I'm putty in her hands.

You think you know a person when you occupy living space with her. When you share flatware and sheets and a sink, whispering good nights and the occasional *I love you* when the mood is right. You think you know what she's thinking most of the time because you luck into finishing a sentence for her once in a while.

You think you know a person until you open your eyes one sunny morning to find her standing over you with a gun pointed at your chest, wearing an evil smile that is altogether unfamiliar to you, yet perfectly at home on her face.

Adrian's always despised guns—at least, she's led me to believe this. Seeing her now, with her dainty finger expertly caressing that trigger like she's just aching to pull it—like she's done it before and wants so much to do it again—so much becomes clear. In a split second, all the deception loses opacity, revealing the disturbing duplicity of everything I held dear in this woman. At once, I realize that, while I've never been happier with my home life than I have been in the last six months, I've also never been more alone—even if my mind has failed to connect those dots.

It's all been a lie.

"I don't understand," I try to say, only my words blur together into an unintelligible mass of collapsed syllables.

Her eyebrow raises—the one with that tiny, sexy scar—in mild amusement. "You know," she says in a breathy growl, "Another day with you and I might've used this thing on myself." She jiggles the gun for emphasis and it gleams in the morning sun. Above, the ceiling trembles as our upstairs neighbor makes his morning pilgrimage to the vending machine in the hall.

Adrian notices as well and begins to chew her lip—perhaps contemplating her next move, perhaps relishing her power in the moment. I see frustration gathering behind those beautiful eyes, and with a start I realize that my fate isn't sealed just yet. Adrian can't shoot me without alerting the neighbors, and she knows it. Emboldened by this glimmer of hope—however fleeting—I snap into a side roll toward the side of the bed.

And smack my head against the nightstand.
That'll show her.

I don't offer any resistance as Adrian handcuffs me to the headboard, though a yearning glint in her eyes dares me to. With me secured, she pulls the drapes and leaves me alone in the darkened bedroom. Her muffled voice creeps from the living room, speaking to someone in short bursts. I have no idea who she's speaking to, and I'm too distraught to care.

After a few minutes, the front door shuts with a faint click, and she's gone.

In a fog of helplessness, I submit an emergency transmission on my NanoPrint and settle in to wait for salvation. A half-hour later, when the cavalry has yet to bang down my door, the fog begins to lift, and I realize that I may be in serious trouble.

How long can I lay like this before I die? I wonder. The nexus returns an array of unpleasant figures, none of which bode well for me.

I close my eyes, defeated, swaying to the mournful heartbeat pulsing in my head.

I awaken with a start. The bedroom seems darker, yet daylight still silhouettes the window drapery in a burning rectangle. I doubt I've been out for long. Adrian hasn't returned, which doesn't really surprise me—neither does it make any sense. The throbbing in my head has calmed, but an area just above my right temple feels as though a giant bug is perched there, its spiky legs latched into my skin.

An hour crawls by as I lay motionless, arms pinned uncomfortably to opposite sides of the bed. My scalp stings; my head aches fiercely.

My heart is completely broken.

Though I know it only adds to the torture, I pass the minutes revisiting my fondest memories with Adrian. It's funny how obvious the warning signs are in retrospect. I've been such a fool to miss them. I don't want to jump to any hasty conclusions, but I have a sneaking suspicion that *Casablanca* isn't really her favorite movie.

My anger feels so palpable that I might well rip myself free by its power. Yet before I can put this theory into action, the bedroom door bursts open and I'm blinded by the overhead lights. For a fraction of a second, I feel hope surge through me, because—in a confused daze—my rescue seems more logical than reality. But the fantasy passes quickly, and I'm deflated by its absurdity.

As my eyes slowly adjust to the lights, I discern the shape of a man standing over me—thick and powerful. Squinting in the brightness, my eyes slowly dilate until a face slips into gradual focus. Smiling down on me, it fills me with immense dread, yet I can't look away. Peering deeply into this man's eyes—empty, reptilian things—I realize there are far worse horrors a man can experience than a quick death.

The shame of peeing one's pants, for example.

The gears of my mind are beginning to shudder and creak to life in a groggy slush. I suppose I'm not completely surprised that he's here—on some level, I think I've understood since the day Keith invoked the man's name that he was somehow at the bottom of everything. I have to assume that Mitzy marginalized his significance because she simply didn't know better. Or, in the grand scheme of things, maybe she was right. Only, scaled down to real life, it doesn't matter much who's pulling the strings—when you're looking down the barrel of a gun, the triggerman is considerably less significant than the velocity of his bullet. There's no room in that equation for politics or puppetry.

I don't care what brought this devil to my door. The

inescapable truth is that no one crosses Palmer Gunn and lives to tell the story.

I have no reason to think I'll be an exception.

Mr. Gunn has me delivered to an old warehouse, where he promises we can *talk as loud as we want*. Once there, the door is locked and three of his minions immediately start to work me over. No effort is made to restrain me—save for the beating itself, that is—but I doubt I'd get far anyway. I lose consciousness almost immediately, but I don't think that stops them. When I come to, they're still going—grunting and yapping like a pack of wild dogs—only they've moved from my ruined face down to my hands, snapping fingers like pretzels with their booted heels. My screams are blood-curdling, and I'm as traumatized by the sound of them as I am by the pain that spawned them.

Then, as suddenly as it began, the beating stops. Whimpering like a starving puppy, I try to open my eyes; one is unresponsive, but the other permits a sliver of light, just enough to see that we're not done, merely on a break. My attackers have retreated to make way for their boss, who is standing over me again with pistol in hand. He rests the weapon against my forehead and smiles.

Despite the horror of all this, I'm not really afraid. The worst is over, after all—dying should be easy by comparison. Gunn doesn't pull the trigger, though. Rather, he hunches at the waist and speaks—and what he has to say is far more menacing than the prospect of death.

"I'm gonna start with her toes, understand?" he says. I don't, though my face is surely too swollen to express it. "Then I'm gonna fillet her legs, and work my way up north."

I stare at him through the slit of my eyelid, dripping blood on the concrete floor in a steady trickle.

"And when she thinks she can't handle any more, when she's

ready to beg me to just end it all? I'm gonna light that little hag on fire." The pistol leaves my head, though I scarcely notice. Gunn chuckles in a low, wheezing vibrato, scratching his chin with the barrel of his gun. I guess it's too much to ask for him to pull the trigger while he's at it. "Any idea what something like that feels like, kid?" he whispers. "To be on fire? To feel the flesh melt right off your bones?"

I have no idea who it is with such a lovely evening ahead of her, but I'm truly afraid for her. I open my mouth to speak, but I have no words. Not that it matters—my tongue is too swollen to permit intelligible speech, anyway.

"Poor little Mitzy," he says wistfully. I feel my heart lurch in my chest and I groan. I don't know which Mitzy he's referring to, and it doesn't even matter. I'm petrified by the thought that either one should suffer, particularly on my behalf.

"Of course, it doesn't have to be that way."

I spend a few blurry nights in a hospital. Doctors dope and stitch me up without a single question—my condition must be self-explanatory. Throughout my stay, I'm in and out of consciousness as steroids and stem-cell injections are administered to my throbbing hands. On what I estimate to be day three, I'm discharged with a clean bill of health. I step into the sunshine, more or less healed on the outside, still aching on the inside.

My muscles are weak, rendered flaccid by days of inactivity, but the sun feels fantastic on my skin. Tears spring to my eyes, and I make no effort to hold them back. Birds are chirping; a river barge bellows a tenor hello.

I can't believe I'm still alive.

Looking around, I tap my implant to establish some bearings in this unfamiliar part of the city. Glancing behind me, it occurs to me that this place can't be a hospital; it has the look of an abandoned office building—decrepit, unkempt and utterly forgotten—and there's no listing for it in the nexus directory. Pondering this, I hobble on stiff ligaments—wobbling like a weak-legged fawn—to the curb. There, I slump to the sidewalk in an exhausted heap to wait for a tram. Everything feels off, like my brain is free-floating in fluid, bouncing around as I move and sending out fragmented signals.

Three hundred years later—or eighty-five minutes, for those who prefer to split hairs—I reach my front door. My condo is trashed. Adrian—or perhaps Gunn's guys—has taken the liberty of picking my belongings clean of anything worth saving before fleeing the building. I half-expect to find a note from Adrian—some weak attempt to justify what she's done, some impotent apology—but then I remember: she probably thinks I'm dead.

Worse, she wanted me dead.

This thought swells in my chest, and it hurts. It hurts so badly that I truly wish I was dead, because the pain of betrayal can't follow me there.

Now that I'm home—in my comfort zone, despite the state of disarray I've found it in—my mind finally begins to make a contribution to my survival. For the second time in my life, I enable the privacy settings on my NanoPrint. Similarly, I clear my MentalNotes, in case they're in some way accessible. I know this won't befuddle anyone with direct database access, but it feels like something. When I've finished, I step into a steamy and precarious shower, reveling in the hot spray even as I gasp with every painful move.

My body is healing, I know, yet my heart festers in its wounds. How could I have been so blind? Adrian walked into my life within hours of my discovering Arthur's list. She pretended to like the things I like—real coffee, old movies, et cetera—and I bought the lie wholeheartedly. I forsook the physics of romance in fair trade for keeping Adrian in my life. I am—and will surely always be—the polar opposite of the man whom women are purported to desire. I lack the credit account, personality, physique, sense of humor, style, and charisma to explain how someone like Adrian could be in any way attracted to me. I know this with certainty now, and I must've known it on some level then, too. Maybe I was just afraid of jinxing my profound luck, of allowing my objectivity to crowd out the woman of my dreams.

I don't know why I'm beating myself up over this—I feel like I've been adequately punished for my stupidity, already—especially now, when I should be concentrating on more important things. I have precious little time to work with, and absolutely no game plan. If I don't come up with one soon—now, in fact—bad things are going to happen.

I agreed to Gunn's conditions under extreme duress, yet I'm no less ashamed of myself. If only he'd just shot me dead. If only that devil hadn't dangled hope in my face. If only I had been a better person—a stronger, braver man—in that moment, I'd have left this world with some dignity—if not peace—and my worries would have died with me.

But that's not what happened. The despicable truth is, I begged for my life. And, like some demigod, Palmer Gunn granted it—with some strings attached. Thanks to my weakness, I've been dealt an impossible decision. Somehow, I have to locate Mitzy—or *Misty*, if you prefer—and personally deliver her to Gunn. If I fail to do this, Misty's young, beautiful—and completely unwitting—scapegoat will die in her place. Either way, I'm pretty sure my life is over. Actually, that might be the worst part of all—not my death, but that I would sacrifice another human being, just for the privilege of living a few more days.

With a gun to my head, I was revealed to be a hopeless coward. But now that I'm free—if only for a short while—I intend to redeem myself.

I don't know how, but there has to be a way.

Thirteen

They'll be following me, I'm sure; waiting for me to clear a path straight to one Misty Edwards. I'm expected to deliver her myself, but guys like Gunn don't leave much to chance. And with good reason, in this case. I have no intention of looking for her, much less giving her up. Right now, I have more important concerns. Misty is safe enough for the moment: her whereabouts are a mystery to us all, and frankly she's proven far more industrious than anyone might have imagined.

As for Mitzy 2.0—*my* Mitzy?

Thanks to me, she's in imminent danger, and I can't protect her on my own. I need help, yet I have no one. For all my uncertainty, one thing is quite clear: I need to get moving. That's easier said than done, I'm realizing. After all, where can anyone go to escape the watchful eye of the nexus?

With nothing concrete in mind, I hurriedly pack a duffel bag with clothes and toiletries. Glancing around my condo, I'm overwhelmed with a sense that, once I walk out the door, I won't be returning. I'll miss it, I know. As the seconds pass, I feel more and more frantic about my presence here, as if the devil himself will burst through my door any time now—and with every moment that I survive here, the odds seem to increase that the next moment will find me dead.

Still, I risk a few minutes to do something I should've done days ago. I launch the network settings on my portable terminal and disable all wireless access. It's useless now, except as a reader for Arthur's file—the ridiculous text file that started it all.

It's pouring rain as I leave, fat droplets pelting off the pavement like marbles. I could kick myself for overlooking this detail, because I'm not dressed for it and it might ultimately slow me down. But it's too late to change clothes; I've already given myself more time here than my better judgment can tolerate. I cover my head with the duffel bag and barrel into the rain.

I catch a tram to the nearest shopping mall, where I buy a hot cup of coffee. I find a seat in the crowded food court and sip from my cup. I'm soaked, and I'm freezing, but the coffee helps. For a while, I practice being anonymous—it shouldn't be too hard, considering that I've all but perfected the art of invisibility with the ladies—but right away I seem to catch someone's eye. There's a man hovering by the entrance of a vitamin outlet. That alone is a red flag—I mean, who window shops at a vitamin store?—but there's something else. Every few seconds, he looks around as if he's waiting for someone, and his eyes pass innocently over me. What bothers me is that his gaze seems to linger just over my head, or next to me, for no reason—there's nothing beyond me save for an unadorned wall. I'm not positive, but I strongly suspect he's one of Gunn's crew, keeping watch over me. If so, I sincerely hope he doesn't find cause to come after me; he's built like a rhino—all muscle and girth, and the knobby angles of a brawler—and I'm pretty sure he'd mash me to a pulp just by brushing against me.

It's hard to not get freaked out by this stuff. Days ago, the worst of my problems amounted to keeping my transgendered boss's first names square. Given everything that has happened, and knowing what I know now, I'll be shocked if I'm still alive by dinner. Speaking of food—and despite the stress of this entire situation—I'm suddenly starved. The aroma of Indian and Italian cuisine isn't helping, either; my stomach is cursing like a sailor.

I get in line at Kombal's, a small but very good Indian restaurant. I'd like to tell you all about their food—how they're one of the few places around that still slow-cooks food using pots and pans rather than hydration racks and tablets, for example—but I'm busy giving mister rhino my own inconspicuous looks. I don't need anyone to tell me to keep him in sight; if a guy like that gets hold of me, I'm done.

And worse, so is Mitzy.

I eat my food with gusto, biting back the sour tang of guilt. I scan Arthur's dirty file on my pocket terminal as I chew, seething at the number of revered names who have conspired to hold my company hostage. Abruptly, I set my fork down and blink; my mouth comes to a halt in mid-chew as a name chimes a tiny, barely discernible bell in my memory: Mannford Waters, GFL. I don't recognize the man, but the company is more familiar than most.

Global Freight and Logistics isn't just our top transportation provider, it's also our sole vendor for atmospheric and interplanetary transportation. Anytime IDS develops new satellite technology—which happens annually, at a minimum—GFL is tasked with transporting our new hardware to the Unified Space Station for setup. The cost for this service is the single-largest expense on IDS's books; when tax season rolls around, it never ceases to raise eyebrows with our auditors.

In a way, my awareness of this is why I'm so surprised to see GFL listed here—they're already making a killing off us, so why the extra racket?—but as I think it through, some of the tangles start to come unraveled. It's a given that GFL is extorting us along with everyone else on the list. But that may not be the end of it.

Now that the gloss of my trusting nature has begun to wear thin, it's not terribly difficult to imagine that someone has been padding the freight charges all along. IDS is a relatively small company; for my theory to hold any water, I have to stomach the notion that someone I have known and trusted—for many years, in all likelihood—is a criminal.

Speaking of criminals: I glance around with startled, snapping movements, searching for my watcher.

But he's gone. I'm not sure if I should be relieved or alarmed.

I've decided to warn Mitzy—2.0, that is. It's probably a foolish plan, I know, and there's no easy way to do it. If I knew her well, I might just send her an encoded contact request, wrapping a heads-up in code-speak—you know, the way they do in old spy movies? I doubt I'm clever enough to come up with any sort of encryption that would fool anyone and still make a bit of sense. Especially since I've only met her once; anything along those lines will only confuse her.

My next thought is to enlist a messenger—someone from her work, from her neighborhood, perhaps—to convey these sinister tidings. But again, I'm a victim of my limited experience with her; she might take it as a joke, or worse, a threat from me.

It seems the only way to communicate the depth of her endangerment and to be taken seriously is to do so in person. I'm loath to approach her, though, because I feel as though any contact with her might draw unwanted attention from Gunn. I know this is foolishness; Mitzy's already in his crosshairs, after all. I don't doubt for a minute that she's being shadowed just as I am. If I don't work something out soon, shadows will be the least of her problems.

Just as I did only a week ago, I board a plane to Vegas. None of the passengers strike me as particularly suspicious, but I'm no safer or more hidden here than on the ground. As long as my NanoPrint is in me, I'm a sitting duck. I check Mitzy's daygrid every few minutes to make sure her schedule hasn't been interrupted—my working assumption is that any abrupt change in her planner is an indication that she's been threatened, or even abducted.

The plane ride ends without incident. When I step off the plane in Vegas, however, things quickly begin to fall apart. Suddenly, Mitzy's daygrid goes blank; her schedule has been completely cleared. A few minutes later, as I'm headed toward her apartment on an empty tram—I guess most tourists prefer the posh comforts of a shuttle—her status abruptly switches to private. Maybe she simply detected my trace on her profile and has merely reacted as any sane woman would—who wants some creep following her every move, after all?—but given all I've been through today, that seems an awful lot like wishful thinking.

My heart is pounding so hard that it pulses in my ears, yet all I can do is sit on this stupid tram and wait. Its maximum intracity speed is thirty-five miles per hour, and—though fortune has found me alone in the vehicle—its snail's pace is killing me. I'm seventeen minutes out and counting. If Gunn is as efficient—and ruthless—as his namesake implies, I'll never make it in time. I feel tears gathering; my hands begin to sweat and shake. Coming here was a monumental mistake. I know that now.

Long before the tram even reaches her building, I sense that I'm too late. Giving credence to my suspicion, the already subdued magnetic propulsion of my tram flags—still a full block away— allowing an emergency shuttle to land and pass by at ground level, sirens blaring. My flesh screams to get away from here, because whatever fate has befallen Mitzy is certainly preparing to afflict me, too. Still, she might be injured—I can't just leave her. As the tram regains speed, I coil by the door like a caged animal, poised to erupt the moment the door opens. But just as we approach the building, I glimpse confirmation that—for all my good intentions—I've doomed this poor woman. There she is, splayed across the entry steps in a pool of blood. Nearby, pedestrians are covering their eyes in horror, some crying and shouting. Paramedics are speaking to a bystander, who points to an upper story. Following the trajectory of his finger, I see the broken window through which this young lady was thrown for my rashness, my crank stupidity. The door to my tram opens and in rushes the sounds of weeping and unease, the coppery smell of death. I remain affixed to my seat. "Airport," I whisper. The door swooshes shut and my tram takes off again.

Just as I round the corner and the building pans from sight, I begin to cry.

Nearing the airport, I begin to feel in my bones that I'm verging toward yet another mistake; they'll be waiting for me there, and the time for negotiating has expired. I have nothing to lose now—and they know it—so their next move will be to take me out. I should be afraid, and I guess that on some level, I am. But more than fear, I feel anger—anger so great that it couldn't possibly have originated from within me; it must have seeped into me right through my shoes, for surely I'm not capable of such murderous thoughts on my own.

A few blocks from the airport, I finally get my mind in gear. According to the nexus, there are three GFL docks in Las Vegas. Two are located at the extreme poles of the city, and I decide they're satellite locations; I need the hub. "Global Freight and Logistics," I say. "East Flamingo Road." The tram slows and adjusts fluidly to our new destination. I'm momentarily grateful that I managed an empty tram today; there's no forgiveness for indecision in a full tram.

The transportation facility is only a few minutes west of the airport. I wish I had more time to plan this, to work out the finer details. The Global Freight and Logistics sign peeks above the palm trees; it's neon, just like everything in Vegas, and designed centrally around a slick logo depicting a vintage gridded globe with an airplane bursting from its core. I instruct the tram to deposit me at the fence line, and from there I hike to the office entrance. Inside, I approach a receptionist and ask if they're hiring. They are always hiring, she assures me. I'm painfully nervous, because I'm flying by the seat of my pants.

Have I mentioned that I'm a terrible liar?

I have almost no idea what I'm doing here; my gut—which led me here so adamantly—suddenly has nothing to offer on the subject. The receptionist, a cute redhead with violet bands tattooed around her neck, asks if I would like to speak with the hiring manager. I agree that I would. Before I can second guess this sloppy ruse, a clean-cut black man five to ten years my junior approaches, sizing me up with every step.

"Terrell Webster," he says in introduction, a lean, confident hand reaching to shake mine. "Wilson Abby," I offer in return. An alias will do me no good—my NanoPrint will betray me, even in privacy mode. Our hands clasp, and at once his eyes lose focus; I can tell he's checking me out on the nexus.

"Any particular reason you're in privacy mode, Wilson?" he asks. There's nothing threatening in his voice, but his eyes are wary.

"Yeah, sorry about that. I don't want my boss to know I'm here, you know?" I say. My voice shakes slightly. As usual, my problem with lying has never been the lie itself, but the delivery. In this case, I'm lucky to have a legitimate excuse for being anxious. Surely a hiring manager has heard this line a few times before.

"Understandable. No sense losing your job just for weighing your options, right? Well, come on back and let's talk."

In his office, I try to spin as little yarn as possible, painfully aware of how hopelessly shady I sound. I can't stay here long; any minute now, Gunn's people are going to close in on my location. But I have an unshakeable feeling that my salvation lies here, somewhere.

I think what I need is a tour.

"So, how many docks do you have here?" I ask, leaning back in my chair and peeking out the office door, as if to procure a wider view of the dock.

"Five hundred in this building, but this is one of three on the campus. In terms of dock doors, this is the largest freight facility in the state." I nod appreciatively and peek out the door again.

"How'd you like a quick peek behind the magic curtain?" asks Terrell with a conspiratorial wink.

Thank God.

The loading dock is massive. I feel as though I've stepped into a new world filled with crates and girder winches and automated forklifts. Terrell takes me down one side of the warehouse and points out some of the cutting edge technology they employ here— self-leveling pallets, cold-storage modules with redundant, self-maintaining temperature controls, and a bot for every task imaginable.

"This place is a modern marvel of ingenuity," boasts Terrell. "The freight comes off the trucks on the east side of the dock, gets scanned at the doors, and our system automatically determines everything from there: what bay to stage the freight in, what sterilization procedures are appropriate—everything down to the best load pattern to maximize capacity for our outbound loads. Manifests generate automatically, and they're extremely accurate. Then, the bots load it all out on the west side of the dock."

"That's amazing," I acknowledge, though my gaze is locked at the end of the dock, where a series of small planes and spacecraft are dipping and bobbing under the weight of automated forklifts.

"You might notice a conspicuous lack of people out here, right?"

I hadn't, though it's quite obvious, now that he's brought it up. "Yeah. I kind of expected a higher ratio of people to bots."

He laughs, his chest swelling with pride. "This place can just about run itself; we're the only transportation company in Unified America utilizing some of this technology. Not sure why—our competitors all have a death grip on outdated technology, like it's their lifeline or something. They just don't seem to get that manpower and brute force don't cut it anymore. It's only a matter of time before they go under."

"Huh. I guess I have to ask, then: if this place pretty much runs itself, what exactly are you hiring for?"

"Good question. Let me show you."

Terrell leads me toward the center of the dock. We wind through a labyrinth of freight racks, each stacked fifty feet high with pallets. "This is where people come in," he says, pointing to a large bay of freight whose packaging has been disturbed—forklift holes, broken pallets, torn shrinkwrap. "Most of our customers load their own freight on dropped trailers; we just swing by and pick them up at the end of the day. Sometimes, this is what the freight looks like when it gets here."

"So you guys repackage this stuff?"

"When we can; our guys survey the damage and determine what we can handle, and what we can't. It's really more about liability than capability, if you know what I mean."

I don't. I'm too busy sweating in my shoes, thinking that Gunn is going to step onto this dock and murder me in a matter of seconds. I need to abort this ill-planned tangent; I'm not sure what I was hoping might come of it, but so far I've only managed to waste time.

"Listen, Mr. Webster, I've gotta get back," I say, trying to sound apologetic and hurried at the same time. The latter is easy to accomplish; I'm practically vibrating in my shoes trying to stifle the primal urge to run.

"Sure, I understand. Why don't you give me a call when you have some more time to talk? We really could use some reliable help around here. Supposed to be someone working right now, but he was a no-show."

"I hear you. Sounds good," I say. We're venturing single file back through the freight racks when Terrell suddenly stops in his tracks ahead of me.

"Can I help you, sir?" he calls out. I peer over his shoulders and feel my entire body tense.

"You guys hiring?" a tall, muscular man asks. Terrell is suddenly glowing; I nearly pee my pants as I recognize the rhino man from the shopping mall.

Terrell steps toward him in a brisk, confident stride, reaching out for what must be his trademark handshake. I think I hear him say "Terrell Webster," but I can't be sure. I'm twenty feet away by then, running faster than I've ever run in my life. I'm somewhere near the center of the dock, which means the nearest exit should be one of the dock doors on either side of the warehouse. But I'm not interested in those. I push toward the back end of the warehouse, where I can just make out the profile of a small spacecraft through a dock door. The other craft are gone now—and if I don't hurry, this one will be gone, too. Behind me, I hear Gunn's man on my tail; his feet clap like bare hands against the concrete floor, applauding the approach of my untimely death. I've got a good fifty-yard head start, though.

I reach the dock door and leap into the gaping maw of the spacecraft. Inside, a robotic forklift is lowering a final crate into position; I surge past it into the safety of the cargo bay. It's dark in here, and though I'm thankful for this small favor, I have no idea how far into the chasm I've ventured, much less how much farther it extends. Fumbling around with my hands, I manage to locate and unlatch the lid of a large crate. Inky darkness veils its contents, though a quick inspection by touch reveals a fair amount of empty space within. But it's a big risk; there's no telling what's in there, and the last thing I need is to crawl into a crate of razor blades.

The man is standing in the dock door, now. I can see his eyes, piercing and cold—the eyes of a predator. They slip over me and keep going. I'm protected in the darkness—for now. He takes a step into the bay. With an inner groan, I realize that I don't have a choice anymore; all I can do is cross my fingers that I'm not escaping death in one form only to encounter it in another.

I slip into the crate and gently lower the lid back into place. It's very warm inside and I doubt my panicky breathing is helping. In mere seconds, I'm drenched in sweat. My back is lodged against something blunt but painfully invasive. I hear the forklift retreat, and the entire vessel rises a few inches as the seventy-five-hundred-pound machine backs out onto the loading dock. A full minute passes in silence. I'm contemplating a quick retreat back onto the dock—where I can hide among the pallet racks—when the ship comes to life. I hear the muffled grunt of hydraulics as the cargo door closes, and suddenly we're moving.

I think I'm sharing real estate with some sort of oversized pipe fitting; my fingertips explore what feels like a merging of short pipe sections, budding with bolt heads around their union. Plastic banding spans the cubby in a stiff web, binding the freight to the bottom of its crate. The protrusion against my back gouges my ribcage incessantly as my weight shifts to the jerking of the vessel.

As far as nonlethal hiding places are concerned, I couldn't have chosen a more uncomfortable one to stow away in.

Fourteen

The moment the aircraft becomes airborne, my predicament escalates from haphazard to lethal. As the landing gear retracts, the air begins to jettison from the fuselage, depressurizing the bay. The gap between my crate and its unlatched lid hisses with the outflow of my modest air supply. Forget about the freight digging into my back; that's merely an inconvenience. The ship's cargo bay may have protected me from a brutal death at the hand of a cold-blooded killer, but its price of admission looks to be equally fatal.

I struggle to leverage the lid back against its rubber seal, but with only slick surfaces to grip from the inside, I'm just wasting precious time and energy. I'm guessing I have less than a minute before the air is sapped completely from this enclosure. If I'm still curled up here when that happens, I'm dead.

I give an experimental heave against the crate lid. Though it's already open a little, it resists opening farther; either the exponential increase in hull pressure is weighing it down or I've already grown weak from oxygen deprivation. Frantically, I try again, putting every ounce of strength and stamina into a single, desperate effort. My heart soars as the lid grudgingly lets go, releasing its compression with a muffled *poof.* Suddenly, I'm gasping in a vacuum. In my panic, I forfeited a brief and valuable opportunity to catch a good breath; thanks to this oversight, my lungs are now starving. I've got to get out of here.

Now.

In spite of these frightful circumstances, I've been granted a small favor. The fuselage, which was cloaked in complete darkness earlier, is now dimly lit by a series of tiny beacons lining the walls. On its own, the light doesn't save me, but without it, my doom would be a foregone conclusion. A variety of freight containers form a neat, forklift-sized corridor through the bay. It seems to extend for miles, terminating in a blurry pseudo-horizon. It's too far, I know. Yet what else can I do, but try? Flailing down the path like a wounded animal, I feel as if my chest is pressing in on itself, squeezing out my last bits of life like a twisting sponge. I'm down to seconds, I think. My skull is stinging at its core, infusing with a sweet fog—*Sleep*, it seems to say; *It'll all be better if you just sleep.* Spots appear before me, dancing with colors that can only be the conjurations of a dying brain.

And then I see it.

Straight ahead of me is a hatch—it's right there, so close I can almost touch it. Like a runner digging deep in the last few yards of a marathon, my will to live transcends my weakness. In a final bound, I surge forward, drunkenly stumbling against the coveted exit.

I pull at the lever, summoning what little strength I have left in me—which is frightfully scant—and it proves just enough. With a hissing release of suction, the door opens. Just a little, but I'll take what I can get. Clean, breathable air sucks past me into the cargo bay, along with the shrill whine of an alarm. I drop to my knees and cram my face into the makeshift airway. My lungs drink greedily, slurping oxygen like a heavenly brew. The fog in my skull thins, burning off a little with each breath.

That was close.

I'm surprised at how little time it takes to regain my strength; in less than a minute, my body has all but forgotten its near-death experience. I turn my attention again to the hatch; like my crate lid earlier, it's been unlatched, yet hijacked by the immense hull pressure. With fresh air in my system, I'm reinvigorated. I lean hard against the riveted steel, pushing with the heels of my hands until it eventually gives. When the space is wide enough to accept my head, I wedge my body firmly into the gap and begin wriggling therein, gaining a centimeter here, an inch there. Cool atmosphere screams past me into the vacuum of the cargo bay, whipping my hair painfully about.

And just like that, I'm through, plopping into the tail end of a short hallway. At second glance, I realize the end of the corridor doesn't terminate immediately, but adjoins a perpendicular hallway. I take a few steps into the passage, passing a deep cubby inset into the wall; the space is lined with orange storage lockers, the floor littered with all manner of cordage and packing materials.

I'm not sure where to go from here, only that I can't remain static for long. The shrill breach alarm blares around me, filling me with a new sense of trepidation. I'm retracing my steps to the open cargo bay, reaching out to shut and latch the door behind me—I wasn't born in a barn, after all—when I hear something new. From beyond the corridor, approaching footsteps thump a deep, sinister cadence below the noise. I shouldn't be surprised by this development—of course the ship would be manned, and the alarm continues to cry for human attention—but my opportunity to think this through fell into neglect as I was fighting for my life. As a result, I have no plan; I'm at fate's fickle mercy.

Almost immediately, a lone, grumbling voice joins the choir. It sounds close, and it sounds angry. On impulse, I throw myself into the storage cubby, where my body lands in a hapless jumble amidst a pile of loose netting. I'm not at all hidden, here; at best, I'm slightly camouflaged by clutter.

"Of course I'm sure it's closed," says a man just as he bursts into the corridor. "We couldn't have taken off if it was open!" He's dressed in a flight suit, his facemask dangling on a tassel from his helmet. As he nears me, he exclaims: "What the—it *is* open. How'd that happen?" For a terrible moment, his words seem directed to me. But then he scurries past me and I realize I've gone unnoticed for the moment.

He regards the open hatch and throws up his hands. "I'm telling you, it was shut and latched." With a stiff yank, he grizzlies the door open and peers inside. He's a short guy, but there's no question he's strong—stronger than me, anyway. I hear his voice again, but this time his words are absorbed into the intense cross-breeze rushing from the ship's interior into the low pressure of the cargo bay.

I'm not sure what I'm waiting for; this guy is perfectly preoccupied—with his back to me, at that—yet I lie frozen in this corner, where I'm vulnerable for discovery at any moment. Abruptly, the man secures his facemask and hurls bodily into the cargo bay.

This is it, I realize. I won't get a better chance to make a move.

I climb hastily to my feet with my eyes locked on the open door. Suddenly, the trajectory of the aircraft lifts and topples me back to the net pile. At once, the man reappears through the door and latches it in a tantrum of exaggerated motion. The alarm silences. I flatten myself into the netting, as if I might will my body into a state of invisibility. "You trying to kill me, or what?" he snaps. "Give me a second to get back on deck, would you?" He storms past me, disappearing into the small hallway from whence he came. When he's gone, I can't help but laugh.

Holy scrap, that was way too close.

I'm not out of the woods just yet, though. Any second now, the craft will change slope again, this time almost vertically, to punch through the atmosphere. Once the shift is in motion, I'll go bowling around like a piece of trash in the wind. Milliseconds after this realization hits me, the floor pitches again and the craft's engines graduate from a low whine to a deafening hurricane.

Without really thinking about it—almost instinctively, really—I enable my NanoPrint's inner-ear stabilizers.

See how easy that was, Adrian?

I'm in mortal danger, yet all can I can do is bury my fingers in the netting and hunker down to weather the storm. As the ship accelerates, I begin to slide toward the rear of the vessel. Our trajectory is rising acutely; with a stab of fear, I discover that my grip won't be able to support my weight for more than a second or two. While I still have the strength, I begin to loop the thin strands of netting around my hands. I hear the roar of friction against the ship's hull as we accelerate even more.

I'm not sure why, but the interior lights are fading; it's almost like—

When I come to, my feet are afloat in midair, hovering eighteen inches over the floor. My hands are entangled painfully in a chafed knot of vinyl netting, anchoring my body to the floor. The g-force must've knocked me out; without an oxygen mask or a flight suit, it's a minor miracle that I'm alive at all. Nevertheless, I haven't survived unscathed: my head is spinning and my stomach is threatening to follow suit. Sure enough, the slightest movement causes me to vomit, soiling my little nest with miasmic bile.

The room is spinning so fast. Why won't it slow down?

Closing my eyes, I attempt to consult my NanoPrint settings— my inner-ear stabilizers are enabled, aren't they?—but my implant isn't responding. I know it's still running, because I can feel it tingling beneath my skin as it calls out to the nexus. Yet, try as I might, I can't get it to acknowledge me.

This can't be good.

I get almost no time to contemplate the meaning of this, because the ship's reverse thrusters suddenly engage in sequence, slowing the craft for docking. The pilot is a surgeon with the controls, so deft that I don't even realize it when we've finally docked. My only clue is that the outer cargo door begins to retract as the telltale clatter of forklifts and pallet jacks resounds through the nearby bay.

I keep expecting the pilots to burst into this area—if they do, I guess I'll be completely out of luck—but after fifteen or twenty minutes, I decide that the ship's crew has exited by some other route. The spinning in my head has slowed considerably; it's not altogether gone—I feel like I might toss my cookies again without much provocation—but it's much more tolerable now. My muscles quiver like gelatin as I disentangle myself from the nylon web and scramble to my feet. I'm tempted to reenter the cargo bay, since I'm at least somewhat familiar with the lay of the land; the sound of human voices within dissuades me. There's really no other choice but to follow the nearby hallway into the depths of the ship, trusting that a way out will ultimately reveal itself.

With every bound, my nausea abates; I feel almost human again—for all of two minutes. Just as I'm congratulating myself for so expertly dodging the proverbial bullet, faintness begins to take hold of me again.

I just can't catch a break.

I'm not sure, but I think I'm breathing the wrong kind of air; I feel it moving gingerly past me, as if the entire craft is being purged of its atmosphere. Is it just me, or does this ship seem unusually determined to kill me? The hallway funnels through a narrow hatch into the control room. I slip inside because there really is no other place to go; thankfully, the space is unoccupied. With the engines at rest, the ship is dead silent, save for the gentle breeze rustling my hair.

At first, I'm unclear what the air is moving toward, until I see the door. I'm not sure how I missed it, actually; it's just ahead of me, situated directly opposite the one I've just entered through. More notably, it's boldly placarded in large, green letters:

EXIT.

My heart quickens; my mouth hikes in a dumb grin. The door is ajar, beckoning me like a beautiful siren.

I ought to be grateful—if not downright excited—to have found a way off this deathtrap; instead, though relieved, I feel my smile falter, bending under the crushing weight of cynicism. If I step off this craft, it won't be onto the safety of an airport tarmac, where shuttles and city trams idle in wait for someone to please. Outside this cosmic portal, a spiraled umbilical intercourses with the Unified Space Station. I can easily discern the bizarre, slinky-like structure through the door opening.

I can't believe I'm in freaking space, dang it. Not on some orbital pleasure cruise, mind you, but skulking around on a GFL freighter like a diseased ship-rat. I don't have any business out here, disconnected from my world.

And I'm pretty sure I'm not in for a pleasant reception.

On the other hand, I know what awaits me if I stick around for the return trip. It's not the sort of trade I like to make, but I'm forced to weigh probable disaster here over certain death back home. Either way, I can't remain here for long; I need air—real, life-giving air—and I have my doubts that I'll make it off this ship at all if I don't get some right now.

Wheezing, feeling weak—and a little confused—I forget for a moment that gravity has more or less abandoned the equation of walking in space; carelessly, my leading foot pushes off with too much vigor, launching me into a flying leap. My head rebounds off the ceiling with a dull *thunk* and sends me flailing back to the floor. My hands extend instinctively to absorb the impact, but instead skate down the back of the copilot chair. The friction flags my velocity; I still hit the floor with bone-jarring violence, but it could've been worse.

I sit up and blink as my body begins to gently levitate from the floor. My scalp smarts and my neck is rapidly stiffening, but my pride is perhaps damaged worst of all. I'm reminded of a time when I fell down the escalator at the downtown Hyatt. Arthur was there, along with close to a hundred gawking bystanders, who apparently had never fallen in their life; Arthur was never a fan of slapstick, but I remember he laughed his butt off as I bounced down those stairs like a beach ball. I realized then that even the best of friends will laugh at your expense; that doesn't mean they aren't still your friends. At least this time I looked miswired without an audience.

At once, I notice my periphery shrinking, which I figure can't be a good thing. I should make a frantic dive for the door, yet it doesn't seem that important anymore. Plus, it seems so far away, and it's sliding farther and farther into the horizon. My mind seems to detach from reality, floating over a fuzzy plane of existence where everything's trivial and time is a fixed point. Or a circle. Or a point in a circle.

Here we go again.

I'm seated in a folding chair at the center of what might normally be a conference room; the furniture has been removed, but its feet have left behind subtle impressions in the carpet. I count the former locations of twelve chairs and a single long table. My head feels better. Similarly, all traces of nausea have vanished, though my stomach now cries out in ravenous neglect.

I can't say for sure how I came to be in here, but I must have been carried; I certainly didn't walk in here on my own, anyway. I'm not restrained, which doesn't actually mean much, when you think about it. Not many prisons require restraints these days; the landscape of the moon, for example, is enough to deter escape from its penal colonies. Likewise, I'm as good as restrained here. Beyond these walls is infinite, empty space—as good a deterrent as any desert or glacier.

I've been pouting for several minutes about my sour luck when I notice an unopened bottle of water at my feet. My lips are dry; my stomach feels like a sprung steel trap in my belly. With trembling hands, I rip open the bottle and drink greedily, downing more than half the bottle in one long pull. My tummy gurgles with delight.

"Good, you're awake," says a disembodied voice. The odd shape—sort of ovalish, only bisected off from center—and emptiness of the room makes for an interesting set of acoustics; I can't place the origin of the voice, because it seems to have spawned from the air itself. I drop the bottle and stand in one startled motion, poised to—well, I'm not sure what I'm gearing up for; it's just one of those primal reactions that prepares your body for fight-or-flight while your mind flips a coin. At least, that's what mine is doing.

A man steps into the room from a side door and approaches at a distance, careful to stay well outside of my reach. It strikes me as humorous that anyone would think me worthy of such caution, yet my amusement doesn't reach my lips.

There's no telling how long he's been there; I didn't even hear the door open, and that bothers me. I wonder if others are standing by invisibly, watching me like a rat in a death chamber.

"You gave us all quite a scare," he says. He's reedy-framed, I note, built for perching over a microscope rather than grunt work. Even in my weakened state, I know I can overpower him if I need to. Still, glancing into his eyes, I see a fierce spark of intelligence that warns it would be a grave mistake to underestimate him.

I haven't spoken a word yet, in part because he hasn't actually said anything requiring a response, but more so because I'm busily processing my surroundings. I steal a glance through the open door, preparing to bolt the moment an opportunity arises.

The man smiles—not unkindly, but knowingly. "The crew's out there," he assures me in a calm, reasonable tone. "You won't get far." Abashed, I nod my understanding and then, unsure of what other options remain, I drop back into the chair. My water bottle lays empty on the floor; its spilled contents have left an oblong spot on the carpet.

"Name's Hollister, but everybody calls me Hal."

I nod and open my mouth to speak, but for a terrible moment, I can't tease my name from the slush of my fragile mind. Ah, but there it is. I'm still me.

"Wilson," I reciprocate.

He takes a couple of timid steps deeper into the room, peeking over his shoulder as someone passes by the open door. "So, Wilson. Why don't you tell me what you're doing here?"

I laugh humorlessly. "Trust me—you wouldn't believe me if I did."

"Try me."

I pause for a beat, then offer a noncommittal shrug. What can I possibly say? We lock eyes and I sigh; for a split second, frustration flexes in his jaw. "Just so we understand each other," he says with sharp annunciation, "you aren't walking out of here until I'm convinced that you aren't a threat to this facility. So I suggest you start talking."

Nothing in his demeanor is in any way threatening; firm, sure—but not at all hostile. He's a model of self-control, and I don't doubt him for a second. I'd like to level with this guy, but the truth is simply too unbelievable. I feel I have no choice: I have to lie.

"I work at the GFL loading dock," I tell him. "I must've bumped my head in the cargo bay and lost consciousness." I don't even know where that came from, but it sounds thinly plausible. In another spurt of genius, I add, "I've never been popular with the guys I work with; this might even be their idea of a prank, knocking me out and all."

Fifteen

The only thing more ridiculous than my laughable inability to deceive is that I repeatedly bother to waste my breath trying. Had this particular fib fallen from the lips of someone else—anyone else, in fact—Hollister might have bought it. As far as fibs go, this one is completely within the realm of possibility, after all. Alas, just as always, I've betrayed my duplicity with a barrage of tells—any one of which would tip off a person with half a brain. One look at Hollister reveals that he knows I'm blowing smoke. As sure as he senses that his cunning is more powerful than my physical prowess—which is average, at best—he also senses that I'm grasping at straws, even if he doesn't yet understand why.

I should've taken his warning more seriously; I should've told him the truth. Sure, it may have damned me as much as the lie, but at least the absurdity of my plight would be to blame rather than my shameful failure to follow basic instructions.

Wordlessly, Hollister frowns and walks briskly from the room. Unthinking, I rise to follow. At the door, he turns and—surmising my intentions—shakes his head with an ironic frown. I'm struck by a barely containable compulsion to tackle him—or something likewise radical—before he can depart, leaving me otherwise helpless to do anything at all.

But I don't.

Hollister shuts the door, and as the locks engage in a tribal symphony of clinking finality, I hear my window of opportunity slam shut. A half hour later, he reappears; this time, he's trailed by seven other men, each visibly more dubious than the previous, as if ordered by their useless ability to exude distrust.

"Wilson, I'm offering you a final opportunity to plead your case," he says calmly—condescendingly, really, as if addressing a child. "Just so we're clear, I don't believe a word you've said so far."

I swallow, my tongue grating like dry sandpaper against the roof of my mouth. No point in defending my honor, I suppose. "What are you going to do with me?"

"Well, let me just say this: we don't have the resources to hold a prisoner, and we have no intention of risking your return to Earth if there's a chance you'll endanger our flight crew. You're a liability, and the rules out here aren't very forgiving."

I swallow again. "What exactly are you saying?"

"I'm saying that if we can't be satisfied that you're not here to harm us, we'll have no choice but to dispose of you."

I feel the blood trickle like cold acid from my brain into the hollows of my shoes, scouring the pipework of my heart with the stinging burn of dread. I'm not sure what to envision, exactly—the phrase *disposed of* leaves much to the imagination: banishment into space, perhaps; incineration with the weekly trash?

Oh, God.

I don't even realize that I've begun to speak until I pause in midsentence to take a breath. I don't bother to correct myself now, though, because it's clear to me that my body has wisely deduced—even before my feeble little brain could form a sound conclusion—that there really is no other play left.

The truth shall set me free—if there is freedom in death, as there is in vindication, anyway.

Nevertheless, I spill the beans, every last one. When I've

138

finished, my face is shiny with sweat and unashamed tears. Hollister glances about the group, betraying nothing of his opinion on my narrative—at least, not that I can discern. Yet, almost in unison, they clear their throats and leave me to stew in my own fear.

An hour passes, and then another. My mind crowds with disorganized thought; my NanoPrint can do nothing to channel them, and they bounce around like rubber balls with infinite momentum. Without warning, the door opens again, and Hollister enters bearing unexpected gifts: another bottle of water and a meal-supplement pill, both of which must be of considerable value in space. His face is unbearably impassive. I can't stand not knowing what's in store for me—surely the not knowing is even worse than the fate itself.

"Please," I whisper. "Tell me what's happening."

Hollister scrutinizes me with a tired sigh, scrunching his eyebrows indecisively. "Here's the thing, Wilson: more than one of our group suspects you're either a terrorist or spy."

"What?" I gesticulate. "You've got to be kidding!"

Hollister laughs dryly and shows me his palms. "You don't have to convince me on that point; I know who you are."

My face must look thoroughly confused, because he motions toward my wrist, where my NanoPrint continues to whir but makes no progress in reaching the nexus. "I scanned your implant while you were out cold."

"Then you know I'm not a spy!"

"No, I don't believe you are. Truth be told, I think you're simply in the wrong place at the wrong time."

Thank goodness. "Hollister, if you believe me, you've got to help me."

"I wish it was that simple, believe me. But if any part of what you've told us is true, we're no better off than if you were a terrorist. Surely you've considered what will happen if it gets out that you've been here?"

"I won't say a word, I swear it!"

"You don't have to, don't you see? If you don't think someone with the resources of Palmer Gunn can reach you here, you're sadly mistaken. And he'll burn right through the rest of us to get to you." I don't dispute this point, though I don't really grasp it.

"We're all bachelors here," Hollister elaborates, "with the exception of Dr. Wan—though he would sooner die in space than spend a day on Earth with his wife. Nevertheless, we all have loved ones of one form or another back home. If Palmer Gunn has any reason to believe you've survived your journey here, he'll have just as much reason to believe you've infiltrated our ranks and won an advocate among us." He pauses to scratch the back of his head, a fleeting shadow of shame scampering across a pair of wiry eyebrows. "I don't wish you any harm, Wilson—really, I don't—but I won't put my family at risk for your sake. None of us will."

My body grows numb with dull resignation. I'm about to die, and now that I know it for sure, I begin to wonder about things I've taken great pains to keep under the rug.

What do I have to be proud of in my life?

What if there really is a god? What if we've all talked ourselves out of the truth?

Before I can give these questions much attention, Hollister gives me an ounce of hope. "You do have one option, however."

A maniacal guffaw escapes me, fresh tears glazing my vision with a blur of uncertainty. "I'm not a picky man, Hollister."

He chuckles sympathetically, a dry hack like corn stalks rubbing in the wind. "Somehow, I thought you'd say that."

He raps sharply on the door with the back of his knuckles. Moments later, another man pops his head into the room. Hollister acknowledges him with a curt nod, and the stranger shuffles inside.

"Kurt Grogan," he says, approaching me with an outstretched hand. "Pleased to meet you."

I shake his hand, though I'm thoroughly confused—and just as suspicious.

Hollister notes my wariness and coughs out a brittle laugh. "Mr. Grogan here's in the market for some help, Wilson."

I glance at him, raising an eyebrow.

Grogan takes over, nodding appreciatively to Hollister. "I run a research lab, and it just so happens that I need a lab technician."

My incredulity is rewarded with a crooked grin. "I know—you're not a certified technician. But the truth is the work isn't as technical as the title implies. Just follow instructions, and leave the science to the researchers. Pay's pretty good."

I smile cautiously, thinking this sounds a little too good to be true. "Okay. So, what's the catch?"

Grogan shrugs and puts his hands into his pockets. "No catch." Then, as if it's only just now occurred to him, he adds: "Of course, the lab's on Mars."

I blanch. "Did you say Mars?"

"I did."

"I can't go to Mars!" I exclaim, eyes bouncing from Grogan to Hollister and back again.

Grogan cackles. "Sure you can—the way I hear it, you don't have much choice."

Part Two:
The Red Planet

Sixteen

We leave around dawn. Hollister sees me off with a limp handshake and a tired smile. His colleagues are undoubtedly fast asleep at this hour, but I'm sure they send their best wishes. Sunrise out here is a bit like a flashlight creeping from behind a brick wall—not at all the beautiful terrestrial display I've grown up with. The turning of the day is so unfamiliar—and unexpectedly bland—that it seems a little moot. My usual good-morning stretching of limbs and coffee-induced leap into the day certainly isn't triggered, anyway.

Then again, the lackluster sunrise is truly the least of my concerns; I have to assume I'm fixating on it because I need the distraction. I'm doing the best I can to stave off tears, but it's hard. My whole body has begun to shake and no amount of effort is enough to control it. I absolutely can't believe this is happening. I'm not a brave person; I'm afraid of a lot of things, many of which would only embarrass me to confess, yet this is more frightening— and equally exciting, if I'm being honest—than any fate I've ever imagined.

Grogan's ship begins to accelerate with maddening sluggishness, which conflicts with my heightened state of anxiety. I watch the Unified Space Station shrink until it's a faint twinkle against the Earth's atmosphere. This alone takes half an hour; at this rate, I'll need a denture fitting by the time we finally reach Mars; hope they serve dinner at four p.m., too.

"How long will it take?" I ask Grogan. My voice wavers, and though I'd rather not air my terror for all to see, I don't know this guy well enough to care what he thinks of me.

"Four days. It'll take a couple of days to reach light speed, and a couple more to decelerate again."

"Huh." Nowhere near as long as I feared, yet still a surprisingly lengthy trip. "Why does it take so long?"

"Well, it's not the ship, if that's what you mean—this baby can go from zero to light speed and back again in about four hours, but you'd be a quivering pile of gore within the first fifteen minutes. Biological masses can't handle the g-force, so we have to taper out the acceleration and deceleration over a few days."

It has never occurred to me that g-force exists in space; I guess I've always attributed it to planetary gravity—shows you how little I know about physics. Once upon a time, I flaunted this ignorance like a badge of honor because it struck me as evidence that I wasn't a complete nerd.

Our velocity might be a little underzealous this early in the trip, but I'm already feeling pretty queasy. Maybe it has less to do with our speed than the realization that I'm headed into an immense blackness as deep as infinity, and that I'll never see my home again.

Either way, I've felt better.

"So tell me more about this job," I say, perhaps more out of need for distraction than genuine curiosity. Grogan sighs and rubs at a sore spot at the back of his neck.

"Not much to tell, actually. A lot of mindless busywork. We're employed by an R&D company out of China. PRMC—that stands for Planetary Research and Mining Company—set up shop on Mars a few years ago to develop a proprietary species of medicinal plant. Sounds illogical, I know; but it turns out Mars is an ideal setting for our research."

"Why is that?"

"Well, for one, the plant has some chemical properties that make it desirable as a toxicant."

"So you can't legally grow it on Earth," I infer.

"Yup. We initially suppressed those qualities in the genome, but they turned out to be necessary for the more desirable medicinal properties to maintain the intensity we're after."

"So why Mars? Seems a little out of the way; why not the Unified Space Station, or even the moon?"

"Good question. It would certainly be more convenient, wouldn't it? Thing is, PRMC already had a base in progress on Mars. About a decade ago, the company was contracted by the Unified Government to gauge the potential for harvesting iron from Mars. Only, halfway through construction of the research facility, the price of iron dropped in half back on Earth, and the government suddenly pulled out."

"Leaving your company holding the bag?"

"Exactly. A blessing in disguise, if you asked me. Mars's iron content is limited to its surface, anyway, so it was a short-lived venture at best. A few years, and the whole planet would've been stripped."

"Why only the surface?"

"Well, unlike Earth, Mars doesn't have an iron core."

Just like everything else I've heard today, this is news to me. I hope I'm not accentuating my ignorance with questions that any ninth-grader can undoubtedly answer, because they're coming either way. "Okay, so where'd the surface iron come from?"

Grogan takes a deep breath. "Asteroids," he replies. His expression is patient, though an undertone of irritation is beginning to leak from the seams. For the moment, he's taking it all in stride, but I figure it won't be long before he blows a gasket. "The generally accepted theory is that enough of them have blasted Mars over time that the surface has become impregnated with bits of iron shrapnel. The planet's atmosphere is mostly carbon dioxide, but there are traces of ice in the soil. They're apparently enough to allow oxidation, hence the red surface."

"Huh," I mutter in comment, feeling more intellectually outclassed than I have in days. "So that venture failed before it could even take off, and PRMC figured, why waste a half-built facility?"

"That about sums it up. It sounds dramatic, I know, but that kind of stuff happens every day in the industrial sector. You gotta roll with the punches to stay afloat, and that means making tough decisions and finding creative ways to make money with what you've got."

I have a million more questions, now that my interest is engaged, but I figure they'll only draw more attention to my stupidity. I suspect most will resolve themselves soon enough, if I just give them a chance. One, on the other hand, has wormed its way to my tongue, and I'd be remiss to let it die there, unspoken. I clear my throat, aware that I'm about to broach what is likely to be a sensitive subject.

"So, uh, who am I replacing?"

Grogan blinks, the corners of his mouth bending into a suspicious frown. His eyes narrow a tinge, and I know my hunch was dead on. "What makes you think you're replacing anyone?"

"Just an educated guess; I figure if you were recruiting under any other circumstances, you'd need to be a lot pickier about your prospects."

Grogan smiles, cheeks flushing like I've just taken his queen with my knight.

"His name was Lawrence Montague; most of us just called him Monty. He was a good guy." He looks away.

"What happened to him?"

For a moment, Grogan doesn't respond. Shaking his head, he allows his gaze drop to the floor, where it lingers for an uncomfortable five count. When he looks at me again, his eyes are hard, distant. "Mars isn't an easy place to live, Wilson. I hope I haven't oversold the place; it's cold, dirty, and completely unforgiving. You let your guard down for a second, and you're dead."

"Is that what happened to Montague? He let his guard down and was killed?"

"I've really said all I can about him, Wilson. I'm really not permitted to discuss it. Suffice to say that ours is a dangerous job. If you're careful, you'll be fine. If not, you'll be putting your life—and the lives of your coworkers—in jeopardy."

I gulp, hoping my consternation isn't plainly visible on my face.

"One other thing," Grogan adds with a tight smile. "Maybe it goes without saying, but if anyone asks where you came from, I recruited you through our USS Moon mining operations liaison. I don't know what you got yourself into back there, but I don't need my crew getting caught up in it. I was in a pinch, you were in a pinch; don't make me regret taking a gamble on you. Got me?"

I do. I wasn't feeling great earlier, but adding this conversation into the mix has me feeling a bit ill. Grogan senses my unease—or notices my greening pallor—and fetches me a bottle of water, along with a small pill. I look at him with weak amusement—a pill, for crying out loud? He's got to be joking. I haven't seen one of these since I was a kid.

"If you want to feel better, take it," he says. "Your implant won't do you any good out here, in case you haven't already figured that out."

Nodding dumbly, I swallow the blue tablet with difficulty, grimacing as it snails bitterly down my throat. "I guess these things take some practice," I remark around a garbled cough.

Armed with Grogan's meticulous directions, I eagerly set out to find the dorms. It doesn't take long, though I get the feeling one might easily become lost here. It's only been a few minutes, but already a heavy shroud of drowsiness has settled over me. It's a sensation completely unlike anything my NanoPrint has ever triggered, and not necessarily in a bad way.

When I locate the dorms—a long hall of quaint, spartan rooms lined with steel-framed bunkbeds—I fall into the first bunk I encounter. One moment I'm sulking against a bare mattress, remembering with stinging eyes and an aching heart the smell of Adrian's skin, the feel of her lips against mine—the next? Well, somehow I'm waking up. Time is a tangle of incongruities on this ship—no clocks, no nexus to keep me in synch. I have no idea how long I've been out, though the rumble in my stomach hints that it's been a long time.

Rising groggily to leaden feet, I'm drawn to the window. Peering through the thick resin portal, I notice that the tiny pinpoints of light outside have begun to grow tails. Soon, they'll be stretched taut like ribbons through space. We must be traveling hundreds of thousands of miles per hour by now.

I'm suddenly terrified by our velocity: what if we collide with a piece of passing debris? At this speed, it would surely punch right through us like a bullet through a foil balloon. I wonder: would the ship explode on impact, or would it implode from the rapid loss of pressure?

I take a leisurely half-hour tour of the vessel, noting countless unmarked doors and hatches throughout the maze, wondering what mysteries lie beyond them. It's a large ship—equipped for a sizeable crew, if needed—yet Grogan and I haunt it alone. At some point during my outing, I realize that I no longer have any idea where I am. I continue to poke along through endless corridors— each seemingly identical to the last—because there's really nothing else I can do, but I'm getting a little freaked out. When I find Grogan sitting in a small cafeteria, I take great pains to appear blithe, but I'm actually trembling with relief.

"Ah," he exclaims. "Sleeping Beauty awakens at last." He cocks his head curiously, appraising me with a raised eyebrow. Suddenly, his mouth forms a ridiculous smirk. "Got lost, huh?"

I can't help but blush, my sheepish smile slipping into a thin line of mortification. "How long was I out?"

"Oh, the better part of a day, I guess." *Good grief—I gotta get some of those pills.* "You want another pill?" he offers with a wry grin. A bona fide mind-reader, this guy.

"No, thanks," I laugh. A few more of those, and I might never wake again.

"You sure? Gets pretty boring out here—no shame in sleeping through it."

"I'm all right. I feel like I've been asleep for a week, anyway. I'll be lucky to sleep at all tonight." I stifle a yawn. At once, a terrible thought cuts through the billowy veil of grogginess. "Now that I think about it," I say with a halfhearted—and completely disingenuous—chuckle, "I guess I'd rather be asleep if there's any danger of us crashing into something out here."

Grogan laughs, a youthful cackle, full of zeal and the sort of abandon that I've never committed to in the best of circumstances. "I know, it's hard to get used to. But eventually you learn to trust the ship, and you stop worrying about stuff like that. It'd take a rock the size of a couch to make it past the magnetic repulsion systems, and anything that large is easy enough to circumvent."

I smile, though inside I'm terrified. Weighed down by doubts, I realize there's really nothing I can do to protect myself; like it or not, I'm at Grogan's mercy. My worries—however plentiful—are worthless out here. Regardless of how many I manage to accrue, they have no power over fate.

Or do they?

Seventeen

It's been two days, and I'm starting to see what Grogan meant about boredom on this trip. Who knew that a spaceship could travel at near light speed with so little noise or vibration? It's so quiet I can't even think straight. I never realized just how vital the white noise of my implant was to my sanity until it was stripped away. I find myself humming to fill the void, sometimes talking quietly to myself—full conversations, I mean, that go nowhere.

What're we gonna do now, buddy boy?

Dunno; what's there to do on a Monday?

Monday? Wait a second, now; today's Tuesday, isn't it?

Actually, now that I think about it, I'm pretty sure it's Wednesday.

Okie-dokie. So what're we gonna do today? Not much to do on a Monday, is there?

Grogan may be a space veteran, but he's no more immune than I am. At first, I worried about wearing out my welcome with him, so I gave him wide berth to do his thing without me underfoot. Since then, it has become clear that he's as starved for conversation as I am. We're the only living things on this ship, after all, and if serendipity hadn't chosen to cross our paths, he'd be here all alone.

Speaking of my host, you'd think Grogan has spent his entire life in space, for he seems almost childishly uncultured about life on Earth. You mention something like digital flavors or the new cinema add-on and he's completely lost. His implant has been idle for so many years that he literally can't remember what it feels like anymore. Hearing this, I'm both terrified and lustful of that possibility for me. Mine is still oscillating under my skin, sending out tiny bursts of signal to the nexus, waiting for a reply that isn't likely to come. I wonder how long it'll continue before it finally gives up. I ask Grogan when his eventually shut off, but he can't remember.

That evening, we've just sat down to eat something when Grogan drops a bombshell onto the table, something I've never seen outside a museum—something that would get him a stiff fine and a week of community service back on Earth. It's a book—I mean an actual, printed book. He tosses it next to his plate like it's the most normal thing in the world, like paper is a plentiful commodity. It's black-bound and thick. It isn't until he opens it and begins reading that I realize it isn't constructed of paper, as I first thought. The text is imprinted on some sort of synthetic material that resembles paper, but has a slightly translucent quality which differentiates it from the real thing.

Grogan looks up at me, as if he can feel my eyes bugging. "Pretty cool, huh?" he says. "My brother got this for me last year."

"I didn't even know they printed books anymore." For that matter, who knew there was even a market for them? "Where'd your brother even find that thing?"

Grogan shrugs with a faraway smile and scratches the scruff on his neck. "Beats me. Apparently, they can have just about anything printed and bound. I have seven more."

My disbelief must've been palpable just then, because later, when we've finished eating, Grogan retrieves all seven in a haphazard tower, supported by his hands at the bottom and his torso at the top.

I'm speechless. On Earth, I could access any published work in a split second via the nexus. But I've never been much for reading—I'm far too lazy. Why read a story when you can just watch the movie? I've never been ashamed by this; at least, not directly. I'm no different than most in this respect, really. But under the circumstances, I'll take any form of entertainment I can get my hands on.

My never-ending hankering for movies—especially old ones—is certainly more significant than is probably healthy. I've inadvertently soaked up tidbits of the antiquated film vernacular and made them my own. With my NanoPrint out of commission, I realize I may never watch another movie again.

First my coffee, and now my movies? Jeez, what's left to satisfy my addictive proclivities? I guess I'll have to get used to using my imagination on Mars.

"Try this one out, if you want," Grogan offers, nodding toward a slab on the top of his pile. The book looks as if it might slide off if I demur, so I pluck it off the stack and admire its heft. "It's one of my favorites," he confesses, watching me flip curiously through the fine pages.

Fahrenheit 451.

I glance at Grogan for more encouragement. "What's it about?"

He sniggers and shakes his head. "I don't want to spoil it for you, but I can promise you'll never take reading for granted when you're done."

It would be rude not to accept it, and I certainly have nothing better to do. So I acquiesce, retiring to my dorm to read a printed book for the very first time.

The ship is slowing now. The sensation is subtle, but I feel as though I'm perched on the edge of my axis, leaning slightly to compensate for the disturbance in gravity. Grogan pops his head into my dorm to inform me that we'll be landing in a matter of hours. I feel a quickening pass through me as I imagine dry ground beneath my feet. Bolting from the bed, I abandon the novel to peer through the window. I'm expecting to see something telltale of the end of our journey, but all I see are white threads of light, which shorten almost imperceptibly as I track them. I feel the now-familiar symptoms of motion sickness creeping in, but I'm reluctant to take another of Grogan's magic pills—I don't want to experience my first glimpse of the Red Planet from its surface after waking from an eight-hour coma.

I leave the dorms behind and move to the flight deck, where Grogan is busy pushing all sorts of buttons and checking gauges. For the first time since we embarked on this journey, it dawns on me that this entire ship—which is easily the size of my entire condo building—rests under the exclusive control of Grogan; through this lens, the man looks strikingly different. I don't know why he should impress me more now, but he does. As he goes about the cabin, making adjustments here and there, I'm a little awestruck that he seems to know what every little control—of which there are many hundreds, if not thousands—is for, and how it should be managed.

Out the front portal, I can see Mars ahead. It's a surreal moment, catching my first view of the planet; it's a rare experience that I proudly share with few men. And just like Earth, Mars's strangeness is unbelievably beautiful from space.

I'm so caught up in the view that it almost doesn't register with my consciousness that my NanoPrint has just gone quiet. When it finally dawns on me, I'm not sure if I should laugh or cry; I want to do both. My fingertips travel tentatively to my wrist, as if to confirm or deny what I already know to be true: that my last link to the only world I've ever known has just been severed.

Eighteen

The countless images I've absorbed of Mars over the years have grossly underprepared me for the real thing. It's not that they've built up grandiose expectations; on the contrary, actually. Everything I've ever seen of Mars has depicted a generally bland ball of dirt and ice—a planet only a scientist could love.

In reality—at least, in my view of it at this particular moment—Mars is nothing like that. Well, in a way it is—but it mostly isn't. Laying eyes on its surface for the first time, it's clear that no picture will ever do this place justice. You need the face-to-face depth of true binocular vision to fully appreciate its grandeur.

I've never seen a desert before today; I can't count Nevada, since every square inch of the state is covered in solar panels and rainwater collectors. Though the term—desert, I mean—implies a certain barrenness—which is of course fitting—the surface of Mars is teeming with mountains, valleys, and some of the most dramatic rock formations I've ever seen. They're like the fingerprints of the cosmos, left behind for my humble amazement. But all of this is incidental to my expectations when compared to what I see as I follow Grogan out of the cargo bay and onto the gritty surface of Mars.

At first, I think I'm misinterpreting what I'm seeing—perhaps my oxygen mix is too rich, and that my mind isn't processing things correctly—but when Grogan comes to a halt and I nearly ram him from behind, I realize that I'm not imagining anything.

"Oh my God," he exclaims. "What've they done?" Directly ahead of us, the ground is punctured in a neat row by an array of bizarre plants. How they got there, I can surmise from Grogan's reaction. How they've managed to survive there, on the other hand, is something I'm incapable of wrapping my mind around.

Grogan storms toward the nearest building, unleashing a few expletives along the way that tell me someone just made his scrap list. The airlock is barely large enough to accommodate the two of us, and I'm quietly grateful that we're at least helmeted right now—I can't speak for Grogan, but I haven't brushed my teeth in days. I feel the pressurization of the room change, and with a hiss, oxygenated air blows into the lock.

Until now, I suppose I've envisioned a small complex of cluttered labs, overcrowded by bumbling scientists. But the reverse seems to be the case; the complex is huge—even larger inside than out, because the lower third of the structure is buried in the ground—and seemingly void of human habitation. Grogan leads me deeper into the complex, which is effectively a large honeycomb of modular rooms. The farther he takes me, the more startled I am by the gluttonous ratio of person to square inch.

As if reading my mind, he explains: "Isn't normally like this, in case you're wondering."

I nod, forgetting that he can't hear my body language. "Is it lunchtime, or what?"

"Not even close," he grumbles. "Think it's more of a case of *when the master's away, the cats will play*." I'm thinking he must mean *when the cat's away, the mice will play*, but I hold my tongue.

We've been here for nearly ten minutes before we finally see another human being. I can tell that Grogan's relieved, yet his relief is shadowed—or even masked—by irritation.

"What's going on around here, Winkley?" Grogan demands as he fumbles to disengage his helmet. I follow suit with my own and instantly wish I hadn't. The air is stuffy, thick with the funk of body odor and mildew—and something else, something sewery.

"Gross," I gag. "What's that smell?"

Grogan regards me with surprise, as if he's only just remembered that he didn't arrive here alone. He wrinkles his nose and defers to Winkley. "You smell something?"

Winkley, who seems grateful for the momentary lapse in his rear-chewing, smiles broadly. He's short and husky, maybe in his midforties. He looks at me with an amused grin and makes a show of sniffing the air. "Not a thing, boss. You?"

Grogan claps me on the shoulder and says, "Don't worry, newbie. Just a little methane—you won't even notice it in a week or so."

"I find that hard to believe," I gag.

Winkley dials down his smile, just a notch. "Seriously; something about the soil here; it deadens your olfactory glands. Pretty sure most of us could walk right over a dead skunk and wouldn't even smell it."

I grimace in disgust, and in dismay. How sad that will be, to lose the ability to smell my own need for a shower. For now, I guess the upside is that no one's likely to notice the neglected state of my breath. That aside, what I wouldn't do for a toothbrush!

"Where exactly is everyone?" Grogan wants to know. "And what are the BPs doing outside?"

Winkley cringes, as if he's been waiting for one or both of these questions with trepidation. "Yeah, that. Well, let's see: Rogers and Cutterly are both recovering in the infirmary—I think the stitches came out earlier—and Fiona's probably in her lab."

"And the BPs?"

"You'll have to ask the missus about that, boss. I'm out of the loop on that one."

Without another word, Grogan sheds the remainder of his

atmospheric suit and stomps past Winkley, pushing farther into the complex.

Winkley whistles a sigh through his round nose. "Always a treat, that guy."

"He usually this tense?"

"Only when he's awake. Actually, he's perfectly happy on his ship. Me? I need a little ground under my feet."

I nod, thinking, *Here, here.*

I get the impression that first names are silent with this group. Maybe it's a blue-collar thing. If so, it's all the more important for me to tread carefully; a name like *Abby* begs for mockery in a group of working-class men. Perhaps wisely, I introduce myself as Wilson and then begin the difficult process of removing my suit. It's a substantial set of gear; thick, stiff and heavy. "Man, this thing's a beast," I wheeze.

Winkley snorts. "You won't complain the first time you're actually outside for more than a few minutes."

"What do you mean?"

"These babies aren't designed for occasional use in low-atmospheric conditions; they're built to withstand serious abuse in the worst of conditions. Even then, when they're all that's between you and Mars, they don't seem like much. You end up out there"—he gestures with a hooked thumb out toward the dirt—"without one of these on? You're done for."

I swallow, my mouth suddenly full of cotton.

"Never mind the air supply; even if you got past that, the temperature out there is all over the map—thirty degrees Fahrenheit one minute, seventy below the next. If the cold doesn't get you, the solar winds'll impregnate you with radiation. Believe me—we're lucky to have these."

I am sufficiently convinced on this subject and decide to bite my tongue, lest I say something else I'll immediately regret.

Grogan returns, and he's not alone. As his associate steps into the room, my breath snags in the mousetrap of my throat. She's startlingly beautiful, and her presence seems blatantly at odds with the drabness and stench of this place. She's like a rare and exotic flower growing inextricably from a trash heap.

My reaction is lost on no one, least of all Winkley. He laughs boisterously at my expense, remarking: "Don't worry, you'll get used to her, too. Eventually, you'll start to see her as just one of the guys."

I sense a thought gathering on my tongue—the kind one might playfully consider inside, but would never speak aloud—and though I know I'll regret it if the words slip into open space, I realize I can't stop them.

"Let's get started, then," my traitorous mouth defects. "You wanna play fort in my room?" *Oh, Wilson; you sad, little idiot.*

The room resounds with a sharp intake of breaths—including my own—followed by a terrible period of dead silence. My ears burn as if aflame.

Keith would be so proud, you loser.

In unison, we dance a nervous shuffle until—at once—Grogan erupts into a blasting guffaw; Winkley squeezes out a weird laugh between clenched lips, sounding remarkably like a fart.

While welcome, the merriment quickly dwindles to a timid clearing of throats, ushering in a terrible spell of sheer awkwardness. All eyes shift to the woman, whose face seems paralyzed in an expressionless mask. Slowly, she trains her magnificent green eyes on me in a challenging squint—the way gunslingers do in old movies, just before they start counting off steps in a duel. It might be my imagination, but I think I detect a faint smile behind that façade, begging for freedom. I feel my heart swell in a lovesick hiccup.

The last thing I want right now is a shootout with the village supermodel, so I do my best to backpedal.

"Listen," I plead, "I'm sorry. That just went right past my filter before I could stop it." I'm speaking both literally and figuratively here; throughout my life, my NanoPrint has helped shape my thoughts, funneling them into socially acceptable parameters. Now that it's gone, I'm finding it incredibly difficult to do things the old-fashioned way.

"Grogan," says the woman, though her eyes remain firmly locked on mine, "who is this Neanderthal?"

Winkley snorts with a hearty slap to an ample thigh.

"This raving misfire is Wilson," Grogan responds, his voice aflutter with bridled amusement. "Fiona, meet your new help."

Nineteen

Mars has a daily sun cycle very similar to Earth's. I consider this to be good news, because my body craves a normal sleeping routine, just as it does air and food—and without the sun to set the pace, my systems are hopelessly without tempo. I experienced this firsthand aboard Grogan's ship, trekking through space for the better part of a week with no distinct night or day. Since then, I've learned that recovery is a game of inches; it may be weeks or even months before I fully recuperate. Nevertheless, with an actual dusk and dawn to aid me, I'm at least headed in the right direction.

Shortly after settling in, I discover that my body burns through much more energy here than it ever did on Earth. I'm a little surprised by this. After all, the gravity here is a fraction of Earth's; by my estimation, things ought to be less taxing.

As usual, my estimation is faulty.

For example: walking from one building to another nearly drains me. In theory, it should be easy—a leisurely series of bounces, like tiptoeing across a swimming pool—but in reality, the task is made much more difficult by my cumbersome atmospheric suit, and by my inability to reconcile the energy requirements of walking outside with those of inside—the same pressurizing system that keeps indoors livable makes it impossible to ever really acclimate to conditions outdoors.

Another contributing factor to my exhaustion is the food. I've always been pretty thin, yet I don't doubt I'll be much thinner a month from now. Food is strictly rationed among us. We don't skip meals—nothing as drastic as that, so far—but our portion sizes are just a little smaller than our bodies crave; as a result, we're always hungry. I'm told this is one of a few things I'm not likely to get used to.

Probably the worst part of living on Mars is the cold. Really, I never minded the cold on Earth. That's not to say I wouldn't prefer a constant seventy-five degrees with a light breeze over the discomfort of a snowstorm, but I distinctly remember looking forward to winter as much as I did summer. The contrast of seasons gave me something to look forward to year-round.

In many ways, Mars is similar to Earth. It's considerably smaller, but otherwise fairly comparable. Climate, however, is not an attribute they have in common. The day I arrived here, temperatures hovered around the low forties. When I awoke the next morning, I could see my breath; the thermometer had plummeted to twenty below during the night. I'm told Mars has its seasons, but when the daily forecast has a standard deviation of plus or minus a hundred degrees, seasons don't count for much.

The complex is heated, but it doesn't cope well with temperatures this extreme, and I'm told I haven't seen the least of it yet. Our climate control system was undoubtedly designed in the comfort of a board room back on Earth, relying heavily on some under-the-gun assumptions regarding the anatomy of Mars. Few of these assumptions were accurate.

Our heating system utilizes ambient ground heat, which is absorbed by a buried array of fluid-filled manifolds. This concept has proven wonderfully reliable on Earth and has been refined over hundreds of years to the extent that supplemental heat sources are literally a thing of the past. In terms of engineering, it works because the planet's core and subcutaneous layers remain at a fairly constant temperature. Apparently, there was reason to believe that Mars would behave likewise.

As it turns out, Mars does not.

Something mysterious is amiss at the heart of this planet. Whatever the anomaly is, it causes the ground temperature to be far more dynamic than anyone expected. It's as if the soil has little or no insulating properties.

With all that said, our system does manage to reap some heat—enough to keep us from a popsicle's fate, anyway. Since the day when Grogan first soiled his boots with smears of Martian rust, he's been working toward a more effective heating solution. Without help from his Earthly engineers—who purportedly washed their hands of the situation, calling it an issue of comfort over survival—it's been an uphill battle of trial and error, importing refined system components one piece at a time from Earth.

I shouldn't complain, and believe it or not, I don't. Not out loud, anyway. I've taken a recent liking to sweaters, which were fair game for ruthless mockery back home. Even still, layered heavily in synthetic wools and insulating polyesters, the cold has found a grudging home in me, leaching into my bones with a constant ache.

Yet if I take a moment to forget about the daily strife of Martian life—which I do on the rare occasion when I'm not freezing or starving to death—I can't help but marvel at the ingenuity that made living here possible. It's usually the simplest of solutions that amaze me, possibly because they often seem the least obvious to me.

If you aren't already aware of it—I certainly wasn't, until Winkley took pity on me—Mars has no magnetic field to speak of, and therefore, virtually no ionosphere to deflect solar winds. This oddity has proven to be a real challenge to operations, particularly concerning communication. Now if left up to me, we'd simply shout above the winds. Or play charades—that could work, right?

Fortunately for all of us, this dilemma was put to bed long before I came along.

Turns out, the solution was underfoot all along. Engineers realized that Mars's iron-rich soil was an ideal conductor, just waiting for someone to exploit it. The boots of our atmospheric suits are treaded with metal cleats, which ground to tiny microphones and speakers built into our helmets. As long as our feet are in contact with the ground, a circuit is created, allowing communication to occur across vast distances, and for our precise locations to be continuously monitored from the control room. The corroded state of the iron is overcome by extreme cold; evidently, some minerals become more conductive at subzero temperatures. Overall, this solution seems to be every bit as reliable as it is low-tech. You gotta love that kind of simplicity.

Nineteenth-century technology applied to a twenty-second-century problem.

There's something else on Mars that I never tire of admiring. Fiona, though a little standoffish at times, isn't merely beautiful, she's also brilliant, and a pleasantly considerate boss. Struggling to establish a new, working sleeping cycle, I'm often late to the lab in the mornings. Yet Fiona doesn't harp on me. Neither does she hold it against me that I have absolutely no education or training that might benefit her research.

For the most part, my lack of training hasn't yet proven detrimental; the type of busywork I'm tasked with requires more common sense than intellectual prowess. Good thing, too; I still haven't normalized to the manufactured atmosphere in the complex—I get dizzy a lot, and my thoughts tend to wander into a soupy haze toward the end of a long work day. Blessedly—or sadly, depending on my mood—the putrid stench of trace gases and the inevitable odors of confined living become a little less noticeable every day.

Fiona delegates a variety of remedial tasks to me, each of which is vital to her research and utterly meaningless to me:

preparing BP7 samples to record various chemical measurements (crushing the scrap out of plant cuttings and pouring the pulp into little cone-shaped vials); measuring pH and alkaline levels of soil samples (dipping a little probe into cups of dirt). It's mindless, repetitive work, yielding no gratification save for my proximity to Fiona.

BP7 represents Fiona's seventh run of blood plant hybrids, so named for the bloody color of their roots. Evidently, it's been a rough progression:

BP6 wouldn't reproduce past the second generation, and it matured too slowly;

BP5 succumbed to Mars's intense radiation;

BP4 choked on the extreme iron levels in the soil and wasn't able to photosynthesize;

And so forth.

Fiona's been here for three years. She's never spoken of what brought her here, or of the life she must've left behind. I wonder about these details, in part because I have a lot of time to think, but especially because she's so beautiful. I don't mean to belabor this point; I only mention it now because I find it hard to imagine why someone like her would want to be here. Why this life of unnecessary seclusion, of concentrated loneliness? Surely she could have her pick of any of the more desirable laboratories on Earth.

If you're musing that I'm overthinking this, and that my naiveté is flavoring my conclusions a bit heavily, I'm not about to argue. I've yearned for companionship my entire life—like some drowner jonesing for the perfect fix—yet I've known all along that not everyone is likewise burdened. Maybe Fiona simply isn't driven by the need for love.

Fiona and Grogan have a complicated relationship, from what I can gather. No one talks about it, but there's clearly a history there; the evidence is hard to ignore. For example, Grogan's constantly griping about the BP7s' migration from the lab to the

Martian surface. I'm not sure his argument is completely without merit—what do I know?—but his admonishments only manage to come off as petty. Fiona greets them like she's humoring the rants of a child: her eyes hard, unwavering, and more than a little condescending. It isn't merely that Grogan's opinions carry little weight with her; the two seem embattled over absolutely nothing at all. They're like an old married couple.

There is one thing that really bothers me about Fiona: she's excruciatingly vague about the big picture of her research, which is really the only vantage from which I can hope to grasp what we're doing. She numbs my mind with technical explanations for experimental procedures, yet she offers up nothing to illuminate the basis of her work.

If her experiments were designed to prove that plants can grow on Mars—with a little help, of course—they've done that. If the intention was to establish a stable species on Mars, they've done that, too. Unlike its predecessors, BP7 has yielded some extremely promising results.

So what exactly is left to prove?

Yet Fiona continues to refine her experiments, repeating them in new—and ostensibly meaningless—sequences. Even after three long years of research, she shows no intention of leaving; I'm not sure if this is an expression of will or resignation. I always figured the purpose of science was to learn things, not to invent new ways to demonstrate what you've already learned. But—again—what do I know?

Grogan is not only closemouthed on the subject of research, but when I dare to ask for his input, he looks at me as if I've just asked an engineer to explain the nuts and bolts of botany—which, I suppose, is exactly what I've done.

My options are slim at this point, so I'm reduced to pumping Winkley for information. My new friend is willing, if not completely able. I start with the basics.

"How can they grow here with no oxygen?"

"I wish I knew. There are trace amounts in the soil, I guess, but nowhere near enough to explain how they thrive. Fiona's really the only one who completely gets it. I have a nutshell understanding of it, though: the extreme iron content of the soil seems to accelerate growth and toughen these plants when it should probably kill them. From what I can tell, the BPs aren't merely tolerating the iron, they're actually feeding on it. They photosynthesize during the day—just like their Earth cousins—but unlike anything I've ever seen, these guys don't shut down at night. They store enough energy during the day to carry them through the dark hours. They're like little biological batteries."

"That's pretty amazing," I say.

Winkley nods. "Yeah; kind of scary, too, when you think about it."

My lips form a lean frown. "What do you mean, scary?"

"Just think about what these things could do on a planet like Earth. BP7 has all the hallmarks of an invasive species, but worse than that, it feeds on iron, man!"

"Yeah, I guess that could be a problem."

Winkley rolls his eyes. "Uh, you guess? Think it through, man. You have a plant that needs oxygen, but somehow manages to survive on trace amounts. Imagine how much more it would thrive with an endless supply! What it *does* seem to need is extraordinary levels of mineral sustenance, and it's willing to burn right through the night to get it."

"Okay, so on Earth you'd have a plant that gets more oxygen than it needs. And, I guess it's able to leach the soil of its mineral content. Not sure I see the big deal—Earth's mineral content was pretty much wiped off the surface over fifty years ago."

"Exactly. So where do think these guys'll have to go for dinner?"

I submit my trademark dumb expression in response.

"Infrastructure, man. Building foundations, railways. Pipelines. Wire grids. Fences. Bridges."

"The nexus framework?"

"You got it. In a few years, that entire planet of yours would be stripped. Technically, you could harvest the plants to get the minerals back—if you were really determined—but it would take a concerted global effort to pull it off. You gotta admire the destructive capabilities of these things."

I'm truly disturbed by this analysis, and I don't want to minimize its significance, yet I'm more disturbed that Winkley has so blithely detached himself from his planet of origin—because deep down, I know that I'm headed down that same road. And my acknowledgment of this truth fills my aching bones with unrelenting sadness.

Cutterly and Rogers are still on the mend, though I guess they've left the sick bay behind for the comfort of their dorms. I've met the two, however briefly, in the corridors of the research base; they have a haggard look to them, and neither seems interested in me at all. They spend a lot of time resting. I still don't know what happened to them—their hands are pink with the gristle of freshly healed wounds, and Cutterly walks with a slight limp—but I'm guessing their poor states have something to do with Montague.

I've dubbed this place the b-hive; the other guys just call it *base* or *the office*. Pathetic. I guess with all the activity going on here, there isn't much energy left for creativity. I'm a little concerned: if these people rub off on me, Fiona and I may someday have four sons named Dave.

It could happen, right?

Anyway, the complex does resemble a bee hive, thanks to its modular design. I'm told it's actually the second facility to be built on Mars, the first of which was found rusted to the ground when PRMC's mining team first arrived nearly a decade ago.

I spend a lot of time thinking about that first facility, wondering what it was here for, what happened to its inhabitants. The longer I'm out here, the more vulnerable I feel. Anything can happen here—there's no nexus to guide my steps, no government agency to intervene on my behalf if I make a mistake. Not even my NanoPrint can aid me here. I find myself agonizing over safety procedures—obsessing over every detail, no matter how minor— because I'm scared to death that my bones will be picked clean by Mars's unfettered winds the first time I slip up. Grogan insists this attitude is a good thing, that my fear will keep me alive.

I'm not so sure. It causes me to hesitate now and then, and hesitations can be lethal.

Sometimes I miss the nexus—the music and movies, the endless array of useless, encyclopedic information I used to take for granted—all streamed to my implant, where I can no longer access it. I've become very aware of my implant's silence; my hormones are virtually out of control, my emotions subject to manic extremes. The subtle chemical nudges I've grown up with are now completely gone, leaving me a little dazed, overwhelmed by the excess of social cues I'm now expected to make sense of. I find, at times, that I even miss the constant white noise of its workings. I'd definitely give Marilyn a fat digital kiss if she were to bound from my periphery.

I think about Mitzy a lot, though I try not to. The guilt I feel is enormous. Somehow, though, it grows a little dimmer every day. At times I'm not even sure what's nagging at me, and then I remember. I consider it a good day when I'm smart enough to think about something else.

More than anything, though, I just miss Earth. Strolling through the city in streetclothes, sipping coffee that doesn't taste like scorched plastic. Stretching in the womb of a sunny afternoon, smelling the breeze of a breathing planet—all the things I once took for granted. It hurts to think on these things. Remembering is like probing a festering wound. Yet, if not for those memories, I'd have nothing but rust and rock to occupy my imagination. My life has ventured down a new path. It's hard to accept that I can't turn back, but I must.

In the grand scheme of things, these are trivial annoyances.

The thing that truly keeps me up at night—drawing sweat from my pores, despite the relentless cabin chill—is Montague. I can't tell you how many hours I've stared at my darkened ceiling, trying to work out exactly what happened to the man. It's odd, isn't it, that I should be so concerned for a complete stranger? I think so at times. Other times, I suspect I'm not really worried about him at all, but indirectly worried about myself.

Because if Montague—a trained Martian professional—was indeed wiped from existence for a single moment of carelessness, I'd say I'm on borrowed time.

Twenty

It's been two months, and for the first time since my arrival, I'm terrified for a very tangible reason.

A moment ago, I stirred awake to a nearby hissing—a gentle but incessant serpent-song that initially only just penetrated my slumber. Then, just as it set me to the sniffling and tossing and turning of near-waking, I realized something was truly wrong and sat upright in bed. I don't understand what I'm hearing now; instinctively, though, I know it's something that shouldn't be here. From the adjacent room—Winkley's quarters—I hear a sudden shout, followed by the bump and crash of a person in distress. I'm on my feet in a flurry, bolting to the door in a mad dash of adrenaline. Surging into the darkened hallway, I nearly plow into Grogan, who rudely elbows by me without warning or apology.

Emergency or not, the guy rubs me the wrong way sometimes.

"What is it?" I whisper to no one in particular, not at all sure why I'm whispering. "What's going on?"

"We're losing pressure," says Fiona from the darkness. A moment later, her body catches up to her disembodied voice and floats by like a pale ghost. Winkley's door swings inward and out he comes, boiling from his room as if on fire and running for dear life. "It's broken through!" he wails, and his voice is so shrill, so haunted, that my own fear—which is as much a product of confusion as anything else—suddenly takes on a more formidable form.

Silhouetted against the glow spilling from Winkley's doorway, Grogan pokes his head inside and gasps. Stepping back, he blurts out a word I've never heard before, though from his derogatory tone and the slight twitch of Fiona's mouth, I divine that it's an otherworldly brand of cursing. To lighten the mood, I'm tempted to ask for a definition as he barrels past me down the corridor toward his quarters, but the look he gives me in passing stifles my curiosity, sending me scrambling in a stew back into my own room. Behind me, Fiona steps through my door and flicks on the overhead lights.

I blink and swallow.

Fiona looks good in here—like she belongs more than any fixture or piece of furniture; oh, for her to be here with me under any other circumstances! As usual, my unchecked hormones abound with no sense for timing. She registers the phantom hissing just as it is joined by a similar but distinctly separate instance of the intrusion. I look up to its source and puzzle over what I see there. A tiny dot—scarcely the size of a grain of sand—has appeared on my ceiling. It's only discernible at all because the ceiling is white, and because its presence is loudly betrayed by the screeching escape of air pressure.

"In here, too!" Fiona hollers.

A moment later, Grogan squeezes past us. Wordlessly, he steps onto the foot of my bed and slides a small dual syringe from his pocket. He unlids it with his teeth and squeezes a dollop of clear epoxy into the hole, instantly quieting the squeal of airflow. The second hole proves more difficult to locate; following his ears, Grogan crawls under a built-in desk and contorts his body into an awkward Y—one foot cutting the air, the other drumming against the floor—to reach it. Seconds later, the hissing ceases.

Winkley's room is in much worse shape. There must be ten

holes in there, two of which are large enough to put a finger through—if they weren't already occupied by vinelike tendrils.

"It's the blood plants," I say blankly, finally putting two and two together.

Grogan looks at me irritably, releasing an exasperated sigh through his nostrils. "Nothing gets by you, Sherlock."

Later in the morning, following a quick breakfast—which is uncomfortably overshadowed by a mounting sense of anxiety—we venture outside to assess the damage. Under the dirty scrim of Martian dawn, a mighty wind abuses us with bits of rock and iron; they snap and pop against our suits like angry hailstones. As we round the perimeter of the b-hive, Winkley cries out and stops dead in his tracks. Timidly—fearfully, really—I approach my friend and peer over his shoulder; the view beyond doesn't make any sense.

Ten weeks ago, the blood plants were individually rooted specimens, spaced evenly apart near the complex. Today, they form a giant mass of purple leaves and overlay a network of long, probing fronds. The fronds have crawled up the b-hive walls like jungle vines, all but obscuring the structure underneath.

"They're out of control," Winkley mutters. Nearby, Grogan engages Fiona pointedly in a long, intense glare, which she breaks off with a scowl. Even through the reflection of red rock on her facemask, her cheeks are visibly aglow.

"Real men don't need to say I told you so," she admonishes, and departs the group. Grogan moves to follow, but falters after only a few steps. I guess real men don't need to say they're sorry, either.

Winkley chuckles, but it's a nervous tic rather than an expression of amusement. With his back to us now, Grogan's face is hidden; still, as he stomps off through the Martian gales, I'm pretty sure he isn't smiling.

○————‖ < > ‖————○

Winkley and I are having quite a time uprooting the BP7s. There's no point in hacking them down; like all hearty weeds, they'll simply grow back with more determination. We're resigned to prying the vines from the building—one at a time—and then digging up each plant at its root. It's more difficult than it sounds; the fronds aren't merely growing atop the metal—they've actually penetrated it. Even the superficial vines are stiffly adhered to the paint by tiny clawlike roots. With every shaking of the plants, however gentle, a thin cloud of dust scatters into the wind, adhering to our statically charged suits like a misting of red paint.

When we're done, the BP7 corpses lie in a single violet mound piled nearly ten feet high. On cue, Grogan joins us and unceremoniously douses the vegetation with something that might be lye. I'm sure we'd all prefer to see it torched, but fire doesn't work on this forsaken planet. I suppose we could drag them into the waste incinerator inside the b-hive.

Yeah, right.

I can't see her, but I know Fiona's watching from somewhere nearby, slumped before a foggy portal, perhaps, with tear-filled eyes. I feel sorry for her, realizing that these plants—however bizarre, in my estimation—represent three long, cold years of effort for her. Even as her specimens are abandoned to the chemical appetites of Grogan's mysterious white powder, I know Fiona's contemplating what went wrong, and what she might tweak a bit for round eight.

I'm the first to flee the scene, my sore back and guilty conscience leading me to the airlock, where I hastily shed my dusty suit.

Back in the dorms, I take an extra-long shower, well aware that I'll endure a butt-chewing for this discourtesy. I truly don't care. At the moment, the scream of my fatigued muscles overpowers the voice of reason. For all my effort, I feel like I can't get clean; it's as if the Martian dirt has come to life and burrowed into my pores to escape the steaming spray. My skin is beet-red when I finally give up the cause.

Pressure-dried and dressed, I lie down on my bed, hoping to doze off my unease. But it's no use; I'm just too freaked out.

When I walk into the cafeteria for lunch, I'm the first to arrive. For a moment, I'm elated: my frequent tardiness has kept me from first pickings since the day I arrived. But then, as I look around, I realize something's not right. For starters, there's no food. Combined with the absence of people, I'm forced to acknowledge that something is definitely amiss.

I work my way back through the corridors toward Winkley's room, hoping he might provide a reasonable explanation for the state of things—he is our unofficial cook, after all—but his room is empty. The complex is unnaturally quiet, I realize. Save for the occasional creaking of structure bending against harsh winds, there are no audible signs of life or machine.

Growing anxious, I head toward Grogan's room, and then Fiona's. When I'm satisfied that the dorms are in fact empty, I move on to the labs.

They're empty, too.

There's only one place left to search; I'm beginning to wish I'd remained in that shower, for I know that whatever awaits me can't be good.

As soon as I approach the infirmary, I realize that things are worse than I could've suspected. Inside, Grogan and Fiona are suited up, which doesn't make any sense—until I see Winkley. My heart lurches at the sight of him; he's out cold on a cot, skin ashen and lifeless, chest rising and falling with ragged irregularity. Fiona is examining him frantically, taking readings with instruments that are vaguely similar to ones I've seen on Earth, only smaller and sort of abbreviated. Her expression loops fluidly from grim to desperate to stricken to grim; her hands flutter like boughs in a spastic breeze.

From the depths of my genome, a primitive need to protect this beautiful woman is ballooning in my cells; I step toward the door, drawn to her as a moth is to flame. Grogan spots me from the corner of his eye and turns to face me, shaking his head before I even reach the door. "Get outta here, Wilson." His voice is muffled through the glass, but quite intelligible.

"But what happened—?"

"Go! We'll talk later, okay? Not now."

I hesitate; I'm reluctant to leave Fiona or Winkley in their respective states of need, and honestly, I simply don't know where else to go. I can't bear to sit in my room alone, not now; I need to *do* something.

A rustle of movement startles me from behind, causing me to lurch in place. Turning my head, I see that it's Cutterly. He's a bit of a creeper, that one; I wonder if he's been here all along, or if he just walked in. I'm just about to ask him this when Rogers abruptly rounds the corner. I can't help but notice that these two look remarkably better than they have in weeks—well rested, vibrant skin color, all that.

I wish I could say the same for Winkley.

Grogan taps on the window and shouts for us all to clear out. His eyes linger on me, smoldering, as if he somehow blames me for this.

We file into the cafeteria with Cutterly leading the charge in a limping shuffle; all I can think about is Winkley—his slackened face, the deathly grayness of his skin; it's Arthur all over again. We sit without speaking, each lost in his own chaotic thoughts. It's well past lunchtime, but I don't suppose any of us feels up to eating.

Forty minutes later, Fiona and Grogan quietly join us; even before they reach their seats, their expressions betray poor tidings.

"He's not getting enough oxygen," Fiona explains weakly, dropping with defeat into an empty chair; her eyes are pink at the corners, swollen with gathering emotion.

Cutterly voices my exact thought before I can get it together. "What do you mean, like asthma?"

"I don't think so; his esophagus doesn't appear to be swollen. I'm hardly an expert, though."

"What happened, exactly?" Rogers wants to know. "He seemed fine this morning."

Grogan takes the baton. "We don't really know, guys. At this point, we don't have much to go on. I found him unconscious in the airlock, and we've been working on him ever since."

Cutterly: "When?"

"Maybe ninety minutes ago, give or take." That would put the discovery with me stepping into the shower on a timeline, I realize. I don't know why this detail should bother me, but it does; I feel terrible guilt wrap around my neck and make itself at home with a squeeze.

"He was the last one in," Grogan adds, heading off the next logical question.

"Think he might've taken off his helmet before the lock was fully pressurized?" asks Rogers.

Grogan shakes his head. "At first, that's exactly what I thought. But if that was the case, he'd have come to in a matter of minutes. He's been out for quite a while now, and—" He looks at the floor, his head swaying in a weary arc. He steals a glance at Fiona, and I notice his eyes have taken on a glassy sheen. I feel bad for him.

"And what, Grog?" Rogers probes.

Fiona picks up where Grogan left off. "He appears to be in a coma. If so, there's no guarantee he'll come out of it. Even if he does, we're likely to see some brain damage. We're really not equipped to deal with something like this."

Cutterly is breathing heavily through his nose, bouncing a nervous knee with such vigor that it quakes the entire table with every upswing. "So, what then?" he demands. "We can't just cross our fingers that he'll get better on his own; we need to get him some help."

Grogan seems to have regained his composure, regarding Cutterly with what might be frustration or irritable agreement. "Our thoughts exactly," he says. "But the question is, where do we take him?"

"Back to Earth, of course!" Cutterly exclaims.

"Can't do that," whispers Fiona. "The USS would never allow it."

"What does that mean?" I hear myself chime in. "Surely they'll want to help." Then again, they didn't exactly fall over themselves to help me out, did they?

"Keep up or stay out of it, Wilson," snaps Grogan. "Or better yet, why don't you let the adults talk for a while?" I feel myself bend under the jibe; on Earth, I was someone worthy of marginal respect—at least, that's the way I remember it. Here? I'm the lowest man on a sinking totem pole. And, for reasons that escape me, Grogan has made me his personal whipping boy. I'm prepared to lash back—I have plenty to say, believe me—but I choose to bite my tongue. Sooner or later, we're gonna have to put this business to bed—Grogan and me—but Winkley is the obvious priority right now.

"Ease up, Grog," snaps Rogers. "He isn't the only one who's not getting it."

"It's an infection, isn't it?" Cutterly quietly interjects. "Some sort of lung infection?"

Fiona nods with a noncommittal shrug, adding: "Could be. The USS won't risk introducing an unknown infection into their facility; we're on our own, boys."

Rogers and I breathe a mutual, "Oh."

Twenty-One

For most of the next morning, I camp outside of the infirmary, gazing impotently through the window upon the inanimate form of my friend. I feel like I should cry—my eyes seem hard at work trying—but I'm dried up, as if my soul has shriveled into a husk. There's a stifling tightness in my chest, too, as if it's piled with bricks. I can't even remember what life was like before death left its slimy fingerprints all over me.

It seems the Abby curse remains in full effect, even on Mars.

"How are you doing?"

The voice catches me off guard—I didn't even hear her come into the room—yet my reflexes are silent, numbed in the pickling elixir of shock. I tell Fiona that I'm fine, lying with uncharacteristic ease. I figure it's what she wants to hear, anyway; she has enough on her plate as it is.

"Listen, Wil, I need to ask you about this morning. Did anything—*happen* out there? Anything out of the ordinary?"

I glance at her, my cheeks heating at her affectionate shortening of my name—what can I say? Love has no regard for things like timing. "What do you mean?"

"I don't know," she admits. "I suppose I'm grasping at straws."

"Well, for what it's worth," I say with what I hope is a charming smile, "I think you're doing a great job. Under the circumstances, I mean."

She looks at me blankly, like I'm miswired—and frankly, I'm beginning to wonder if I am; Asperger's can set in at any age, right? "Sorry," I cringe. "I just meant—" Suddenly my thoughts flicker and I feel my cheeks burn all the more. "Wait a second."

Fiona's face seems to unfold, eyes brightening with newfound hope. "You remember something?"

"I think so. There was a lot of dust," I say.

She nods encouragingly. "What else?"

"That's it," I say. "I mean, it wasn't like normal dust, you know? It was a lot stickier. And I'm pretty sure it was coming off the plants."

"Off the plants? What do you mean, like spores?"

"I don't know. Maybe."

Fiona's gaze loses focus as she ponders this. "This is incredible," she mutters after a moment. I wait for some further explanation, and she suddenly laughs. "Don't you get it? The BPs are supposed to be apogamous!"

If we had crickets on Mars, this would be their cue to accentuate the dumb silence. "Sorry, Doc," I offer in their stead. "You're way over my head." I catch a faint waft of her scent—a subtle blend of wildflowers and something rich like coffee, only not—and sigh. Funny, I don't smell much these days; I suppose that only makes her smell all the sweeter. Of course, it's possible that I'm imagining she has a smell at all. As Fiona has explained more than once, pheromones don't necessarily require a discernably pleasant aroma, though the two often share company.

"Okay, Wil, time for some Botany 101." If it was anyone other than Fiona talking, I'd be fumbling for an excuse to get out of here right now. But the truth is, I'd endure a lot worse than a mind-numbing lecture for the tradeoff of her company. And it certainly beats the heck out of watching Winkley die.

"Your rapt pupil awaits, my dear."

Fiona smiles, eyes twinkling with scientific zeal. My heart skips a beat.

"Okay, so most plants are agamospermous—meaning they reproduce sexually—you know, flowers, pollen—birds and the bees and all that? The blood plants are genetically modeled from fern DNA; specifically, a species that naturally reproduces apomixously—that is, without traditional fertilization. On Earth, this was an evolutionary adaptation to harsh, dry environments, since normal reproduction in ferns requires enough moisture for sperm to literally swim to the egg for fertilization."

"Whoa, that's weird."

She shrugs with a mild frown. "Not really; on Earth, farmers replaced agamospermous crops with genetically engineered apoximous varieties more than seventy-five years ago. Since then, regions once considered unfertile are consistently yielding substantial harvests. It was sort of an agricultural revolution; I'm surprised you're not familiar with it."

Translation: *Third graders know this stuff; why don't you?* I shrug and bow my head in shame. Fiona sighs, slides her bangs behind her ears, then clears her throat.

"Well, anyway, there are two types of apomixous behaviors in ferns: apogamy and apospory. Apogamous plants grow from spores and seem to be regular plants. When they mature, they send out spores—seeds, if you prefer. From the seeds grow what are called gametophytes; they're sort of like plant versions of a larva—not actually an adult, but a stepping stone toward adulthood. Okay? So, the gametophyte eventually buds off a sphorophyte, which grows into the final adult plant."

I raise my hand. "Uh, is there gonna be a quiz over this?"

"Funny. Just keep up, would you? The thing is, the sphorophyte isn't really a fertilized child in this scenario—the gametophyte has literally cloned itself, so it's an exact copy of the mother plant, right down to the DNA. If you didn't know better, you'd think they were behaving like regular plants, because the reproduction happens on a scale that's really only observable under a microscope. With me so far?"

I pretend to snore.

"Come on, it's not that bad," she giggles.

"Seriously, Doc, you lost me at 'aprogilous.'"

"It's *apoximous*, you dunce."

I bat my eyes. "Sorry, we can't all be pretty *and* highQ."

"Stay with me: we're halfway there." I nod, but who am I kidding? "Okay," she continues, "aposporous plants are a little different: they reproduce by sending out antheridia and archegonia—that's the sperm- and egg-producing organs—on the edges of their leaves. If enough moisture is present, the plant literally reproduces with itself. This is the behavior we've engineered into the BPs; I wanted to maintain some control over reproduction, and controlling where spores land is impossible. And up to now, the aposporous genes seemed to be paying off in the lab."

I've understood almost none of this nonsense—classic Fiona-speak, by the way—but I'm able to glean the barest sense that the BPs have unexpectedly changed behavioral patterns—on their own, and seemingly in a single generation.

"Okay," I cede. "So, what happened exactly—I mean, what changed?"

"Well, I'm guessing the lack of moisture in the Martian soil triggered a mutation. To accelerate its maturity, I introduced a bamboo gene into BP7's profile; it's possible that the new gene is conflicting with properties in the base genome. Regardless of the catalyst—if my theory holds true—BP7 somehow morphed from a strain that doesn't reproduce using spores to one that does."

"Huh. Am I safe to assume that's a bad thing?"

Fiona nods emphatically, kneading her forehead with the back of a white-knuckled fist. "Well, yeah. That means that every place a spore lands becomes a potential growth site for a gametophyte. In other words, we lose a fair amount of control over when and where the BPs grow—outside the lab, anyway. Based on what we've seen so far, they may be hard to keep under control." She pauses to catch her breath, and for a moment, she looks as if she might cry. "Beyond that," she says, voice suddenly wavering, "there's something else."

I'm hearing her words just fine, but her mannerisms are quickly gathering my undivided attention; they belie the woman hiding inside the scientist, and I'm transfixed by this rare glimpse of her. I'd just as soon drop this subject—it's obviously hurting her—but her eyes are pleading, begging for permission to confess something terrible—something that might just change my perception of her irreversibly.

"What is it, Fiona?"

She swallows, hands wringing at her midriff. "Well, spores can sometimes trigger allergic reactions when inhaled." A fat tear spills down her ivory cheek. "There are species of mold on Earth, for example, whose spores are toxic to humans."

I can't bear to see her so distraught. I want to reach out to her, to offer the comfort of my embrace—my lips, even better—but from some isolated fold of my brain, I recognize that I've slipped into the drunkenness of lust, and that—however much I'd like to imagine otherwise—Fiona hasn't shown a single shred of interest in me outside the scope of research. I've confused her momentary vulnerability with something else, that's all; I've projected my own need for affection onto her.

Despite my inner turmoil, the implication of her words isn't lost on me. I'd be lying if I said it wasn't greatly blurred by the chemical shadow of my insistent hormones, yet I'm not completely oblivious of it; I suppose it just seems a little too alien to apply to real life, for the moment.

Graciously, Fiona seems to intuit nothing of my heartache; she looks at me for a few seconds—probing my poker face for any sign that I fault her for Winkley's condition—then shifts her gaze right through me. I can almost hear that brilliant mind crunching away like a supercomputer.

A faint *beep* seems to draw her back into the moment. She smiles sheepishly and, wiping her cheeks dry with a sleeve, turns to the sick bay window. All I can see of her now is a diffused reflection in the glass. Her eyes widen suddenly, darting about the inner room with progressive urgency.

Something's wrong.

I try to follow her gaze as it bounces from one piece of equipment to another, but the machinery is largely foreign to me; I don't know what I'm looking at. At once, her expression collapses; she surges against the window like a crashing wave, pounding on the thick glass with her palms. "No!" she cries. Then, as quickly as it came from nowhere, the tide of her anger recedes, exposing an immense tide pool of sadness in its wake.

"What's wrong?" I mutter.

Fiona sags on her feet and—with motherly kindness—rests a protective hand against the window, sobbing quietly. In a whisper so faint it might've been a breeze, she answers me.

"He's gone, Wil."

Fiona's words don't immediately register—he's right there; can't she see him?—yet even as I struggle to process her meaning, she barrels into the sick bay, pulling on her helmet and facemask almost as an afterthought. Through the glass, I hear her sniffle and whimper. As she approaches Winkley, the obvious finally dawns on me, and my heart falls into my stomach like a great, aching boulder.

Fiona makes an adjustment to a nearby monitor—for a brief, hopeful moment, I think maybe I've misunderstood—and then, disheartened by what she sees there, she powers off the device with a deflated sob. Dropping to her knees, she rests her head against

Winkley's cot and begins to weep.

I feel my own tears coming to life, yet—to my eternal shame—I can't tell if they're intended for Winkley, or if Fiona has drawn them out of me. Without forethought, I take a step toward the sick bay door. I can't explain why, but I feel duty-bound to comfort her, to save her from this misery. My foot has scarcely left the floor when a hand grasps my shoulder and—with unnerving strength—restrains me from walking.

"Don't," warns Grogan. His voice is firm, yet full of uncharacteristic kindness. "There's nothing you can do for him now."

Him? I try to pull away, heaving against his iron grasp. I'm more than a little disturbed that I can't break free; he's either far stronger or more desperate than me. Either way, I'm not moving without escalating this confrontation. "Please," I whisper.

Grogan's grip relaxes just a little, but remains affixed. "It's too dangerous, Wil. We can't risk contamination."

I realize that he's right. Too, I recognize how warped my thinking has become that Fiona's temporary emotional state has somehow won priority over the death of a friend.

Good Lord, what is happening to me?

Grogan once warned me that Mars is an unforgiving planet. I never imagined how stark that truth would prove to be. I wonder if he shared this wisdom with Winkley, and if not, if it might have made any difference. I guess I'll never know.

We bury Winkley's body a mile from the b-hive, alongside a mound of eroded stones that can only belong to Montague. I feel filthy for my participation in this ritual. It's a perversion, to my mind; I realize people used to bury their dead on Earth, but it has been taboo for much longer than I've been alive. If asked why, I could only venture a guess; maybe we ran out of virgin ground—

who knows? All I know is that I'm incapable of overlooking the lingering mores of my Earthly culture; they're too deeply engrained in me.

My psyche retches at what we're doing.

Actually, now that I think about it, I suspect the source of my revulsion is broader than mere social peeves; maybe some part of me—a part I never knew existed, perhaps—finds it deeply sacrilegious that Winkley will never *return to the earth*, so to speak. Flesh doesn't decay here, you see; there are no bacteria on Mars to aid in decomposition.

I deliberately mention this to Grogan, hoping that he'll suddenly realize the obscenity of what we're doing and call the whole thing off, but he merely shrugs, explaining that corpses do decompose—to some extent, anyway—by means of dehydration; their fluids are gradually absorbed into the soil, or sapped by the dry winds. He offers this as if it should be some consolation, and thank goodness—I feel so much better now.

Rogers and Fiona have remained behind at the lab, scouring the airlock and the infirmary with harsh cleaners to kill off any invisible spores. I'm glad for their effort, though I suspect no amount of sanitation will let me sleep tonight; I expect my skin will itch with phantom creepy-crawlies well into the wee hours of the morning, and I doubt I'll be alone with that affliction.

Cutterly doesn't say a word, but his demeanor reveals that he's been greatly affected by the loss of Winkley; maybe he's as horrified as I am by what we're doing—after all, unless he lived under a rock on Earth, he must've grown up under the same umbrella of social norms as me.

When Winkley is no longer visible for the mountain of dirt and vesicle-pocked stones, I approach Cutterly. I feel compelled to console him—I know, I'm a regular camp counselor lately—so I place a timid hand on his shoulder and give it a gentle squeeze, the way Stewart once did when my childhood pet goldfish went to visit relatives while I was at school, and never came home.

Cutterly looks at me wordlessly; his face is a collage of dark expressions—far too complex to interpret without a glass of Chardonnay and a pair of snooty bifocals.

Burning eyes flicker to Grogan and then back to me; to Grogan again, and back once more—if Cutterly was a dog, I'd think he was trying to tell me something.

What is it boy? Farmer Tom fell in a well? We'd better get help in a flash!

"Let's go," Grogan says, voice cutting through my inner monologue with an edge of—what is that, *warning*?

Cutterly's gaze—already burning like an incandescent filament—brims with hot loathing, shifting to Grogan again. The two lock eyes; the intensity between them borders on explosive, a violent chemical reaction brewing between polar elements.

Clearly, I've misinterpreted Cutterly's emotional condition; he doesn't need a hug, he needs a Grogan-shaped punching bag. Or a nice sedative, perhaps.

He gives me a polite nod—which is the closest Cutterly and I have ever come to exchanging niceties—and begins limping back to the b-hive, dragging his shovel behind him like a broken rudder.

Jeez, what's with those two?

My assumption—and also, my hope—is that BP8 will now enter the works, and that Fiona will revisit the drawing board with a more careful approach. I don't blame her for Winkley's death—how could she possibly have prepared for that?—but surely it has instilled a renewed sense of caution in all of us.

Dang, I hate being wrong.

Despite the havoc it has wreaked upon us, Fiona considers BP7 to be a success; it has proven to be stable and hearty, and it demonstrates many of the precise characteristics sought after by our employer. As for the danger it apparently poses to human life?

Well, that's merely a reason to be more cautious.

What can I say? I'm freaking speechless.

In the wake of Winkley's death, we've implemented a minor litany of precautionary procedures. Firstly, our suits must be thoroughly sterilized following any direct contact with the plants. Secondly, no suit is to be brought across the airlock threshold into the complex. Thirdly, we must all endure weekly physicals, including minor bloodwork. Finally, all interaction with the BPs is to take place in the safety of groups—no solo excursions.

These protocols give me some peace of mind, but they are sharply eclipsed by a sense of general unease, knowing that—as if this planet doesn't already pose enough physical danger—a new and formidable killer is among us. And though it hasn't been said aloud, it's evident to me that our lives are of little value to PRMC when measured against that of their new—and deadly—cash cows.

During breakfast, Fiona announces that today begins a new phase in the development of BP7. We've officially left the research phase behind us and will now concentrate on domesticating BP7 for mass production.

I'm completely taken off guard, and thereby horrified. I've never been clear on the endgame of our research until now. Looking around me, assessing the reactions of my coworkers, I realize that I'm completely alone in my distress. There's no point in arguing the absurdity of it all; unlike me, these people have known since day one where this was headed. If any one of them harbored any reservations, he or she wouldn't even be here.

After eating, Fiona leads us to the future site of our new BP farm. She and Grogan have carefully chosen acreage that is far enough from the b-hive to minimize the potential of the crops eating our buildings, yet close enough to comfortably reach on foot. There, we spend the next several hours plotting a matrix across the ground, marking points with aluminum spikes, which are then tethered together in a grid of white vinyl twine.

With the field mapped, Fiona delegates the excavation of shallow, evenly spaced pits throughout the matrix. It's brutally laborious work; the ground is densely packed with permafrosted lava rock, which hardly lends itself well to shoveling. Also, I'm an office geek, remember? I'm not built for manual labor.

We pause briefly for lunch—with emphasis on *briefly*; even before our soup has begun to cool in our bellies, we're hard at work again. By evening, we've carefully loaded the new farmstead with BP cuttings. Then Fiona departs for the lab, leaving the rest of us behind to tidy up. Nobody complains, but I think this entire exercise strikes most of us—Grogan included—as an unnecessary waste of energy; based on what we've seen of BP7, it doesn't need our organized assistance to grow—and tidiness will certainly go out the window once the cuttings begin to take root, if the wind doesn't first undo our work for us.

Twenty-Two

Returning to the b-hive, we almost don't notice it. It's easy to miss, really: we're each exhausted and walking directly into the wind; the sun is low in the sky, painting unfamiliar faces on otherwise familiar landmarks. If not for Rogers's keen eye, we might have overlooked it altogether. Even with him frozen in his tracks, pointing across the wastelands like a petrified road sign—*See it? It's right there, man*—I still don't see it right away.

At first, my gaze is drawn to the horizon, where one of Mars's odd moons is perched; its tiny, angular physique dots the sky according to a schedule that I find impossible to nail down. But then I see something—a mass that closely resembles a boulder, or perhaps a crater lip—rustling in the wind.

"What the ... ?" says Grogan. He shields his facemask against the blowing dust, as if he distrusts what he's just seen. "Fiona," he barks. A few seconds pass, and then our helmet comms come to life with her disembodied voice.

"What is it?"

"Can you take a look out the window of the utility room for me?"

"Uh, sure. What am I looking for?"

"You'll know it when you see it."

Thirty seconds tick by in silence, and then: "Okay, I'm back. You gonna tell me what's going—dear God!"

"We're still a bit far off, Fiona; please tell me that's not what I think it is."

"How did this happen?" she demands. The anonymity of our wireless comms does nothing to soften the edge of her agitation.

Cutterly laughs ironically. "You're asking *us*, Doc?"

We adjust course slightly; fueled by the adrenaline of discovery—or perhaps our morbid curiosity—we pick up speed. The wind relents a little, and soon the details begin to fall into rapid focus. Even from a distance, the sight spooks me; it's a tangled network of vines and leaves, thickly projecting from the ground in a volcano of rusty fauna. Unlike the other blood plants I've seen, this one truly lives up to its namesake—its leaves are the color of brackish gore.

"Isn't that the graveyard?" Cutterly mutters. I glance around to get my bearings and, though everything looks a little foreign in the windy dusk, I think he's right.

Grogan apparently agrees. "Fiona, the BP seems to be growing near Winkley's grave."

As we near the gravesite, however, it becomes clear that the plants—two or three, I think—aren't merely growing *near* Winkley, but *from* him. His body has literally been dragged to the surface, crimson foliage spilling from him as if from some sort of organic flowerpot.

I feel my gorge rising—never a good thing in a pressurized helmet, incidentally—and quickly look away. Poor Winkley; he didn't deserve this.

"Cripes, how the heck did that happen?" groans Rogers. "There wasn't anything growing here a couple of days ago."

We'd all like the answer to that question, naturally. But Grogan wants to know more than the rest of us; that, or he's simply determined to show us up. Whatever his motivation, he steps casually into the foothills of this nightmare, nudging scouting fronds aside with the cleats of his boots.

He should be frightened—horrified, really—to be in the thick of such a grisly abomination; I'm about to pee myself just for watching, for crying out loud. But Grogan's indifferent; he might as well be looking for four-leafed clovers in there, the way he's hunched over, poking around with his facemask afloat in a sea of sickly leaves.

"It's the spores," he finally announces, standing erect again. "Thing's growing right out of his lungs."

Fiona pipes in with a long sigh: "I guess that confirms my theory: Winkley must've breathed in the spores and suffered an allergic reaction."

Uh, or the spores germinated as he lay choking for breath.

Grogan looks at us each in turn, gauging our take on Fiona's flimsy explanation. He's not buying it—and as far as I can tell, neither is anyone else out here. Nevertheless, I think we're each too disturbed by our own theories to argue.

Everyone but Grogan, that is. "But I thought the plants fed off the iron in the soil?" he insists.

"They do."

"Isn't blood colored red because it's rich in iron?" I offer helpfully.

"That's true," Fiona agrees. "But I don't think that's relevant." *Well, excuse me for trying to help.* "I think these things can feed off just about anything. I'm headed to the lab to prepare a sampling kit." With that, her audio signal whispers into electronic silence.

Rogers swallows in a nervous gulp. "Want me to take care of it, boss?" His expression screams *Please, say no!* but I have to credit him for asking.

Grogan stares at the defiled corpse. For a second, his hardened façade slips and I plainly see that he's conflicted; I'd like to take heart in this, but the mask is back almost immediately. It bothers me that he's so concerned with maintaining appearances—there's nothing wrong with showing you're human once in a while, is there? "Nah, just leave it."

Cutterly stiffens. "We can't just leave him like this, Grog. They're—*eating* him."

Grogan appraises him blankly. "You got a better suggestion?"

"We could use the incinerator," Rogers pipes in.

"Yeah, that's more flattering—torch him like a cube of trash. Nice." Grogan turns away with a dismissive shrug. "He's too big to incinerate anyway. Unless you want to hack him down to size, of course." Before I can even register the terribleness of that thought, Grogan turns back to the group, mouth stretched in an odd, dark smirk. "Even better, maybe we could drag him to the caves, huh?"

Cursing under his breath, Rogers kicks a rock, sending it through the air in a wide arc. The wind catches it just as it meets the ground and propels it back toward us, and then past us, until it's swallowed by the approaching darkness.

"Um, what caves?" I want to know.

Cutterly and Rogers share a scant glance. This isn't lost on Grogan, who snorts dryly without an ounce of amusement. "They're more like skylights than caves," he explains, lips skewed in a mischievous smirk. "Big holes that open straight down into old lava tubes. You get too close to the edge, and the ground'll collapse and take you with it." He pauses, leveling a cold gaze on Cutterly, and then Rogers. "Isn't that right, fellas?"

Cutterly scowls; Rogers turns beet red. *What in the world is this all about?* I wonder.

Grogan turns to me and says: "Hope you don't fancy yourself a spelunker, Wil; as far as hobbies go, caving is a killer around here. Just ask these guys."

Cutterly's eyes darken. The air is suddenly electric with hostility.

"Uh, okay," I mutter.

"Drop it, Grog. We've been over this; it was our decision to make."

"No, Cutterly, it wasn't. Monty made a flippant decision that cost him his life, going into that stupid cave; your little rescue mission was even more irresponsible—it tied up company equipment and endangered personnel. You two nearly shut this entire operation down." He crosses his arms—for effect rather than comfort, I gather from the stiffness of the gesture. "I'm glad you're both still around—don't get me wrong—but we've barely been getting along while you two heal."

Cutterly scoffs and shakes his head with disgust.

"Cutterly, you may never walk the same again—you know that, right? And you, Rogers: how are you supposed to man the rover controls when your hands are too scarred to even feel what you're doing?"

Rogers's face—normally bland, if not placid—contorts, twittering from the exertion of restraining himself. "I'm guessing they'll be fine to ring your little neck, don't you think?"

Grogan shuffles back unconsciously, eyes glazed—cold, yet bewildered—gloved hands forming clumsy fists. "Don't forget who you're talking to," he chides, his voice reedy with breathless uncertainty.

Cutterly takes a broad step toward Grogan, towering over the younger man like a minor giant. "Let's get something straight: we don't work for you, Grogan—we tolerate you. And lately, our patience is running on fumes."

As Grogan opens his mouth to offer a retort, I realize that he's not backing down—his ego has overtaken his better sense—and that the situation is about to irreversibly escalate. A scuffle out here has death written all over it. I've got to do something.

"Everybody just cool down, all right?" I plead. "We need to get inside; it's getting dark." Cutterly and Rogers eye me in cold tandem, but they seem to relax.

This bizarre tantrum explains a lot, I suppose. Then again, it raises even more questions than it answers. More than anything else, it exposes Grogan as opportunistic and downright cannibalistic when crossed. I'm not completely surprised, though I'm greatly disheartened.

"Fine," he growls, and though his voice is dull with the hollow timbre of defeat, there's something hiding within it—something snide and childishly retaliatory. Just before he turns away, I catch a scarce glimpse of his filthy smirk. "The nearest cave is a little over seven miles northeast of here, and Rover 5's half taken apart," he says. "Which one of you wants to dig up Winkley and carry him?"

Grogan waits for one of us to volunteer, his back still to us. The wind whooshes along the ground in a gentle rasp. We're Martian statues with nothing to say.

"That's what I thought."

After only two weeks, the crop field has me completely freaked out. The cuttings germinated overnight, sending forth sprouts that have doubled in size every day since. As of this morning, one plant can no longer be discerned from its neighbor, having forfeited its individual identity for the greater community of a giant purple rug. Frequently, the winds pick up spores and blow them around like bits of quartz in a sandstorm. It isn't hard to distinguish them from the Martian dust, now that we're aware of their presence; they have an effervescent quality that reveals itself as the particles tumble through the air.

We continue to adhere vigilantly to our sterilization protocols, and every cough or harrumph is worthy of a sideways glance. I'm tormented by nightmares of ghoulish vines bursting through my chest, sending my heart into the air like a grotesque cork. It's no way to live. As tired as I generally am, the ball and chain of constant fear leadens my every step.

It's Saturday. Not that weekends bear any significance in the employ of PRMC; basic survival here is a full-time affair, so we're never really off the clock. I really shouldn't complain—what the heck is there to do around here for fun anyway? Free time is pretty useless—but I find myself more and more agitated these days. I'm tempted to sleep through breakfast this morning, because the only thing more valuable to me than food is rest. But, while sleep is hard to come by, it can wait. Breakfast, on the other hand, won't— my coworkers will divvy up my rations without a second thought if I'm more than fifteen minutes late. I should know—it's happened on many occasions.

With the groans and popping joints of a much older man, I dress for another day in paradise.

"How do we know when they're ready to harvest?"

I hear the question even before I set foot into the mess hall. It's a subject I've been meaning to raise myself—I just haven't gotten around to it yet—so I'm glad to hear it spoken aloud. Ignoring my arrival, Fiona looks at Rogers with mild irritation, as if she's been waiting for—perhaps even dreading—this very question. "It's tough to say," she replies. "My guess is we'll know when we know."

"Uh, what does that mean?" I ask, sliding into my chair. It troubles me that our scientific leader can't answer such a basic question with any certainty. My breakfast—faux scrambled eggs, strips of pseudo-bacon, and black coffee—is cold. But at least it's still here.

Not surprisingly, Grogan snaps to Fiona's aid. I find myself rolling my eyes. "There isn't any precedence for this, guys. Nothing like BP7 has ever been engineered before, much less agriculturally harnessed."

Cutterly doesn't buy this, especially coming from Grogan. "It doesn't strike me as very safe to experiment on this large of a scale. Shouldn't we be doing this in the lab where it's easier to control?"

"In a perfect world, absolutely," answers Fiona. "But we have a couple of problems. First: time. We're coming up on our yearly review; if we aren't prepared for show-and-tell, we're looking at another year before we get another chance to present our findings." She pauses to sip her coffee. This is a perfect opportunity for someone to argue, yet no one does. "Locally, we have a much more immediate problem: BP7 seems bound and determined to pollinate. At the moment, I can't simulate that in the lab."

"What are you talking about?" I demand. This differs greatly from her previous explanations. "I thought they were asexual?"

"I thought so, too; by all appearances, the BPs had switched between two asexually reproductive behaviors. But subsequent tests have indicated something else entirely: BP7 has actually adapted to sexually produce."

"Whoa, hold on a second," interjects Cutterly. "I don't mean to sound negative, but with all the guesswork going on, maybe we need to take a step back. Just seems like—"

Grogan holds up a hand, tapering Cutterly off in midsentence. "Fiona assures me this is actually to our advantage," he explains. Despite the hostility between Grogan and the other men, Cutterly and Rogers now seem to hang on his every word. I swear, there must be something in the water here.

I'm not as easily swayed, and it bothers me that the others are. I suspect my incredulity is further bristled by decaffeination—I don't care much for black coffee, and I despise it cold.

"I can't see how," I grumble around a mouthful of rubbery eggs, eyeing Fiona with mounting suspicion. Her cheeks flush, and she nods.

"A lot has changed since we last discussed this, Wilson. When I first became aware of BP7's adaptation—"

Adaptation? Is that a watered-down substitution for mutation?

"—I feared the plants might be more difficult to contain. But since then, I've come to a less worrisome conclusion."

"Based on what evidence?" Rogers wants to know.

"Based on the discovery that the specimens we've planted possess antheridia, but no archegonia."

Blank faces all around.

"They're all males."

Rogers chuckles, but it's full of nerves rather than humor. "You're kidding, right? I mean, what about the spores? Males can't produce spores, can they?"

"What we're seeing blowing around out there isn't spores; it's sperm. BP7 is behaving more like a simple animal than a plant—coral, for example. It's relying on the wind to facilitate fertilization in the same way coral rely on ocean currents to randomly disperse sperm across a reef."

"I don't understand," Cutterly interjects. "What about Winkley? You said he breathed in spores."

"He did. I studied many of them under magnification during the days that followed, and believe me, there's no doubt. This is something different; our crops have definitively traded spores for sperm."

Grogan clears his throat. "Fiona, you didn't alter the genetic profile of the cuttings, did you?"

She shakes her head. "Of course not. It's as if the cuttings retained an imprint of their death, like they knew on a cellular level that their spores had tried and failed."

"That's ridiculous," Grogan mumbles.

Here, here. It would be very easy to get hung up on this explanation—I feel the seams of my gullibility popping against it, in fact—but it hasn't escaped my notice that she's sidestepped Grogan's larger implication—that the reins of this scientific venture have slipped from her fingers. Even simpletons like me can guess our fate if the BPs manage to snatch the upper hand. Still, I'm compelled to throw Miss Lovely a bone. Maybe I've misunderstood her, after all.

"Just to be clear," I say, "what you're telling us is that the BPs were originally engineered to reproduce asexually, but somehow they began producing spores. Then, after we wiped them out, the remaining cuttings somehow learned from their mistakes—seemingly, anyway—and mutated again to produce sperm rather than spores. Am I on track?"

"That may be oversimplifying things a bit, but in a nutshell, yes."

"That's oversimplifying?" Cutterly chuckles. "Jeez, Doc; I'd hate to hear the complicated version." He smiles, stretching cheeks that aren't used to being stretched. He's trying to smooth down ruffled feathers, I know. I appreciate the effort—as does Fiona, I'm sure—but it isn't working. Even Rogers looks like he just swallowed a bug.

Grogan's expression is particularly brooding. "And on top of all that," he injects, "this new strain needs to pollinate to reproduce, and we don't have any females to pollinate?" He laughs. It's a hollow, condescending sound that—despite the frustration I know we're sharing—grates against my nerves. What's with this guy that he's so determined to belittle others? He was on her side not ten seconds ago. "Sounds to me like you've lost control of this, Fiona. At best, we're at an impasse."

Fiona blushes. She wants to retaliate, I can tell. She certainly has the intelligence to match Grogan's wit, yet she opts to keep her cool. Does she have something up her sleeve, I wonder, or is she legitimately ashamed? I feel torn to pick sides; logically, I'm with Grogan—the state of our work couldn't be more precarious—but my heart is rooting for Fiona. She seems to intuit my sympathy and rewards it with a sidelong glance, embellished with a mysterious smirk.

"Not quite," she replies, eyes narrowing in challenge as they return to Grogan. "As luck would have it, we do have a female specimen in our midst."

Blank faces all around for a long second, followed by another.

"The graveyard," Rogers suddenly whispers. His cheeks are pale, eyes sparkling with disquiet.

I look into Fiona's face, waiting—wanting desperately—for her to debunk this obscene suggestion, yet her head nods in assent. This revelation strikes me with such force that I'm jerked to my feet.

"You've got to be kidding!"

I sulk to the window and look outside. I can't see the graveyard plant from this vantage—I'm on the wrong side of the hive—but I can make out its shadow. In the last couple of weeks, the freakish thing has reached fifty feet tall, and half again as wide. By all appearances, it has completely broken free of its genetic lineage—it's a bona fide tree now, with a base nearly two feet across. Something about it frightens me more than anything else here. I can't put my finger on what has my warning bells clanging with such concentrated vigor—this BP is only one compared to an entire field of creepy flora, after all—but I feel that much more at unease now, realizing that something so sinister has become integral to our corporate success.

Actually, in the days that follow, I suspect Rogers and Cutterly may have become even more wary than me—and that's saying something. This isn't a conclusion I've reached on a hunch, either. The evidence is in plain sight, and it's impossible to ignore.

First, neither is willing to approach the graveyard for any reason. Instead, either I or Grogan must check the tree for new buds, which are indicators that pollination has occurred. This doesn't seem like a fair division of labor, but neither does it seem worth making a stink over.

Secondly, I've walked into the utility room on more than one occasion to find one or both of them staring out the window at the massive plant—not as if transfixed, exactly; it's more like they're keeping a watchful eye peeled, waiting fearfully for something to happen.

The thing that has me wholly convinced, though, is their daily visits to the infirmary. While the rest of us are checked out weekly, as has been routine since Winkley left us, Rogers and Cutterly insist on a daily battery of tests. It isn't lost on me that they haven't encouraged me or Grogan to do likewise—they're as thick as thieves, those two—and my gut tells me they know something. They know something that I don't, and I have this nagging sense that if I'm going to live much longer, I've got to find out what it is.

Twenty-Three

Grogan left this morning for one of his ambiguous supply runs. I watched his ship burn through the atmosphere and imagined I was aboard, headed back to Earth. Though I knew quite well that nothing good would come of it, I allowed myself a few minutes to long for home—for the taste of real food, the smell of flowers, the feel of a woman on my arm. Even the all but forgotten vibration of my NanoPrint. The sting of this careless reminiscence has left me emotionally perforated, as if each memory has punctured my heart until it can no longer retain any peace.

The mother plant appears to have reached her full height, finally. It's over a hundred feet tall now. With Grogan gone, Fiona assists me in deburring its trunk of gametophytes, which will be transplanted later to the crop field—as if we need more. Thanks to similar efforts, our garden of once-lonely sires has slowly garnered female companionship, the largest of which is already twenty feet tall. The females are easy to spot: like their mother, their leaves are blood red, void of spore nodes, and a little smaller than those of their male counterparts.

The BPs don't make me as nervous as they once did, yet I'm continually repulsed by the mother plant, knowing that she's grown to such extraordinary size from the nutrient-rich innards of my friend. Winkley's body is gone now, every bit of him absorbed greedily by the plant—flesh, bones, even his clothes.

Filling my bag with tiny gametophytes—doing my best to forgive nature for her ugly ways—I suddenly glimpse something that nearly causes me to stumble over my own feet. Fiona sees it too and, being farther away than me, says, "Is that ...?"

Her thought is left hanging, but I think I know where it was headed. As I blink to reset my vision, however, I realize I have no idea what I'm looking at. From the corner of my eye, I see Fiona drop her bag and bounce toward me. Her smile is manic, strangely inviting. Confused, my pulse quickens, my arms open instinctively to accept her embrace.

I can't believe this is happening!

But she brushes past me as if I'm not even here.

Man, I'm an idiot.

Oblivious, Fiona hastens to examine the true object of her affection, which resembles a mango—or perhaps a small coconut—dangling overhead from a thick branch. It must've grown there overnight—it certainly wasn't there yesterday. It's too high above the ground to reach, so she peers up at it, standing on a swollen root at the base of the tree to get closer.

"It worked!" she gasps. "I can't believe it!"

"What is it?" I inquire, still quietly mortified.

She doesn't answer me. Instead, she bounces back to the b-hive, leaving me alone with the only other woman in my life—who, incidentally, would surely eat me if she could only get her hungry roots into me. I'm surprised by this, and a little hurt—Fiona's normally a stickler for detail, and she's broken one of her own highest commandments by abandoning me. In this way, it's like I never left Earth—who knew the saga of rejection would follow me all the way to freaking Mars?

Several minutes later, she reappears—not with help, or even a sampling kit, mind you—but with a mop handle, of all things. Before I can even guess at her intentions—and without so much as a trite apology for deserting me—Fiona begins swinging ineffectively at the melon with her stick. It's truly comical to watch—if she was one of the guys, I'd happily offer some crude commentary—but my mother raised a gentleman. Well, technically Stewart and Arthur did, but I suppose my mom got the ball rolling.

Nevertheless, I take over and knock the bulb free on my second try. It lands with an audible *thunk,* sending plumes of dust into the air before bouncing to a stop at our cleated feet. Fiona bends to retrieve it, beaming through her faceplate. I can't help but beam, too—I'm feeling unnaturally proud of myself, and who knows: maybe she'll want to reward my considerable contribution.

But alas, I'm forgotten again, almost instantly. Fiona examines the fallen gourd with unbridled curiosity, cooing and grinning down on it like a mother over her newborn. My mouth forms a childish scowl.

"Fiona?" I grumble. She turns to me and, seeing my consternation—along with no small amount of dejection, I'm sure—her smile flickers, exposing—what is that, embarrassment? Guilt? "What's going on?" I demand. "What the heck is that thing?"

"It's a seedpod, Wil."

"A seedpod," I parrot. "Why would a BP produce both gametophytes *and* seeds?"

Fiona giggles and bats her gorgeous eyes. Dang, she's too cute. It's like trying to stay mad at a puppy: my heart bubbles over like a cauldron on a roaring campfire.

"Don't look so grim, Wil—" *Grim? My lust face looks* grim? "—this is what we've all been waiting for."

"I don't understand—we've been waiting for it to change reproductive behaviors ... again?"

She caresses the swollen pod for another moment, gloved fingers bumping over rounded striations on its surface, and then turns to face me squarely. "That's not what this is, Wil. *This,*" she says, drawing attention to the pod by raising it between us, "isn't an unplanned mutation."

I shrug. "Okay, I'll bite. So what makes you so confident?"

"Easy: I designed it this way. Normally, flowering plants provide fruit or nectar as an incentive for insects and animals to participate in their pollination. But for a long time, we've been able to genetically encourage the growth of seedless fruit—useful to us, useless to the plant. Same thing here, only somewhat reversed."

Sigh. "As usual, Doc, you've completely lost me."

"What I mean is, this seedpod serves no reproductive purpose to the plant."

I hope my denseness is at least remotely endearing, because it's about to rear its ugly head again. "So, uh, what exactly is the point of it, then?"

"Don't you see, Wil?" *Honestly, do you really have to ask, my dear?* "This is what we've been working for since day one—this is literally the fruit of our labor."

Inside the pod, small capsules resembling the seeds of strawberries are suspended in a dense, gelatinous pulp. While they look convincingly like seeds to my unscientific eye, they don't quite fit the formal definition—according to Fiona, anyway—since they're incapable of germination. Nevertheless, for lack of a better word, I can't help but think of them as seeds.

Remarkably, each one concentrates BP7's enhanced medicinal properties into a very tiny—and naturally stable—package. The industrial payoff is huge: these seedlike capsules take up very little space, they're relatively easy to harvest, and they're naturally resilient against even the most extreme elements. And, of course, the plants themselves need not be hacked to pieces in the process of reaping, so the production cycle can be repeated outside of seasonal confines.

Fiona is on cloud nine. Her smile hasn't lost its edge for a single moment since that seedpod first caught her eye. I'm proud of her, knowing just how much hard work and dedication she's invested in the BPs. Still, I feel sorry that she's more or less alone here, with none of her colleagues or family to share in her hard-won victory.

Now that the hard part is behind her, I hope Fiona can finally cast off her lab coat and relax a little. She's certainly earned a little R&R. Who knows, maybe she'll finally notice that Wilson Abby isn't just an undereducated employee, but a man who would bend over backwards to do well by her. I warm at the thought, and it's a nice feeling that I'd love to hang onto. But then Rogers opens his big mouth during dinner and upends my tottering sense of emotional balance.

"Gonna miss that lady," he garbles around a mouthful of gruelish custard.

My appetite falls away like a crumbling glacier into my stomach. "What do you mean?" I squeak.

Rogers frowns, one eyebrow pushing his forehead into a series of porous foothills. "Normal people don't stick around desert scrapholes any longer than they have to, Wilson. You think a woman like Fiona doesn't have other options in life?"

"I guess so," I admit. "I never really knew what to think."

"Well, once the seedpods start growing en masse, her work here is pretty much done. She'll still need to publish her research, I guess, but she can handle that from home. I figure she'll be outta here on the next supply run."

If I was alone right now, I'd throw a proper fit. Hearing Rogers's terrible prediction, realizing that the only thing worth waking up for on this forsaken rock will soon be gone, I want nothing more than to wallow in self-pity. But I'm not alone, and my pride is sufficient to keep tears at bay—for a while, anyway.

"What about the rest of us?"

With a grunt, Rogers drops his fork to his plate. "We're here for the grunt work; doesn't look like that's going away. The company'll probably start retooling the lab for production, and some unlucky, lesser-credentialed earthlings'll end up out here to manage things. As for you and me? We're fixtures here, I'm afraid." He opens his mouth to take another bite, but hesitates, adding: "Well ..."

"Well, what?"

"I mean, assuming we manage to stay alive."

I make two discoveries upon Grogan's return. First, he is no happier than I am regarding Fiona. His face is a slab of granite, and that's precisely how I know. I've been around him long enough to recognize that he's a surly little baby about the little things. The big things? He bottles them up to drink alone.

My impression upon arriving here that Grogan and Fiona have some sort of history between them has only grown more robust over time. The weird charge between them is sparking brighter now than ever before, though I'm no closer to understanding its origin.

My second discovery is a little harder to interpret, though it's easy enough to describe. Even before Grogan's ship landed—just as it began rasping against the atmosphere, forming a burning speck against the sky—I felt something I haven't felt in a very long time.

My NanoPrint came to life.

I'm not really sure what that means; it feels much like it did when I first left home, oscillating as it sends out connection requests to the nexus. There is a subtle difference, though. This time, it feels as though it has somehow connected to something.

Only I'm pretty sure it's not the nexus.

The mother plant—the Queen, as I've begun to think of her—is putting out seedpods like crazy now. We've given up transplanting her budding offspring to the garden; Fiona is confident that we already have enough specimens to sustain long-term production. Unfortunately, the gametophytes continue to pop up daily—not only on the Queen, but on her daughters as well—and must be meticulously collected and later destroyed, lest they be allowed to grow unchecked.

In the garden, The Princess—the largest of the Queen's female brood—has peaked out at just under fifty feet. She hasn't yet produced any seedpods, but we have no reason to think she won't. If Fiona's assessment is to be believed—and I have to admit that she isn't often wrong these days—it makes little difference. The Queen is producing far more seedpods than we need for the moment. It's already a formidable chore to keep track of them, so I'm in no rush for the other females to mature.

In addition to the Princess, there are four more females over ten feet tall now. Added to the hundred-or-so males in the garden, we've got a regular orchard going here.

A macabre alien orchard of flesh-eating produce. Good times.

I've noticed that every time I walk by Grogan's room, my NanoPrint whizzes into high gear for a few seconds. Wonder what that's all about?

Twenty-Four

It's been a month since the Queen gave up her first fruit. Though I've done all I can to slow time, it has bested my feeble efforts. Today is the big day: Fiona is leaving us. To say that I'm a little bummed is understating things a fair amount, and I see my sentiment mirrored all over the hive:

Rogers keeps clearing his throat. Cutterly looks as if his dog's about to be put down; I've seen him grimacing and shaking his head in slow sweeps when he thinks no one is looking. I'm not doing so hot myself, but I'm trying hard to put on a stoic face. Grogan's void of emotion again, yet somehow he looks the saddest of all. Unlike the rest of us, however, he gets a few more days with her en route to Earth.

Lucky pile of circuit scrap.

When the moment of her departure arrives, Fiona gives us each a hug. Her smile is bittersweet, eyes bright and hopeful, yet glassy with the regret of opportunity cost. When it's my turn, I'm given a priceless peck on my cheek, too. Suited up, we escort Fiona to the ship and settle into a stiff line to witness her exodus from Mars. I stand with Rogers and Cutterly just outside the airlock and watch as the ship departs, taking with it my only chance to ever procreate—unless the Queen and I both lower our standards. My tears flow, and I don't care who sees them now.

When a Gaussian tendril is all that remains to commemorate the lovely Fiona, we all head into the airlock and begin sterilizing our suits.

I walked past Grogan's room this afternoon, and my implant went berserk again. Since that moment, I've been contemplating something I would never have dreamed of. Once Rogers and Cutterly are asleep, I plan to reconnoiter Grogan's dorm.

I have to admit that I've been a basket case since I began to entertain the thought. It's so contrary to my nature that my body seems determined to shake some sense into me. Case in point: when dinner comes along, my hands are so jittery that I knock my plate off the table. Given the scarcity of food, this is an unforgivable sin—Grogan would undoubtedly blow a gasket, if he was here. Rogers offers me some of his—an unexpected kindness that catches me completely off guard—until Cutterly points out that, with Fiona gone, we have an extra ration. It's true, I realize. Not that we're free to go off the deep end by any means, but her cabinet is half-stocked with rations. I pick through them and settle on some chicken piccata. The capers are bland, the chicken like wet leather—but at least I'm not eating off the floor. I wonder if I'm imagining the taste, or if I should expect everything else about my life to lose its redeeming qualities as well in the drab shadow of Fiona's absence.

There's not much on the agenda today; operations are more or less on hold until Grogan returns with instructions from PRMC. In the meantime, other than the usual morning chores, I'm left with nothing to do but hang out with Cutterly and Rogers in the commons. They've been so standoffish since my arrival that I've always assumed they were jerks—maybe they are; it's still a little early to say—yet whatever the case, the guys are downright chatty today.

My mind is clattering at full capacity, struggling to map out the particulars of tonight's pilferage, but I feel that I've stumbled upon an opportunity—one that I'd be remiss to pass up. If I play my cards well, these guys might just shed light on something that has bugged me for too long. I decide to try my luck.

"So, Cutterly, what's up with you and Grogan?"

Cutterly looks at me sharply and sighs mightily through his nose, jowl lines deepening. "I'm not sure what you mean."

"I mean, you two seem like you don't like each other much, that's all."

Rogers guffaws. "Ha! That's like saying you might have a little crush on Fiona."

Wow. Have I been that obvious?

Ignoring my crimson-cheeked mortification, Cutterly tosses his head forward and growls. "Fine. We don't like each other. You saying you're sweet on him?"

I bat my eyes and cross my legs effeminately. "Heck yeah, have you seen him in his tighty-whities? Smokin'."

Rogers rolls into a ball with laughter; even Cutterly cracks a smile—adding to a sparse handful that has ever touched his weathered face in my presence—but it's short-lived, waning into the usual frown almost instantly.

"Listen, kid," he says, "seriously, you need to watch him."

The air seems to thicken a little—not to the point of suffocation, really, but just enough that I become conscious of the rise and fall of my chest, as if it might cease altogether if I divide my attention. My smile fades into nothing; even Rogers quiets down, clearing his throat to soften the jagged edge of awkward silence.

"Uh, why?" I want to know.

"Let's just say Grogan can be ... dangerous."

"Dangerous? What does that mean?"

Cutterly shakes his head; he's said all he's gonna say.

"C'mon, guys," I groan. "You can't throw out an accusation like that and expect me to know what to do with it. What do you mean by *dangerous*? Like, irresponsible, or throw-you-under-the-bus dangerous?"

Cutterly exchanges a glance with his pal.

Rogers chews his lip, eyebrows scrunched thoughtfully. "Might as well, Cutt," he mutters with a halfhearted shrug. "The cat's half out of the bag, anyway."

With a somber nod, Cutterly coughs and then addresses my question with one of his own. "Who do you think Winkley is buried next to?"

"I don't know," I confess. "I'm guessing not Montague, though, right? Grogan said there wasn't anything left to bury."

"Nope, not Montague."

"Then who?"

Setting his fork down, Cutterly leans forward, lowering his voice to a conspiratorial whisper. "Winkley wasn't our first BP victim," he says, smiling as my eyes bug. "Didn't know that, did you?"

I shake my head no, too stunned to speak.

He nods. "Guy named Emmers. Died in his sleep."

"What makes you think it was the BPs?"

"Well, for one, he wasn't even forty years old. And he was in better shape than any of us."

My eyes narrow. "You sure it wasn't a freak heart attack or some—"

"We did an autopsy," Rogers pipes in.

"What? You mean you, like, cut him open?"

Rogers nods somberly. "Well," he says in corrective drawl, motioning to Cutterly with his chin, "not *us*—Fiona did."

God help me, I can't help the image that fills my head: Fiona wielding a bloody scalpel, digging around in a heap of glistening organs. I shudder at the thought, feeling as though my skin is itching to crawl away from me. It dawns on me at once that these two are messing with me, that this is just a little belated hazing. *Oh, they're good. They almost had me.*

"Really," I say with a wry, knowing smile. "And what, pray tell, did she find?"

"Poison in his blood, bits of chewed up BP2 in his stomach. Mixed in with his salad greens."

My smile twitches. "He *ate* it?"

"Yup."

If this is a joke, it isn't very funny; apparently Mars warps one's sense of humor over time. "And you think it was Grogan?"

Cutterly shakes his head and reclines in his chair, folding beefy arms across a barreled chest. "I don't *think*, man—I *know*."

"Okay, so how do you *know*?"

Cutterly's face darkens; I get the feeling this guy isn't used to others questioning his judgment. "What," he snarls, "you saying he did it to himself?"

Realizing that I've inadvertently offended the man—a man who could pulverize me into a pile of Martian dust with very little effort—the fragile remnants of my smile flee. "Whoa," I say, putting my hands up in the universal signal for conversational surrender. "I'm not saying that, I'm just trying to understand why Grogan would do something so crazy, that's all."

Cutterly grunts, then picks up his fork again. For now, I'm forgiven—or on probation—but my suspicion that this is a joke is fading fast. "Emmers didn't like Grogan at all," explains Cutterly. "He thought there was a conflict of interests with Grogan working here—you know, because of Fiona—so he filed a complaint with headquarters." He puts away half an entrée in a single bite and begins chewing fiercely.

I can't help but smile; Cutterly's just confirmed my longtime suspicion that Grogan and Fiona were once an item. On the other hand, this whole Grogan thing isn't quite adding up, which waters down my sense of satisfaction. "Seems like kind of a weak motive, don't you think?"

Cutterly swallows his cud and snatches up a napkin, wiping his mouth with a muffled chuckle. "You kidding? Think about it: this place is his whole life, man—it's *all* our lives; we don't just work here—this is it for us. I can't speak for you, but the rest of us don't have much choice about being here. Grogan does. For whatever reason, he's sacrificed a lot to be here. And there's no way he'd let anything jeopardize his position."

"Are you saying that by getting rid of Emmers, Grogan's problems with headquarters went away?"

Rogers chuckles. "He's still here, isn't he?"

I shrug noncommittally. "I guess so."

Cutterly sighs. "You think anyone on Earth gave Emmers's complaint a second thought after he killed himself?"

"Killed himself? I thought you said—"

My objection is cut off by a dismissive wave of Cutterly's huge hands. "I'm just telling you how Grogan spun it—convinced pretty much everyone, too. Just not us."

"Wow." I honestly don't know what else to say.

Rogers clears his throat and leans forward. "Listen, Wilson, just don't let your guard down around the guy if you can help it. That's all we're saying. We don't need another grave out there."

A thought occurs to me. "Wait a second—you don't think he had anything to do with Winkley, do you?"

Cutterly glances at Rogers and they both shrug. "No telling," Rogers replies. "Personally, I figure I'm better off assuming the worst with him."

Man, these cranks are wound tight; can anyone say paranoid?

We stay up much later than usual, sipping hot tea—warm whiskey, in the case of Rogers—until I'm half-convinced these guys are on to my plan and have decided to keep me well within their line of sight. But then, at nearly one in the morning, Rogers passes out on the table. Cutterly is annoyed by this, because the head of his buddy plopped to the table precisely as he was delivering the punch line of a ridiculously long and circuitous joke. I suppose I may never know what happened to that robotic fish and his left-handed pharmacist.

Declining my help, Cutterly drags the limp, snoring bag of drunken flesh that is Rogers from the commons to the dorms. Heart racing, I retire to my own room, leaving the door slightly ajar. My breaths ebb and flow in ragged succession. I hear Cutterly shut Rogers's door and then relocate to his own room. Through the crack of my own door, I can just discern a slice of lamplight against the hallway wall—Cutterly's light. Ten minutes later, when his light finally extinguishes, my breathing finally returns to normal.

I'm as ready as I'm gonna get.

Creeping from my room, I stand in the empty corridor for a long moment, listening for any excuse to abort my mission. Nothing but the tranquil hum of forced air and a faint whisper of night wind outside. On tiptoes, I pad down the hall toward Grogan's room. The darkness is like pitch, so thick and impenetrable that I'm forced to navigate by touch; fortunately, I have a pretty good memory for the lay of the land in here. There's not much at this end of the hall: a few dorms—one Grogan's, one formerly Fiona's, the last used for storage—and a common restroom that, until now, was our unofficial women's room. My NanoPrint begins to hum, and I know I'm close. Seconds later, as my fingers graze the latch to Grogan's door, I suddenly wonder if I've gone crazy.

What am I doing here? I'm no prowler, yet here I am sneaking around like one, preparing to break into my boss's dorm. And for what—idle curiosity? What would Stew think of me now?

I'm almost hoping the door will be locked—that's perhaps the only scenario in which I'll walk away with both my dignity and a clean criminal history—but alas, it opens on well-oiled hinges, beckoning me inside. I hurriedly oblige before I can change my mind, shutting the door behind me as noiselessly as I can manage. I flick on the light and look around. The space is much larger than I imagined—easily twice the size of my own dorm. The room is halved by a muted seam along all four planes, perhaps the ghostly footprint of a removed wall. On one side of the line is a tidy bed, a desk with a blank surface, and a dresser; it's a depressing, militaryish space, devoid of any personal identity whatsoever. In its own way, the opposing side of the room is just as bizarre: it has been modified to resemble a control station of sorts, sporting monitors, gauges, meters, toggle switches, buttons—you name it. I'm betting Grogan can control every inch of the b-hive in some capacity from here.

I'm not sure what to do now; my implant is busily humming away—kind of annoying really, now that I've grown unaccustomed to the thing—yet I'm not at all sure how to identify what's causing the activity. I wander toward the wall of electronics, hesitating with it just out of reach; I'm not sure why, but something inhibits me from approaching any closer, as if even the slightest movement of air against the circuitry will set off an alarm. This is probably an irrational fear, but it might also be the sound warning of my trusty gut—under the circumstances, it's difficult to distinguish between the two.

Better to err on the side of caution.

Stepping away from Grogan's altar of gadgetry, I steer toward his dresser. Nearing the plain chest of drawers, my implant seems to go crazy, and the feel of it—a frenzied wiggle, so tantrum-like that it could almost be a living thing—sends my blood into an excited boil.

There's something here, no doubt about that.

I find it in his sock drawer—a little plastic container that hinges open like a miniature suitcase. Inside are two identical, rice-sized bits of loose metal. I've never actually seen one before, yet I innately know what I'm looking at. These are NanoPrints—though

I have no idea who they belong to, much less what they're doing here. I pick one up delicately, bringing it closer to my eye, like a jeweler examining a gemstone through a loupe. It's too small to discern much detail, but I can just make out the tiny trademark fingerprint stenciled on one side. Between my fingers, the implant suddenly begins to vibrate in short pulses, and my own responds in similar pulses as they shake hands.

The pulses graduate until my NanoPrint is virtually dancing under my skin, hiccupping like an old combustion engine with a maladjusted carburetor. I can feel it accepting an xchange profile just as it sends out update requests to the nexus, choking on a bottleneck of unheeded threads. My daily schedule loads and attempts to fetch the availability of my favorite restaurants and retailers, and that chokes, too. Even as I'm overwhelmed by the piling of failed functionality, I sense something flicker in the background: a file has just downloaded to my MentalNotes. It's not large, and it's definitely not one of mine. Something has copied to my implant almost faster than I could detect.

Unrelated to the NanoPrints, a feeling of unrest begins to settle upon me, bristling the hairs in my pores as if I'm being watched. Nervously, I check the door. I quietly rejoice that it's safely closed, yet I feel no less probed by invisible eyes.

Gaze darting about the room, it suddenly occurs to me that I've been terribly naive to believe I could invade Grogan's privacy without his knowledge; not only is he an engineer, he's an adamantly secretive person. On Earth, people like him monitor every inch of their living and working spaces, especially in their absence. Why should Grogan behave any differently here? I can easily imagine that my digital likeness has been recorded to a hard drive somewhere, waiting patiently to betray my crooked ways.

Man, I'm a crank idiot.

Afraid now, I drop the NanoPrints back into their box and return it to the drawer where I found it. I can't wait to investigate the file in my MentalNotes, but I don't dare linger here any longer.

It's all I can do to keep from sprinting for my room. But I've got to leave this place with the same cunning—or better—with which I entered it. There's still a chance I might get away with this—not that I've ever been lucky—and the last thing I want is to squander that chance out of carelessness.

As I tiptoe down the hall—my fizzing stomach lurching at my esophagus—something I should have predicted happens: my NanoPrint abruptly goes still again. Repeated efforts to access it fail until the scope of my predicament gradually sinks in: if I'm going to access that file, I'll have to do it from Grogan's room—for reasons that I can't fathom in the heat of the moment, my implant doesn't seem to function away from it.

Though my flesh cries out for permission, I'm given no chance to panic because just then, a voice accosts me from the inky corridor, very nearly squeezing the pee from my bladder like a rolling pin against a jelly doughnut.

"What in deep space are you doing, Wilson?"

I stiffen with such a start that blurry spots glide into view. *Pardon me while I have a heart attack.*

"I asked you a question," the voice hisses. It's Cutterly, I realize.

"Give me a second," I gasp, doubling over to catch my breath. True, I'm stalling for time, but I'm also genuinely struggling to keep from fainting. "Holy pile of circuit scrap, you nearly scared me to death," I confide in a wheezy slur. "I was just looking for something to read."

"In Grogan's room?" I can't see much of Cutterly—just an ambiguous outline against the darkness—yet I can physically feel his presence nearby. I'm not sure why, but it comforts me as much as it frightens me. With that said, my heart is racing.

"Well, yeah," I say, noting that apprehension has boosted my voice half an octave. "Where else am I gonna find a book?"

Cutterly is quiet; the darkness veils his expression, but I sense that he's mulling over my explanation. And that he's found a hole in it. "So what'd you get?"

"What do you mean?" I quip innocently.

"You said you were looking for a book in there; so what book did you get?"

"Oh, yeah—that. No luck. Grogan must've taken them along for him and Fiona to read." That much is true, anyway; I didn't see any books out in the open. Of course, now that I'm on the defensive, even the truth sounds shady.

Cutterly sighs, and though a sigh can't always be translated into words, this one manages to say a lot. Have I mentioned that I'm a terrible liar? It's been so long since I bothered, I suppose I forgot until I opened my mouth to try. "Listen, Wil," Cutterly whispers. "I don't know what you're up to, but I get the feeling you're playing with fire."

"I'm not up to anything, Cutt."

"C'mon, crank. It's almost two in the morning—in my experience, only prostitutes and cat burglars are running around this late."

I realize the opportunity is untimely, but I find it impossible to pass up this invitation to poke a jab—I mean, silver platter, and everything. "Got a lot of experience with prostitutes in the wee hours, do you?" An amused snort escapes me, but that's about it. Would've been more satisfying with a better audience, I guess.

Cutterly doesn't laugh—shocking, I know. His breathing deepens, though, a powerful, cavernous sound when juxtaposed against my own choppy respiration. For a long moment, neither of us speaks and I begin to wonder if he's fallen asleep.

"He'll know you were in there," he finally says. "You realize that, don't you?"

My skin prickles. I had nearly convinced myself that I was being paranoid. The back of my tongue turns into cotton, and the compulsion to run becomes almost unbearable. But where would I go?

Afraid my voice will betray me, I don't reply; instead, I nod my acknowledgement, realizing too late that he can't see me.

Cutterly chuckles—maybe he can see me after all; that, or he's simply interpreted the truth from my silence. "When I said to watch out for Grogan, I didn't mean to do it from his room."

This bit of dry witticism strikes me as mildly funny—and that's being generous—yet before I even realize what's happening, a raging flood of nervous laughter explodes from me, resounding through the hallway in a single, crashing tidal wave. I can't help it; since this afternoon, the tension has slowly built up in me until it simply had to break free. Better laughter than tears, I suppose—or worse: vomiting, or even explosive diarrhea. Anyway, drunk or not, Rogers couldn't sleep through that.

When my fit has subsided, Cutterly clears his throat uncomfortably; fumbling in the darkness, he lays a calloused hand on my shoulder. "Go to bed, Wilson," he says. "Too late to do anything else." Inexplicably, the man's voice is more gentle and fatherly than any I've heard in a long time. Unexpectedly, tears gather in my eyes, mercifully cloaked in deep shadow.

For no reason, I'm reminded of the one fight I ever picked in my entire life. I was twelve. In the throes of some preadolescent identity crisis, I guess I thought I'd give bullying a try. Uncle Stewart came to my rescue just as our inhumanly scrappy, eleven-year-old next-door neighbor was cocking back an oversized golf club to literally bash my head in.

I vaguely remember Stew carrying me home, then, cradling me in his arms like a baby. I was beaten to a bloody pulp; Uncle Stew cleaned me up and then spanked me with his belt until I swore to never provoke violence again. I'm not sure which of us cried harder that day.

A year later, incidentally, that same kid lit a neighborhood dog on fire before disappearing into some psychiatric care facility—

I'm pretty sure his helix was missing a few hundred spokes. Even now, I shudder to think what that freak would have done to me, if not for Stewart.

Jeez, I'm a wreck tonight.

I hear Cutterly shuffle toward his room, and as I follow through the darkness, exhaustion abruptly hits me like a brick wall—and I mean with a vengeance. My NanoPrint'll have to wait until tomorrow.

I'll be lucky if I make it to bed before I crash.

Twenty-Five

It's after four. I don't even remember my head hitting the pillow earlier, only awakening later in a confused panic—and since then, I'm not sure that I've actually slept for more than a few minutes at a time. Despite the dope of fatigue, my consciousness porpoises in and out of slumber, broken up by short spells of lights-on disorientation. I can feel my brain cranking away at the gears even as I try to shut the machine down.

I suspect I won't get another wink of sleep until I get a look at that file—and frankly, trying to rest is wearing me out even more than staying awake—so I sit up in bed. I've had a minor epiphany, by the way: I don't need Grogan's room—there's nothing special about it, except that it's much more spacious than mine—what I need are those loose NanoPrints.

Wearing only my boxers, I once again traverse the darkened hall to Grogan's room. As before, my NanoPrint hums to life, which reaffirms that I'm not endangering myself for no good reason, and thereby emboldens me. Leaving the door wide open and the light off, I creep to the dresser and slide the sock drawer open.

Snatching the plastic container within, I shut the drawer and return to the hall. Seconds later, I'm back in my room, simultaneously elated and achingly tired. Just as I hoped, my implant remains active. Grinning at my success, I deposit my plunder on a nearby desk and settle back into the warmth of my bed.

It takes some effort to interact with my implant—it's fighting like crazy to run routines that require a connection to the nexus, and as a result, very little RAM is available for my discretionary use. Still, a little perseverance eventually pays off.

I can't help but laugh at my last MentalNote, logged forever ago. "Whatever you do," it warns, "don't eat the sushi at Jin-Jing's. Ever again."

Fuzzy with sleepiness, or perhaps the hypnotic allure of nostalgia, I scroll past my remaining notes and browse my implant's file directory, where the file in question is likely hidden among thousands of audio, video, and document shortcuts. I sort them by modified date, sending the newer files to the top. First in line is a file whose date stamp completely baffles me.

My God, have I really been here that long?

I don't recognize the file extension, but thankfully, my NanoPrint does; almost instantly, my internal audio/video routines mount the file and begin transcoding. Closing my eyes, I hiccup with surprise—Arthur's face appears on my retinas, his voice in my ears as though he's sitting beside me. For a moment, I'm confused—outside of text mode, MentalNotes records the comprehensive experiences of one's sensory organs, so I expect to see what Arthur saw when he made this note, rather than the man himself—but then I understand.

Art's looking in a mirror.

"If you're watching this, Wilson, things have probably gone badly for me. I've put a program on my NanoPrint—yes, I may be a dinosaur, but I can still throw a program together with proper motivation." He smiles, knowing I'd poke fun at this paltry attempt at humor if I was there. My eyes are welling with tears, but through the magic of my NanoPrint, the video feed maintains crystal clarity.

"Anyway, should anything happen to me, my implant is programmed to automatically seek out yours and launch a file transfer; I can't risk it within the nexus because it isn't safe, so the only way it's gonna work is if you get near enough for a handshake. I installed an old http server on it, so it should stream the files without interference from the nexus. The files should self-decrypt on your implant."

Files? Huh, I only saw one. Consulting my NanoPrint's file directory, I discover that there are, in fact, hundreds more files with today's time stamp; I guess I grabbed the first one that caught my interest and never looked back.

Arthur pauses and takes a deep breath, peeking over his shoulder to make sure he's still alone. The diluted odors of urine and tile cleaner fill my nose, and I see stalls behind him. Is he in a public restroom?

"Gotta apologize for the venue; privacy is a rarified commodity in this building. Anyway, whew! Kind of a bleak, longwinded preamble, huh?"

He peeks over his shoulder again and back again. This is a nervous Arthur I've never seen before.

"So here's what's happening: IDS has a regular soup kitchen going; more than a decade ago, the same people we rely on to protect the nexus got their claws in us, and they've been squeezing us for ransom ever since. And unfortunately, it gets worse. Lately, I've had some very heavy people leaning on me—you remember Premiere Global, right? Bunch of sweethearts, let me tell you. Anyway, they want me to slip something past nexus security, and the word *no* doesn't appear in their vocabulary."

Arthur's cheeks burn red, as do mine; he's given in to their demands already, I know, and I can see that he's ashamed. Lord, this man gave up his most prized possession to protect me—his integrity; it stings to see how deeply that sacrifice pierced him in life, because even on my best day, I'll never deserve it. I feel a sob collecting in the back of my throat, curling into a little ball that refuses to be swallowed.

"I don't have time to explain anything in detail," he apologizes, "but what I can tell you is that things heated up about a week ago. One of these lovely parasites—our good and faithful vice president, if you can believe it—just up and doubled her monthly demand. Out of nowhere, I mean—I guess campaign season is upon us again. Next thing I know, others have found out and decided to follow her lead.

"So, now we're stuck, Wil; IDS can't maintain those kinds of payouts and still turn a profit, but without the blessing of these bloodsuckers, we're dead in the water. Once Premiere figures this out, I have a feeling they're gonna try to take me out; I figure I'm more of a liability than an asset to them, now."

Arthur sighs, stress glistening on his forehead like drops of morning dew. "There's something else, too: I've been doing some research—the kind that might well get me into trouble, I'm afraid—and I stumbled across something huge. I found a link between Vice President Carlisle and an exceptionally unsavory character." Arthur swallows and blurts a jittery guffaw. "Crank, I never saw this one coming: her stepbrother? His name is *Palmer Gunn*—I'm guessing you already know who he is, so I won't belabor his significance. Naturally, Carlisle has gone to extraordinary lengths to cover this up. Imagine what that kind of information could do to her if it was made public! Anyway, the evidence is still out there in the nexus—for those of us who know how to be thorough, I mean. It's all in the files, Wil.

"So, one of two things needs to happen, now: either we fold up tent, or we do the one thing that might still save this company: we have to—*I* have to—blow the whistle."

He tosses his head back and looks at the ceiling for a moment and says, "Crank, I can't believe I'm doing this." Running tremulous fingers through a shag of silver hair, Art smiles sagely. It's a sad, defeated smile that unleashes the sob within me in a sharp gust. *How I miss that man!*

"Okay, so tomorrow morning, I'm going to release a set of data packets on the nexus. They'll be anonymous, but that won't fool anyone for long. If all goes as planned, they'll flood the media torrents before anyone can interfere—and everyone in the Unified World will know exactly what these people have been up to. I wish I could be sure that IDS will survive this—even if every detail falls into place flawlessly, there's no guarantee we won't go under while the government tries to piece the evidence together. But I've gotta do something, you know?"

Clearing his throat, Arthur grimaces slightly. He grunts as if recovering from a kick to the diodes, then looks down. His left hand—no, I guess it's actually his right—seeks out his other arm and begins kneading at its bicep, perhaps rubbing out a sore spot.

"Okay, so there it is," he says with a weary grimace. "If you're watching this, it's likely that I didn't succeed. But *you* still can, and here's how: if my files have all made it across, you'll find an executable named *pedestal*. Execute it from your implant, and the program will do the rest—it'll scourge the nexus like wildfire."

At once, his face softens, abruptly drained of the adrenaline which has been driving his monologue thus far. He looks so alone, so vulnerable. My heart breaks to see him like this; though he was alive and kicking, I know his mental state was eclipsed by the deterioration at work in his body. Man, I'm not sure how much more of this I can take.

"I know this is a lot to ask of you, Wil. Maybe it's too much— I guess that's for you to decide. If you don't want to be a part of this, no one's gonna blame you—least of all *me*. And if that's your prerogative, the best thing you can do is delete these files. Every last one, Wil—no souvenirs."

He looks away from his reflection now, eyes settling on his wringing hands.

"I know you must feel betrayed that I've kept this from you for all these years, and I'm truly sorry. It hasn't been an easy secret to keep, believe me. There's no one I trust more than you—"

Without warning, Arthur spins to look at the bank of stalls, gaze snapping to and fro. "Who's there?" he barks, breathing heavily again. His behavior seems manic to me, verging on explosive; I'm flushed with unbearable guilt that he's become so rattled, and that I never knew. "I said who's there!" he shouts.

Suddenly, the entrance door creaks open off to his side; with blurring speed, Art swivels his head toward it. "Well, well," an obnoxious voice intones, "I thought I smelled an old fart."

My mouth drops open. Through Arthur's eyes, I'm watching myself—albeit a younger, healthier, and better-dressed version— strutting into the bathroom like a miswired fool. "Guess who just got IntelliQ approved for portal testing?" I spout through a smirk. Arthur's gaze—and therefore my field of view—snaps back to the stalls, where a door is creeping open.

"C'mon, Art. Don't hate me because I'm efficient," my digital self says. "And beautiful." But Arthur's glued to that stall door, huffing like he's been running sprints. He takes a step toward the open stall, and when he peeks in, I nearly shout in dismay from my bed.

I recognize the neatly plucked eyebrows first, then the fat cheeks.

"So we going, or what?" I say—the recorded me, not *me*— "Gizi's or bust, Art."

"Sure," Arthur replies, eyes still locked on Keith; my ex-boss lingers in the protective seclusion of his stall, wearing a lipsticked Mona Lisa smile. One look into his reptilian eyes reveals that he knew exactly what was coming—that Arthur would depart the equation soon enough; I feel like I might vomit. "Let's get going, birthday boy," Art says, snatching an absorbent towel from a dispenser by the sink. As he wipes the sweat from his face, the recording ends, disengaging my senses to the unlit throw of my dorm.

It was a long time ago, but I remember that day well. We had a nice lunch at Gizi's—I had manicotti, Arthur: fettuccini alfredo; I recall that Arthur even ordered me a little cupcake with a candle in it and conned our waitress into singing Happy Birthday. Back at the office, we finished out the work day as usual, with me none the wiser to his demise. Later that evening, Art bowed out early from an impromptu poker game at my apartment because he wasn't feeling well.

The next day he was dead.

I'm crying profusely now, hot tears cutting rivulets down gaunt cheeks. I've always disliked Keith, but it seems I was too morbidly fascinated with his eccentricities to discern the larger truth—that he truly was a malevolent fiend, with no moral compass and no respect for human life. If I had the means, I'd risk life and limb hitching back to Earth just for the pleasure of kicking the snot out of that androgynous pile of rotten circuit scrap. He once warned that I'd regret calling him out, that I'd wish I could take it all back.

He was wrong.

My only regret is that I let my social sensibilities keep me from doing more than smarting off to her—I mean him. It.

Breakfast is a tram wreck: Rogers is teetering on the verge of vomiting, and keeping from falling asleep in my eggs is quite a feat. Cutterly cackles as he chews, grinning broadly at the misery of his pathetic underlings; *You've brought this on yourselves*, his smile seems to chide. I'm relieved that he seems to have forgotten our hallway run-in last night, yet I haven't stopped thinking about what lies in store for me once Grogan returns.

After breakfast, Rogers unpacks his proverbial luggage in the kitchen sink; he seems to feel better afterward, except that—big surprise—now he's starved. Cutterly has little sympathy, though; the breakfast ship has sailed, so Rogers'll just have to wait until lunch.

There's a lot of work to do this morning—operations may be officially on hold, but the Queen hasn't slowed down production for our sake. We pass the morning down the usual checklist of pod-picking and garden cleanup, bickering all the while. In the short time since Fiona left us we've already slipped into gross inefficiency. I guess we took her direction for granted—

Pick that one right there, please.

Leave that one until tomorrow; it's not fully developed yet.

—and without it, we find ourselves taking liberties that I suspect she would never have tolerated.

No one's interested in killing himself over the seedpods, yet they've been growing higher and higher up the tree with the passage of time, as if the Queen derives some pleasure from making life more hazardous for us. Incidentally, if you've never attempted to climb a tree in an atmospheric suit, let me assure you that it's much more challenging than you might imagine. Nevertheless, we gather what we can; maybe we pluck some that aren't quite ripe, and maybe we leave behind a few that are.

I guess we just don't care.

In our defense, it's not like our jobs come with any built-in gratification. Unlike Fiona, spending our waking hours in the company of killer hybrids doesn't fulfill a lifelong dream; nor does a single one of us care about the advancement of science, particularly where these vegetative freaks are concerned. Save for survival, we have no personal stake in our activities here.

Accordingly, we make do with the bare minimum of effort, carrying out our meaningless tasks with the zeal of robots. Lazy, sloppy, grudging robots. Okay, now that I've said it aloud, I realize we sound more like grumbling kids at self-esteem camp, the ones who only show up at all for the free food. Blessedly, I'm too tired to feel ashamed.

The next several days flip by like carbon copies. We've become a quiet bunch, lost in our respective thoughts regarding the barrenness of our future. I can't speak for the other guys, but I'm feeling very aware that Fiona was the celestial body whose gravity kept us all in the same orbit; without her around, we've drifted into disconnected trajectories, and who knows if we'll ever cross paths again.

Each of us mourns Fiona's absence in his own way—some more intensely than others—and I wonder if our indifference to busywork isn't fallout from her leaving. I'm pretty sure that's the case with me. If Cutterly and Rogers weren't here to ogle me along, I'd probably sulk in bed until my limbs shriveled up like jerky.

Twenty-Six

Grogan returned this morning, and he wasn't alone. Four PRMC "consultants" have joined us and are presently poring through the campus with a fine-toothed comb. Officially, they're here to streamline operations, to promptly retool the facility for full-scale production. Based on what I've seen so far? They've come all this way just to throw dirt in our faces—"This doesn't meet minimum code requirements," and "That conflicts with Interplanetary Settlement Safety code ten sixteen point four." Bunch of cranks, as if PRMC even bothered to put us through any training before putting us to work. Of our original group, only Fiona and Grogan have so much as laid eyes on a representative of our employer.

Until today, that is.

The worst of it is my new roommate. With all the new bodies, we've had to play musical rooms a little; Rogers and Cutterly are now sharing a dorm—let me tell you, that didn't go over well—two of the new guys are bunking together in what was once Cutterly's room, another has taken over Fiona's old room, and I'm sardined with a mammoth, muscle-bound crank named Skelly. He snores and farts in his sleep, and that's truly the best I can say about him. One other thing, though: sometimes if I look at him long enough? A faint, familiar bell tolls in the recesses of my memory. But then he smirks, remarking something snarky, like, "You guys have really made a mess of this place," and whatever familiarity I felt a moment before vaporizes into childish brooding.

You're the one poisoning the air supply, farthead.

On their second day here, the four stooges accompany us to the mother tree to oversee the morning harvest. I hate working with people breathing down my neck—once upon a time, Keith used to do it whenever I let a deadline get too close, and it drove me crazy, then—but these guys have it down to a meticulous science. They're always there—even if I manage to forget it for a moment—just watching pensively, waiting for the tiniest excuse to belittle my efforts. It's clear to me that these cranks aren't interested in making better employees of us; they point out our shortcomings with relish, yet share no corrective wisdom. I suppose they might be building a case to have us replaced—maybe back on Earth, some NFL team's only chance at dodging prison for a regrettable gangbang is a stint on Mars.

Stranger things have happened, right?

Nevertheless, climbing a predatory tree on Mars when you're nervous is never a good idea. But what can I do? When the first of the Queen's seedpods bursts, I happen to be perched precariously in her branches—only a few feet away from the explosion—something like ten feet off the ground. One of the consultants is admonishing me for this risky and ill-planned solution to plucking high-hanging fruit when a blast like gunfire sets my ears to ringing; seeds pelt off me hard enough to sting right through my suit.

I react.

Dropping to a crouch, I throw up my hands to shield my face. Alas, built for more substantial gravity, my muscles grossly overcompensate. I feel the sharp tug of a sheared branch on my sleeve as the overzealous kinetics of my body betray me.

Somewhere in my little pea-brain, I know I'm in trouble. But it's too late to change my mind. My mass is already committed to motion; momentum has already been established. The fabric of my sleeve rips with a sound like the biting of an apple. An instant loss of pressure deflates my suit, hissing against my ears.

Ten months on Mars is nothing to sneeze at, yet it can't even begin to compete with a lifetime of primitive, earthly instinct. Adrenaline takes the reins and commands me to act. I obey—opting for flight over fight—stepping back and away from the commotion.

Into the comforting safety of thin air.

For once, I'm thankful for the diminished gravity here. My impact with the ground hurts, yet it's mercifully understated—more like tripping over a curb than falling from a tree. That's not to say that I'm out of mortal danger, however. Panic burns my cheeks as stark reality dawns on me: I have precious seconds to live, barring some sort of superhuman intervention.

This is it, I realize; this is my Montague moment—a single, damning mistake that will end my life. I zigged when I should've zagged, and there is no such thing as forgiveness.

Desperately, I struggle to plug the hole in my sleeve with a fat, gloved hand; the rush of air from my helmet reduces to an irregular hiss, but it doesn't stop.

This really is it.

Martian winters are a six-month affair without a single redeeming quality—no snowmen or hot chocolate, for example. More to the point, it's something like seventy below outside. With my air all but gone, I'm sucking down more freezing carbon dioxide than oxygen; my lungs are simultaneously burning and starving to death.

And to make things worse, it's getting too dark to see much. *Is it really nighttime already?*

There are few places I prefer to avoid more than the infirmary. Yet here I am, nursing the worst headache of my life. My lungs are sore, but they're medicated and recovering nicely. No concussion, incidentally, just a bad case of whiplash. Actually, my only real concern is my arm; an area the size of my palm was frostbitten deep into the muscle of my forearm—a little Martian kiss, Rogers calls it. Though it's heavily bandaged now, I've been assured it'll heal quickly. In fact, the wound isn't supposed to scar much, thanks to hourly administrations of some acrid stem-cell ointment. Considering the severity of the wound, I find this prognosis a little hard to believe. Drawing from the confidence of my coworkers, though, I've become cautiously optimistic. I guess we'll see what we see.

The least of my long-term concerns—and the one thing I can't seem to rise above—is the unbearable pounding in my head. Ironically, we can reattach a severed limb here if need be, yet the best we can come up with for a headache is some aspirin.

Skelly's been hanging around more than I'm comfortable with. My first impression was that he was genuinely concerned for my well-being—probably from a liability standpoint, since my injuries were sustained on his watch—but I realize now that he's *waiting*. For what, exactly, I can't say.

Cutterly tells me that once the first pod exploded, a chain reaction ensued and eight others burst in rapid succession. Fortunately, no one else was hurt and—aside from me—everyone walked away no worse for the wear. The seeds, on the other hand, are everywhere; apparently, they've even managed to slip into the joints of our atmospheric suits and hitch a ride right past the sanitation blowers, which is no small feat. From what I hear, Skelly washed one out of his hair, and Rogers found one between his toes on the evening of my accident. Obviously, they're sticky little things.

I know they're supposed to be harmless, but still—can anyone say *cree-py*?

I'm looking forward to tomorrow, when I'll be officially

released for duty again. Not that I've been dreaming of work; the sick bay just doesn't inspire a lot of peace or confidence, you see. Right now, for instance, I'm lying on the very cot where Winkley died. And I was put here by the same entity that feasted on my friend's remains—the circle of life has never seemed so perverse.

I don't remember falling asleep, yet I must have—because if I had been awake, I would surely have seen him. Even in the darkness, which is sparsely weakened by a constellation of subdued LED indicators, I can clearly discern a humanoid shape hovering over me like some deathly chimera. My mouth is gagged by a fist-sized wad of gauze, hands bound snugly to my cot. He's leaning over me now, blasting me with fetid breath.

"Evening, Wilson," whispers the indistinct silhouette. "Thought we might have a talk."

"What're you doing?" I try to demand, but the sounds that emit from my mouth are muffled and utterly unintelligible.

"Hold your horses, now. Let's go over the rules first, okay?" His smile is bizarrely pronounced, white teeth floating like disembodied dentures in a caricature of shadow. Still, while the dim light has diffused this man's other features, his voice betrays him. A jolt of recognition surges through my body.

"You ready for rule number one?" Skelly wants to know. Noiselessly, he crosses the room and clicks on a small reading lamp. It provides scant illumination, but it's enough to see that he's holding up a finger, preparing to tick off his list. Gagged and restrained, all I can do is nod somberly.

"Good," he says, voice bouncing whimsically, as if praising a toddler. He returns to my bedside, kneeling into an eclipse with the lamp. "Rule number one: make any effort to scream, I squeeze the life out of you. No second warnings." *Oh my God, what is this?* Oddly, Skelly plugs his extended finger into his ear and digs around for several seconds; it emerges shiny with a balm of wax. Though nauseated, I manage the decorum to bite back my disgust. I swear, though, if this crank farts right now, I'm gonna lose it.

Skelly unfolds a second finger and brandishes it in my face. "Rule number two: don't you *dare* lie to me. I'll know, believe me—and you'll regret it." I wish I knew what this was about, because I'd happily give him whatever he wants. This charade—oh God, please let this be a charade—isn't necessary. If only he'd ungag me, I'd convince him of this.

"Pretty easy to remember, Wilson. Even for a scrap putz like you." He digs in his ear again. *Gross—somebody has an ear infection; serves him right.*

"So, you ready?"

I nod yes, but I'm not. I'm not at all prepared for whatever this crank has in store, because—try as I might—I can't even imagine what he's after. Honestly, what could I possibly know that warrants this kind of extreme interrogation?

"Good," he says, yanking the gauze from my mouth. "Tell me about Arthur."

With a tongue too parched to swallow, I can only stare at him in dumbfounded silence. A moment ago, I was prepared to be the voice of reason—indeed, my survival seems wholly dependent on it. Now, though—hearing Skelly's words—I feel hopelessly disoriented as past and present collide, scattering logic like bits of cosmic shrapnel. Despite appearances, I'm sufficiently motivated to obey his every instruction, yet the best I can muster is a whispered, "What?"

Lodged in a lamplit eclipse, Skelly's floating teeth disappear behind an implied frown. "Don't make me repeat myself, Wilson. I'm not a patient guy."

Oh God, how I wish I could give him what he wants! The problem is, my mind is awhirl with fragmented thoughts, and I can't seem to bring two together. He might as well have said, *Tell me about shoes.* I mean, honestly—where do I begin? What *about*

Arthur?

Skelly sighs. "Not real good with instructions, are you?" At once, calloused fingers latch around my trachea like steel cables and begin to squeeze. The discomfort is immense, indescribably terrible; it isn't only the frightening deprivation of oxygen—which, in addition to paralyzing me with fear, adds a sharp sting to the three-day pounding in my head—but also the sickly sensation of my throat crunching against my spine. Instinctively, my body thrashes and bucks to no avail. The inhuman noises escaping me—wet, primal grunts of a dying animal—horrify me as much as my murder. My eyes ache, bulging in their sockets like champagne corks. From nowhere, brilliant, white light begins to vignette my vision, enveloping me in contradictory heat and cooling numbness. The panic is quickly subsiding, I realize, as is the pain. I'm strangely comforted, at peace. No longer afraid, I cuddle into the welcoming bosom of death to rest.

Goodbye, Mars. Goodbye, Queen. Goodbye, bone-chilling misery.

Dying is easy, I realize—frightening at first, to be sure—but so much easier than living.

And then it's all over.

Only I'm still alive. The warm light has vanished and my body cries out in pain once again, erupting into a coughing fit. Skelly's iron grip has released me, freeing his hands to slap my cheeks.

"Wake up, kid," he snaps. My eyes flutter and his ugly face blurs into view, poised mere inches above my own. Chuckling at the sight of me—gasping and coughing through a throbbing trachea—Skelly probes in his ear again: "You ready to take me seriously now?"

Heaving with uncontrollable sobs, I've truly had enough—live or die, I just want this to be over. Tears crawl down my temples and into my ears like wet insects.

I can't explain why, but my mind chooses this moment to dredge a gem from the vault of my most precious memories,

Mitzy's porcelain face grins nervously at me, glowing gently against a neon backdrop; unaided by the recall of my implant, her features shift in and out of mental focus. She's just confessed that her spastic dance moves have kept her single; I think this was the moment when I first had an inkling that this girl was special. Because she was a dork, just like me.

I know I'll never see Mitzy again, that I'm destined to die alone on this planet. But seeing her face has ignited a stubborn flame in me, and it occurs to me that I still want to live. To remember her again, perhaps; certainly because I fear that death will put even more distance between us.

"Last chance, kid. Start talking."

So I do.

Skelly watches me as I talk, his expression disclosing nothing. Lacking direction, I impart everything I can remember about my friend, from the day I first met him in the prime of my adolescence to the day he died in that pathetic hospital, alone. Skelly nods encouragement, absently plumbing his ear while I revive the details of Arthur's missing NanoPrint and its baffling reappearance here on Mars. It finally dawns on me that this must be what he's after, so—with gathering confidence—I tell him all about Art's MentalNote and his files, sparing no detail.

I'd tell Skelly so much more, if only there was more to tell—after all, every moment I'm talking is a moment I'm still alive—but I've said all there is to say. Well, almost. What little I've left unspoken is mine alone; it's nobody else's business that Arthur meant more to me than my own parents, that he was a greater man than any of us will ever be.

Long after my monologue has tapered into silence, my roommate continues to appraise me, as if to grant me ample time to recant my story, or perhaps to add a guilty postscript. When I do neither, he rises from my bedside and begins to pace the room, pinky corkscrewing into the side of his head.

"So your implant contains copies of Arthur's files?"

He asks this question with a dazed smile, savoring the feel of the words as if they're a bit of sweet poetry. "Yes," I mutter.

"And you can read them? They aren't encrypted?"

I cough, my throat gritty like a gravel road. "I think they were decrypted by my NanoPrint." Even as I divulge this small truth, I sense that my eagerness to please has only sealed my fate. As if to prove me right, Skelly produces a knife from his boot and saunters back to my bedside. His black eyes are shiny and giddy, like this is the real payoff—the violence, the gore of what remains to do.

"That's good, Wilson; very good." He waves his knife before me, flaunting it like a banner; steel serrations flare in the lamplight like the hypnotic taunting of a metronome. "I'm afraid this may hurt a bit, though."

The door latch rattles without forewarning, but it's locked. Skelly swivels toward the sound, smile never fading. Despite my fear—or perhaps because of it—something happens as I numbly consider this crank's ugly profile: countless threads of disconnected thought mysteriously converge.

And I remember.

My mind travels back through time, where he shadows me at a shopping mall, and then later, chases me across a freight dock. His hair is much shorter now—almost militarily trim—and he's lost some weight, but there's no doubt that it's him. Skelly raises his hand to worry at his ear again and seems to remember at the last second that he's holding a knife. He chuckles sheepishly. "Dang it, got a crank gnat in there, or something."

Funny, we don't have bugs on Mars.

The door latch rattles again, and this time a muffled voice whispers frantically, "It's me—Grogan. Let me in."

My heart leaps in my chest. *Grogan—oh, thank God!* I'm not sure that Grogan can take this guy—especially considering Skelly's armed—but I'll take absolutely any help I can get. Even if it only buys me a few more seconds of survival. And, though it shames me to admit it, even if it costs Grogan his life.

Skelly approaches the door without an ounce of concern, flipping and slicing his blade through the air with too-practiced ease. Something about his nonchalance seems to contradict common sense, but I can't spare a second to work out the what or why. He unlocks the door and Grogan spills inside as if he's been trying to shoulder his way in.

"Watch out!" I bark. "He's armed!" Unthinkingly, I've broken rule number one—*no second warnings*—and I know what comes next. But Skelly doesn't rush me with his wicked blade. Rather, he rolls his eyes. Again, logic wavers.

Grogan glances at me, then back to Skelly, who shrugs, as if to say, *What can you do?* Grogan sees the knife—surely he must see the knife—and isn't alarmed. He shuts the door quietly and locks it behind him. As the lock clicks home, so do my thoughts.

I understand now.

To Skelly, Grogan growls, "What're you doing?"

Skelly shrugs. "I'm just about done here."

"Fine, but what's with the knife?"

"We need his implant," Skelly replies, grinning mischievously.

Grogan's cheeks flush red. "You crank idiot! We need the implant *in* him; take that thing out of him and no one'll ever be able to read those files. Their decryption could be tied to his vitals or something."

The larger man crosses his arms, eyes narrowing. "My thoughts exactly."

"Skelly, you're not using your head, okay? Gunn wants the files—all of them—and not just to destroy them. There's something in them that he wants, and I mean to give it to him."

Skelly smirks with disregard. "Believe me, he'll be happy just to know those files'll never see the light of day."

"Listen, Skelly, that's his decision to make, not ours."

Skelly shakes his head—no, it's more of a twitch—and digs in his ear again. Suddenly, he doesn't look so good. His arms fumble behind him as if clearing a path, and then he collapses to the floor, landing solidly on his rear.

"What's wrong with you?" demands Grogan. "Are you drunk?"

Skelly shakes his head emphatically—wait, nope; just more twitching. "Something's wrong," he murmurs. A tear streaks down one cheek and disappears into a heath of dark stubble. "It hurts."

"What is it?" Grogan rushes to him, grasping him by the shoulders. "Did you take something?"

In response, Skelly slumps forward into a moaning heap. Flustered, Grogan storms to my side, jabbing an accusatory finger at my face. "What'd you do to him?"

I'm as alarmed as he, even if I'm also equally relieved. More than anything, though, I'm angry. "You mean other than lay here tied to this scrap cot?" I seethe. "I guess you're not only a backstabbing traitor, you're also a stupid moron."

Twenty-Seven

Throughout the b-hive, the corridors are still; it's very late—or early, depending on your perspective—and with the exception of our shuffling footfalls, the silence of the dorms is broken only by the monotonous pulse of snoring. Skelly remains in the sick bay, unconscious.

"You're bunking in my room tonight," Grogan whispers. "I don't trust you to be alone."

"Trust *me*?" I scoff. "That's a laugh."

Here's the thing: Skelly is a dang scary crank—he's a muscle-bound killer, and he works for a man who has carved out a wide niche in infamy. And given that Skelly's stuck here on Mars with no entertainment, I don't have any doubt that he'd dismember me just for kicks. In stark contrast, Grogan—at least, in my estimation—is nothing but a loud-mouthed, nerdy tightwad—just like yours truly—and I'm pretty sure I can take him. Actually, if I'm being completely honest, I've been sort of hoping to find out since the first time he belittled me in front of the others. In front of Fiona.

The only thing holding me back now is the long arm of uncertainty. What if the other PRMC consultants are working for Gunn, too? Will they come running to Grogan's aid? Are they, like

Skelly, itching to cut the life out of me? Though my ego wants so much to provoke confrontation—to prove itself more worthy of Fiona, I suppose—I must admit that I'm not ready for the answers to these questions.

A few feet from Grogan's bed, I lie on the hard floor, watching tiny green diodes blink happily from the control panels across the room. Angrily, I seethe the seconds away until dawn finally begins to stir the darkness.

If there's any silver lining to be found on this situation, it's that Grogan probably hasn't slept a wink either; the comforts of mattress and pillow are poor substitutions for a clean conscience. It's a small consolation.

It blows my mind that this crank—a man I've disliked on such a trivial level—has emerged from this chapter of my life as a villain. Maybe I'm jaded—forgive me if I feel a little entitled to some cynicism—but I honestly didn't think he had it in him. This makes twice that I've underestimated the nefariousness of a coworker.

Just as the sun breaches the horizon, Grogan rolls out of bed, rudely jostling me with a bare foot—rude not necessarily for any use of excessive force, but because Grogan knows perfectly well that I'm already awake. "Get up," he says in a hoarse bark. "We're leaving in an hour."

True to his word—yeah, I know; *now* he bothers—fifty-five minutes later, we're headed toward the airlock, showered and sparingly fed. The others are still asleep, which is as Grogan planned, I'm sure. All the while, a voice harps at me: *Why are you going along with this? This crank has no power over you!*

I can't really blame the unknown for ignoring that voice—not exclusively, anyway. Sure, Grogan could call for backup and I'd be swarmed with members of his sleeper cell, but what does that really matter? Dead today or tomorrow—what's the difference? I suppose if it's going to happen anyway, I'd rather die on Earth than here.

On our way out, we stop by the infirmary to check on Skelly. Just to be clear: I don't give a strand of rotting circuit scrap about his well-being. He's a murderer, and while I doubt I could ever bring myself to kill another man, I can certainly let this one die without blemishing my conscience. Nevertheless, for reasons that are presently his and his alone, Grogan seems almost desperately concerned about him, and I suppose my morbid curiosity is sufficient to tame my indignant tongue. As it turns out, my curiosity and Grogan's ambiguous agitation don't come close to preparing us for what we find.

Skelly's lying on his side, just as we left him. Completely relaxed, his body is a still life of tranquility—motionless, arms tucked snugly against the contour of his torso, legs extending the lazy, serpentine flow of his spine. From the neck up, the view sours with eye-puckering intensity. The space once occupied by Skelly's head is now an eruption of blood-red vegetation, every blot of skin obscured by ghoulish shoots of sinister foliage. Sprouting from his ear—and undoubtedly rooted into the depths of his tiny brain—is a female BP7.

I've been wrong before, but I'm betting that our debarking from Mars is now on the backburner.

"So the buggers are completely bypassing the gametophyte phase now," Cutterly notes with a grave frown. He's still sweaty from an excursion outside, during which he and Rogers grudgingly buried Skelly near the mother tree. It's the first time I've seen either approach the Queen since Winkley's death. "The Queen's acting more like bamboo than fern anymore."

If we were solely interested in producing the BPs en masse, this observation might actually raise our spirits. But for the moment, the name of the game is containment—and I have a hunch that we've already lost our grip, even if no one's willing to admit it.

Rogers clears his throat and says: "Spent two hours uprooting saplings yesterday from when the seedpods blew. Half a dozen sprouted on our roof—even a few on our walls. Sent out roots right into the metal." As if on cue, the distant pop of an exploding seedpod resounds outside. He smiles nervously, larynx bobbing in his throat as he harrumphs a very Rogers harrumph. "It's only been a few days and some were already three and four feet tall."

A couple of our consultants pale noticeably.

"Those seeds aren't supposed to be able to germinate," I remind the group with a hint of irony. "Sounds like Fiona jumped the gun a little, doesn't it?"

Cutterly grunts in agreement.

"Kind of weird," I add. "Don't you think? That she would invest so many years in her experiments and then fly out the coop when all that remains is a few more weeks to confirm her findings?"

"Uh, I think the saying is 'fly the coop,'" offers one of the consultants.

"What's a coop?" Rogers mumbles to no one in particular.

Grogan coughs and when I glance at him, his eyes are smoldering as if screaming for my silence.

My eyes roll sharply to the ceiling. "Whatever," I growl, both at the unwanted—and unverified—correction of phrase, and at Grogan's wordless, nonsensical threat. "Seems like she ought to have known better, that's all I'm saying."

Following a long pause, one of the PRMC guys tosses in his two credits—and to my ear, it's the best advice I've heard in a while. "If we're gonna keep the blood plants in check, we need to get a greenhouse erected immediately. Maybe structured with acrylic or carbon fiber—something with little or no mineral content. At the very least, we should layer it with something they can't eat through. Probably ought to do likewise with the rest of the buildings as well."

If my death warrant hadn't already been signed, I might feel relieved that someone is finally pushing a proactive agenda. It sounds like a practical solution to me, one that any engineer ought to approve of—or at least weigh in on—yet ours provides no assessment whatsoever. For all intents and purposes, Grogan has left the building; he stares into space as if half-asleep.

Cutterly gives him a gentle elbow. "Okay there, Grog?"

Grogan blinks and quickly recovers. "Sorry about that. Great idea. I'll look into it ASAP."

For the first time since I learned of his duplicity, I begin to wonder about his motivations. He's been here for half a decade, after all. Currency has no value among us, so what's the appeal?

Not long ago, Cutterly revealed that our original crew—Fiona, Rogers, Cutterly, Winkley, Montague, and even Emmers—was staffed primarily of exiles, each of whom was running from something. Just like me. Grogan is the definitive exception. Now that I think about it, this place seems to drive him crazy. So why has he stuck around for all these years? And for him to have turned on me so suddenly, something must've changed.

Pondering this, I scrutinize the engineer, trying to glean something from his expression that might reveal the truth. To my surprise, I *do* see something there, and though I'm no student of psychology, the panic welling up in his eyes sheds a glimmer of light on things.

Don't get me wrong—I'm still screwed, but I think I might understand a little of *why*.

When Grogan announces that we're headed out soon, it becomes very clear that I was right to wonder about the new PRMC crew. Two are visibly nonplussed at the poor timing as well as the flimsy explanation that came with our unplanned departure. The third, though—a mousy little guy I've hardly noticed until now—smiles serenely. I'm not surprised when Willace—no, it's *Wallace*—conjures an excuse to accompany us, nor am I immediately concerned. A moment later, though, he engages

Grogan in a stony glance, punctuated by a snide wink. In that instant, despite my initial impression of him, I know I'm in the presence of something evil—a killer like Skelly, only worse; you see a troll like Skelly coming, but a guy like this slips right under your guard and slits your throat before you even realize he's a threat. Stealing a glance at Grogan, I see that he's equally unnerved.

We leave just after lunch. Though I've scarcely gotten to know them, Rogers and Cutterly are as close to friends as I've got, and this is the last time I'll see either of them. At the mercy of my fragile emotional state, I give them each a handshake—heartier than usual, and embarrassingly tearful—and wish them the best of luck. They look at me as if I've gone a little daft. Neither has bothered to question the nature of my trip. They've been fed a lie—that we're off to fetch supplies for the new greenhouse, and that I'm tagging along for my own amusement—one that apparently doesn't quite jive with the finality of my farewell. Cutterly walks away in a chuckle, but it's a nervous sound—the kind you make when you only half get a joke and you're trying feverishly to figure out if it's actually funny. Rogers hesitates, lingering as if he senses something amiss. I wish I could confide in him—to warn him, really—because I doubt he's immune to the craziness that somehow managed to follow me here.

But I can't say a word.

Wallace is sentinelled nearby, lancing Rogers with a glare that eventually sends the much larger man away in a scamper. How I ever misread Wallace so grossly, I'll never know; I can't even begin to reconcile him with the harmless creature I perceived him to be only a short while ago.

Twenty-Eight

The ramp leading into Grogan's ship creaks under our combined weight as we crowd the airlock. Wallace stands at my back, literally breathing down my neck. I feel hyperaware of his presence, that he could kill me quite effortlessly if he chose to; just a quick, well-placed blade—or maybe a little pinprick of cyanide—to the back, and I'd be gone before I knew what happened. I'm probably being irrational, but I can't help but feel that I'm willingly marching into the maw of certain death with nowhere to run.

Without speaking, we shed our atmospheric suits; a few seeds shake loose onto the floor, sending a universal shiver through our ranks. As much as the little things freak me out, I willingly help Grogan gather and dispose of them. Left unchecked, something tells me they'd have no problem taking over this ship. Minutes later, we're punching through the thin atmosphere and into frictionless space. I walk around with trembling hands in my pockets, waiting helplessly for what I know is coming.

Grogan tries to persuade me to take a pill; I decline out of sheer spite. I have no intention of making this easy for him; I won't let that crank forget what he's doing to me, not even for a second. I know I'm getting to him, too. He's pacing the flight deck—not nervously, exactly, but with considerable agitation. Beneath the skin of my wrist, my NanoPrint tingles a *hello*, so I know Grogan has Arthur's implant nearby, probably in his pocket. Wallace is always around, but just as he did on Mars, he hangs just outside our periphery where it's easy to forget he's there.

Eventually, boredom sets in. I follow Grogan around the deck like a hungry dog, poised just outside kicking range. When this fails to goad him sufficiently, I start in with the questions. I'd like to say I'm interested in some real answers, but the truth is that I'm much more interested in pestering Grogan than entertaining more of his lies.

"You must be the greediest crank I know; riding around in a ship the size of a freaking apartment building, and you're ready to sell out your friends for a few lousy credits?" I'm posturing, of course, yet I'm a little taken aback by the sincerity of my own bitterness.

Grogan snorts and scratches at his scraggly chin. "Oh, Wilson. I can see those little gears trying so hard to get in motion, but they're just too slow to build any momentum." He chuckles and shakes his head. "It's almost endearing."

"Thanks for caring, scrapbag."

His expression darkens. "Yeah, I guess you're just lowQ enough to think I'm enjoying this—like I have even the tiniest choice in any of this."

"Everyone has a choice." I say this with conviction, but on some level, I suppose I know better. The most damning choices aren't usually choices at all.

"Sorry, Wil. I like you. Always have, despite what you must think." His face falls, and I don't doubt his sincerity. "If there was any other way out of this," he says, "I can promise you I'd have taken it."

"Forgive me if I'm ungrateful. So, what's the payoff, then? You serve me up on a platter, and you get what?"

"I can't talk about this with you, Wilson."

"Why not? I'll be dead in a few days anyway, right?"

Grogan looks at me with unusual ferocity. I can tell he wants to come clean, but something's holding him back. His eyes flicker to Wallace, who's leaning against a portal, watching the shrinking silhouette of Mars.

"You don't mind, do you, Wallace?" I ask.

Wallace sighs and glances slowly at Grogan. If there's a message buried in their glance, I can't read it. But Grogan swallows audibly and nods.

"Fine, you wanna know? I'll tell you."

I hold out my hands, palms up. "By all means, please."

"If I bring you in, Gunn'll release them."

"Release who?"

"My brother and sister."

My bitterness loses some toxicity at these words, because I realize that—yet again—my perpetual demise has contaminated the well-being of another. I'd much rather blame Grogan, but it's clear that I'm to blame for this predicament. "I didn't even know you had a sister."

"Yeah, well. Like I said: you're a little lowQ."

"What's her name?"

Grogan looks at me like I'm truly miswired and chuckles. And then he turns my world upside down. "Her name's Fiona, idiot."

I'm speechless. I scarcely manage a choked, "What? But ... what?"

"She didn't want anyone to know because she was afraid it would complicate things."

"That's ridiculous!" I declare.

"Not really. You know she's the only woman at PRMC with a research grant to herself? You can't imagine how prestigious her reputation will be one day, given what she's accomplished on Mars."

I did not, but he's left an opening, and I can't resist taking a jab. "You mean, genetically engineering an invasive plant that could destroy a planet, and then abandoning her post before it's safely contained?" Even as I speak the words, tasting their truth as they pass my tongue, I feel guilty for thinking such things about Fiona. The beautiful Fiona, who still visits my dreams with disturbing regularity.

Grogan ignores me, completely unruffled. "And I'm guessing you probably didn't know that I'm the youngest engineer alive with his own twelve-tier spacecraft?"

Again, news to me. I'm not even sure what a twelve-tier spacecraft is; this one only has two levels. I guess it explains the inflated state of his ego, however.

"Think about it: it doesn't matter which angle you take, most people would assume there's some nepotism at play here; and once the accusation is out there, the facts become irrelevant. Truth is, we're both just equally ambitious. I didn't influence her placement on Mars, and she sure didn't influence my fleet status. When she was awarded this opportunity, I just wanted to be close by to protect her. So I put in a requisition for the route through the USS; they never asked why. Eventually, I switched my domicile from Earth to Mars so I could stay there more regularly. She'd never admit it, but I've saved her life on Mars more than once."

I look at him, mouth agape. He laughs.

"Funny part is, everybody else had us pegged in a matter of days. I think Fiona always resented my being there, like I was trying to keep her on a leash or something. And I guess sibling rivalry is hard to mask."

All I can think to say is, "Oh." I want to point out that I'm an only child and wouldn't recognize sibling rivalry if it slapped me in the face—but what's the point, really?

"Don't feel too bad; seems like she tried a little harder to keep up appearances around you. Truth is, I think she might've had a little crush on you."

Even now, given everything I've learned, I still feel my blood pressure rise at the thought. "Now you tell me." Despite my hormones at work, something keeps floating to the top of my mind, bobbing to and fro amidst all this new information. "What about Arthur's implant? How'd you end up with it?" I ask.

"On that last supply run before Fiona left, Gunn and a few of his guys were waiting for me on the USS. They'd already roughed up a few of the staffers there. A guy named Hollister—you remember him, don't you?—they broke every finger on his right hand for trying to hail me with a warning."

"Oh my God."

"Anyway, I guess you didn't cover your tracks very well before I took you on. They knew everything there was to know before I even docked the ship. They made me watch a MentalNote recorded by my brother. They were holding him in an old warehouse; I couldn't actually see him, but I got the sense that he was in pain."

I'm so ashamed for what I've brought on Grogan that I could cry. But first, I have to clear something up. "You said you brought Arthur's implant back with you, right?"

"Yup."

"So what's with the other one?"

"Another coworker of yours—didn't catch the name. Once Gunn and his guys got beyond Earth's atmosphere, I don't think they could tell the implants apart anymore, so they just sent them both on." I guess it escaped their notice that the USS has an implant reader on board.

"What about Fiona? How'd they get her?"

Grogan blushes, eyes glassing over. "Pure stupidity on my part; I tried to smuggle her to safety."

"Safety? What's safer than Mars?"

"Once that first seedpod appeared, I knew the company would send out a few reps; it's a very big deal to them. I had a hunch Gunn wouldn't pass up the chance to get his clutches in a little deeper, so I convinced Fiona to vacate and return to Earth."

"She didn't want to go?"

"No. She didn't think we had a firm enough grip on the BPs yet. She was right, of course; I didn't care. I just wanted her somewhere safe from Gunn. I was going to pull some strings to hide her until things blew over."

"And they got her anyway?"

"On my return trip, I got word that she was captured back on Earth. Some men grabbed her the moment her shuttle landed."

My heart lurches; if I wasn't already dead, I'd be as committed as Grogan to save her.

"So that's it," I say. "You hand me over, and Gunn sets Fiona and your brother free."

"Yeah."

"And what makes you think he's gonna let them go? From what I've seen, Gunn doesn't much care for loose ends."

"I'm not an idiot, Wilson. I can't be sure what'll happen when this is over; but there's no question what'll happen if I don't cooperate."

I can't argue that point. I glance over at Wallace. He's watching us with idle amusement, one hand unconsciously splayed against the portal window. "How about you, Wallace?" I ask with a smirk. "What would you guess our friend's odds are?"

Wallace chuckles and scratches a dimpled chin. "Better than yours, kid."

Twenty-Nine

I feel for Grogan; really, I do. And even more for Fiona. But I've grown pretty weary of playing the victim lately. So when Wallace needles me in the back with a stiff knuckle and says, "Why don't you rustle us up some dinner?" I invite him to kiss something unsanitary. I'm not sure if I'm trying to provoke him, or if I literally don't care what happens to me anymore. Regardless, he only smiles and retorts, "Well, somebody better do something before I get too hungry; you don't want me getting irritable."

Grogan stands and disappears into the kitchen in my stead. A few minutes later, he serves up our dinner—grilled chicken breast, steamed vegetables, and buttered dinner rolls—and we all eat in silence. I do the best I can to enjoy my food—it should be easy, considering it's the first taste of meat I've had in months—but there's a pit in my stomach that isn't at all interested in food. Every second that we travel through space, I'm that much closer to death.

After we eat, I borrow a book from Grogan and retire to an empty dorm to read. It takes every ounce of wit I have to concentrate, because Wallace has followed me into my room and commandeered a nearby bed, from which he can keep an eye on me. I wonder if he'll be the trigger Palmer eventually pulls to take me out. He certainly seems up to the task—and chomping at the bit to carry it out.

"Wow," I say. "My own personal watchdog."

"Don't worry, kid. My bite is much worse than my bark." I need no further convincing.

Two hours later, I'm mercifully engrossed in the story—thank goodness for the escape of fiction—and it nearly escapes my attention that Wallace's breathing has deepened to a gentle rumble. Eventually, I notice and permit my gaze to slide from the pages and across Wallace's sleeping form. He's positioned on his side, facing me. Even asleep, this guy manages to terrify me. I have no doubt that he'll awaken if I get up, so I stay put. Better to let sleeping dogs lie and all that. I don't have the energy to read anymore, so I lie back on my pillow, book resting on my chest. Closing my eyes, I do the only thing I can do right now. I wait.

I don't know what time it is, but Wallace has abandoned his post and is in the bathroom adjoining our dorm. He's been in there for a while now, grunting occasionally.

We're eating breakfast. Well, Grogan and I are eating breakfast—Wallace is staring at a plate of scrambled eggs and bacon as if it has just flagellated. "You see that?" Wallace whispers.

I glance at Grogan with a question mark in my eyebrows.

"Okay there, Wallace?" asks Grogan nervously.

"It's telling us the way, but we're not listening."

I have something witty and nasty to add, but I swallow it with my eggs. Wild animals are at their most dangerous when they're wounded, after all. Wallace glances at Grogan, and then at me. His skin has taken on somewhat of a translucent quality, and despite the cool in here, his upper lip is brimming with droplets of sweat.

This guy does not look good.

"What did you two do to me?" he hisses. Grogan stops in mid-chew; he looks truly frightened and scoots back in his chair until he's in danger of toppling backward. I'm feeling particularly dark—and for once, I'm not at all afraid. Again, though, until this guy's down, he's still too dangerous to unleash.

Grogan turns to me and asks, "What should we do?"

"I don't know," I admit. "He probably just needs one of those motion sickness pills."

Grogan nods hopefully, remarking, "Yeah, good idea."

"I'm not taking any pills, so don't bother getting up."

"But you look really sick, Wallace."

"I'm fine. Your cooking blows, that's all. It makes everything sound orange." Well, I don't begrudge him that point. My eggs are a little runny, though I think they sound more yellow than orange.

I finish my breakfast with a smile working like crazy at the corners of my lips. Grogan notices—I can tell because he looks at me as if I have a death wish—but doesn't say anything. Wallace has fallen asleep at the table, slumping haphazardly against the back of his chair.

When we're done eating, Grogan pulls me into the kitchen and yanks me away from the door, against the wall; he's sweating and breathing in short bursts. "You figured it out, didn't you?" he whispers.

"Yeah, I did. I know I can be a little dimwitted—but I'm not a complete misfire."

"Okay then. Keep cool, though. Don't give him any reason to freak out."

I agree, but I have to ask: "I'm not complaining or anything, Grogan. But surely you know that if Wallace looks like this when we get to the USS, Gunn's gonna take it out on your family. How do you know you haven't just signed Fiona's death warrant?"

"Don't worry about it, Wil. Actually, if you think about it, this only makes me look better; I singlehandedly brought you in when

Gunn's own guys weren't up for the challenge."

"But why even risk it?"

"Because no matter what happens, that freak can't be allowed to continue terrorizing people. I had the chance, and I took it. No regrets."

I can only stare at him, this man who I've clearly underestimated.

Grogan swallows and blinks, eyes utterly haunted. "He's done things you can't imagine, Wil."

I open my mouth to rebut, but then clamp it shut again as another thought occurs to me. "Grogan, about Skelly—was that you, too?"

"Nah, that was just nature finding a way. It gave me the idea for Wallace, though."

I nod and breathe a deep sigh. "Well," I add, nodding toward the doorway. "I guess this guy had it coming. You hear the way he was bagging on your cooking?" Through the door, we hear a loud thump as Wallace collapses to the floor.

Wallace sleeps most of the morning away, stirring now and again only to slip back into an uneasy slumber. By lunchtime, it's all over. I find him in a bathroom stall, propped up on a toilet with a network of leafy vines exiting both ends. Too late to turn back now, huh?

Grogan and I drag him to the airlock and release him into space. With horror—and a little fascination—I watch as he disjoins the ship in a lazy tumble. At near light speed, the corpse will reduce to vapor upon collision with even a single speck of dust. I turn away, knowing I'll never free my mind of that image if I witness it firsthand.

I can't believe I've played a part in the death of another human being. I suppose the circumstances might justify our actions—to some extent, anyway—yet I'm overwhelmed by sadness over what I've done. Not remorse, exactly. Just shapeless guilt for breaking the code of life.

Thirty

I'd like to think I'll find within myself a previously unknown font of self-preservation, but the truth is that from here on out, everything is out of my control. My fate has been in motion for a long while now. In the background of my waking moments, I've heard the telltale clinking of its gears; too bad it's taken me this long to distinguish it from the noise of circumstances. Even still, I think I've known all along how it would end, even if I hoped for something better. I imagine Grogan is thinking something like this, too. If I thought it would help, I'm pretty sure I could take him in an all-out fight, if by no other margin than the depth of my desperation. But at best, that would only delay the inevitable; even if by some miracle I could figure out how to fly his ship, I'd have to land it eventually. And when I did, I have no doubt Gunn would be waiting. Besides, as much as I'm viscerally driven to save my pathetic life, I can't sacrifice Fiona's any more than Grogan can.

In a way, I think this situation is even harder on Grogan than me. After all, as much as I feel caught in the middle of a tug of war, Grogan has much more to lose than I do. Because when I leave this life, no one will miss me and my pain will have ended. Grogan, in contrast, has loved ones relying on him—the combined weight of their lives is upon his shoulders, and that's got to be more of a burden than any man should ever have to bear.

The ship is utterly silent as we dock at the USS. I lie in my bed, trembling. The bandage on my arm is gone; my fingers trace circles around what was a crispy crater, yet I'm too distraught to be amazed. I can't see much through the window portal from here, but I can just discern the glow of Earth's atmosphere creeping into the corner of the pane like a peeping Tom. The floor shudders faintly as the ship mates with the Unified Space Station dock, then I feel more than hear a series of clicks as locks engage to solidly couple the two masses together.

Ten minutes pass, and I'm ashamed to admit that I spend them weeping. Grogan knocks gently on the door, which is already ajar, and peeks his head in. I wipe my eyes with my shirtsleeve and take a deep breath.

"It's time," he says.

I nod. Shuddering, I get to my feet. My knees wobble like jelly. Grogan approaches and—with unexpected and blessed kindness—takes my arm, gently guiding me from the dorms. Wordlessly, the engineer leads me through the ship to the airlock, which has already pressurized with the USS. I follow him through the hatch, inching toward my death.

Despite my frightful state, I can tell Grogan's only marginally better off—he stumbles often; his breathing is taxed, rasping with worry and sorrow.

And then, just like that—with no shoe-clopping preamble of gathering dread—there's Palmer Gunn. I suppose I was more than half-expecting another throng of his meatheads, not the main man. But here he is—and he's utterly ecstatic at the sight of me.

"Well, well, well. Long time no see, Mr. Abby," he remarks. He sounds ridiculous, like a bad caricature of some film mobster. "So happy you accepted my invitation," he adds. Good grief, this guy needs to work on his presence; scary or not, I can't imagine how he's managed to get this far, talking like that. If he had a gun in hand, I'd more than half expect him to add, "Say hello to my little friend," in a thick, Cuban accent. For once, my internal filter catches these remarks before they can slip through to hasten my death.

Grogan squeezes my arm—the closest I'll get to a goodbye from my friend—and then takes a deep step back. It dawns on Gunn now, for whatever reason, that things aren't necessarily copacetic, even if his evasive quarry is finally within his grasp.

"Where's my boys?" he grunts at Grogan.

Grogan shows the palms of his hands, shaking his head pleadingly. "They didn't make it, Mr. Gunn."

Palmer Gunn steps toward Grogan and his face darkens like the night itself. "What do you mean, *they didn't make it*?"

Grogan swallows visibly, but holds his ground. "I'm sorry, sir. They didn't acclimate well to Mars. Despite my best efforts, neither took our safety protocols seriously."

Gunn takes a second step toward Grogan, who looks like he might vomit. *I'm right there with you, buddy*. Gunn grabs a fistful of shirt and draws Grogan in until only centimeters span the gap between them. "You kill my boys, kid?"

For a brief moment, it occurs to me that even if he's armed, Grogan and I might stand a chance against this guy—he's alone here, after all. But against all logic, he instills something that surpasses fear, something that seems to psychologically eliminate any possibility of ever prevailing against him.

One moment, I'm thinking, *He doesn't look that big*. The next? If I had a loaded gun in my hand, I'm fairly certain I'd hand it over without a fight.

"No! Of course not," Grogan yelps.

Gunn drills him with his eyes and then lowers his voice to a guttural whisper. "If I find out different, things are gonna get really messy for you, got me?"

Grogan nods, eyes bugged like his head is in a vice. Abruptly, Gunn releases my friend, who stumbles back and to the floor, and diverts his attention to me. "He tellin' the truth?" he demands.

I suppose he has good reason to think I'd betray Grogan— after all, the man has betrayed me—but Gunn has miscalculated. "Yeah, he is. They both died from exposure to one of our research specimens," I say. Grogan swallows and looks at the floor, nostrils flaring. "Truth is," I add, "I was ready to make a run for it. But this crank dragged me in, even after those other guys died."

Gunn looks at me with eyes like needles, probing deeply into me as if to unearth a hint of deception. But he finds none because, though I'm a terrible liar, I'm telling the truth—if stretching it a bit. Gunn seems satisfied. With lightning efficiency, he fastens an iron grip on my upper arm.

"Time to go home, Wilson."

Part Three:
Prodigal Son

Thirty-One

I haven't grasped the depth of my longing for Earth until I've returned to the protection of its atmosphere. I've forgotten how rare and beautiful this planet really is, bejeweled in mesmerizing shades of aquamarine and jade, liquid with symbiotic life. For a brief moment, my fate seems inconsequential. Drawing near my homeland, I'm helplessly transfixed by the sheer beauty of it, the fantastic variety of color and textures, the sedimentation of living layers held firmly in its bosom.

Suddenly, hot breath is on my neck and Gunn's gravelly voice blasts past the turbulence of reentry, through my blissful reverie. "Soak it in, kid. May be the last thing you ever see."

We land at a small airfield near Houston and I'm dragged across an empty tarmac toward a transit bay. A shuttle awaits us. As I step inside—with the brusque assistance of Gunn—I find that I'm not the first passenger. For a split second, I'm relieved that she's here, that she's survived Grogan's gamble. But as Fiona affixes her eyes on mine, I see something in them that I never expected, something that breaks my tired heart.

"Sit down," Gunn snaps. I obey, and the shuttle begins to move. My eyes are glued to Fiona, and for once, there's no lust there.

"What is this, Fiona?" I ask. Her mouth forms a sad frown and she shrugs. For a moment, I wonder if I've misinterpreted the situation. I've been known to do that now and then, after all.

"I'm sorry, Wilson. Things weren't supposed to play out like this."

"Oh, spare me," Gunn interrupts with a groan. "Don't go getting sentimental on me now. We got things to do."

"You aren't going to kill him, are—"

"Now? Relax, lady. If I wanted the kid dead, he'd be dead already. I'm not done with him yet."

Fiona seems guardedly pacified. "Mr. Gunn, we need to contact my brother. He did his part and got Wilson here; he needs to believe you've done your part."

Gunn rolls his eyes. "Ah, screw your brother, lady."

"Mr. Gunn, I won't let you turn my brother into a liability. If he thinks I'm still in danger, he's going to reach out for help. We don't need that kind of attention. Need I remind you of what's at stake here? If any of this gets out, none of us are safe."

Gunn takes a step toward Fiona, glaring down at her diminutive form. "So maybe I'll just take him out then, huh? Lure him to the surface and trigger a little stroke or something."

Suddenly Fiona is a very different creature than the woman I thought I knew. "Listen up, you psychotic bully," she seethes. "I'm to report to the president of Unified America in less than an hour. If I even suspect my brother is in any danger, you're going to feel her wrath." She pauses briefly, then flashes a terrible smile. "Big sister can be ruthless."

Palmer Gunn scowls and seems to loom over her like a great gargoyle. He wants to hurt her, I can tell. But instead, he matches her terrible smile with his own and chuckles. "Fine. But don't think you can throw your weight around to save this one." He gestures at me with a dimpled chin. "Once we scrape his NanoPrint, he's dead. I got orders, just like you."

My eyes glaze over with shock. What could the president

possibly hold against me?

Fiona looks away, out the window at the airfield on the horizon. "I know," she mutters. She turns to me, but she avoids my eyes. "I'm really sorry, Wilson."

My brain is overloading from the sheer contrast of stimulus I've experienced in the last twenty-four hours; I feel like I'm so close to understanding it all, yet—as always—my mind is incapable of drawing the pieces together. My thinking muscles are just too tired, cutting off in midthought, merging ideas that don't belong together. I think of Wallace and the bizarre fragmentation of his mental processes under the influence of a BP7 seed, and I can't help but draw some similarities between that and what I'm experiencing.

It's then that something occurs to me, something that perhaps should have long ago.

"PRMC," I say. "It's a Miritech company, isn't it?"

Fiona swallows visibly, steeling herself for something. Her face begins to smooth into an expressionless mask. "Always a few steps behind the pack, Wilson."

Ignoring the jab, I put a hasty conclusion into words before it can fall apart. "So, I've been working for the vice president all this time?" I consider this for a moment and realize that I've overlooked the significance of her earlier remark. "Wait—Carlisle. She's not just the vice president anymore, is she?"

Fiona looks at me appraisingly with eyes turned to stone, and then shakes her head as if annoyed. The longer I look at her, the less I can reconcile her with the woman I once knew. "How do you even manage to dress yourself in the morning?" she mutters. Her demeanor has now completely transformed. My ears burn, my heart turns to lead in my chest.

It's not merely that I've been chastened that saddens me just now. I know it's in my nature to cringe against such treatment when perhaps I ought to keep my chin up. But I think it's her blatant and immediate disentanglement from me as a person—as a man who has both consciously and unconsciously yearned for her affection, if not her respect. I know I've probably read or dreamed things into our relationship over the previous months—I'm a man who doesn't take hints well, after all—but until right now, I haven't realized just how prolific her deception has been. And how ugly she really is to deliberately turn on me rather than put up an ounce of fight for me.

"Does that make it easier for you, kicking me while I'm down?" A shimmer of guilt ripples across her face, but it's fleeting. She masks it with a bland smile and turns away, dismissing me.

"Go ahead—convince yourself that you hate me, if it'll make this easier."

Gunn sighs nearby and rubs at his temples. "Would you two love birds knock it off? You're giving me a headache."

For a while, we comply. But with the passage of each second, my anger swells until it can no longer be contained. Spite takes my reins, and it has a smart mouth.

"Too bad about Mars, huh?" I remark, eyes boring into her with a glare that smolders with radioactive intensity. "All those years of hard work down the drain."

She considers me with a flicker of uncertainty, trying to resist the bait. But she can't. "What's that supposed to mean?" she sighs with feigned disinterest.

"It means your seeds—the hallucinogenic fruits of your labor—they're not sterile." Her expression turns to steel, and for a split second I fear I've only demonstrated my modest intelligence again. But then, her eyes narrow and her mouth curls into a terrible sneer.

"You're lying," she says, but the waver in her voice and the fresh desperation in her eyes betray that she knows better. I'm not capable of it, after all. Particularly to her.

Suddenly, behind the exhilaration of this small victory—and just above the merry gliding of the shuttle above the city—I feel a

long-forgotten tingling on my wrist.
  And everything changes.

Thirty-Two

My NanoPrint is suddenly humming full blast, laboring to download thousands of unheeded notices. At once, my senses are overloaded with auditory and retinal signage. Wincing, I struggle to dig through it all, sweeping aside the nonsense to reach my file directory. It's no good; my implant is all but locked up. Still, I'm not completely out of options. If I hurry, maybe I can—

>>*Oh, Wilson. I've missed you sooooo much!*

Marilyn slides from my periphery into the center overlay of my vision at half opacity.

>>*Say, handsome—why don't I configure all these new add-ons for you? I know how you like it when I—*

Dang it—not now, Marilyn! I give my digital personal assistant—who is even more beautiful than I remember, I can't help noticing—a mental shove aside; she responds with a sexy pout before blinking out in a blast of trademarked, skirt-lifting wind. Before I can regroup, her head reappears.

>>*Maybe later?* she whispers with a long-lashed wink, and then she's gone.

Breathing heavily, I manually add a single request to my process queue. Sequences process there so quickly I almost lose track of my request immediately. Once I find it, I realize a minor adjustment is needed. I open the request to edit and increase its priority rank to *urgent*, which sends it closer to the top of the queue. I still can't predict when my request will engage—native implant updates are inherently profiled with the highest priority, so they supersede all other processes. For the moment, all I can do is wait.

Our shuttle glides onto pavement with a slight jolt, though I hardly notice.

Fiona sees the strain on my face and visibly tenses.

"What're you doing?"

"Nothing," I mutter. A mist of sweat at my hairline channels into a single, telling droplet down my cheek.

Fiona rises to her feet, but there's nothing she can do.

"Stop him," she barks to Gunn.

With startling speed and agility, Gunn is instantly on me, gripping my arms and screaming obscenities in my face. He gets one of my fingers into his meaty fist and yanks it back—seriously, what's with this guy and fingers? "Stop!" he growls. My brain explodes with agony, and I shriek—but I cry out as much in victory as in pain. My implant has finished updating, and even as it bombards me with a year's worth of notices and unsolicited spam—I almost laugh at the number of Nike ads in my system—and while Gunn has his barbaric way with my poor, defenseless fingers, I sense my implant bulleting through its queue and finally preparing to process my humble request, and then—

Executing file pedestal.exe.

Gunn begins punching me in a bone-jarring frenzy, as if he can somehow sense that the moment is irretrievably slipping through his fingers. With each blow to the head, my vision dims. "Just kill him," Fiona pleads, and for a moment I'm flooded with burning hate. "You know I can't," Gunn hisses. "Get up front and engage the jammer." He catches me with a clean right cross to the jaw, and the world fills with black stars, which suck at the light and swell like black holes.

At a run, Fiona disappears into a control chamber at the front of the shuttle. A second passes, then another. Though hurt, my head is clearing. Gunn locks eyes with me, probing for some sign that my inner workings have been interrupted. Arthur's program stalls; my retinas alight with connection errors, weighing down my spirits like Jovian gravity. Just as quickly as they were born, my hopes blink out of existence.

Fiona reappears and announces, "It's on." I stare at the ceiling with my best poker face, but Gunn sees through it. Smiling, he manhandles me into a seated position, rubbing and flexing the pink knobs of his swelling knuckles. "Cripes, that was close," he says with a relieved chuckle. He offers this observation to me, it seems, as if I'm supposed to nod my head in lighthearted agreement.

Without warning, the shuttle gains momentum, and Gunn's smile falters; the whine of the shuttle's twin engines rises to unfamiliar heights as old warehouses and private airfields begin to race by.

Gunn turns to Fiona with a sharp rebuke. "What'd you do? Why are we speeding up?" Fiona pales with uncertainty. "I don't know, I just..." She dashes to the control chamber, footfalls vibrating through the floor.

Suddenly, our center of gravity shifts dangerously off kilter as the shuttle confronts a corner too quickly. Gunn teeters on his feet, grabbing at a luggage rack overhead to remain standing. A second passes and it feels as if we're about to roll. Instead, the shuttle straightens and stabilizes on its axis. Still, we don't lose velocity.

"It's the nexus jammer," Fiona calls out, voice ringing with growing panic. "I think it's interfering with the shuttle's navigation link."

Gunn bolts to her aid, cursing the "Chinese piece of scrap" with each step. He disappears into the control chamber, and for a scant moment, I consider the wisdom of trying to lock them both in. Even as I contemplate this, the shuttle begins to slow. Looking around, I realize just how old the vehicle is; the once-white interior moldings have yellowed with time. The seat cushions are quilt-like with worn, vinyl patches. This thing could easily have retired from public service ten years ago or more. Now that I'm paying attention, I notice that a fine, faraday mesh has been applied to the interior; but it's a sloppy installation—frays of thin copper wire protrude here and there, trailing like wisps of shimmery hair.

I rise on wobbly legs and peer out the window, placing a trembling hand against the scratched resin for support. Outside, the scenery has transitioned to old refinery tanks and stacks of rusting shipping containers. The vehicle encounters a bump in the road, and I feel the window panel give a little under my hand. My gaze slips to a lever set into the base of the window frame. There, a small red sticker reads, "Emergency Exit Only. Alarm Will Sound."

"Sit down, you little twerp," Gunn snaps from the doorway at the end of the aisle, but I pay him no mind. Sparks are popping in my head, burning holes through the cloudbanks of my rattled brain.

I reach out and rotate the lever with detached curiosity.

"Don't you freakin dare," Gunn bellows. I turn to smile at him just as he begins a clumsy scamper toward me, propelling his considerable girth forward against the seat backs along the aisle.

Crawling bodily onto my seat, I lean into the window and give it a single, desperate shove. With a sucking pop, the panel falls away, granting entry to a wind of hurricane-like ferocity. An alarm trills, blasting through the wild rush of air with piercing tones. Just as Gunn grabs for me, and before instinct can betray me, I hurl into empty space.

My shirt immediately catches on something, and my body hinges back toward the shuttle, bouncing against its outer shell. For a brief moment, I hang there, confused, watching the ground whiz by like an endless conveyor belt. But then I feel strong hands hauling me back in, and I kick out my feet in frustration. One buries itself into something soft.

And suddenly I'm falling.

The concrete rushes to meet me and I feel a leg snap in greeting. My body tucks into a ball, arms enfolding my head, knees cinching into my stomach. The pavement rushes by, clawing at my skin, skipping angrily against my bones.

Soon the spinning world begins a merciful fade to black, a color that ushers in neither pain nor pleasure—merely stillness and relief. I feel a tickle in my consciousness as my implant awakens and busies itself with some forgotten task. My body impacts with a curb and a hundred swords pierce my ribs.

It doesn't matter, the pain. Despite it—and maybe even because of it—I'm smiling. For the first time in my life, I've done something that might just make a difference. It doesn't bother me at all that I can't remember what that is, even less that I won't live to see the result; it's enough to have done it, to have faced the pain I've always been afraid of and to have remained resolute.

I welcome the emptiness now. I chose it, just as it chose me.

An unpleasant stinging calls me to the surface, but it's small. So small, I can't bear the notion of crawling from my pillowy darkness to fully acknowledge it.

"Is he dead?" a small voice asks, white light peering down at me as if through a pinhole.

"Close enough," is an even smaller reply. The blackness flickers red as the stinging becomes something duller, something harder to ignore. But I persevere, pushing away the color and drawing blackness about me like a warm cloak.

A watery mumble from far, far away.

"Mind your business, buddy," says a passing breeze.

There's a pinching now, but it can't be my pain. It's just too small, too distant to do more than send a ripple across the void.

"Hurry up," whispers the tiniest, faintest voice that ever was. "I hear a siren."

Yes, hurry up.

The soft down of the void calls to me, drawing me back into its loving bosom. My senses fade, and all is still now.

I regain consciousness in what appears to be a hospital—but I've fallen for that before. Outside my door, the hallway is bustling with excited chatter. A doctor peeks in; finding me awake, he steps briskly to my bedside.

"Mr. Abby, how are you feeling?"

I look at him, mind murky, ears ringing. He looks familiar, but I'm not completely here yet. "Do you remember me?" he asks. I look at him closely—he blurs in and out of focus, yet I have no doubt that I know him, even if I can't place him.

"Yeah. Not your name, though. Just the face."

"Good, that's good. I'm Dr. Seymore. You were admitted to my care this morning with some pretty significant injuries." He pauses to make sure I'm following him; I am. With every second, things are coming back with more clarity.

"Gunn? Fiona?" I croak.

"Don't worry about them right now. That situation is under control."

"What do you mean?"

"Mr. Abby," Dr. Seymore says. "I'll let the authorities go over that with you in a little while. Right now, I need to address your physical well-being. And you're still in the woods."

"Am I dying?" I whisper. It certainly feels that way.

"Well, no. Not exactly. You're pretty banged up. Nasty head wound, plenty of broken bones. But those should heal up quickly. Not to minimize your injuries, but you have a more pressing concern at the moment."

"I do? What is it?"

"Well, to be blunt: it's your NanoPrint. It's been removed, and not with much precision."

For a moment, I'm awash with déjà vu. I look at him, remembering more and more his plump face. The moustache is gone, thank goodness. He smiles, and his genuinely caring nature cuts through time; he's a sight for sore eyes. "Seems like that's been happening a lot on your watch, Doctor," I point out.

He laughs and shows me his palms. "No argument here. Now, Mr. Abby." He peeks over his shoulder with abrupt nervousness and, finding no one in earshot, lowers his voice conspiratorially. "What should we do about your NanoPrint?"

A groan passes through me. The very thought of breaking in a new implant—regrowing nerve filaments for the next decade, reconfiguring globals and profiles that have taken a lifetime to refine—makes me want to vomit. But what can you do? I give the doctor a muted shrug. "It's not like I have much choice. Can't function without one, right?" I remark tiredly.

The rotund doctor chuckles appropriately and then begins rocking on his heels, appraising me curiously. For a few seconds, he just looks down on me, smiling a weird, pensive smile that reminds me of Stewart. Then, nodding to himself, he swallows and takes a deep breath. "You'd be surprised," he says in a voice burbling with excitement like a soft melody.

For a moment I'm not sure what to make of this—neither his mannerisms nor his words make much sense—but understanding does eventually sink in, and once it does, I can't help but wonder how in the world I ever missed it. Even in my groggy state, it's just so obvious now.

"Oh, man," I mumble. "You're a crank dodger."

He gives me a shrug, coupled with a twitchy grin. "Afraid so," he whispers, patting his pants pocket, where his disembodied NanoPrint must reside. A flicker in his smile betrays that he's already second-guessing the wisdom of this confession.

"Don't worry, Doc. Your secret is safe with me," I promise.

His smile gains a firmer footing, and I think we both must feel a little better. "Good to know," he says. "So, now that you know your options, Mr. Abby, what would you like to do about your implant?"

I lie back and close my eyes, smiling with strange relief at the calm, uninterrupted flow of my thoughts. "Not a thing, Dr. Seymore. Not a single thing."

On the upside, Arthur's program worked its magic like a charm. Though only time will show just how brilliant it was, it sparked an immediate wildfire of fuss. On the downside, the program seems to have positioned me at the center of scrutiny; government officials swarm over me like angry flies for the next several days. They squeeze me for every detail I can muster about my experiences with Fiona and Palmer Gunn, who remain on the run.

Not surprisingly, my relationship with the government proves to be all give and no take. I'm given absolutely no information in return for my cooperation. When Gunn is finally captured at a private club, I learn the details from a gabby nurse rather than from the investigators who have promised to keep me in the loop.

Still no word on Fiona.

The building super has to let me in to my apartment, since I no longer have an implant to verify my identity. Actually, I more than half-expect my condo to no longer be my own—after all, I've been gone for the better part of a year. If not for my savings, my monthly autodraw against the lease would've failed at some point, and my belongings might've been recycled.

"Good grief," the super gesticulates as I stand in his doorway. "I saw you on the news a couple of days ago, but until this moment I didn't recognize who you were!"

"I've been on a little diet."

A few minutes later, I'm standing in my condo with the door open behind me. I linger a few feet into the entryway, statuesque, held upright by luck and gravity. I can't explain it—I'm afraid to go forward into this strange capsule of modern convenience that I once called home. It doesn't draw me in like an old friend—it holds me at bay with a cold hand, as if it somehow knows I'm not the same man who left here so many months ago. I push inside anyway.

The place is less trashed than I left it, thanks to my automaid, but at some point I'll need to do some serious spring cleaning.

A long, hot shower does wonders for my aching bones. I'm grateful that modern medical technology has the ability to heal bones so quickly, but the accompanying aches are unbearable without the pain management services of an implant. Dr. Seymore has kindly provided a bottle of pain tablets, which are supposed to help. Unfortunately, they're so large I can't imagine how I'm supposed to swallow them.

After a quick shave, I feel a little more human—and very emotional. In my dresser, my clothes are dusty and stiff. Actually, my entire wardrobe is useless. I've lost twenty-five pounds since the last time I bought clothes, and they weren't pounds I could afford to lose. I pace the condo in my boxers, looking at this and that, my mind bobbing to and fro to connect the dots of time, dragging memories from the forgotten caverns of my former life.

I find myself standing in front of mirrors throughout the condo, taking in the disturbing gauntness of my abused body, wondering, *How long have I looked like this?* I'm not only frightfully thin, my eyes are piercing. They're haunted. The boyish naiveté that has always been a fundamental element of my appearance—for better or worse—has been bleached away, exposing a hard, even cold, wisdom.

Despite my initial impressions of Mars, when I thought it a remarkably beautiful place, I've grown to loathe it. Everything on

Earth seems unimaginably beautiful by comparison. There was a time when I took that beauty for granted—and why not? It's everywhere on this planet—but I can't do that anymore. To look at me is to know that I no longer belong here, that I'm no longer fit to mingle with beautiful things. Against my will—and outside of my awareness—I've been infused with ugliness, the ghostly drabness of Mars that I learned to despise. So I will drink up loveliness like a man dying of thirst, and I won't waste a drop.

I sit at the foot of my bed wondering what I'm supposed to do next. My doorbell rings, a shrill tone I can only equate to a dying animal.

I vaguely recognize the inspector from my interrogation following Stewart's death, but I don't bother intimating this. "Mr. Abby?" he says, his voice arcing to a question mark.

"That's me," I say. He pores over my features, into my eyes, and hesitates. "I know, I've looked better," I admit. Only, just as the words pass my lips I realize that he's not merely taken aback by my unhealthy appearance; he literally doesn't recognize me. I remember him now—Rackley, right?—but he's not able to reconcile what he sees in front of him with the man he was so interested in last year. I'm a shell of my former glory, and it didn't add up to much before. It doesn't bode any better for me that I'm standing here dressed only in my boxers.

I invite him in, and he declines. "Just wanted to drop this by to you. We recovered it this morning from one of Palmer Gunn's confiscated properties." He holds out a small plastic bag, and I reach out to accept it.

It's my NanoPrint.

"I suggest you make arrangements to have it implanted again very soon," he warns. "You wait too long and it'll deactivate on you."

I nod blankly, staring at the tiny gizmo in my hand—an invention that has been my crux and my salvation, my strength and my weakness. I mutter my thanks, and Inspector Rackley makes a hasty exit.

Well, that's one way to clear a room—just strip to my boxers.

I use the toilet and set my NanoPrint on the counter by the sink—wait, reverse that.

Bedtime, take two.

A knock on the door. This time it's my neighbor, Mrs. Grace. Thankfully, she's old enough to have seen it all and doesn't even notice that I'm more than half-naked. Before I can mutter any sort of a greeting, she snatches me into a heavy embrace, squeezing me hard enough to pop my joints.

"I was sooooo worried about you!" she cries. "I just knew something had happened to you and I'd never see you again." When she releases me, her eyes are spilling tears. And—to my surprise—so are mine. This marks the first physical contact I've had with another human being in more than ten months. Excluding beatings, anyway.

Mrs. Grace invites me over for dinner, with the caveat that I put on some clothes—and I don't mean just any clothes; Mrs. Grace is a devoted disciple of dressing for dinner. Unfortunately for both of us, my clothes hang off me like dusty tarpaulins. I savor a plateful of roast beef and potatoes, wishing my shrunken stomach had room for it all. She's a talker, Mrs. Grace, yet she still manages to put her food away faster than me. I feel so heavy, like my extremities are invisibly mired in elastic. Although it was less obvious at the hospital, this sensation has become more and more noticeable.

"You need to start beefing up, Wilson. You'll never get a girl to marry you looking like this."

I have to laugh.

"I'm serious," she says with a motherly frown. "Don't they have a muscle-stimulus add-on for the implants now?"

I shrug noncommittally. "First I've heard, but I've been out a while. Besides, my implant isn't much help at the moment."

"What do you mean?" she asks, but then her eyes lose focus

for a moment, and I realize she's connecting to my NanoPrint. "Oh my goodness," she observes. "You're here, but our NanoPrints can't shake hands!"

I slide back a loose sleeve and give her a peep of my scarred wrist. "Yeah, I gotta get that fixed."

Mrs. Grace covers her mouth and coos like she's seeing the Grand Canyon for the first time.

"You know, my husband Charles—rest his soul—had quite a physique." My excised implant is forgotten.

"Really?"

"Oh, yeah! He had every woman inside a mile radius giving him the eye every time he stepped out the door. Got pretty old, to tell you the truth. Jealousy takes a lot more energy as you get older."

"Was it genetic?"

"No, I don't think so. His parents were both heavy. But Charles always made time to exercise."

Huh.

Thirty-Three

The next morning, I take a tram to a nearby sporting goods store. I order a beginner's set of free weights, a jump rope, a punching bag, and a few sets of exercise clothes. The saleswoman doesn't say so, but she's surprised at my zeal. "You don't get a lot of that?" I have to ask.

"Nah, ever since that muscle-stimulus add-on was released, things have been pretty slow. But that'll change. Everyone's getting all pumped up chemically because they don't know any better just yet. Won't be long before that blows over."

"What do you mean?"

"Well, the thing about building muscle is that it makes you stronger, and it changes your metabolism."

"That's a good thing, right?"

"It can be, but not in this case."

I don't get it. Shocker.

"Think about it for a sec. You got some guy relying on his night-burner to keep his waist trim, right? Then he decides thin isn't enough and throws muscle stimulus into the mix. Now, he's burning off calories at the same time his muscles are trying to grow, just spinning his wheels, you know? So he's gotta eat more, right? To fuel all that muscle growth? Next thing you know, he's ripped like crazy, but he's got a caloric imbalance that leaves him starving and exhausted twenty-four seven; built like a tank, but can't even take the stairs in a fire drill."

"Whoa."

"Eventually people'll figure all that out and some guy's gonna walk in here and say, 'Hey, what can I do to not feel like circuit scrap all the time, but still look like this?' And I'll say, 'Never leave to your NanoPrint what you can do for yourself.'"

I smile; that could've been Arthur's mantra.

When the lecture's over, I head to the nearest mall and buy some new clothes—I don't go overboard, because if all goes well, I'll be back in my old ones in no time.

Just before dark, the delivery crew arrives. When they've finished storming my apartment with the clinks and clanks of iron, my spare room looks like a boxer's private gym. I lean against the doorframe and just stare at the equipment for a long, long time.

At eight o'clock, Mrs. Grace invites me over for a slice of pie. I'm pooped and take a rain check.

I'm just lying down when there's a tentative knock on my door. Now, I would hate to speak ill of Mrs. Grace, who is literally the only person on Earth to me right now, but if she's standing at my door with a slice of pie, I'm going to be more than a little peeved.

But it isn't Mrs. Grace. At once, the person I find at my doorstep is infinitely familiar, and hopelessly foreign.

"Hey, Wil," says Tim. "Remember me?"

I feel all my fatigue vanish into the night, swishing around my legs, whipping through my hair at the welcome sound of his voice. Before I can think better of it, I step out and pull him into a mad bear hug—I know, Keith would be so proud.

He looks a bit embarrassed when I finally let him go, but he'll get over it. I invite him in and we drink hot tea in my kitchen.

"You look older," I observe. His hair's a bit long—more hip than shaggy—and the boyish cheeks I remember well are all but gone.

"I *feel* older, Wil. You look like circuit scrap."

"I feel like circuit scrap." With no real forethought, I add, "And by the way, It's Wilson now."

Tim blinks as if taken aback, then up go the hands in theatric surrender. "Well, excuuuuse me," he balks, still smiling. "Didn't realize you were suddenly a grown up."

I shrug, offering a crooked smile. "Had to happen eventually." The truth is, I'm not exactly sure where this came from; I can only say that *Wil* suddenly feels wrong. It belonged to someone I used to know, a kid I can no longer relate to.

"Maybe you should start calling me Timothy."

"Sure, no problem."

Tim mouths the word a few times—Timothy… Tim-o-thy… Tim-ooo-thee—but wisely calls the whole thing off. "Nah, that wouldn't work," he explains. "I'm a monosyllabic type of guy, and unlike some people I know, I'm okay with it."

Crisis averted.

A gap creeps into the conversation, but there's nothing awkward about it; it's merely an agent of reflection. I'm compiling a mental tally of the many ways in which we've both changed since I last saw him, and I suppose he's doing the same.

Tim takes me in with a sad sigh, and then breaks the silence. "You know, I thought a camera was supposed to add ten pounds. So when I saw you on the news, I was thinking, *Get some more cameras on this guy, would ya?* You look a little better in person, but not by much."

"Always the charmer, Tim."

"Yeah, well. Gotta be me. Stopped by the hospital a few times, but they had you under lock and key." Learning this warms me.

We settle back to shoot the breeze for a little while, and I ask about IDS.

"We're hanging in there, but the writing's on the wall. We'll be lucky to survive another year."

I was afraid of this. "I imagine there were some pretty traumatic hiccups after Gunn's extortion ring was exposed, huh?"

Tim shakes his head with an ironic smile. "Actually, no. Not really, anyway. Our stock plummeted like crazy for a couple of days, but it stabilized. It's really undervalued at the moment, but our real problem is that without Arthur and Ryan—and you, for that matter—we've lost all our government contracts. It's hard to maintain consumer confidence when your top dogs have slipped the leash."

"Can't say I'm surprised, but I am sorry."

"Don't be. The truth is, with all those kickbacks out of the equation, we'd have a good chance of squeaking by—if it wasn't for Keith, anyway."

At the mention of that name, I feel darkness gather in our midst. "What do you mean?" I ask, wishing we could talk about something else.

Tim looks at me without speaking for a second, then shifts his eyes to his hands, where his fingers are drumming against the side of his mug. "You'd think with all that's happened, I'd have learned to keep my nose where it belongs."

"Uh-oh. What'd you find?"

"You ever notice how high our GFL invoices have been?"

I think I see where this is going, but I nod my head and keep my trap shut.

"Well, with Gunn out of the picture, I thought it might be worth looking at one of their competitors. I just couldn't handle the thought of paying another dime to Global Freight, knowing how much they've sucked out of us over the years."

I nod again.

"Anyway, so when I got an idea of what we should be paying, I made the mistake of pulling our old invoices to make sure our accounting system didn't have a bug in it or something—I mean, we're talking a hundred and fifty thousand credits every year, when everyone else is charging fifty."

"So what did you find?"

Tim hesitates and his cheeks flush with heat. "Well, you."

I laugh, first because it must be a joke, then because I realize it's not. "What in the world are you talking about?"

"Well, obviously you didn't do it—and if it comes down to it, I can probably prove that much. One of the payments was authorized by your implant signature, but it couldn't have been you. The profile IDs match and all, but according to your proximity stats, you and Arthur were setting up a test partition in Dallas the week you supposedly signed off on it."

I try to remember, and though I can remember taking such a trip, I can't lasso in any detail about the time period.

"Okay," I say. "So where does Keith come in?"

Tim sighs. "That's the part I'm not clear on. I know it's him; I just can't prove it."

"How's that?"

"Well, I did some digging—the kind that could get me fired, by the way—and I found that Keith and our GFL rep have spent a lot of time together in the last several years. Fishing trips to Canada, a safari to Africa."

My tea is gone and I switch to coffee. Tim switches to lite beer and starts pilfering through my cabinets for something to snack on.

"Is he a man or a woman?" I ask. He pauses with a hand still in my pantry.

"What? Who?"

"The GFL rep," I say with a sly grin.

"What difference does that m—" Tim's eyes narrow and then squeeze shut. "Oh, c'mon, Wil!" he explodes. "I mean, Wil*son*. That's just nasty."

I burst out laughing. "Sorry, I'm just saying. Even the genderless get lonely."

Tim shivers. "Well, I'm pretty sure that's not what's going on."

Maybe it shouldn't matter, but that actually seems to make me feel a little better. "Good to know. So that's all you have to go on?"

"Basically." He stares at the floor for a moment, snacks no longer on the menu.

"Still thinking about them?"

"Can't wipe the image away, you jerk. Why would you even go there?"

"That's what friends are for, you know?" I slap him on the shoulder and laugh again. My face hurts from smiling so much; I haven't had this much fun in a long time. "Anyway, I see your dilemma. So what're you gonna do?"

Tim breathes heavily through his nose and slaps a hand on the countertop. "I don't know. I guess I figured it was time to enlist some help."

"From who?" The police? The FBI?

Tim tosses back the dregs of his beer and burps. "I'm looking at him."

Thirty-Four

At seven thirty a.m., I drag myself out of bed and into my brand-new home gym. Just looking at all this stuff wears me out. I take it slow—not only because it's the recommended approach, but because I'm too wimpy to do it any other way. Ten push-ups—performed with the form of a narcoleptic misfire—ten sit-ups, a set of six bench-presses of sixty-five pounds. When I'm done, I feel as if I might faint, so I drop to the carpet and lie there for a while.

Eventually, the spell passes and I'm able to stand without seeing spots. I look back at my home gym and think, *You don't look quite so scary anymore*.

I don't want to sound ungrateful for the things Tim has done for me as a friend and a coworker over the years, but to say that I'm reluctant to grovel for my old job back at IDS is grossly understating reality.

I'd just as soon beat myself in the face with a dead cat.

In the end, though, I decide to do it—not only to help out Tim, but because I've never stopped hating Keith, never stopped longing for the day when he's brought to justice.

And the idea of hastening that day is too appealing to turn away.

I have every reason to think that Keith will show me the door as soon as I peek into his office. In the best of times, we were never really on the same page. In the worst, I'm pretty sure he'd have killed me if he thought he could get away with it. But he doesn't kill me or give me the boot. On the contrary, he jumps up as if I'm his long-lost brother and yanks me into a horrific back slap.

"Oh, man, Wil. It's good to see you. Figured we'd seen the last of you around here."

It's Wilson, I think—and only just refrain from actually saying out of habit. Oddly, it doesn't really bother me. I don't give a pile of circuit scrap what Keith thinks of me, so he can try to belittle me or ingratiate himself to me all he wants. Looking at him, though, I realize this is going to be much harder than I expected. When I consider all the damage he's caused to my life—betraying Arthur and getting him killed, dragging me into the fray of his iniquity by first sneaking the list onto Arthur's drive and then setting me up as a patsy for his own embezzlement schemes—it becomes utterly impossible to keep from diving across his desk and beating the life from him. I let my eyes settle just over his shoulder, where they can see something other than red.

"So what brings you by? You looking for a job?"

I nod, because it's all I can do to bite my tongue.

"Hm," Keith remarks. "Let me think."

For a split second, I worry that he won't rehire me. But Tim has convinced me that he will, and the more I consider Tim's logic, the more certain I become that he's right. IDS is months away from filing bankruptcy, and when that happens, the attorneys are going to swarm in and pick the books to death. It won't take long before one of them discovers what Keith has done; he may have doctored things a little, but he won't fool a professional for long.

Unless…

If he can get me back on board, he'll have an opportunity to either turn me or further incriminate me. And if by some miracle I manage to help him turn the company around along the way, IDS might just escape bankruptcy—and that means the GFL gravy tram might just continue its midnight run moving forward. There isn't much of a downside, when you think about it. The downside to not hiring me, however, is much steeper, because as long as I'm out of his sight, I'm unpredictable.

"Got it!" he announces. "There's still your IntelliQ program—it never reached the test partitions."

Despite why I'm here, I have to admit I'm more than a little offended that my work didn't warrant any attention in my absence. I'm also relieved that it still has a fighting chance of hitting the nexus. Even now, I have absolute confidence that it's a cash cow waiting to be born.

"Really?"

"Yeah, without you or Arthur around, nobody was brave enough to take the reins."

This isn't an unreasonable explanation, but I know feces when I smell it. I start to throw in a jibe, to point out that my program is no different than any other we've developed here—we have programming standards so that personal bravery never has to be a factor when projects are shuffled around.

Again, I bite my tongue.

"Let me just make a couple of phone calls, Wil—" *It's Wilson!* Sorry, old habits die hard. "—and I'll give you a shout. You mind waiting out in the lobby for a few minutes?"

An hour later, I'm dusting off my old desk—my office has become a catchall for empty boxes and backup journals—and trying to remember how to program.

After work, I eat dinner with Tim at his apartment. It's the ultimate bachelor pad—ugly but super-comfortable furniture, an entire shelf of his fridge devoted to beer—and it's somehow even more depressing than mine. Maybe because I know it'll probably always be a bachelor pad. The centerpiece of his dinner table is a pewter dragon-foot with talons wrapped around a crystal orb. I'm reminded of a nature show I saw when I was a kid where a male bird spent days making a nest to impress a female, only for some reason, the female was more disturbed than impressed by his handiwork, so she flew away, leaving the male to cock his head, as if to say *What just happened? Is it something I said?*

Still, Tim wears bachelorship well. He's content to watch cheesy movies and read nouveau graphic novels. Unlike yours truly, Tim's just fine with who he is. As I'm thinking this, he takes a gulp of his beer and says, "So, you'll never guess who Keith-sha"—that's Tim's newfound remedy for the Freudian slip—"called today."

"Do tell, please."

"Robert Marlin, our GFL rep."

"Really? Do we even have any projects going that require hardware updates at the USS?"

"Nope. He's just counting his chickens, I think. If we can get your IntelliQ project wrapped up, he'll have an excuse. Our equipment's fine, but it can always use a little beefing up. You just wait: he's gonna start turning the thumbscrews on you any day now."

"Fantastic. So what am I supposed to do? I mean, has anything changed since I left? How do we get the programs on the test partitions without Arthur?"

"Well, I won't say the problem's gone away, but it's nowhere near as dire as it once was. We hired a private nexus consultant to help us with that."

"So what's the holdup? I mean, why didn't you guys get the IntelliQ program up and running? It was already approved for testing before I left."

"To be honest, I really don't know. I've asked myself that question over and over. We'd be rolling in revenue if we had, that much is certain." My cheeks warm that at least someone has some confidence in my work.

"Okay. So if I can get things worked out with this consultant, we can get the program up and running. And then Keith will start running his scheme again."

"That's my guess."

"Okay, so then what? How can we bring him down?"

Tim runs his fingers through his hair. "Well, I suppose that depends."

"On what?"

"How's your programming these days?"

Yikes. "You mean in general? Pretty rusty, but it's coming back."

"Well, get to practicing. Because I've got a program in mind, and there's no room for sloppy coding."

I'm intrigued.

Thirty-Five

I'm feeling energized by my workout this morning. It's only been a few days, and I'm already seeing a little difference—I'm *feeling* a huge difference. I'm starving at breakfast, putting away more food than I've put away in a single sitting since I can remember.

For the first time in a really long time—long before Mars, in fact—I feel really good, like I'm advancing toward something positive. At the same time, I'm stressing a little over my implant. The truth is—as much as I have avoided acknowledging it—I have no interest in getting it back. Sure, it was convenient and made life so much more fluid, but I'm enjoying the peace of its absence from my body. My head is so clear. No more retinal signage or daily planners, for example. On the other hand, I can't just forget about it, either. It remains in my pocket most of the time, which allows me to access my apartment and office doors, transact credits, and satisfies my legal obligation to remain accessible to the nexus.

The problem is, my implant is useless in every other capacity, as long as it remains outside of my body. No contact requests—who knows how many have racked up over the past year?—no optional add-on updates, credit account accessibility, et cetera. I can get over not knowing where people are at any given time—in fact, I've always felt pretty slimy about that part of the nexus's functionality—but never knowing who's trying to reach me or the state of my financial affairs is an affliction I'm not able to cope with.

Fortunately, I know a guy.

As I pass through the lobby of my office building, I realize I don't need any coffee for once. I'm plenty awake and feeling fantastic. There's a line at the elevators, and for the first time ever, I blow it off to take the stairs.

Just as Tim predicted, Keith is primed to pressure me about the IntelliQ project. I take it in stride—it's much easier to tolerate Keith when his behavior follows my plan.

"We need this thing done yesterday, Wil. Sorry if this puts you on the spot a little, but if you pull this off, IDS may survive the year. If not, well I'm sure someone's already brought you up to speed—we're barely hanging on right now. I had to let someone go yesterday, in fact."

I can read between the lines—he unloaded another programmer in order to make room for me on the books. It angers me that Keith would toss that upon my shoulders, when we both know who actually hopes to benefit from it. I feel my old irritability stretching its wings, ready to take flight. It slips through my fingers before I can get a hold on it.

"Is that supposed to be flattering, that you fired someone to hire me on? Jeez, man. You should've just turned me away—I don't have any seniority here anymore." *Oops. That's not helpful, is it?*

I feel the temperature of the room cool a few degrees, but Keith keeps a firm grip on his composure. Glad one of us is in control of his faculties today.

"Sorry," I murmur. "I'll make it my top priority, believe me."

Keith steeples his chubby fingers and watches me contemplatively. "It's okay, Wil. I need to ask you something, though."

"Okay, shoot."

"I've never been one to question my employees' personal decisions, but I gotta admit it makes me a little nervous that you're always in privacy mode lately."

Oh, scrap.

"It's your right, don't get me wrong. It just creates an impression, you know? Like you're hiding something."

I gulp.

"Just something to think about, that's all."

I retreat from Keith's office like a kid who just got busted cheating on a quiz. I don't really care what Keith thinks of me, but he's right about one thing: privacy mode will do me no favors right now. Too bad I can't do anything about it, with my implant rattling around in my pocket like a loose coin.

I poke my head into the rack room and when I catch Tim's eye, I don ear protection and slip inside. He drops what he's doing and follows me at a short distance to the back of the warehouse.

The moment I'm certain we're alone, I say, "I need a favor, Tim."

"Yikes. Those are words I never want to hear from you."

"Nothing big. I just have a little problem with my NanoPrint."

"What kind of problem?"

"The kind where it's in my pocket instead of in my body."

"What? You've got to be kidding."

"I wish, buddy. At least, I do right now. Anyway, my problem is that I can't access anything on it, and I need to figure out how I'm gonna stay on top of the day-to-day stuff without it."

"Is that even possible?"

"Sure. Dodgers do it all the time, right?"

"Yeah, but that requires some illegal hacking. This is crazy, man. I'm surprised it hasn't deactivated yet."

I don't need more fuel for stress at the moment; I feel my

blood pressure rising like a balloon. "Listen, can you help me or not? I don't need to hear how messed up my life has become to know it's messed up."

"Simmer down, toots. Let me think on it for a little while."

I leave him tapping his fingers against a server rack and return to my office. It's absolutely filthy; I guess the cleaning crew hasn't figured out that it's in use again. I spend half an hour scrubbing things down, coughing and sneezing at all the dust I stir up.

Just as I sit down to appreciate my work, Tim pops in— sweaty and breathing heavy, as if just returning from a run—and deposits a small device on my desk. "This should help."

"Care to elaborate?"

"I do not. Just keep it near your NanoPrint and you'll be able to access everything manually."

"Whoa. I didn't think implant readers were legal."

"Strictly speaking, they're not. This is a law enforcement model."

"How'd you get your hands on it?"

"Don't ask, all right? The less you know, the better."

He walks me through a maze of touch screens. I'm sure that as soon as he walks out of the room, I'm going to forget a step and have to track him down again, so I ask for repeated demonstrations until I'm vaguely competent at navigating the menus.

"Tim, what am I gonna do about this, I mean long-term?"

"Get it reinstalled, man," he says with a shrug, like it's the most logical thing in the world. "Not that big of a deal."

I consider it for about two seconds before I feel a bad taste rising in my mouth.

"What if I don't want to?"

He pauses. "Then you've got a problem. No telling when it's gonna happen, but eventually that thing's gonna deactivate and you'll lose all access to the nexus. How long's it been now? Three or four days? I can't believe it's still running, man."

"It's been a week, actually. How long does it usually take?"

"Dunno. Hold on a second." His eyes lose focus for a few seconds as he consults the nexus on the subject, and suddenly his mouth curls up in a smile. "Normally twelve hours. Sounds like your implant has gone rogue."

"How can that happen?"

"Human intervention is my guess. I'm thinking it's time we took a look at it—maybe we'll find something on there that explains things."

Tim calls up my files on his reader and begins sifting through them. Hundreds of updates await my attention—they downloaded to my implant as I reentered the planet, but they've yet to be installed. Tim gets them going and continues plunking around.

"I wonder if my privacy mode has anything to do with all this," I offer helpfully.

"Maybe. But I doubt it. Looks to me like someone's hacked the access point to your vital stats."

"Who could do that?"

"There's only a handful of people I can think of," he admits with a frown, but his eyes are sparkling. "And one of them was Arthur."

We move on to my financials, and right off the bat, we stumble across something that absolutely floors me: evidently, I have received substantial credit deposits for every month I spent on Mars. Grogan and I never discussed compensation in any detail—after all, what choice did I have?—so I'm a little surprised—pleasantly so—to see a handsome sum piled in my personal escrow account. It occurs to me that this might well be the breadcrumb trail that led Gunn to my interplanetary doorstep. Tim and I do some quick and dirty math and find that I did better financially on Mars than either of us has ever done on Earth; it doesn't hurt that I wasn't in a position to spend anything there, either.

But that's just the beginning.

The real surprise is revealed in a little something left behind by Arthur's *pedestal* program. Gunn's guys managed to scrape off

Art's files before I got my implant back, but they clearly didn't find everything there was to see.

Tim looks paler than I've ever seen him. I peek over his shoulder to see what's got him so freaked out. At first, it looks like something has glitched. Tim spends a great deal of time chewing his lip and tapping around on the drive with shaky fingers, bobbing his head and saying things like, *No freaking way, man!* And, *Are you kidding me?* Eventually, he looks at me and guffaws. Closing my door, he leans back against it and says, "You're either unbelievably lucky, or you're seriously screwed."

"What does that mean?" I demand.

So he shows me.

One of Arthur's parting gifts: embedded in his *pedestal* program was a procedure that shuffled eleven million credits— roughly one month's extortion payouts—from IDS's capital accounts into an unnamed offshore account. Because of the serendipitous timing of this process, the payout log has the appearance of transacting as usual, just before I dropped Arthur's bombshell on the nexus.

Technically, the payments stayed right on schedule—they just fell off the radar before anyone could claim them. When Arthur's program was finished, it wrote out the account information, including its private-access credentials, to a commented field of a user-preferences file—one of thousands on my implant. This one only captured Tim's notice in the first place because, like me, he's in the habit of sorting files by time stamp, and this one was near the top of the list.

Counting all those zeros, my eyes glaze over. "Oh. My. God."

"Guess you're buying dinner tonight, huh?"

Thirty-Six

I'm too tired to watch a movie tonight—after a shameful display of fresh-seafood gluttony with Tim, it's all I can do to stay awake on the way home—so I settle for the news. For once, I'm glad I bothered. The networks are saturated with constant tidbits on Palmer Gunn. After years of fruitless investigation, the FBI finally convicted their man—thanks to Arthur. Evidently, as the nexus was permeated with Arthur's whistling from the grave, hordes of victims came out of the woodwork to testify against Gunn, documenting his otherwise untraceable hand in more crimes than anyone could've imagined.

An added bonus: Palmer Gunn's blood link to our dear president has also made mountainous waves. Coupled with her implication in the IDS extortion ring, it has secured her membership in one of this continent's most exclusive clubs: the impeached presidents. Her administration is crumbling at this very moment, and the new regime is chomping at the bit to take control. I doubt they'll be any less filthy than her, but I must admit I feel considerable pleasure to witness—and even play a role in—her fall from grace.

Incidentally, Miritech was ripped to shreds at the first sign of President Carlisle's demise, and all of its subsidiaries are rapidly disappearing into vapor. I still know nothing of Fiona's status, and I'm loath to drag Tim into my world of espionage to find out. All that aside, I continue to lose sleep over a single, haunting thought: did any of the blood plant seeds make it back to Earth?

Speaking of Tim, he explained over dinner that I can have an anonymous token issued on Arthur's phantom account, since I'm in possession of all the necessary information. The token can be retrofitted to just about any inanimate object, though they're most popularly fitted to jewelry. I've decided to order a handsome watch—for this purpose, and also because I have absolutely no sense of time without my NanoPrint. Normally, this is an option reserved for corporate entities. But eleven million credits tends to sway customer service a bit.

I'm grateful to have Tim by my side through all this—not only for his technical expertise, but because he's one of a handful of people on this planet who I believe is trustworthy enough to be a part of this without undercutting me for a piece of the pie.

All of this amounts to one thing: I'm comfortably financed—wealthy by most people's standards, including my own. Perhaps I should be excited by this—and I suppose I am, at times—but I'm equally terrified. I fear that at any moment, Palmer Gunn, or perhaps the FBI, is going to kick in my door and plunder what's left of my earthly life. Rationally, I know Gunn is no longer a real threat—even his own cohorts have abandoned him at this point—but there remains a scrim of uncertainty over the money, which prevents me from relaxing completely. I don't dare spend a single credit.

So I work out instead.

I've often heard people say they'd continue to work for a living, even if fate called their number in the lottery and bestowed unimaginable wealth upon them, because they enjoy working too much to leave it behind. It hasn't taken me long to learn that I would not be at home among these people. Now that I'm ostensibly well-to-do, I'm finding it increasingly difficult to drag myself to work. I'm still very much motivated by my yearning to bring Keith down, yet every day at work feels like precisely that— another day at work. I know my presence is serving a purpose—at least, I think it is—but I'm wondering if it's possible to just buy my revenge.

Apparently I can afford it.

I've been working closely with our nexus consultant, and with his considerable help, we're finally making some progress in moving IntelliQ towards public consumption. The programs are actually on the test partitions now, where the nexus can scan for memory leaks. This is a far cry from our endgame, though. Assuming we bridge this phase, there still remains the formidable task of installing and securing the library on our nexus portal. I'm happy to defer to our consultant for this, and I have every reason to believe he'll pull through. IDS is truly at his mercy, because if by chance he fails, I'm not gonna be much help.

If we weren't so close to making this all come together, there's a chance I'd drop everything. I hate to think that I'd selfishly leave Tim in that sort of a bind, but I suspect I'd find a way to minimize the guilt. Maybe I'd buy him a set of dragon-wing placemats to complement his dining room decor.

"Hey, Wil—I mean Wilson," Tim says, "don't want to freak you out or anything, but I just found something I thought you should know about."

"Jeez, what now?"

"It's Mitzy."

My breath catches in my throat. "Oh, scrap. Did they find her?"

"What? Did who find—wait; wrong Mitzy. I'm talking about the other one. Miss Victoria's Secret?"

"If you're going to tell me she's dead, it's okay. I already know."

Tim gives me a blank expression. "Dead? What are you talking about?"

"Gunn's people got her. On the day I fled the planet—I saw her dead on the sidewalk."

"Well, that's pretty bizarre, considering she left you a contact request four days ago."

I've taken a recent liking to watching the news. I used to despise learning about the depressing state of the world; these days I devour current events like candy. I suppose, if I'm being completely honest, I'm more than a little hopeful I'll learn something about Fiona; after all, if Grogan was to be believed, her research is supposed to be the stuff of legends here on Earth.

But I never hear anything.

I've been home for more than a month now, and I figured I'd be back to normal by now—and for the most part, I am. Yet as I sit before one of my Viseon walls this Saturday morning, sipping coffee and thinking that life has finally taken on a sweet hue, something threatens to rip it all to shreds.

It's a text ticker, crawling almost unnoticed across the bottom of the screen. A woman on the screen is talking about the local reception of a recent tax proposal—I'm sure you can imagine how that story's flavored—and I'm so busy enjoying the sweet deliciousness of my coffee that I nearly miss it.

"Two youths found dead in public restroom outside Houston. Cause of death attributed to germination of unknown seeds within victims' digestive tracts, which later ruptured."

Oh, no.

Moments later, Tim's unshaven face has replaced the news broadcast on my wall. To his annoyance, I've called him to put his researching abilities to work on his official day of rest. He returns the favor by taking his sweet time to oblige me, poking away at his keyboards and subjecting me to some New Age gothic scrap in the background that makes me want to claw my ears out as the minutes tick by.

It's not that I blame him for minimizing the significance of this situation; I've done my best to describe the horrors of the blood plants, but until you've experienced them for yourself—until you've personally witnessed the death and flowerpotting of a human being—it's pretty hard to wrap your mind around.

"Not much more out here than what was already reported."

"Anything about the victims themselves?"

"Like what? What're you looking for?"

If I'm on the right track here, I believe Fiona's little experiment slipped past Miritech's dismantling and into the illicit drug scene. "Did they fit the profile of a drug user, or what?"

"Can't tell from this. You know how it goes; no one wants to be the mudslinger in this type of thing. The story is the deaths, not the victims themselves."

I don't disagree completely, but I imagine the families of the victims would have a very different perspective on this. One thing I know for certain?

I've got to do something.

Thirty-Seven

I've talked myself out of it twice now, but as they say, third time's the charm. When I step into the police station—for the second time in my life—it's as if no time has passed at all since Stewart was killed. The memory of his murder is abruptly fresh on my senses and I find myself tearing up before I can prepare myself to bear the burden. And my frayed nerves aren't exactly helping. The last time I sat in a room with Rackley, he set on me like a bloodhound. Drawing his attention again—intentionally, no less—might prove to be my dumbest move yet.

I half-expect—or perhaps just hope—for Inspector Rackley to be out of the office—after all, it's hard to inspect crimes from a cubicle—but he's in and agrees without hesitation to see me. I've changed physically over the course of the last month; my morning workouts, along with a newfound appreciation for earthly portion sizes, have transformed my body into something that I'm somewhat proud of. Everyone seems to have buffed up these days, but just as that sports store lady warned, the indiscriminate increase in muscle mass looks pretty odd, and the add-on's conflict with the night-burner has already diminished its popularity. I haven't yet reached a state that's noticeable to the opposite sex, but those people who have known me long enough to have some frame of reference are slack-jawed every time they see me lately.

Rackley's no exception.

This time, there's no question that he recognizes me—unless I'm misinterpreting his speechless moment of doe-eyed awkwardness. I explain to the inspector why I'm here and his shock only intensifies. I can't tell if he's disturbed by the frightfulness of my claims, or if he's merely blown away that I'd expect him to find them credible. Bear in mind that of all the inspectors in this great city, I have the least amount of credibility with Rackley. Not only was I once listed chiefly among suspects in his little black book, I spent a fair amount of time being uncooperative back then, rather than making an effort to set his mind at ease.

When I've finished my narrative, which sounds startlingly fictional to my ear—and downright disingenuous, for my occasional nervous stammering—Rackley tosses his pen onto his desk and stares at me like I have a third eye.

"Mr. Abby," he says with a sigh, "you seem to be smack dab in the middle of every nightmare coming across my desk lately." I resist the urge to point out that the happenings of Houston are surely not landing on his desk, but his point is well taken. I smile crookedly with a shrug.

What can you do?

I leave with no real understanding of Rackley's intentions. I've just given him notice that a travesty of unprecedented proportion and oddity might well scourge the planet of human life, yet even I recognize the distinct ring of implausibility in my claim. The truth is that I'm not capable of doing justice to the extraordinary potential for disaster; I'm at the mercy of Rackley's intuition here, and that scares me. It isn't that I don't trust his abilities—though neither do I have any faith in them, considering I know next to nothing about the man—it's that I don't trust his willingness to overlook his warped—and perfectly justified—perception of me to see the truth.

As I'm heading home, I pass a bar and my step falters. It's a dirty hole-in-the-wall, the same I once made Adrian's acquaintance in. I have no desire to repeat my business there—the booze was nasty and the company was decidedly deadly—yet, as did Rackley, this place takes me back to before I left this planet and returned as a husk. I catch my distorted reflection in the filthy window and I'm reminded that things aren't all bad—I look and feel better, and I'm sitting on more credits than I'm capable of burning through without concentrated effort—but life remains a lonely affair for me. It's a depressing part of my psychological makeup, that I crave the affection of a woman so acutely.

Still, I've had a lifetime to accept it. Somewhere along the line, I think I became numb to its implications regarding the larger picture of who I am. I feel like that has changed—like I have changed. Since the other night, I've been thinking about Mitzy almost nonstop. I'm so sick of being yanked along by the leash of my libido. I've gotta learn how to be okay on my own. Scrap that—I'm already okay on my own. I've spent most of my life alone, and I'm doing just fine. I've just gotta remember that when it matters.

Nevertheless, I don't care how bummed I feel—I'm not stepping foot in that skunk hole again.

I awake to an irritating trill; I'd cover my ears to wait it out, if not for a nagging sense of unease that has consistently deprived me of a decent night's sleep since returning to Earth. I'm betting on Tim, or maybe even Rackley, but I'm absolutely unprepared for the face that lights up my wall. Literally, I mean: I'm wearing boxers, and my hair looks like I spent an hour with my head out the window in a hurricane.

"Oh my God," Mitzy says with a breathless giggle. "I didn't expect you to answer. I just figured it was worth a try."

My mouth is dry and agape. "Is it really you?" is all I can think to say. She's so alive, so beautiful.

"Yeah, it's me."

I don't even know where to start here, so I just stare at my screen and breathe.

"Look, I'm sorry," she says, her smile dimming to a prim line with every second. "This was a mistake; I should've taken the hint before. I just—I just wanted to see for myself that you're okay."

"Wait, no. I'm, uh, I'm—fine. You're—you look so good."

"I do?" She does. She really does. Yet I'm aware, as perhaps I have always been, that her beauty follows a completely new and unexplored tract of physicality for me. There's a wholesomeness about her, a sweetness that digs through lust and into the soul, where my loneliness has always stemmed. I'm very aware, drinking in her image, that this is a woman who can build me up or tear me down on a level that causes me to shudder.

"Yeah, look at you."

"Not so bad yourself," she says. "I like the outfit."

I'm suddenly very conscious of my scant attire. "What, this old thing?" I can feel myself blushing—and I don't mean just my face.

"So how have you been?"

"Good. Well, actually—you know what? I'm feeling a little bit, uh, naked. Why don't we have lunch and catch up?" I feel stupid as soon as I say this last part—I mean, what exactly is there to catch up on, considering our conversation this morning amounts to nearly half our total history?

"Little early for lunch, isn't it?"

"Well, it'll take some time to get there, you know."

"You mean, you'd just jump on a plane and come all the way out here just to have lunch with me?"

I realize as I ponder her question that that's the least of what I'd do for her, and I don't even know her yet. I recognize just how ridiculous, how unhealthy my willingness is, but I'm in the habit of overlooking such details, and now is no exception.

"Wow, that's really—"

"Creepy? Yeah, I guess it kind of is."

"I was going to say romantic."

"Really?"

Mitzy grins wistfully, pushing a lock of loose bangs behind her ear. "Yeah. But I'm thinking I'll just save you the plane ticket and come to you."

"Here? Oh, uh—"

"How about nine o'clock?"

Nine o'clock? It's eight now. "Uh, do you mean tonight?"

"Are you really this lowQ?"

Boy, I wish I could say I wasn't. "Absolutely."

"See you at nine for breakfast. Clothing required."

Thirty-Eight

At ten 'til nine, my doorbell chimes. Until just now, I've completely forgotten I even have a doorbell. Pretty much everyone I know just knocks. I open the door with an elated snap, butterflies fluttering throughout my body with anticipation.

"Morning, Mr. Abby."

Sigh.

"Inspector Rackley. You have a knack for catching me on my way out."

"We all have our gifts. I just need a moment."

I usher him in, though I'd just as soon toss him off the balcony right now. Inside, I lean against the wall and wait for an explanation. I don't offer Rackley a seat, and he doesn't ask for one.

"So?"

"You watched the news yet this morning?"

"Nope."

He nods and chews his lip.

"Should we reconvene after I do, or are you going to save me the trouble?"

"There's been another incident."

"As in ... ?"

"Your blood plant; four more victims, this time in Dallas."

"Jeez."

"That's not the worst of it."

"What do you mean?"

"I contacted the CDC; they're reporting innumerable incidents of nonlethal contact with the plant."

"Nonlethal contact?"

"It's already establishing an invasive presence in the Midwest, popping up in places where no plant should be able to survive. It seems to grow at an alarming rate, too, and it's got a lot of people on high alert."

"Listen, Inspector, I wish there was something else I could do. But the truth is—"

"Yes?"

"Well, if past experience counts for anything here, it's too late."

Rackley crosses his arms. "What do you mean?"

Before I can answer, Mitzy knocks on my door, and for the briefest of moments, I forget that our world is quite probably coming to an end.

I send a somewhat miffed inspector on his way and escort Mitzy to Enrique's for breakfast. They have the best chorizo omelets—if you're into that sort of thing; turns out, Mitzy's not. She settles for some sort of crepes, which look a little gross to me, but she seems to enjoy. I'm ecstatic to be in her presence, her living, breathing body inches from mine—but beneath the hum of excitement is the gnawing of fear.

"What's wrong with your daygrid? It's always blank."

My cheeks flush. "I'm just that pathetic, I guess. So, what brings you to Chicago?"

"You have to ask?"

"Well, I don't *have* to, but I have to."

"Okay, if you must know, I moved here a while back."

"Really?"

"Yeah, my roommate was killed and I just couldn't stay in Vegas anymore." Her eyes are glassing over.

For a moment, I'm tempted to let this pass; after all, what good can come of her knowing the truth? But as I look into her sweet eyes, I know that—although I never want to contribute to her pain—I'd rather cut her now than destroy her later. We finish our breakfast and return to my condo, holding hands like old lovers. My hand is trembling, and so is hers. I tell myself I'm just freaked out by what I have to tell her, but the truth is that my body is a raging mess of charges. Without my NanoPrint to regulate my chemical processes, I'm left to the underdeveloped power of my will to keep from running.

We sit on my couch, and before I can resolve to speak, she kisses me. It's a long, sweet, passionate kiss that's so visceral and real that I feel as though I'm flying away into a land that is Mitzy and nothing else. When she breaks away, there are tears gathered at the corners of my eyes. Not the sort of reaction women are looking for following such an event, I gather from her reaction.

"Listen, Mitzy. There's something I need to tell you." I squeeze her hand, because I know well that she'll pull it away the moment she has an inkling of the truth.

She looks into my eyes, and seeing the intensity therein, her already drooping face falls a little more. She gives my hand a squeeze, and it seems to say, *Don't, Wilson. Whatever you're gonna do, just don't.*

Even now, knowing full well that I'm safe from Palmer Gunn, I'm afraid to speak of the past—so many people have died because of my loose lips. Yet I can't allow myself to walk away from this—especially not now, with so much death looming on my doorstep. If I'm to be the man I aspire to be, I have to come clean. I have to do it, and my future with this lovely creature cannot be a consideration in that decision.

So I close my eyes and, taking a breath so deep that it hurts, I begin.

It's after one in the morning, and I'm not sleeping. I'm lying here, doing my best to believe that life has meaning—that tomorrow has even the slightest chance of being better. But I'm no better at lying to myself than to anyone else. I'm not buying what I'm selling.

I expected Mitzy to be horrified by what I had to tell her—by me, and the senseless misery that my existence has inadvertently dragged into her life—and for once, I was right. The tears come now, and as each worms past my temples and tickles at my ears, I feel exhaustion gently push me into the consoling embrace of the darkness. As it turns out, there's no sleep aid quite as powerful as grief. I sleep for the better part of the next twenty hours.

I'm being punished, I decide, though for what exactly is a question I can't seem to resolve. I've always felt I was a good person at my core, so why all this? It's a cruel thing for Mitzy to step in and out of my life with such brutal efficiency. But even if I don't feel deserving of my fate, I know it's a powerfully toxic force, and I don't mean just in terms of the drama it has cast over Mitzy's life. I get this strange sense, deep in my heart—where logic and culpability carry no weight—that I simply don't deserve her. Maybe not because I'm particularly bad, but because I'm simply not good enough. It's something I struggle to wrap my mind around, because it transcends the intellectual properties I rely on to make sense of the world.

Incidentally, I never felt this way about Adrian. Don't get me wrong: I often felt that she didn't make any sense in my life, as though we were an obtuse mismatch that favored me immeasurably, but I never felt that she was a better person, and therefore more deserving of happiness than me.

I leave a contact request with Tim, who's doubtlessly immersed in a nexus game against some kid in Japan or something. I ask him to give me a holler without expressing a reason, because I don't really have one. I feel as though my heart has been gouged, not in a deathly blow that will kill me quickly, but more like a sickly puncture that will bleed me out slowly.

With little else to do, I spend the rest of the day working on my secret program.

It's not a terribly complicated program, but it contains more straight code than I've written in a long time. I'm used to tapping IDS's immense corporate library of code classes—as in families of program functions rather than the instructional venues you might be thinking of—and in doing so, I'm spared the nuisance of reinventing the wheel throughout my projects. The problem with that approach to this program is that accessing those resources will leave an imprint in IDS's system, registering the codebank to a project that isn't supposed to exist. For Tim and me to circumvent the logs, I don't have to just reinvent the wheel, but also the axles, and even the roads.

Fortunately, the pitiful state of my social life leaves plenty of time to work it all out. I just hope that in the end, we reap some fruit for all my efforts. The plan is to create an irresistible trap. My little program will carve out a new asset repository in our accounting system and hopefully entice Keith into making a grab for it. There's a lot of opportunity for error—not only in the program, but with our lone participant, who must do her—I mean, his—unwitting part precisely.

Mrs. Grace stops by at seven thirty and invites me over for dinner. I decline without an excuse. She gives me a sweet hug that shows me she's a very perceptive woman. She reminds me of my Aunt Gertrude.

I sit on my patio and sip tea, lonely and afraid—no longer only for myself, but for the world. For Mitzy, and Mrs. Grace. For Tim. And Misty Edwards, wherever she is these days.

Thirty-Nine

In the movies, the faceless government comes for you in the middle of the night. In real life—at least in my own case—they come in the middle of breakfast. And they don't bother knocking.

Before I can begin to react, I'm whisked from my condo and into a private tram, accompanied by three men who can only be described as nondescript and cold-blooded. They don't speak a word, though one allows me a brief glance at his badge. He looks at me with great suspicion, and I realize that his credentials are probably readily available to my NanoPrint, which I must access manually.

I'm driven to an unfamiliar part of downtown and into a parking garage. From there, I'm hustled through darkened hallways and stairwells without explanation. On a seemingly empty floor, my captors finally come to a halt. They deposit me in a small room that could easily be mistaken for a storage room but for the keyless entry scanner on the door and a large, worn table within. I'm left for an hour or more without a word, though I hear the occasional muffled voice outside the door.

I'm lost in thought when the door finally swings open. The man who enters is a stranger to me, yet I recognize his kind of boldness and charisma, having seen it similarly at work in Palmer

Gunn.

"Mr. Abby," he says blandly. "I appreciate your time this morning."

Though he's done nothing yet to cause me alarm, I sense that this is a man I should be hesitant to upset. But I'm compelled to test the waters.

"No need for thanks; I wasn't given much of a choice."

No smile, no frown.

"I'm Special Agent Eugene Dryers of the Chicago field office of the Federal Bureau of Investigations. In a moment, we'll be joined by Dr. Roger Tisdale of the CDC. He's come a fair distance to speak with you, on the recommendation of a local inspector. I would appreciate your full cooperation."

"I'm not sure what help I can be, but I'll give it a shot."

Dryers nods curtly and promptly departs. Five minutes pass, and then he returns with a companion and a few folding chairs.

"Dr. Tisdale, Mr. Abby." I unconsciously rise at the introduction. A moment later, we're all seated with the scarred table between us.

And the interrogation begins.

I withhold little, though I make every effort to veil the status of my NanoPrint. When it's all over, Dr. Tisdale is escorted from the room. Dryers remains behind, deadpan eyes locked on mine like magnets. I have nothing to hide—not really, anyway—yet the silence in here is disarming, and the urge to fill it with something is all but overwhelming. But I'm not a complete idiot. I hold my tongue.

A full five minutes of wordless silence passes, at the end of which Dryers rises from his seat and leaves me alone, yet again. I smile inwardly that I've withstood round one. A half hour later, when my stomach is beginning to rumble, Dryers returns with a soft drink and a sandwich and hovers in the farthest corner of the room as I eat. The moment I've finished, the door opens and we're joined by a new face.

I very nearly fall from my chair as she steps inside, appraising me with the unimpressed disinterest of a complete stranger.

"Wilson," she says with an empty smile.

"Well, if it isn't the brilliant Fiona."

"I prefer Dr. Grogan, thank you."

No point asking if her snooty title gets her special treatment in prison; obviously, she's managed to dodge that bullet. "So who'd she roll over to save herself?" I ask Dryers.

"Dr. Grogan is here to discuss matters regarding the blood plants. No questions outside that scope—personal or professional—will be answered."

"Naturally," I say with a wry smirk.

Fiona sits across from me and clasps her hands in her lap. It's funny: despite our history—the countless hours cramped in close quarters together—I feel that I'm seeing her for the very first time. She looks almost exactly the same—all the features align with what I remember—but somehow, her beauty has worn away.

"Since you returned to Earth, have you been contacted at any time by Kurt Grogan?"

"No."

"Have you seen or heard anything that might indicate his whereabouts?"

"Fiona, are you a doctor or a detective? These questions have nothing to do with the blood plants."

"Just answer the question, Mr. Abby," commands Dryers.

"Fine. No. I haven't seen Grogan since he apparently fled for his life." Glaring at Fiona, I add, "What happened, did he turn out to be a *liability* after all? You did this, Fiona—all of it."

Dryers levels a gaze on me that could peel paint off metal, but Fiona's jaws clench, and I know I've scored a point. "That's enough, Mr. Abby. Just answer the questions asked, and that's all."

Fiona clears her throat and purges her face of all emotion again. "Have you personally witnessed the effects caused by the ingestion of a blood plant seed?"

"Yes," I cede with a frown. Until now, I haven't considered what I could possibly contribute on the subject of the blood plants—particularly with Fiona in the picture, considering she's the foremost expert. Then the questions become more open-ended, and I'm gradually filled with horror by their implications.

"Please describe your observations."

"Well, first the guy seemed to be hallucinating—pleasantly so, actually." I level my gaze on Fiona. "But you already know all about that, don't you, Dr. Grogan?"

"Mr. Abby, please."

"Fine. When the high passed, he had a stomachache. Diarrhea. Probably some cramps, too, though I can't know for sure. He did a lot of grunting in the bathroom."

"What else?"

"That's about it. Except for the obvious: a plant grew out of his mouth and his rectum."

The room is silent, and I know they're visualizing what I've spent many hours trying to forget.

"What kind of plant?" Fiona asks softly.

"What are we talking about here, guys? A blood plant."

"Please describe the blood plant."

"What is this, Fiona? You know what the blood plants look like! You created them, for crying out loud."

"Please, Wilson. Just answer the question," Fiona says. "What did it look like?" Her eyes are hard, but I see something uncharacteristically vulnerable—perhaps even desperate—hiding in the creases at their corners.

Something clicks, and I finally understand.

"It was red, Fiona," I say in a measured whisper. "A female. Do you realize what you've done?"

She rises to leave, cheeks dappled with chagrin, and Dryers follows her lead. Just as they reach the door, Fiona turns to me and says, "One more question, Wilson. Did you have any seeds on your person when you returned to this planet?"

"You mean when I was kidnapped, dragged here, and then beaten nearly to death a few feet away from you? No, I didn't have any seeds."

When they leave, I feel a sense of satisfaction for having gotten in the last word. But as I'm escorted from the room, down a long hallway, and into a small infirmary filled with medical instruments and a foreboding gurney-style table, I realize I've still managed to come up short.

I may have gotten the last word, but the government always gets the last laugh.

On the way home, I nearly vomit from overstimulus. Under the skin of my wrist, my NanoPrint hums away, prickling at my heightened senses with overwhelming determination. My government escorts more than half-carry me into my condo, and if not for them I'd have surely collapsed on the sidewalk. Once home, they shoulder me roughly onto my couch and then leave me to suffer, slamming my door on their way out.

It takes several minutes of painful, concentrated effort to discern what's wrong. My NanoPrint has been reset to the factory default so that all processes—of which there are thousands—are allowed to pester me at once. Slowly but surely, one at a time, I disable feeds and unfamiliar add-ons until I can finally begin to think straight. At some point, my brain gives up and puts me out for a while.

When I regain consciousness, I give Tim a call. Before I even open my mouth to speak, he says, "Oh, no." I must really look terrible. "I'll be right over."

Waiting in dull misery, I enable my nexus assistant, thinking maybe Marilyn can help get my settings back in order. But it isn't the lovely Marilyn who heeds my beck and call. It's Astrid Electronica, my NanoPrint's default nexus assistant.

Oh, no.

Astrid is kind of hot—in a weird, over-pierced, Hollywood kind of way—and you would think she has to be pretty cool to get the default slot, right?

Yeah, not so much. I gave her a shot years ago, and I'm not sure that I'll ever really recover. For example: once, she asked how I was doing—which seemed nice enough on the surface—so I replied that everything was white as rain. This was her idea of gentle, constructive criticism:

>>*What, you got a broken helix or something? It's* right *as rain! No wonder you're single, crank dummy.*

Not only is she a mean-hearted bully, I'm still more than half-convinced she's glitched. I mean, what's right about rain? It's not a right or left kind of thing. But it *can* be white. Right?

Sigh. What can you do?

Taking a deep breath, I rip off the proverbial band-aid: *Astrid, oh queen of the digital world, will you please configure my implant defaults?*

>>*Oh, sure, Wilson.* She slides into view and beams me a winning smile.

I blink. *Wow.* Did old Astrid get updated, or maybe replaced with—

The smile abruptly winks out, and she begins to bow sarcastically.

>>*Your wish is my command, oh wise master. What, like I'm some kind of freaking genie? Like it's my job to do your stupid busywork? You're such a lazy misfire.*

Ah, it's like she never left. Good times. *Fine, Astrid. I think I'll just disable you, then.*

>>*Yeah, right. You wouldn't know how, Mr. White-as-rain. You're too stupid to—*

_open NanoPrint admin
_config nexus attributes
_modify globals

... Modifying nexus globals is highly discouraged. Erroneous configuration may result in unpleasantness such as poor connectivity or physical death. Are you sure you want to proceed?

_confirm;

>>Whoa, there, boy toy—wait a second, would you? Let's just settle down.

_open global preferences

_disable NanoPrint digital assistant

>>Did I mention you're a crank loser? Astrid growls.

"You did," I say aloud.

_apply settings

... Configuration saved.

_exit

Astrid sticks out her tongue, flips me the bird with both hands, and storms off my retinas in a barrage of profanity.

Classy, I know. Seriously, does NanoPrint hate consumers or something? Please tell me I don't live in a world where people actually enjoy being treated like that.

I spend the next half hour configuring defaults on my implant, starting with my nexus assistant. There are a ton of new add-ons, but I ignore them for now; Marilyn can take care of those later. For now, my brain needs a hammock and a cool breeze. I lie back on my couch and close my eyes.

>>Oh my goodness, Wilson ... you look so tense. Would you like me to sing you to sleep?

Marilyn, as if you even have to ask. Oh, how I've missed you.

Alas, just as I begin to nod off, Tim is at my door. Immediately, I start to recount my experience with Fiona—because what could be more newsworthy than that?—but he cuts me off and turns on the actual news. "Wait, wait. You gotta see this, Wilson."

It's on virtually every channel, filling my entire wall with footage of a giant blood plant heavily laden with seedpods.

"—in the Dallas metro area. Reports of similar plants are

coming in from all over the continent, Richard, and the concern is that this plant isn't only invasive, it's deadly. As of this moment, seven deaths have been directly linked to the ingestion of seeds from this plant. Local authorities in Chicago are already discussing possible defensive measures, should these dangerous plants make an appearance—"

"Oh, scrap. We're so screwed," I moan.

"Is this as bad as it looks?"

"Worse, Tim. Those things are more aggressive than you can imagine."

Tim's face falls, but he's holding fast to a tiny thread of hope. "Yeah, but it's still early, right? Maybe there's still a chance we can wipe them out before they get fully established."

"No, Tim. You're not getting it. That plant?" I nod to the Viseon wall, where an aerial view of a large specimen has burst through the roof of an apartment building, as if climbing toward the sky. The visible portion is easily forty feet tall. Even from a distance, the seedpods are clearly distinguishable. "Every one of those seedpods contains thousands of seeds. And they're capable of germinating just about anywhere. If even one of those pods ruptures, that entire city block will look like that apartment building in just a few days."

"Surely it won't be allowed to get that far along? They'll probably torch the building or something, don't you think?"

"Maybe. But as long as a seed—or even just a leaf—survives, it'll just grow back. Either way, it's too late. If we're seeing this one, you can bet there are more out there that haven't been discovered yet."

"*—sources at the FBI and CDC have independently corroborated speculation that these plants may have been engineered and then accidentally released during the production of an innocent pharmaceutical product—*" Hah! Innocent, my butt. "*—Little is known at this point about the—*"

I power off the Viseon wall and collapse in a heap onto the

couch.

The silence afterward is heavy with dread. To lighten the mood—and because I feel that I've patiently waited my turn—I spend the next ten minutes recounting every detail of my abduction and subsequent release for Tim's wide-eyed amusement and awe. When I'm finished, I sport my newly stitched wrist as evidence.

He whistles. "That kind of sucks. At least you get Astrid Electronica back though, right?"

I can't help but groan.

Tim looks at me blankly. "What's wrong with Astrid? She's awesome."

There are simply no words, so I wave off the subject and mumble, "Forget it."

For a moment, Tim looks ready to push it—because the sweet Astrid is so worthy of defending, I guess?—but his face abruptly slips into dismay.

"Aw, scrap," he moans. "You know what this means, don't you?"

I do not. "Other than an end to the peace and quiet I've come to know and love?"

"It means that we just lost our edge, man; everything we've been working toward to get Keith is about to be derailed."

"Um, what do you mean?"

"Think about it, Wilson. Everything you do is gonna be on the record now. All your programs are going to automatically log—even if you don't tap the codebank—and if Keith bothers to check up on you—which you know he'll do—he's gonna get very suspicious, very quickly."

He's right. So great is my frustration that I find I can only nod. Speaking of Keith, he's been very busy spinning more deception since I rejoined IDS. First, he assigned me an accounting code—which I have no business possessing—and began using my code to sign off on minor company transactions around the office—receivables and supply orders, for example. My guess is that he's trying to breadcrumb a verifiable history of my involvement with corporate accounting, thereby establishing my reasonable access to the documents and procedures generated by our GFL transactions. I must say, Keith's being much more careful now than before. Clearly, in my absence over the past year, he's had plenty of time to dwell on how he'd do things differently if given a second chance.

Seeing my name tied to things I've had nothing to do with makes me sick to my stomach. My window of opportunity is closing rapidly. I'm stricken with urgency to vindicate myself, to somehow outsmart the deathtrap I so willingly stepped into. I just wish I knew how.

"What am I supposed to do now?"

"You know, there is one thing you can do," Tim says with a smirk. "But you're not gonna like it."

Forty

I leave a contact request for Mitzy, knowing full well that she won't respond. I have to do something. It isn't just about me, either. My loneliness takes a backseat to panic, considering the impending blood plant pandemic, and—

>>*Oh, silly Wilson ... you're so cute when you exaggerate. Did you mean to say 'impending blood plant* epidemic*'?*

Sheesh, even Marilyn is overconfident.

The point is that I'm desperately driven to warn Mitzy—even when logic says that warnings are completely useless now. Honestly, what would I say, anyway?

"Sorry I ruined your life, but you should really avoid purple- and red-hued vegetables. Oh, and you might want to cut any kind of seed from your diet altogether."

I invited Mrs. Grace over for coffee and cake, and she'll be here any time. I'm not merely stretching my social wings here—and no, I'm not suddenly a baker; I had the cake delivered. I may not be able to warn Mitzy, but I have an opportunity to do so for Mrs. Grace and I mean to take it.

Mrs. Grace is gushing over my physical recovery, and I have to admit that the praise feels good. It's weird—the more in shape I get, the more powerful I feel. I know I'm only a man, yet I sense something much larger building in my depths, growing stronger and preparing to someday rip its way to the surface. Until that day, I'm content to catch an occasional glimpse of myself in a passing mirror and see for myself that I've indeed left behind the skin and bones that was my former self.

We eat cake and sip coffee, and I do the best I can to broach the subject on my mind with tact and decorum—because Mrs. Grace demands nothing less. She's seen the newscasts, just as most of us have. No, she's not worried. Dallas is a long ways away. Her composure feels brittle, though, as if a little calculated pressure might cause it to collapse altogether—and that's not at all what I want. Yet, how can I communicate the horror I know to be true without destroying the peace upon which Mrs. Grace seems to be precariously balanced?

In the end, I realize with sadness that, for all the mounting power of my physique, I'm completely helpless. In fact, the only real power I possess in this matter is to spare Mrs. Grace the gory details of this nightmare. Because if there truly is nothing any of us can do, every day she remains swathed in blissful ignorance is a precious gift.

IntelliQ has advanced to a new stage of testing on our nexus portal. If things continue at this pace, we'll be in business within the month. Company morale is higher than it has been in a long while.

I'm immune.

Among other things, I've been busy stressing about IDS and what to do about Keith. Even with everything else going on, I feel a constant anxiety chewing away at my resolve. I don't know how much longer I'll be able to keep this up.

The secret program I've been toiling with for weeks now—just as Tim predicted—has proven to be completely useless now that my NanoPrint is back in play. My implant doesn't necessarily expose my actual programming, but it logs my time investment automatically, and Keith is already showing signs of unease. There's no doubt he's keeping tabs. If he's highQ—and deep down, I have to acknowledge that he wouldn't have gotten where he is today on stupidity—he won't need to understand exactly what I've got in the works to see a red flag waving.

Man, I hate this. I feel a noose closing around my neck, and as much as I desperately need to breathe, I remain convinced that if I don't find a way to bring Keith to justice, no one ever will. I've got to take him down or die trying.

I could call Inspector Rackley, I know. Actually, I've considered it more than a few times, and all things considered, I think he'd believe me. But the kind of proof he'd need to secure a conviction simply doesn't exist, except in a form that incriminates me. Besides, the moment Rackley starts poking around, Keith will lock things down. If Grogan was here, he'd probably slip Keith a blood plant seed and call it a day.

Me? I'm just not that blasphemous.

What I really need is incontrovertible evidence of what's going on—anything less will only doom me.

In the back of my mind, Tim's words whisper and I'm unable to shush them. *You know, there is one thing you can do. But you're not gonna like it.* Chock it up to old-fashioned greed, but I'm not ready to put my own money on the line as bait. I may not have earned eleven million credits, but I'm having a hard time imagining a future without them. Besides, let's assume everything goes as planned: Keith makes a grab for the money and lands behind bars, where he'll spend the rest of his life lamenting his long-lost Maybelline.

What's to become of those eleven million credits?

Well, they'll disappear into some evidentiary slush account with nary a peep. Eventually they'll find their way into some politician's greedy pockets.

So the question is, is it worth it? The answer should be

obvious. Of course it's worth it!

But, still.

I'm leaving Mitzy another contact request—I know, I'm probably breaking all kinds of unspoken laws of romance, and perhaps even a harassment law for good measure—but my need to protect her has become swollen beyond my grasp on common sense.

When she answers and my Viseon wall flickers to an image of her face, I hiccup in midbreath and manage only to stare mutely at the screen.

"Wilson, you have to stop this," she says. Her eyes are pained and intense; she's dressed, but it looks as though she was interrupted while doing her makeup. She looks beautiful to me—even the unpainted half of her face.

I want to tell her how sorry I am, how truly miserable I feel for causing her pain. I want to tell her that my life has been a flavorless gruel but for the few moments I spent with her. Yet if my motives are pure—and I believe they are—I can't squander this opportunity.

"I know, Mitzy. I just need a second, okay? Then I'll be out of your life forever." Then because for all my talk of pure motives, at heart I'm still a lonely man, I add, "If that's what you want, I mean."

She rubs her temples with her fingers—never the effect I hope for with women, but one I apparently bring out in them—and sighs.

"Wilson, please."

"Just listen for a second, okay? Do you remember what I told you about Mars? The plants, I mean."

"Yes."

"Have you been watching the news lately?"

A pause. "You mean ..."

"Afraid so."

"How bad is it?"

"It's bad, Mitzy."

She leans forward a little, eyes glassy with worry. "Define *bad*, please."

"End of the world bad."

Another pause.

"I'm sorry, I just don't even know how to sugarcoat it."

Mitzy swallows, and I see my fear mirrored in her face. "Is there anything we can do? To protect ourselves, I mean?"

I want to sow a little hope here, to give Mitzy a reason to chin-up, if not to trust me. But I know how cheap and transparent my platitudes will sound, and if these are to be my last words with her, I want them to be the truth. However ugly the truth may be.

"No. I'm sorry."

She nods with bland detachment, and then begins to sniffle. "I have to go to work," she says. "Don't call me again, okay, Wilson?"

Tears spring into my eyes, but I nod my agreement. "Okay. Take care, Mitzy."

"I will."

"And Mitzy?" I croak. Her eyes are wet, but they abruptly harden.

"What?"

"I—I'm just so sorry. For everything. I never meant to hurt you."

She swallows and clears her throat. "I know," she says. "But it doesn't matter."

My screen darkens, revealing my grief-stricken face in its reflection.

Forty-One

When I finally crawl out of bed, the sadness of my dreams—of memories I thought to be buried and forgotten—cling to me. Even from the foot of my bed, I feel that the world has changed. My deadened sense of smell seems to have infected my surroundings. It's as if the shine of life on planet Earth has faded into gray.

I guess that's just what sadness does to me.

I'm like the walking dead all the way to work. I offer and return no greetings, not out of rudeness, but out of a near-physical inability to participate in the banal rituals of life. As I shuffle into my office, my light flicks on. My desk is clean, the carpet vacuumed for once. I realize I've glossed through my routine and forgotten my coffee. I don't really care. I don't really care about anything, to be honest. If the police marched in here right now and arrested me for Keith's sins, I doubt I'd say a word in defense.

I'm sick, I think. Lovesick.

Tim peeks in on me; he notices my state, but chooses to ignore it. "Wilson, you gotta start checking your updates," he complains.

I look at him through corpse eyes and offer a shrug so uncommitted that it's only just discernible.

"Jeez, Wilson." He stomps past my desk and taps my Viseon wall—possibly the first time it's been used in many years. I don't even turn around to see, but I don't need to. The audio is enough to freeze my blood.

"—*first appearance of the so-called* blood plant *in the state of Illinois. This particular plant was discovered growing in the back seat of a tram,*" a woman is saying.

A man volleys: *"Have any definitive explanations been released that might explain how the plant came to be there, and perhaps how long it was there before it was discovered?"*

The woman again: *"As we speak, local law enforcement and nexus administrators are working together to make that determination. This is a fairly small plant by comparison with those we've seen reported in other states, so the assumption is that this is a relatively young specimen—"*

I'm trying very hard to care, and a part of my mind is abuzz. Yet the better part of me is in a thick funk that I can't seem to overcome. It's as if all the muscle I've worked so hard to put on is suddenly dead weight, working hard against me rather than for me.

My NanoPrint hums as a contact request downloads. I've probably got several in my queue; I haven't checked them since yesterday. To drown out the sickness of my psyche, or perhaps the sounds of my collapsing city, I begin sorting through them now.

Two from Keith: one yesterday afternoon, another just before I walked into the office this morning—I delete these without listening to them. One from Tim about an hour ago—*Wilson, I need you to get here ASAP. It's important. And bring your implant reader.*

A final one from Mitzy, just now.

My heart flip-flops so hard I could faint. But then Tim interrupts my thoughts before I can take any joy from the moment. "Keith is really getting busy, man," he warns. "We don't have much time."

I feel my blood warming again. "What'd he do?"

"When I got here this morning, a GFL pickup was already scheduled. They'll be here before lunch today. The invoice is already approved and accounting is processing it."

"Dare I guess who approved it?"

"One Wilson Abby."

This sucks, but we've been expecting it for a while now. "So what's the panic about?"

"Got a call from our nexus consultant after you left last night." His face is suddenly beyond grim.

"Uh-oh. What's the damage?"

"With everything going on with the blood plants? The nexus admins are tabling all asynchronous programs and/or add-ons relative to perishable industries. IntelliQ is double-dinged."

"What? Why in the world would they do that?"

"My guess is, they're trying to avoid a panic."

"What do you mean?"

"If a blood plant manages to infiltrate our food supply, nexus admins wanna know instantly that it's happening, and they don't want to risk the information bleeding out of their loop or lagging because discretionary processes are asynchronously eating up all the bandwidth."

"What, so they're shutting us down?"

"Pretty much."

"Jeez, that seems extreme."

Tim looks at me like I'm miswired. "Extreme? Were you not just listening to the news?"

"Of course I was. Kind of."

"Maybe you didn't hear: three people died in Illinois overnight from those freaking blood plants. One of them wasn't even a drug user; they think it was in his food. And this morning, they found one growing in a fricking tram here in Chicago."

I can put the rest together myself. The moment IntelliQ was put on hold, the future of IDS plummeted. Keith is pushing the satellite upgrades—even when he knows they're useless—because it's his last opportunity for a payday before we go under. As for me? I'm useful only as a scapegoat, so Keith is going to be falling all over himself to bury me.

Probably today.

"Please tell me you brought the implant reader."

I sigh. "Afraid not, buddy."

"Dang it."

The moment Tim steps out of my office, I call Mitzy.

"Did you hear?" she asks without preamble.

"Yes."

"What're we supposed to do, Wilson?" Her face is screwing into a mess of fear. It breaks my already broken heart to see her like this.

"I wish I knew, Mitzy. I really do."

She's crying now, and a head pops over the cubicle wall beside her.

"You okay, Mitz?" asks the disembodied head of an older woman. Mitzy turns to her and nods. "Fine, Beverly," she assures. "I'm fine." The head disappears. Mitzy turns back to me and whispers, "Sorry, there's no such thing as privacy in here."

"It's okay. Do you want me to call you later?"

"No, it's fine."

"Are you sure? I can—"

"Please don't go, Wilson. Please."

My heart lurches. "Okay, I won't."

I've avoided Keith for as long as I can. I catch him just as he returns from a long lunch. I can surmise who he had lunch with—and who picked up the check—from the giddy grin on his face. I glance toward the racks and see that Tim's watching through the window. He gives me a subtle nod.

"Wilson, just the man I was hoping to see. Let's talk."

"Sure thing, boss."

As soon as I sit down, I feel my implant begin to hum—not the brief whir I've come to associate with gathering updates, but a long, grating buzz that tells me Keith's up to something. Keith chats me up about nothing until he senses my patience is wearing thin—all things considered, I'm actually a little proud of him for picking up on this. Then, he gets down to business.

"Listen, Wilson, I guess you probably have an idea of what our future looks like at IDS, considering what's happened and all."

"You could say that."

"I want you to know that I appreciate all your hard work, everything you've done to help save this company."

My implant winds down and is finally silent. Whatever that was, it was huge.

"Did you feel anything?"

"Felt something. I don't know what, though."

Tim rubs his temples, eyes bugging in their sockets. "Man, that was the craziest thing I've ever seen. He overwrote your proximity history."

"He what? How?"

"I'm not sure how, but I know that's what he did. I've been expecting him to try something fishy today, so I've had your stats pulled up since this morning. Yesterday, for example? You left at a quarter to five, but now your stats show you were the last one here, well after six thirty."

"Wow. That's a whole new level of slimy." It's a shame I've let myself forget that Keith has access to all the same technology as me—or Tim. "I can't believe it's even possible for something like that to happen."

"Yeah, it's baffling. Thing is, whatever he just did? It's way above our capabilities here. He's getting help from someone smarter than us."

"What about your implant reader—couldn't he just have gotten one of those?"

"Nope. Law enforcement readers do just that—they read. I'm not aware of anything capable of overwriting stats via an implant. That kind of technology is highly illegal, and it isn't supposed to exist."

"Fantastic."

To my confusion—and irritation, in fact—Tim's smiling. "You aren't seeing the silver lining, my friend."

"Feel free to enlighten me. I'm about to pee myself."

"Let me start with a recommendation. You know your detective friend?"

"Who, Rackley? I wouldn't exactly call him a friend."

"Whatever. I think it's time you gave him a call. But first, you need to run home for a late lunch. And don't come back without that reader."

I'm not hungry, but I obey.

At home, I scarf down a sandwich in less than two minutes. I pack Tim's NanoPrint reader into my pocket and as I head back to the office, I'm inexplicably filled with hope. For the moment, I choose to forget the fate of the world tomorrow—because my own is on the line today.

At ten to five, the front door opens and a surly-faced man stalks past the receptionist and into Keith's office. I don't recognize him, but he has the look of a police inspector. This is it—Keith's going down right where we can all watch and applaud.

But that's not what happens. Rather, the man says something to Keith, who gestures through the door—toward me—with his chin. The man turns to look at me. His eyes are loathing and predatory—whoever he is, something tells me we aren't destined to be buddies.

He closes the gap between us with startling efficiency; his legs are long and bony like a crane, adding to his predatory image.

"Mr. Abby, a word?"

"And you are?"

He produces a badge from his pocket and suspends it in my face, much closer than necessary. "Inspector Filmore."

"All right, Inspector. How can I help you?"

He smiles with a giddy grimace cluttered with bad teeth. "You can start by putting your hands behind your back. You are under arrest."

I suppose I've feared this very string of reality all along, yet I'm more dismayed than ever that it has come to life. That's what happens when you dare to cling to hope, I guess. I'm given no opportunity to ask questions. I'm simply prodded past Keith's office—he's smiling faintly, victory proudly bleeding through his makeup—and into the parking lot.

Sulking in a police tram, cruising to the police station in handcuffs alongside this toothy man who believes me to be something I'm not, I realize that it's all over. Both life as I know it and the life I've been chasing with all my heart are approaching the end.

I'll be imprisoned.

I'll never see Mitzy again.

All the while, blood plants are going to overrun this entire planet, and I'll spend my final moments wondering what I ever did to deserve such an awful lot in life.

Part Four:
The Fall

Forty-Two

I've been in an interrogation room for more than an hour now. Though he was gushing with glee when he tossed me in here, Inspector Filmore hasn't returned to gloat. He's left me instead to the wiles of an old digital clock bolted to the painted cinderblock wall. With little else to look at, my eyes are drawn to it; not merely by the novelty of it, but by the spell of its steadfast pace. The pixellated digits glow faintly, seconds pulsing slowly from double zero to fifty-nine over and over again.

This is how they break you, I realize. With the clock. It's a psychological weapon, relentless and impossible to ignore.

There's a small window across the room, and I stumble to it with relief, leaning against the sill to peer into the bowels of the city. This part of town is dirty, and the view isn't at all flattering. I wonder how long before the buildings are completely obscured by blood plants. Weeks? Months?

The door startles me as it hinges open with an unoiled screech.

"Thought you'd save me a trip, huh?" says a smiling Rackley as he pushes into the room.

"Yeah, you know. Was in the neighborhood, and all."

"Really? My good luck, I guess."

I'm glad he's in a good mood, but I'm already weary of this

back-and-forth. "Yeah. So, here I am."

"Indeed." He looks at me as if seeing me in a new light—though I'm not sure if it's a good one or not. Abruptly, he realizes my hands are cuffed behind me and curses under his breath. He unshackles me with a practiced hand and we sit.

"So, I got your package."

"Good."

"Our techs are going over the data right now. So far, everything you've told me checks out. Can't imagine how, just yet, but your proximity statistics have clearly been altered."

I nod. "So what happens now?"

"For the moment, we sit tight. I wish I could just send you on home, but until this is fully resolved, I'm afraid my colleagues feel you're a bit of a flight risk. You know, given your ... uh, *history*."

"Ah, I see." My eyes flicker to the dreaded clock, and Rackley smiles knowingly.

"It shouldn't be long, though. Filmore may be a world-class jerk, but he's no idiot. Even he's gotta wonder why a multimillionaire would get his hands this filthy over a measly hundred thousand credits."

If I had been drinking something just then, I'd have shot it right through my nose. I try to keep my cool, but Rackley's well trained at reading people, and I know I'm wasting energy. "How'd you find out?" I want to know.

He smiles modestly and holds out his palms, as if to say, I'm a detective—how else?

"It's okay," he assures me with a warm smile. "Your secret is safe with me. Everyone has a right to his privacy. Even rich people."

My NanoPrint has been remarkably quiet in here. I've begun to wonder if the building is wired to absorb—or even jam—wireless communication. I've been alone in here for a good hour and forty-five minutes now, and I'm getting hungry. At seven thirty, Rackley returns.

"You're free to go, Mr. Abby," he announces. Though his words should fill me with joy, everything about his demeanor says that something is very wrong.

"Everything okay?" I ask. "Keith didn't fly the coop before you could nab him, did he?"

"No, no. We got him, no problem." He gives me a forced smile, and then adds, "Frankly, we've all got bigger problems at the moment."

Something tells me I don't need to ask for examples, and the look in Rackley's eyes tells me I should know better than anyone what's happening. "Sorry I can't offer you a ride home," he says with a tired frown. He hands me a plastic bag containing my belongings, and then he's gone.

Along with my gaudy watch, I'm surprised to find Tim's implant reader inside—I guess I more or less assumed it would be confiscated, considering it's not strictly legal for an unconnected civilian like myself to have one in his possession. Obviously, I assumed wrong.

That Rackley's an interesting guy.

Tim's waiting in the lobby for me. When he sees me, he cries out in joy and crushes me with a hug. His enthusiasm fills me with joy, if only for a moment. On our way out, he says, "Guess you've probably figured out what's going on, even if you haven't officially heard the news, right?"

"What's that?"

"Seriously? You haven't noticed?"

"Noticed what?"

"The nexus—it's down."

He might as well have told me the number four has been replaced by purple. "What does that mean, *down*?"

"As in, this entire city is at a complete standstill. Maybe the whole continent, for all we know."

Looking around, I realize that he's right; the streets are filled with stalled trams and helpless, wandering pedestrians. The sky is completely void of shuttles and air traffic. The sounds of industry have vanished. I try to access my implant and I'm able to without resistance, but it's operating on cached data, and most of my add-ons are idling.

"Holy circuit scrap, man."

"I know, right? What do you think caused it?" he asks. For once, I look at Tim like he's the clueless one.

"C'mon, Tim. What do you think?" His smile falters, but it doesn't entirely disappear.

"You don't mean the plants, do you?"

I rotate in place slowly, scanning the panorama for new information. "There," I say with foreboding. I point to a nearby railway bridge. "See it?" He doesn't respond, but I know he sees the blood plant, just as I do. It's radiating like a mass of giant sea stars from the underside of the overpass. My eyes hover there for several seconds and then continue on.

"And there," I add, pointing down a side street to where a manhole cover has been dislodged and is perched atop a bloody mass of leaves in the middle of the road.

"And there."

And everywhere.

It takes us two hours to walk home. Tim lives closer than me, so I drop him off along the way. Since the nexus has gone down, I've been knotted with worry over the state of my world. Why didn't I take the time to ferret out Mitzy's address? I have absolutely no way of reaching her. I can't believe I'm saying this, but I'd give anything for the nexus to be alive and kicking right now. Several times as I walk along, my implant reconnects with the nexus, but only for a second. It's like the nexus has a million shorts in its circuitry. I can imagine laborers and nexus administrators frantically darting about the city, digging up and repairing buried lines compromised by the roots of blood plants, only for new problems to take their places elsewhere.

The next couple of days are quiet, but no less disconcerting. Since I can't call Mitzy, I take to sitting on my patio where I can watch for her. I know this is ridiculous, but I don't care. Mrs. Grace sits with me often, sniffling once in a while into a wad of tissue. If she's intuited my role in this mess, she's been gracious enough to overlook it. I'm glad she's here with me.

Life is funny sometimes.

I'm barely thirty-one, a multimillionaire living in a middle-income condo, wearing the same clothes I wore before I hit it rich. The irony is that, while I've finally decided that the money is mine and can safely be enjoyed, we're on the brink of a plague so devastating that my newfound wealth is rendered moot. I literally can't spend a single credit with the nexus down, and there's no reason to believe things will turn back around any time soon.

I can almost hear Arthur's ghostly voice, as if he's whispering in my ear: *There goes the pedestal, Wilson. Can you feel it crumbling?* I'd cry if I wasn't already laughing so hard.

It's been three days since the nexus went down. The sky has taken on a pale pink sheen. Everywhere I look, blood plants are entangled in the city's bones. I awoke this morning to a resounding blast nearby. When I went outside and down to ground level, I found the sidewalk littered with seeds from a burst seedpod. Before I could return to my condo, a series of similar explosions concussed from my roof. Seeds showered me like sticky drizzle.

Frightened for my life, I stripped nude on my doorstep and left my clothes in a pile. I made a mad rush for my bathroom and pilfered my cabinets until I found a pair of electric clippers. I shaved my head and swept the clippings into the toilet. It occurred to me that I was flooding our sewers with blood plant seeds, but I figured better the sewers than my apartment.

I took a long shower, followed by a thorough swabbing of my ears. It was a stressful event from which I still haven't quite recovered, even two hours later.

I'm sitting on my couch now, trying not to cry for what is happening to my city. When I wipe my eyes and stand to get a hold of myself, I see that two blood plants have taken root on my living room floor—one immediately inside the doorway, the other a few feet farther toward the bathroom. I carefully untwine them from the carpet fibers and flush them, like my hair.

I peek out my door, and just as I expect to see, my clothes are speckled with tiny plants. I scan around me and find that everywhere I look, blood plants are sending up leaves. I use my foot to shove the pile of clothes under the railing and onto the ground below. I hear Mrs. Grace shuffling about next door, and I knock lightly on her door.

She opens it so quickly, I wonder if she's been standing there all along.

"Are you okay?" I ask, giving her arm a squeeze.

"Oh, Wilson. It's so terrible." I nod my understanding, but then, as I glance over her shoulder and into the freakish greenhouse of her living room, I realize she's not making a generalization.

"Jeez, Mrs. Grace! Come out of there!"

She sobs, but allows me to escort her to my own condo, whose walls, unlike her own, are not bristling with the advancing tendrils of death.

On day five, my heart soars. I'm on my patio with Mrs. Grace, just watching the horror unfold—don't think me morbid; there's really nothing else we can do—when a figure appears around the corner.

"Mitzy?" I cry out. She looks up and it's her—it's really her! I traipse the stairs like a dancer, so filled with joy that the creeping vineyard consuming my building might have been the set for some bizarre ballet. I receive her in an embrace so fierce she cries out. I kiss and hug her, and she laughs at my zeal.

In this moment, I don't care about death and the fall of civilization. The world doesn't exist but for this lone woman, who I have somehow fallen so deeply in love with that I can die a happy man, right here and now.

That night, just as the horizon sucks the last bit of light from the sky, we lose power to the building.

Forty-Three

We can't stay here any longer. I've called this place home for my entire adult life, excluding my brief but memorable Martian sabbatical. Funny, though: so few moments of real significance have taken place here that I'm having a hard time scraping together more than a handful of memories worth cherishing. You could argue that my time here with Adrian was significant, and you wouldn't be wrong; but considering how that turned out, I don't care to dwell on the subject. Besides that, this has been my eating and sleeping quarters, my gym, and little else. As a result, I'm lit up by an impression of coziness rather than the emotional series of snapshots one expects when leaving his long-time home. I suppose this is a little sad all on its own, yet it's also a good thing—because leaving would be a somewhat traumatic event, otherwise. And it's important that we hit the road with clear heads.

I'm not suggesting that a safe haven is awaiting us out there, or that we'll be running to anyplace in particular, only that another night here will surely claim one or more of our lives. The blood plants have infiltrated the electrical chases and plumbing of the building and when dawn finally sent light forth through my window this morning, it revealed a network of vines stretching across the ceiling in my bedroom.

This time tomorrow, my condo will resemble a crimson rain forest, and there's nothing I can do to stop it.

Outside, the skyline looks less like a cityscape than a lost ruin. There are occasional pedestrians out and about, but none seem interested in speaking with us—they're skittish and take care to keep their distance from us. It occurs to me that we should take their cue and do likewise.

With no real plan in mind, I suggest we make the trek to Tim's apartment building. It's a good five miles from here, but it's a high-rise—unlike my building—so it makes sense to me that perhaps the plants haven't completely ravaged it yet.

It's a long, laborious hike through neighborhoods that appear to be completely abandoned. A few areas seem virtually untouched by the blood plants; others can't be seen at all for the sheer lushness of the foliage. Once, while crossing an intersection, I step over a huge, swollen vine that has spanned buildings on either side of the street; my foot lands squarely on the torso of a corpse. Her face is buried under leaves and the rest of her is sapped to a dried husk; I'm able to make a gender assessment only by her clothes. I won't describe the sensation of my foot sinking into her flesh because it's important that I push that behind me, lest I lose my mind.

Mrs. Grace, who started off with admirable stamina, has used up her last reserves by the time we reach Tim's building. I'm not sure what to do now; Mrs. Grace won't survive ten flights of stairs, yet remaining at ground level is hardly an option. Even if the blood plants weren't already encroaching into the lobby, I've had the distinct feeling of being watched—if not followed—for a while now. This city has to be crawling with looters and opportunistic vagrants, even if I can't see them.

And we're completely defenseless.

For now, we resolve to rest in the stairwell, which seems clear of vegetation so far. I'm eager to check on Tim. Still, I'm not about to leave my ladies behind to fend for themselves. So I sit on a stair next to Mitzy, whose cheeks are aglow from the hike.

A couple of hours later, things aren't looking any better for Mrs. Grace. She's weakened to the point of no return, at least until we get some food in her. I realize the only option at this point is to carry her. I accept this task with some doubt—I'm tired and hungry myself, mind you—but once I pick her up, I know I'll be okay.

She's startlingly light, like a frail wicker chair covered in soft down. We stop at the second floor and I set her down gently. Mitzy opens the main hallway door and I peek through, peering thoroughly into the darkened corridors. We repeat this process until we reach the seventh floor, glimpsing a few strangers who dart away at the sight of us.

Tim's door is unlatched—not really open, but not firmly shut—so as I rap my knuckles onto the hollow steel, the panel hinges open in a gliding welcome.

"Tim?" I whisper. I'm greeted by silence. I push slowly inside and take a look around. It's too dark to interpret much detail, and it doesn't take long for my imagination to run away from me—the shadows look like human figures in various positions of waiting, ready to pounce on me. I feel the hairs on my neck standing at attention. Before I can chicken out, I dash to the window to open the shades. They aren't shades, though. Tim—or someone—has peeled the Viseon layer from one of his walls and used it to black out the window. I free it from invisible restraints, realizing with detached curiosity that I never figured Viseon fiber to be opaque.

As the sun splashes across the furniture and the walls, the corpses seem to smile at me.

Tim barely looks dead at all, actually; he could just be napping after an afternoon snack, his head resting against a corduroy pillow with a hand forked underneath. But there's no question; just like the others in his living room—three teenage boys and an older woman with long, frizzy hair—his clothes are crusted with dried blood.

"Oh, no," I whisper. There's no sign of blood plants in here, but they aren't the only predators on this planet. I take a step toward him, tears springing from my eyes, and a bullet casing bounces away at the touch of my foot.

A gentle hand settles against my lower back. "I'm sorry, Wilson." Mitzy's voice is so deflated, so broken that I can barely hear it above the hum of death in my ears.

We settle into an empty apartment on the second floor—close enough to the ground floor to make a clean getaway if necessary, high enough to employ a bird's-eye view of the street below. There are plenty of food tablets in the pantry, though we have no way to prepare them. There are old-world staples in there, too—pasta, rice, beans—which seems to indicate the owner of this apartment had the foresight to prepare for hard times. It isn't difficult to conjure scenarios in which he or she was forced to flee without first gathering these survival foods, and while I'm exceedingly relieved to have found them, I'm just as worried at what attention their aroma might draw.

Mrs. Grace has benefited greatly from a few hours of rest and is now bustling around the candlelit kitchen with very nearly a zing in her step.

I don't know what time it is, but it must be very late—or very early. Mrs. Grace is sleeping soundly, the way some children learn to do when surrounded by the constant tumult of bickering parents. I know she's asleep because she snores—gingerly, like grass rustling in a breeze.

Mitzy is awake next to me, on the couch in the living room; we have jittered to consciousness in tandem at the sound. First it was in the halls—a rabid slough of expletives shouted with sneering, and then in gleeful abandon—and then above us, coupled with the explosive sounds of murder.

I've known there were others in this building—we've seen a

few in passing—but until now, it hasn't occurred to me that we are in any real, immediate danger. Mitzy's looking at me, spotlit by the moon through a large window between drapes hanging at half-mast. Her eyes dance across mine, and I sense they're begging for a sign that I have this under control. I give her a reassuring smile, though I know in my heart that we won't last long if this apartment is infiltrated.

If we make it through tonight? I'm going on a raiding party of my own; this isn't a time or place one can afford to remain unarmed—and I have some very important people to protect now.

I lock and deadbolt the apartment door, jolting at every mechanical scrape and click, knowing that if we're heard, this door won't shield us for long. Mitzy and I lie in each other's arms until dawn; a few times, I feel her breathing relax and deepen as she succumbs to exhaustion, and a few times I suspect I've nodded off myself. But overall? I feel as though I haven't slept in a week, and when we finally rise, I see my exhaustion reflected in Mitzy's puffy eyes and slumping posture.

Forty-Four

Mrs. Grace has stayed behind as Mitzy and I venture out to scavenge what remains of the city. Outside, the air is crisp and clear, one of those sharp autumn mornings that could easily take me back to better times if I was brave enough to close my eyes for a moment. We take a fairly circuitous route through the neighborhood, in part to avoid heavier concentrations of plants, and also because I'm simply too unfamiliar with the area to navigate more efficiently.

Rounding a once-proud brownstone, I feel my pulse quicken; up ahead, jutting out over the sidewalk like an armed guillotine, is the unlit sign of a pawn shop. My heart rejoices, screaming for me to abandon caution and make a run for it, but my gut has me hugging the stone-clad building as if I could disappear into the grout lines. I'm rewarded for my caution: as we watch, a trio of unsavory gentlemen suddenly erupts from the storefront and spills onto the sidewalk like gunslinging insects fleeing a plundered nest. We're far enough away that they don't see us, though if any one of them takes a moment to look in our direction with even an ounce of scrutiny, we're completely exposed. They're each weighted down with rifles and bags of ammunition, but they look strong and determined. They cross the street and disappear between two buildings.

"Let's go," I whisper, and we retreat back around the corner.

In another lifetime, alleyways were surrounded in taboo, the proverbial playground for misfits and hardened vagrants. Times have changed. Right now, anyway, this one seems like the safest place to be. I haven't given up on the pawn shop, even if I've forfeited the front entrance. It's dark enough between the buildings that I nearly miss the back door—actually, I do, but Mitzy doesn't. When she elbows me in the ribs and points to the heavily riveted barrier, I see that we have our work cut out for us. I guess I should've expected this—this is Chicago, for crying out loud, and just because crime was at an all-time low not long ago, every right-minded person still locked his or her doors at night—but as I take in the formidable door with its steel panels and industrial-grade deadbolt lock, I feel a wave of helplessness wash over me.

A couple of hours with a grinder and a cold chisel might get me in there—but nothing less. It isn't until I look up that I realize we're not completely out of options. A fire escape ladder is suspended just a few feet above our heads, leading up a series of iron switchbacks toward the roof.

It takes a few running tries to get a grip on the ladder, which is cold and slick with morning dew. When my fingertips finally snag a rung, I seize it and allow my body to counterweigh the springs holding it out of reach. The structure groans a loud squeak of protest that echoes through the corridor like a scream. Glancing down at Mitzy, the panic in her eyes gives my heart a pinch of admonishment.

We scurry up the fire escape like our lives depend on it, because we very much believe that they do. At the first switchback, I manage to get a painted window open. I'm peeking in when Mitzy grabs a handful of my shirt and gives it a swift yank.

"Wilson!" she hisses.

I back out and look at her, and even if I didn't suddenly hear the menacing approach of voices, the look on her face would have explained all. The space behind the window might be a bottomless crypt, but what can we do? I contort my body through the opening and breathe a sigh of relief when my feet clumsily find a floor. Mitzy, who is much smaller and far more limber than me, slips inside with little effort. I ease the window shut and squeeze off to one side. From here, I can safely survey the ground through a gouge in the painted glass. In the anonymity of darkness, I feel overwhelmed with sadness for what has come of not only my life, but the lives of us all, that we should all be reduced to surviving at the expense of others. The voices are just audible from in here, like a radio in a tin can. Moments later, bodies join the noise as a horde of miscreants swamps the alleyway.

"Come out, come out wherever you are," one of them sings.

Mitzy tugs on my sleeve and I shrug it off. "It's okay," I whisper.

I see a pale face peering up at me from the ground and I flinch, but I recover quickly, reassured that he can't see me. Nevertheless, he's spotted our hiding place. Mitzy takes my hand and gives it a gentle pull, but I'm only marginally aware of it. There's a screech of metal on metal below as the ladder is deployed, and I know we're in trouble.

I turn to Mitzy, ready to get her moving while we still have time to escape, but she's not looking at me. Her eyes are riveted to the darkness behind us. She's so still—statuesque and afraid.

Outside, the fire escape clangs and rattles. I need no further inspiration to make a run for it, but Mitzy isn't moving—except for her hand, which has begun to progressively clinch over my own like a tiny vice.

Then I see it. Ahead is an open door, the edge of which is only just illuminated by the light of the window. And just beyond, the highlights of a figure slowly resolve from blackness—and extending from his hands, the barrel of a shotgun is leveled at my chest.

"Please," Mitzy mutters, and I'm not sure if she's begging for mercy or for me to do something.

I take a tentative step forward and the gun becomes more rigidly fastened on me.

"Don't," says a man's gravelly voice. "Turn around and go back out the same way you came in."

I want to cry out that we couldn't even if we wanted to—and believe me, with that gun trained on me, I want to—yet even as the words are forming on my lips, the window behind me shatters and glass showers into the room. Instinctively, I drape my body across Mitzy, who has curled into a ball on the floor with her hands protectively latticed over her head. The subsequent shotgun blast is deafening to the point that whatever sound remains in its wake is so quiet by comparison that I can't hear it. A man topples into me from behind and collapses to the floor, spewing blood from a gaping wound. I can imagine the sounds of his suffering, but all I hear is a single, high-pitched tone that seems to originate inside my own head.

I feel Mitzy heaving breaths and tensing underneath me, and it takes several seconds to realize she's screaming. The sound grows from a faint ringing in my ears to a shrill, visceral wail of fear. With the painted glass gone, the room is flooded with the morning sun.

Shrouded in sun kisses, the person on the floor is revealed to be a kid—maybe fifteen or sixteen—and his time in this life is counting down to mere seconds. Black, arterial blood is gouting from his mouth in weakening coughs, forming a ghastly puddle on the carpeted floor. Outside, shouts volley up and down the scaffolding as this boy's peers abandon him to live another day.

Mitzy is no longer screaming; she's crying softly, seizing with sobs that seem to rattle from the pipes of her wounded soul.

"Please," I say to the man, to the reaper and his fiery bludgeon of death. "We're leaving." I show my empty hands and plead with my eyes. He steps into the room and at once the hellish killer is transformed by light into a short, stout man in his seventies. He pokes the kid on the floor with the barrel of his gun, but the teenager's gone, his essence pooled around him on the carpet.

The shotgun sags in the old man's arthritic grasp, and he unleashes a throaty whimper.

"Mother of God, what's this world coming to?" he whispers. "Just a boy."

When he looks into my eyes, I notice his are gray, like melted pewter. They strobe between dismay and tired acceptance. He's a survivor. And like me, he's not necessarily at peace with the price of living. "What're you two after?" he asks. I'm tempted to lie, to say we were merely chased up here by those little gangsters. But as simple as this task sounds, as I look into those old eyes that are swishing like an angry sea, I know I'm not capable of deceiving him.

"There's a pawn shop downstairs," I say. "We were trying to find a safe way in there."

"What for?"

"We need to protect ourselves." Motioning to his shotgun with my chin, I add: "Seemed like a good place to pick up one of those."

The man sucks at his bottom lip in a toothless grimace of contemplation. "You won't find any in there," he says. "People been lootin' it like crazy for a while, and what little was left got cleared out not a half hour ago."

Mitzy rises tentatively from the floor, her hair twinkling with bits of broken glass. Her cheeks are wet and splotched with pink, but she's already recovering. She's a survivor, too.

"Can you help us?" she asks. Her voice is brittle and childlike, and it pokes at my heart to hear it so vulnerable. "Please?"

Forty-Five

His name is Truman, and—first impressions aside—he represents a dying breed of gentleman. He serves us lunch prepared over an old army stove powered by a little propane canister. I can't even tell you what we're eating—he's mixed tablets together in such a way that all the flavors coalesce into a single aftertaste that no person should ever have to experience. With that said, Mitzy and I haven't eaten since last night and are grateful to have something in our stomachs, however pungent.

"Haven't seen many of you around," Truman confesses. "Good people, I mean."

"Where is everyone?"

"Most folks made a mad dash for the quarantine camps when this all started."

Quarantine camps? I wonder if there's any hope to be found in them. Apparently, my expression asks this very question, even if my voice is too reluctant.

"Believe me," he warns with a bitter cackle. "You don't want anything to do with those, son."

"Why not?"

"Word was, they scrubbed you down and burned your clothes. If you survived the next forty-eight hours without one them dang

351

plants sprouting out of your butt, you got to stay."

"That doesn't sound too bad."

"Yeah, but that ain't how things went down."

"How do you know?"

"Because I was there. Me and my wife."

Mitzy pipes in with, "You have a wife?"

Truman looks at her sharply, then flicks his gaze toward the window. "That place killed her."

"How?"

"Anytime you get a bunch of people together, sickness gets passed around like a bottle. My wife was so busy trying to help people, she didn't realize she was sick." Truman shakes his head and swallows. "She was always like that, my sweet girl. Sometimes I wish she'd been different—because then maybe she might've come out of that place alive. That's the score nowadays, in case you haven't figured it out yet." He looks bitterly at me, and then at Mitzy. "You gotta look out for number one, cause ain't no one else gonna do it for you."

I'm startled by the appearance of this coldness, yet I understand it completely. "Truman, why are you helping us?"

He doesn't answer right away. Poking at his half-eaten food, his face is a mask of regret. Finally, he sets his bowl down with a restrained clatter.

"Because that little girl right there," he says, nodding to Mitzy, "reminds me of my wife as a young lady. And because it's what my Mildred would've wanted."

"I guess things might've gone down pretty differently if I'd left her at home, huh?"

"You can bet your last credit on that."

After we've eaten, Truman takes us downstairs to his store, which has been utterly dismantled. If he's at all torn up about it, he hides it well. He kicks aside the crumbs of his career as if they meant nothing; I guess that without his wife, it is all truly meaningless now.

Just as he predicted, the last of his arms has been plucked and all that's left is meaningless memorabilia from a time when people cared about jewelry and musical instruments and antique power tools. He looks at me with a sheepish smile and says, "How about a nice ring for your lady, there?" My eyebrows shoot up.

"A ring?"

"Well, she ain't wearing one. Might as well make an honest woman out of her. May never get another chance."

I turn to Mitzy and she's gone pink, avoiding my eyes. I allow my gaze to linger until she finally relinquishes and returns a look. The corners of her mouth curl slightly, and I have to laugh.

"What'ya say, Mitzy? Wanna get hitched?"

She rolls her eyes, but she's grinning. "The ring alone doesn't seal the deal, Romeo."

"She's right," admits Truman.

I turn to him and with a disingenuous frown, demand, "Whose side are you on, old man?"

He laughs. It's a warm sound that reminds me of Arthur and Stewart, and Tim and every man I've ever known enough to care about.

"I ain't picking sides, son," he chuckles. Turning to Mitzy, he says, "Seems like you can probably forgo some of the formality, don't you think? I'm licensed to marry, though, see?" He points at the front door, where painted in pseudo-embossed font are the words *Notary Public.*

"Yeah, right. Every girl's dream wedding, in a ransacked pawn shop with no friends or family or dress or anything."

"Better than nothing, right?" I offer.

Mitzy looks at me like I'm in real trouble, but there's a spark in her eyes and a smile that she can't quite keep on the leash. She taps her foot on the floor and sighs. Her grin softens, losing its edge against some thought that has saddened her.

"Not without Mrs. Grace."

Growing up, I used to think Chicago was monikered the Windy City because of the fierce winds that scour boulevards year-round. It wasn't until I was a teenager that I learned it was actually a stab at the local politicians back in the eighteen hundreds, who were reputed to be full of hot air. The thing is, on days like today, you can easily take it literally.

We're all holed up inside today—me, my new bride, Mrs. Grace, and Truman—with the shades drawn, faces wrapped like terrorists with bandanas against any unseen drafts. With every gust, the wind fills the air with pink clouds of spores. Until today, I'd all but forgotten about them, but now I'm reminded of just how dire our circumstances are.

Truman agreed to accompany us here to marry us, and now that he's fulfilled that purpose, he's eager to return home. I can tell he's not comfortable here; his hands are wrapped so firmly around his shotgun that his knuckles have gone white like the knobs of unwrapped bones. Our upstairs neighbors have worked their way down and are at work in the halls, kicking in doors and pillaging their way toward our apartment.

We could hide, and indeed, I did my best to plead a case in favor of it. But even as I defended the idea, I realized that the space is too sparsely furnished to hide with much effectiveness, and it provides no protection from anyone with enough brunt to force his way in. It's a small apartment—two small bedrooms with no closet between them, a hall bathroom, a kitchen that opens into the living room. But for a linen closet in the hallway, there isn't a single crevice large enough to accommodate a person—much less four.

So here we sit, like fish in a barrel.

I found a knife in the kitchen, and I'm holding it in one hand now, my other squeezing Mitzy's with as much reassurance as I can muster. But I'm not fooling anyone. Any moment, that door is going to barge in and we'll be overwhelmed by the violence of people who have not only survived in the absence of order, but have found joy in exploring their unbound proclivities. Until this very moment, it escaped me how reliant we had become on our NanoPrints, not only for access to information, but for the reigning in of our animalistic urges. Our minds have been weakened by the constant crutch of our implants, and with them gone, our thoughts are free to roam into sickly lands.

Outside, the spores of blood plants swirl about, seeking a bare patch to take root, whether it be on earth, structure, or flesh; those bizarre entities destroy everything in their paths, killing in order to thrive. And when a sharp rap resounds on our door, followed by a stout kick, it's now clear that, for all its horror, this is the new formula for life. At its core, there's no love or loyalty in animal survival.

And despite what I've always believed to be true, humans haven't necessarily broken that mold.

On the fourth kick, the doorjamb finally gives and the door rips open with enough force that its knob is buried into the drywall. Mrs. Grace cries out, and I wish I could do something to calm her.

In spill four men dressed in piecemealed outfits, scavenged from bits of clothing that were never meant to coordinate with each other. In front is an absolute bull of a human being with a thick moustache and beard. He looks like a wilderness man, except that in the wilderness, such people live off the land rather than their fellow man.

"Well, looky what we got here," he says. He has a guttural voice, like he's got a bit of phlegm in his throat that needs to be coughed out. He glances around the room, soaking us all in. His eyes come to a stop on Mitzy, and suddenly his hairy face splits in a maniacal grin; even with her face masked, her beauty cannot be belied.

Oh, God help me.

The hulk of a man takes a step toward her, poking at her with a pistol, and though I know he'll kill me, I rise to intervene, brandishing my puny knife like a child's toy. When the blast comes, I'm surprised at how little it hurts—until the man slumps to the floor at my feet, and I see Truman standing nearby, his shotgun trailing a plume of smoke. Half-standing, drenched in the blood of an ogre, I reach down and snatch the pistol from his hand, even as he twitches and groans his way toward death. My shoulder stings and I know I've been wounded, but it's minor.

"Who's next?" Truman growls. There are no takers. Just as quickly as they came, they are gone—leaving behind their dying leader like the cowards they are. Mitzy is weeping and I hold her until she regains her composure. Truman sees to Mrs. Grace, whose kerchief has fallen away, revealing a mouth frozen in a silent scream. Her eyes bounce from the intruder to Truman and back again. I can imagine what she's thinking: All this death—do we really have to kill to survive?

"I'm terribly sorry," he mutters. "I had to do it." Mrs. Grace looks at him with horror staining her gaze and says nothing.

"You saved our lives," I say. I realize as I say it that I'm really speaking for Mrs. Grace's benefit, so that she'll understand that regardless of how disgusting it was to witness, this man's death was a tradeoff for her life—and not only did he give it willingly, he demanded that we act rashly.

With our door obliterated, what little sense of safety we enjoyed is gone. We're afraid to merely relocate to another room, yet we can't leave the building for the spore-laden wind.

It's then that we hear the planes.

Forty-Six

Outside, while the blood plants rule at ground level, the military rules the air. The planes are too numerous to track; each is a fat-bellied beast trailing rivulets of white, which almost immediately diffuse into a sagging fog. For nearly an hour, they circle the city, drizzling their payload over every square inch of real estate. As we peek out our window, I notice we're not the only bystanders. I see darkened shapes in windows across the street—there must be twenty or more—and though I should perhaps feel some comfort in knowing that there are other survivors, that we're not completely alone in this mess—all I can think of is the dead man on our floor. I guess I'd rather that we were alone, if it came with some assurance of safety from others.

Mrs. Grace has been increasingly distant since the onset of the plague, yet she's fixed her attention even more inward in the last hour, and I can't help but wonder if she'll ever come back out again. Mitzy is stroking the elderly woman's thin hair, whispering encouragement into her ear. But it goes unnoticed.

I've resolved to drag our intruder into the hallway, where at least we won't have to look at him. I've heard the term *dead weight* before; until now, it never really registered that mass can change with death. On my own, I can't budge him. Mitzy and

Truman join the cause, and we soon get him out of the apartment. The floor where he died is soaked with gore, though; it's still an improvement, but if my stomach is flopping with disgust, it's probably safe to assume that the others will be likewise afflicted.

Mitzy finds an old welcome mat in the hallway and tosses it over the mess. I laugh at the irony—*welcome to your death*, it seems to say—but the humor of this is lost on the others. Fortunately, I'm allowed to act out of turn in these conditions—we all are. So when Mitzy drags me into the back bedroom where the drapes are still pulled and begins to kiss me like there's no tomorrow, I don't hold it against her. Because for all I know? There is no tomorrow.

And besides, we're married now.

It's getting dark, and I'm spooning on the couch with Mitzy. Truman is sawing logs in a nearby chair, and Mrs. Grace hasn't moved an inch.

At dawn, Mitzy is the first to wake. When she does, she shakes me violently.

"Wake up!" she yelps frantically. "She's gone!"

I do my best to process this statement, which isn't easy to do when climbing up the slick walls of sleep. She's right, I see. Truman is rubbing his eyes, wondering what all the fuss is about. It takes only a second for him to understand what's happened, too—that Mrs. Grace has left us.

Mitzy checks the bathroom as I peek into the hallway. Both are lifeless. At once, my new bride begins to cry. As a man, this is like kryptonite on its own—but combined with my own grief and a dangerously primal need to protect those I care about? It's just too much. These people are all I have left in this world, and I feel that I've let my guard down, to the detriment of someone I made a commitment to protect.

I know what I'm doing is ill-planned and blatantly stupid—but I don't care. I take the stairs two at a time down to the ground floor, cinching a torn bit of t-shirt around my face as I go. It defies logic that anyone would intentionally go out into this nightmare, yet something tells me that's precisely what Mrs. Grace has done. Reaching the bottom of the stairwell, I see that the exit door is ajar. The lobby is dark, but I sense long before I slip inside that it isn't void of habitation. I tighten my grip on the pistol, and I must admit that I feel powerful with it under my command.

I hear a rustling of fabric and from nowhere a man materializes, holding a bit of nail-studded lumber, winding up to whack me. I raise the gun and shake my head. I'm prepared to shoot him, and I realize this doesn't disturb me as it once might have. On the contrary, I feel emboldened to step out of the shadows and into full view of danger. I'm desperate, and I'm armed.

Bring it.

The man falters and then slows to a halt. Now that he's close enough to get a look at, I'm surprised to find that he's not a man at all, but a boy—no more than twelve. He looks at the gun with what can only be described as lust. He wants this power so badly, and his willingness to attack me evidences that, even given his shortage of years on this planet, he's more ready to pull the trigger than I am.

"Get back," I say. He takes a single step back, and then waits. For a moment, I think he's just testing his boundaries—isn't that what kids do? But his face is in constant flux, quaking under the stress of inner battle. He's not just testing me, he's psyching himself up.

He wants to kill or be killed.

"Where are your parents?" I demand, as if it makes any difference—maybe I'm hoping a question or two will distract him from his fool's errand. "Are they alive?"

"Fifth floor, dead."

"How long ago?"

He shrugs, and though it might be a gesture of defiance, I believe him—time has nearly lost all meaning in this new world, with no power or clocks. No nexus.

His hands tighten on the stick again, and everything about his body language says that he's poising for another rush.

"C'mon, kid. You don't wanna do that," I chide.

But apparently he does.

To my eternal shame, I don't even try to outmaneuver or strong-arm him; I just pull the trigger. He drops to the floor with a rustling thud. It's so easy to end a life. My heart is racing now, but I know the real blowback will come later, when I look in the mirror and cringe at the monster I see there, wearing my clothes. I turn toward the front door, and there she is. Leaning against the door, as if waiting patiently for a tram that will never come.

"Mrs. Grace?"

She doesn't respond, but I know she can hear me, can see me. I know she has witnessed the carnage of what I just did back there. She's seen it, and even if she's already half-mad, her body still has the sense to cringe at my approach.

"It's okay, now. I've got you." I'm reaching out to her, wanting to comfort her, to protect her. But as my hand nears her, I realize it's still holding the pistol. I balk and shove it in my belt. Her eyes are molten, brimming with contempt.

"Don't you touch me," she growls. "Whoever or whatever you are, you stay away."

"It's me, Mrs. Grace—Wilson."

She squints at me, scrutinizing the man before her with disbelief.

"No you aren't," she insists. "You're an imposter. You're a cold-blooded murderer."

My mouth drops open; I'm armed for battle, yet I have no defense against this sort of weaponry. She turns her back to me with an indignant swoosh and—just like that—pushes through the door. Before I even register what she's done, she's already vanished into a cloud of spores.

I cry myself to sleep later with Mitzy at my side. Though he's reluctant to draw attention to himself under the circumstances, Truman is clearly beside himself. He wants so much to go home, away from this carnage. Even if it's just an empty building, he's invisibly tethered to it and longs to return.

The sky is clear in the morning, the sun bright and full of promise. Truman has convinced us to relocate to his building; not only will he be in his element and closer to his roots, there's considerably more room there for me and Mitzy.

As we step outside the building, all three of us notice it at the same time, but Mitzy is the first to speak of it.

"Is it just me, or do the blood plants look—sick?"

They do. On the street, smaller plants have shriveled into dried spiders. The larger ones have slackened, and many have lost much of their color. Everything is coated by a mysterious powder. Whatever substance the planes dropped on the city, it seems to be working. It's too early for hope to have any room to grow—but it's something.

We reach Truman's building in no time. Along the way, Mitzy and I often struggle to keep up with him—he may be old, but he's as spry as they come. With smiling relief, he leads us down the alleyway and into the back door of his building. Glancing up, I think about our brush with death the last time we were here.

"We probably ought to fix that window, don't you think?"

Truman grunts, and Mitzy giggles with a half-smile.

The planes are at it again. I wish I knew for sure how effective their efforts have been, but I'm willing to take anything at this point. We watch from the upstairs window facing the street— which isn't painted or boarded up, unlike the back side. I don't know if my optimism stems from any reasonable expectation or not, but to my eye, the plants really do look to be dying off.

Before bed, Truman brings an old shoebox out of a closet. Inside are hundreds of old printed photographs of him and his deceased wife in their younger years. There truly is a resemblance between Mitzy and Mildred; now that I've seen it for myself, it's easy to understand the depth and rapid development of Truman's attachment to my wife.

I fall asleep dreaming of Truman's pictures. Visions ebb and flow in and out of sequence like a wad of filmstrip, and over the course of the night, I experience a lifetime through Truman's eyes. Mitzy wakes me in the morning with a kiss that tells me she's had similar dreams.

I hope we make it through all this. I'd give anything for a chance to make my own memories with this woman, memories that aren't burred and stained by the only existence we've had in common thus far, which can only be described as ongoing trauma. I want to share romantic sunrises holding hands, and dinner at Gizi's on Friday nights, and late-night old-movie marathons when we should be sleeping. I want to give her flowers for no reason, to deliver kisses so deep they solder our souls into one.

I want to love my wife in a world that isn't conspiring to eat us.

I'm thinking about this well into the morning, beyond breakfast and right up to lunch. I'm thinking about it still when something amazing happens.

The power comes on.

Well, it really just flickers on for a second, and then back off again—but you can't imagine the chain reaction of glee in that room. Truman jumps to his feet and shouts for joy. Mitzy covers her mouth and has some sort of bouncing spasm. I'm cautiously optimistic, because one of us has to remain pragmatic, but when it flickers again—this time lingering for a full thirty seconds before losing its grip—I feel my heart bulge with hope. Mitzy is crying, but it's a happy sort of crying. I wrap her in my arms and she collapses into me, a tide of sobs swelling through her and into me as if they are my own.

Forty-Seven

The power's been on for a few days now. We lose it now and then, but it returns fairly quickly. Still, each time it vanishes my heart seems to stop beating for fear it'll be gone for good this time. My NanoPrint has hummed to life a few times—which implies that somewhere nearby, a nexus hub is powering up–but it eventually gives up connecting to anything and quiets down again. Truman doesn't have Viseon walls, but he does have an old plasma television that still works. None of the broadcast stations are fully up and running, but a couple of the regional networks periodically air updates; the trick is to be sitting there when they happen to come along.

From what we can gather—so far all the news has been continental, so we're left guessing about anything local—the blood plants have been nearly eradicated. I have a sneaking suspicion that Fiona may have a hand in our salvation. I'm reluctant to award her any credit, though; she brought this plague upon us, after all. There's been a lot of speculation as to which chemical the government used against the plants—sodium chloride, sodium hydroxide—but whatever it was affected more than the blood plants. I can't speak for the world, but just about every plant on this continent has died a similar death. As hopeful as we've all become, we can't help but wonder what future awaits us; without crops, we're on borrowed time.

Just like everything else, the death count is merely a guess—one hundred and sixty-five million, last I heard—but I have no problem believing it to be in the ballpark. I don't know how the calculations have been reached, so I have to wonder if I've been mistakenly included in that count. Realizing this possibility gives me a little hope that we—the survivors of the blood plant plague—might very well amount to more than anyone dared to hope for.

The governor of Illinois has dispatched military installments throughout the city. There's some sort of martial law in effect, but to be honest, I'm not sure what that's supposed to mean. We're still afraid to go outside for more than a few minutes at a time, anyway. Whatever curfews have been placed over our heads are moot.

Our food is nearly gone, and we've begun to ration it—we should've been doing this all along, I suppose. One benefit of the military installments is that food and medical rations are expected to be distributed regularly—though to where remains an unanswered question—starting in a couple of days.

I keep waiting for the floor to drop away, for everything to fall apart again. Our nation is on the mend, yet there are so many who didn't make it. And though I try very hard to forget it, the life I took will surely haunt me forever. I know I shouldn't complain—I deserve it, after all.

Truman and I have begun fixing up his building. The pawn shop downstairs is in extraordinary disarray. I don't have any idea what I'm doing, but Truman is quite the handyman. He mocks my fruitless efforts at construction, yet he doesn't speak ill of my work ethic or my willingness to learn. I've come to think of him very fondly; he's not really a father figure, but I have an enormous amount of respect for him as a man, and as a survivor. Because when you think about it—and despite his claims to the contrary—he has never needed us. He was doing just fine before we came along and disrupted his solitude.

There's no question that the blood plants have caused more destruction, more death, than any other plague in human history. Yet in the wake of this destruction, a rainbow is bleeding through the dust. Though the plants fed on man and earth alike, it was the nexus that suffered the most incalculable loss. If reports are to be believed—and I must admit that I hope they are—the nexus won't recover. At least, not in my lifetime. The entire network of nexus infrastructure—which took over a hundred years to amass—has been completely destroyed. I admit I have mixed emotions on the subject—but overall?

I'm relieved.

There have always been dodgers out there, weirdos who abandon the data stream to get back to nature and whatnot; and guys like me have always had a good laugh at their expense. But you know what? There's something undeniably fulfilling in learning to be self-sufficient—to not only consume, but contribute. Maybe that's what family has always been about. I never got that impression in my home, but that doesn't count for much. I'm tired of looking down on my family, though. My parents tried hard; they failed in so many ways because they didn't know any better. I've decided—better late than never, I hope—to learn from their mistakes rather than cling to them.

I've decided to forgive them.

That's important, too. Because in the midst of all this craziness, I plan to have a family of my own. I know—who would do that, right? Who would bring a child into this flailing civilization? I suppose I feel something coming, something that will rise above the rubble. Something worth living for. Something worth sharing.

Epilogue

It's a steamy morning—barely eight o'clock and already in the upper eighties. It smells like rain, though no storm clouds are in sight. I sip my coffee and stifle a yawn. My patio is ridiculously small, but it's not bad, considering how little I pay for it. I gaze into the morning sky where the moon is still perched in a waning gibbous against a sea of blue. I look upon its sickly surface, mottled with splashes of pink and brown, ulcered with red sores, and I'm reminded of just how precious time is—and just how close my species came to extinction.

Nobody's completely worked out how the moon came to be infected, but I don't suppose it matters much. While global leaders caucus over the trivialities of politics and commerce, scientists everywhere are screaming at the tops of their lungs that the moon isn't that far away. They're viewed worldwide as zealots, as crazy people who can't bear to let go of the past.

I hate to be negative, but I agree with them. One day, I fear, a little red plant is going to pop up on someone's driveway or something—if one doesn't, something equally life-threatening, and probably of our own making, will pop up in its stead—and the world will be scoured of life once again.

In the meantime, I mean to make every moment count.

"Come inside, Wilson," hollers a voice from downstairs. I sigh and obey dutifully. Inside, I brush my teeth, comb my hair, and dress in comfortable shorts and a t-shirt. Two days ago, every active NanoPrint on the planet was wiped clean.

Well, one might've slipped through the net.

With an enigmatic smile, I wink at the man in the mirror, abstractedly running my fingers across the ragged stitches on his wrist. I think about how much the world has changed in my lifetime, and it never ceases to amaze me.

These days it takes me a little longer to descend the stairs, but I'm in no hurry—I have all the time in the world. The aroma of bacon and eggs sends my stomach into a rumble and I cry out, "Feed me, woman!" Mitzy chortles and greets me with a good morning kiss and an affectionate pat on the rear.

"Not bad," she says with a giggle. "For an old man."

At the kitchen table, my son groans. "Can you guys put a lid on that while I'm here?" He looks so handsome in his suit. I wish he had more time for us, but he's a man now—he'll be twenty-seven tomorrow—and with his own home and career to cultivate, I feel privileged to be a priority at all. Just like me in my younger years, Arthur isn't a huge hit with the ladies. But I know there's a young lady out there with his name written all over her. In the meantime, I'm honored to have him here for breakfast, even if it's a pastime he humors purely out of a sense of duty.

"Now why in the world would we want to do that?" I say.

Arthur chats us up about work, where he's a key player in the restoration of the nexus. I don't agonize over his choice of career paths anymore. It's his decision, however much my paternal instinct seems to whisper otherwise. Mitzy and I raised him to follow his heart, and I'm doing my best to let him.

Besides, admonishing a man at his age will only push him away.

I'd be lying if I said it didn't tear me apart to watch him do what he does. The world is systematically hoisting mankind back onto that precarious pedestal—blindly repeating a mistake that nearly sucked us dry of our ability to be self-sufficient, to be human beings rather than mere consumers. And knowing that my son is subjected to daily propaganda—cleverly packaged, portraying those of us with colorful opinions as crazed radicals—honestly, it drives me nearly mad.

But I believe in my son, and to believe in him is to know that he'll brave the truth, once it's revealed to him.

Mitzy lowers a gift bag onto the table like a crane; expertly curled projections of colorful, tissue–thin cellophane peek through the opening like volcanic ash frozen in time.

"Aw, c'mon, Mom. We agreed you guys weren't going to do this." His words are firm, but they don't really chafe, because his eyes are sparkling with mischief. You can never take the boy out of the man—and birthdays have never lost their importance to us. He rips into the bag like the little boy I'll always cherish.

"Wow, Mom. It's beautiful." It's a matching titanium pen and pencil set engraved with his name, and a leather-bound journal. The pages are of thin, slightly transparent polyethylene, but they'll outlive us all. In a world of virtual keyboards and voice-activated word processing, writing by hand is truly a lost art. Naturally, we've become pretty fond of it in this house. Nothing like a near end-of-the-world experience to bring one back to the basics.

"It's just a little something, hun."

Arthur leans across the table and kisses her cheek. "Thanks, Mom. You really shouldn't have, though."

"Uh-uh," Mitzy rebuts. "I'm not giving up birthday presents, no matter what you say. It's my right as your mother, so get used to it."

I smile at this petty exchange; it's not only their annual ritual, it's mine, too—watching from the sidelines, I mean. When it's over, it's my turn. Taking a deep breath, I gingerly lay a small box on the table in front of my son. I've painstakingly wrapped the box in blue, metallic plastic, encircling my handiwork with a silver ribbon. Mitzy rewards my effort with a smile; she's a keeper of the "it's the thought that counts" principle, so the gift-wrapping is as important as the gift itself.

Arthur tears through the wrapping and opens the box. As he reaches inside, I feel my heart flutter nervously. This is a moment I've at once been looking forward to and dreading. For a split second, I doubt my decision to do this and nearly snatch it from his hands to throw in the garbage. But then I feel Mitzy's hand seeking out mine underneath the table, and I know she's apprehensive, too. That we're in this together, no matter what.

We're doing the right thing.

Arthur may love us or hate us for it; only time will tell. But sometimes doing the right thing comes with a tax, and you just have to grin and bear it. Because without the truth, without an honest acceptance of what has been, we're all destined to repeat our mistakes.

"What is it?" he asks curiously, his fingers emerging with a small device between them.

I swallow thickly, my tongue suddenly a pile of sand in my mouth. "It's a NanoPrint reader." I want to tell him how rare a device this really is, that once upon a time, law enforcement agencies might've been pretty upset to find one in my possession. But that's not the message I want to convey to my son. What I'm trying to share with him exceeds monetary value or novelty, even the thought behind the gift; what I want to share is something so basic that people too often overlook it, though it's the most important thing of all.

Arthur glances at me with raised eyebrows, and I have to smile. It's the same look I get whenever I bomb on a Christmas present, one that seems to say: *Wow, it's a reindeer sweater ... with an LED nose—just what I've always wanted.*

"That's not all, look in the bottom."

His gaze abandons the reader in his hand for a moment and returns to the box. He tips it to its side and a tiny bit of metal tumbles onto the table and bounces to a stop.

"Whoa, is this what I think it is?" His eyes are bright and furiously curious, just like when he was a kid. They flicker to my wrist and back to the tiny implant between his fingers. It may be small, but it's the greatest gift I can give.

He looks at me with a wary frown, and again I feel the flutter of nerves. "But I thought they were all reformatted?" he says. Mitzy swallows loud enough for me to hear.

This is the part I've been dreading the most. How can I explain myself honestly, knowing just how bizarre it will surely sound? What sane person would believe that I had a dream—a dream so powerful and convincing that, upon waking, I immediately rushed to the kitchen and cut open my wrist like a crazy person? And that days later—against all odds, defying logic itself—my far-fetched dream came true? "Mine's a little glitched, I guess," I finally say. It's not untrue—it's merely an abbreviation of a more convoluted truth.

Arthur glances at his mother and then back to me, eyes guardedly intrigued. Mitzy squeezes my hand and I feel her excitement surge into my skin. "So, what exactly is on this thing?" he wants to know.

"The truth," I answer in a firm but kind voice. "The plain, unwashed truth, son."